'We think it would be best if you kept your distance from Lord Nicholas.'

'And if I don't?' But in Thea's heart she already knew the answer.

'Maybe nothing. Perhaps you would fall in love and marry. But if he discovered the truth, would Lord Nicholas continue to look on you with love—or would he turn his back with condemnation and contempt?'

'I could not bear that.' A tear stole unnoticed down Thea's cheek. She knew what she had to do. She must set herself to destroy any vestige of the relationship which might have begun to blossom between herself and Lord Nicholas. It should not be too difficult, should it, to give him a disgust of her if she really tried? To make him wonder what he had ever seen in her?

No one must guess. Not Lord Nicholas. Not ever Nicholas.

And, whilst Thea found herself reduced to the blackness of utter misery, Lord Nicholas Faringdon was equally prey to extreme emotions. Against all the odds he had fallen in love. He wanted nothing more than to ask for the lady's hand in marriage. She fired his blood. She intrigued him. She entranced him. If he had his way, Miss Theodora Wooton-Devereux would become Lady Nicholas Faringdon in the shortest possible time.

A smile of satisfac vas nothing in the ma hat might indicate t his addresses.

Dear Reader

In *The Disgraced Marchioness,* the first volume in **The Faringdon Scandals** trilogy, Lord Henry Faringdon succeeded in finding happiness with beautiful Eleanor in New York. This left Henry's handsome younger brother, Nicholas, to administer the Burford estates in Herefordshire in the name of his infant nephew. I wondered what Nicholas's future would be, bound as he would be by a sense of duty—and so was born *The Outrageous Débutante.*

Nicholas is a typical Faringdon, with dark good looks, unused to having his will thwarted, and driven by ambitions. What will happen when his path is crossed by Theodora, a delicious débutante who is just as strong-willed as he, and certainly given to outrageous behaviour? Will it be possible for Nicholas and Theodora to find any future together after so stormy a first encounter? And when scandal strikes again, far too close to home, can their love even be declared, much less survive? Nicholas has to face the grave demons of his past, Theodora the truths of hers, both of which have the power to wreck any love affair between them. It could all so easily end in heartbreak...

Still the Faringdon history is not complete. Sarah Russell has yet to find her destiny. Although not a Faringdon by birth, her fate will become involved with that of the notorious Lord Joshua Faringdon, the Black Sheep of the family, cousin to Henry and Nicholas. Look out for their turbulent love affair, in *The Enigmatic Rake,* coming soon!

I hope that you enjoy this passionate encounter between Theodora and Nicholas, as much as I did in bringing them together.

Anne

THE OUTRAGEOUS
DEBUTANTE

Anne O'Brien

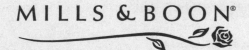

All the characters in this book have no existence outside the imagination of the author, and have no relation whatsoever to anyone bearing the same name or names. They are not even distantly inspired by any individual known or unknown to the author, and all the incidents are pure invention.

First published in Great Britain 2005
Harlequin Mills & Boon Limited,
Eton House, 18-24 Paradise Road, Richmond, Surrey TW9 1SR

© Anne O'Brien 2005

ISBN 0 263 84395 5

Set in Times Roman 10 on 11¼ pt.
04-1205-99802

Printed and bound in Spain
by Litografia Rosés S.A., Barcelona

Anne O'Brien was born and lived for most of her life in Yorkshire. Here she taught history, before deciding to fulfil a lifetime ambition to write romantic historical fiction. She won a number of short story competitions until published for the first time by Harlequin Mills & Boon®. As well as writing, she finds time to enjoy gardening, cooking and watercolour painting. She now lives with her husband in an eighteenth-century cottage in the depths of the Welsh Marches.

Recent titles by the same author:

RUNAWAY HEIRESS
PURITAN BRIDE
MARRIAGE UNDER SIEGE

and in *The Faringdon Scandals:*

THE DISGRACED MARCHIONESS

Don't miss the third instalment of
THE FARINGDON SCANDALS

THE ENIGMATIC RAKE

Coming, March 2006

Prologue

The sun beat down from a sky so pale with heat as to be almost colourless. From the deep ochre sand and rock of the Syrian desert, ruins of a Roman town stood proud, as if grown from the earth. Arches lifted their broken heads to the heavens, columns rose with splintered capitals and walls crumbled into dust. They might have stood there since the beginning of time, and would continue to stand until the hot winds and cold nights reduced them once more to nothing but grains of sand. Nothing moved in the landscape except for a pair of lazily circling eagles and the lizards that basked on the hot stones. Nothing moved until two figures emerged from the distant heat haze, to fly across the firm sand towards the ancient town. A pair of fine Arabian horses, their riders crouched low as they encouraged them to pit their strength and speed against each other. Far behind followed a small group of riders, at a more sedate pace, leading well-laden pack horses.

The two riders drew rein before the remains of a magnificent triumphal arch. The animals danced at the curbing of their energies and tossed their heads. They were beautiful, both satin-skinned greys with the short curved necks and small heads of true Arab breeding. The riders controlled them with ease as the horses resisted the firm hands on the reins and fought to run.

As they finally settled and consented to stand, sides heaving, the riders dismounted. They walked towards the crumbling stonework and, securing the reins to fallen masonry, sank down in the shade. Then they proceeded to unwind the scarves that had been draped around head and face against the sun and sand and to loosen the all-encompassing robes that protected their clothes—to reveal that the riders were female.

'That was wonderful! So much light and space. I love the elemental heat of it—even when my nose is pink and I have sand in my mouth!' The younger woman wiped the back of her hand over her dry lips as she watched the slowly approaching caravan, then turned her brilliant blue eyes on her older companion. 'You have no idea how much I shall miss this place, Mama.'

Lady Drusilla Wooton-Devereux smiled her understanding, in complete accord with her daughter. 'I, too, regret leaving it, Thea. And Sir Hector would not be averse to remaining at the Court of Constantinople for a few more years. But his position does not allow him free choice in the matter. We must make the most of the remaining days here.'

Theodora Wooton-Devereux pulled the long veil completely from around her head, to reveal the interesting fact that her hair was of a rich gold, a burnished cap in the sunlight and cut as short as any boy's. She ran her fingers through the short strands where the wisps stuck to her heated forehead and cheeks. Unconventional it might be—shockingly so, some might say—but it drew attention to the face of a Beauty. Glorious deep blue eyes, the dark, elegantly arched brows, the fine cheekbones and straight, almost masterful nose. Miss Wooton-Devereux's delicious mouth with its full bottom lip curved in unalloyed pleasure. She was without doubt a striking young woman.

'What will it be like in Russia when Papa is sent to St Petersburg?' she asked. 'Cold, I expect.'

'Not so much now in the summer months. But in winter, yes. A land of ice and snow, temperatures so low you could not believe it. Even the rivers freeze over.' Lady Drusilla smiled at the memories, surrounded as she was by extreme heat and dust. 'Your father and I spent a few months there—he was in a lowly position in the diplomatic ranks in those days, of course—before you were born, Thea.'

'How exciting it must have been—you as a young bride. I shall like to see it. And the court of Tsar Alexander, of course. Do you suppose he is as handsome as they say? We shall need furs and woollen cloth, not these wonderful light garments.' Thea leapt to her feet, unwilling to sit longer when energy surged through her veins, and strode around so the robes billowed about her, robes such as a Bedouin in the desert would wear, revealing that beneath them she wore wide breeches as the Turks might, tucked into the tops of long leather boots. 'I think that wherever we go, this will always be my favourite place. Riding for ever with the distance never seeming to come any closer. Sleeping outside under the stars, which shine with such brilliance.' She spread her arms and danced a few short steps of joy. 'But I expect Russia will hold as many delights. How long do you suppose before Papa is transferred?'

'A few months, perhaps as long as six. We should be fixed in London for the time and so will take a house for the Season.' Lady Drusilla watched her daughter, unwilling to curb Thea's delights. But she knew she must. It was more than time for her to remember her duties as a mother to this enchanting daughter.

'Thea—I do not think that you should come with us to Russia.' The words came out as a bald statement.

The dance across the sand stopped. The dancer turned, her face registering a sharp mixture of shock and surprise. A sudden fear.

'Not come with you? But why not? I have always travelled with you. Saint Petersburg cannot contain more dangers than Constantinople, surely. And if *you* are to accompany Papa, there is no reason for me not to do so.'

'It is not a matter of safety. That has never been an issue, as you are well aware.' Lady Drusilla turned her eyes away, unwilling to see the hurt that she must surely inflict. She knew her daughter's temperament too well. Had she not herself fostered the strong streak of independence, the love of travel and adventure? But there were now steps that must be taken. 'It is time that you married, Thea.' She kept her voice light and gentle. 'You are now one and twenty, high time that you were wed. I had been married all of two years when I was your age.'

'There is plenty of time for that.' Thea came to sit beside her mother, intent on persuasion. In her short life she had rarely found it difficult to get her own way. But Lady Drusilla, fully aware of her daughter's tactics, shook her head and resisted the clasp of the urgent hand on her arm.

'No. We have been too selfish with you, my love. Enjoyed your company far too much. I shall miss you dreadfully.' She closed her hand over Thea's, to still the restless fingers. 'But it is time that you had a husband and your own home. Children, of course. We must not leave it longer. It would be most unwise.'

'Mama—do I really need a husband? I would far rather come with you to Russia. Perhaps in a few years when—'

'No! You are older than a traditional débutante for her coming out as it is, Thea, and that is my fault. You should have a Season in London—you deserve one. You are a beautiful young woman and should not be denied a formal introduction to London society. Besides, I want a rich and titled husband for you, so that you might be comfortable.'

'But I am an heiress. I don't need more wealth.'

'Perhaps not. But you certainly need a husband. I do not wish to think of you growing old as an eccentric and lonely spinster, roaming the deserts with no company but your servants, the object of gossip and speculation from everyone you meet. That is not what any mother would want for her daughter.'

'I would not be lonely. I should take a lover!' The lady lifted her chin, deliberately intending to shock her mother, horrified at this sudden arrangement of her future life without any consideration for her own wishes.

'You will do no such thing, Theodora. Your upbringing might have been somewhat out of the way in comparison with that of most young girls, but I will have no truck with the scandalous, the improper!'

'I see.' Thea lowered her chin, her mind working rapidly. 'Does Sir Hector agree with this plan?'

'Yes. Of course. We have talked of it.'

Of course they would have. And Sir Hector would undoubtedly be swayed by Lady Drusilla's forceful arguments. All the joy, all the brightness, seemed to have gone out of the day. 'Very well.' What other could she say? 'I suppose I shall have to be more conventional in London.'

'Assuredly. I think I have allowed you far too much licence in the past.' Lady Drusilla frowned a little at her daughter as she considered her sudden compliance.

'No. Never too much. It has been wonderful, Mama. Can I gallop my horse in London?'

'Certainly not. Nor wear the garments you enjoy at present, as you are very well aware.'

'Or ride astride?'

'Theodora! You must behave with decorum and dignity. Your purpose in London will be to attract a husband, not frighten him away with an exhibition of unseemly manners. I would not wish you to become an object of gossip or shunned because the *ton* considers you ill bred.'

'Oh, dear! It all seems very dull.'

'By no means. I wager that you will find it most entertaining.'

'Well, I shall certainly do my best to make it so, as you know, Mama. I have never yet been bored. I suppose that London can offer as much to attract and occupy me as Constantinople or St Petersburg.'

'Thea!' Lady Drusilla warned as she recognised the glint in her daughter's eye.

'Don't fret, Mama. Of course I shall behave.' After a little thought, Thea's good humour had quickly reasserted itself and she laughed. 'Perfectly, in fact. I shall set my cap at a fabulously rich Earl and ensnare him, just to please you.' Her eyes twinkled at the prospect, but she managed to keep an expression of innocent compliance in place. Perhaps London might not be so dull after all.

Chapter One

In the county of Herefordshire, far removed from the exotic delights and windblown sands of Arabia, Lord Nicholas Faringdon opened a letter with utmost reluctance, a letter that was destined to disrupt the unchanging predictability of his life.

His lordship had spent the morning, unaware of the devious workings of fate, in the company of George Dinmore, agent to the estate of Burford. A fine sense of optimism warmed his blood, as satisfying as the first real heat of early summer that brushed his skin. It was too early to tell if the harvest would be good but the crops were coming on well, the arable fields sheened with bright green. Now it was up to sun and rain and the will of God. There had been too many cold and wet summers of late. But the cattle and sheep were thriving, as were the horses on his own estate at Aymestry Manor. It could not be said that Lord Nicholas neglected his duty to his family in his role as trustee for Tom, his young nephew, who held the title and inheritance as Marquis of Burford.

The little town of Kingshall, its wood-and-plaster dwellings clustered around a central market square, hummed with life. Outside the Red Lion, Lord Nicholas had paused to listen to the landlord, who could be relied upon for knowledge of any local happenings. Nicholas made it his business to enquire and keep abreast of developments or hints of unrest. The local cottage industries were thriving well enough. There was no serious competition here from machines. He knew that if he rode down Back Lane, he would see the women who made the beautifully sewn gloves from the palest, finest of leathers, sitting working on their doorsteps in the sun. But another bad summer, another autumn beset by storms and heavy rain, would push up the price of grain. Lack of food, as Nicholas well knew, led to mutterings in the Red Lion over a draught of ale. The lord would be the easiest target for such discontent when tempers ran high. Lord Nicholas Faringdon had no intention of allowing his nephew's inheritance to be destroyed or compromised in any way, even if his nephew was living in New York with Nell, his mother, and nearly four years old.

As soon as the pasture had opened up on the edge of the town he had urged the young chestnut mare out of her somnolence into an easy gallop. She had willingly extended her stride until they'd flown across the grassland in perfect unity, disturbing a small flock of Ryeland sheep. He rode well, could never remember not being at home on horseback. The speed, the breeze which had ruffled and tugged at his dark hair, the sun which had glittered on the still waters of the mere, had all served to lift his spirits, banishing the niggling worries that had plagued him of late.

He did not know why he had been so beset. There was no obvious cloud of concern on his horizon, nothing which could not be managed between himself, Dinmore and Hoskins, the family lawyer in London. Nicholas had frowned as he breasted a rise and the lovely, familiar view of Burford Hall had opened up before him, its mellow stone glowing in the sharp midday light. For some reason life was a little flat. Even a little lonely. The house was empty apart from himself and the servants and would be so as far into the future as he could see. His brother Hal and Nell, now his wife, were firmly settled in New York where the firm of Faringdon and Bridges occupied Hal's business acumen. His eldest brother Thomas had been dead now more than three years. So the Hall was empty. As was his own attractive manor at Aymestry.

Perhaps a visit to town was the remedy for this vague sense of *ennui*. It was a year or more since he had last taken up residence for any length of time at Faringdon House in Grosvenor Square. The Season would be at its height with all the Polite World in town. It would not do for him to rusticate completely, to become nothing but a county squire, buried in soil and hunting with pretensions to neither fashion nor style. Nicholas smiled at his own harsh judgement. There was little chance of that. He could rise to the occasion as well as any and play the sophisticated man of fashion.

Lord Nicholas's arrival on the sweep of gravel before the steps of Burford Hall had coincided with that of the post boy from Leominster, so that now he stood in the library, wine glass in hand, having leafed through the letters before casting them on to the desk. But not all. One of them, the fatal one, had caught his attention—he had recognised the handwriting immediately. It caused him to groan quietly. He might have wished for a change of pace and scenery, but that did not include the interference of Aunt Beatrice. He could guess at the content before he even unfolded the thin sheets of paper with Lady Beatrice's distinctive scrawl. Carrying it to the window seat, he sat and prepared to read.

My dear Nicholas,
Although the Season has been under way for some weeks, it has come to my notice when visiting Judith in Grosvenor Square that Faringdon House has remained closed up with the knocker off the door and we have not had the pleasure of your company. I took the liberty of calling to ask Elton if he had any knowledge of your sudden arrival—which he had not. I am sure that it is not good for you to bury yourself in the country. You need to come to town, my boy.

I know that it will be no surprise to you if I suggest that matrimony should play a significant part in your planning. You are young, well set up with your own income and property, both of which are substantial, and I do not hesitate to say that you are not unattractive to the opposite sex. It is time that you took a wife—indeed, I consider it to be your duty. Now that Henry and Eleanor are settled in New York—although why that should be I cannot imagine—it behoves you to consider setting up your own nursery. I am sure that you take my meaning. I believe that life can be considered cheap Across the Sea.

How can you expect to meet anyone suitable if you are buried at Burford Hall? Not that it is not a delightful place—I remember exceptional house parties there in your dear mother's day—but not in April when you should be in London for the Season.

I cannot insist that you come to town, of course—

Really! Nicholas's lips curled in appreciation of his aunt's forthright style, against which few members of the family were ever prepared to take a stand.

and I am sure that you can find any number of excuses why your time at Burford is invaluable, but it would please me if you would present yourself in Berkeley Square for my own ball in three weeks. I will take the opportunity to introduce you to this year's crop of débutantes. Some very pretty well-bred girls, who would be valuable additions to the Faringdon family.

There is no need to reply to this letter. Merely arrive!

Your loving aunt

Beatrice

He cast the letter on to the desk to pour a glass of claret from the decanter, which the footman had brought in whilst he read.

Merely arrive!

Well, he had thought of going, had he not? But not if he was to be an object of Beatrice's interest. Like a rare insect under a magnifying lens.

Marriage. Of course she would interest herself. Her advice in the letter was nothing new. But Beatrice—damn her!—had

pricked at his sense of duty and he could not but acknowledge
the weight of her argument. Even so, the prospect of dancing attendance on any number of young girls at Almack's and other
fashionable squeezes filled him with something akin to horror.
Eyed, assessed, gossiped over by their avaricious mamas, his income, rank and future prospects a matter for public speculation.
The daughters hanging on his every word, hoping for a declaration of undying love or at least the invitation to accept his hand
in marriage and take up residence at Aymestry Manor. Or, even
more enticingly, at Burford Hall in the absence of the Marquis.
Thomas, with considerable aplomb and good humour, would
have laughed it off and enjoyed the flirtation and the female flut-
tering for his attention. Hal would have simply made himself
scarce. He, Nicholas, in the circumstances, could do neither. The
bonds around him, the silken ties of family responsibility and
duty, tightened around him even more. Unbreakable, even though
constructed from love and care.

Nicholas poured another glass of claret and frowned into it.
Hal had the right of it when he took himself off to New York.
But, of course, he had Nell with him now, the love of his life.

He supposed he could simply stay buried here, as Aunt Beatrice had so tactfully phrased it. Offer for the hand of Amelia
Hawkes, daughter of the hard-riding, hard-drinking baronet
whose land marched with the Faringdon estate in the west. She
would like nothing better than to be Lady Nicholas Faringdon,
and many would see it as a good match. An excellent rider to
hounds, well connected locally, Amelia would take over the running of Aymestry Manor with the same style as she had run her
father's establishment since her mother's death. She had probably been waiting for an offer from him for the past half-dozen
years, he decided, with more than a touch of guilt. Not that he
had ever encouraged her to believe that marriage was in his
mind—but neither had he discouraged her. With some discomfort he saw the situation from Miss Hawkes's perspective. They
met frequently in the hunting season. He stood up with her at
local assemblies in Ludlow and at private parties. Her father, Sir

William, certainly would have no objection to such a match. Why not offer for the girl and tell Beatrice that she need dabble no longer—it would be comfortable, easy, familiar?

No, he could not do it. He put down the neglected wineglass with a sharp snap. Poor Amelia. He had not been fair with her. The plain truth was that he no longer wanted comfortable, easy and familiar. She was an attractive girl and would no doubt make some man an excellent wife. He liked her well enough. But love? Amelia never caused his blood to run hot or his eyes to spark with the possessive emotion that he had seen in Hal's when he turned his gaze on Nell. Nor was the lady blessed with a well-informed mind. They could exchange views on horses and hunting, the desirability of pheasant at the end of the season when *stringy* could be something of a compliment. But if he ever took the conversation into any other channels—the new ideas on farming—or, God preserve him, the political situation—her eyes glazed over and she had no opinion or knowledge to volunteer. And, he realised as the image of Miss Amelia formed in his mind, she had absolutely no interest in clothes and her appearance, spending most of her days in a riding habit. Nicholas, he discovered with some surprise, since it had never crossed his mind before, was sufficiently fastidious that his future wife must look and play her part with style, whether it be in a fashionable drawing room or on the hunting field.

No. Miss Amelia Hawkes would never be mistress of Aymestry Manor. He supposed it would have to be Aunt Beatrice and the débutantes. He hoped to God that since it was undoubtedly his duty to marry and his heart was clearly not engaged elsewhere, he could meet someone suitable, someone intelligent, stylish and conventional, within a few weeks of his arrival and get it over with. As long as he did not repeat the experience he'd had with Georgiana Fitzgerald. He'd thought he had been in love. The lovely Georgiana Fitzgerald had flirted and smiled, had led him to believe that she would look for more than a light friendship—indeed, a deeper, lasting relationship. For his part he had been entranced by a lively and confiding manner and lovely face. And then, when he had been on the point of declaring himself, she had thrown him over to become the object of interest to an extremely wealthy Viscount on the trawl for a wife. She had wanted a title and fortune, not the heart and devotion of a younger son with a mere easy competence. Nicholas, distinctly disillusioned, had been left to consider the folly of allowing his heart to become engaged when considering matrimony. But that did not make Miss Amelia Hawkes any more acceptable!

On which negative note, Lord Nicholas tossed off the remainder of the claret and left the haven of his library to give instructions for his visit to town. With perhaps, in spite of everything, a lightening of his heart.

Chapter Two

Judith, Countess of Painscastle, sat alone in the supremely elegant withdrawing room of the Painscastle town house in Grosvenor Square. Thoroughly bored. she leafed through a recent edition of *La Belle Assemblée*, but the delicious fashions for once left her unmoved. She closed the pages and frowned down at the fair and innocent beauty who graced the front cover. There was absolutely no reason for her lack of spirits! There were so many possible demands on her time, and all of them designed to please and entertain. A soirée at the home of Lady Beech that very night. Lady Aston's drum later in the week. A luncheon party. An essential visit to the dressmaker. What more could she require in life? She was truly, deliriously happy. But her husband Simon had found a need to visit Newmarket. He would return before the end of the week. But she missed him more than she would ever admit.

Now a married lady of almost seven years, Judith had changed little from the flighty, gossip-loving débutante who had stolen Painscastle's heart. Her hair was as wildly red and vibrant as ever, her green eyes as sparkling and full of life. Only the previous year she had fulfilled her duty and presented her lord with a son and heir. She was inordinately proud and loved the boy beyond measure. But she could not devote all day and every day to her child. She needed something, or someone, to entertain her.

She sighed again, flicked through the pages again, tutted over an illustration of an unattractive and certainly unflattering walking dress with heavy embroidered trim around the hem and cuffs when, on a polite knock, the door opened. Matthews, her butler, entered and presented a silver tray with a bow.

'Forgive me, my lady. A morning visitor.'

She cast aside the magazine at once and sprang to her feet. A diversion!

'A visitor!'

'A young lady. She says that she is unknown to you, but was advised to call by Lady Beatrice Faringdon.'

'Mama told her to come? Did she, now? She did not tell me.' Judith picked up the visiting card from the tray. 'I do not recognise this name. But if Mama sent her… Pray show the lady in, Matthews.'

'Yes, my lady.' There was a stern expression on his face as he retreated from the room to usher forward the lady in question.

'Miss Wooton-Devereux, my lady.'

'Thank you, Matthews. Would you be so kind as to bring ratafia?'

'Of course, my lady.' With a distinct frown, the butler retired.

The lady curtsied. Judith did likewise.

'Forgive me, my lady.' The lady spoke with confident assurance in a low, rather husky voice. 'I know that it is not usual to pay a morning call on someone to whom one has not been formally introduced, but my mama and Lady Beatrice have exchanged some correspondence of late. Lady Beatrice suggested that it would be of advantage to me to make your acquaintance as we are to be here in London for a little time. Being of a similar age, you understand.' She saw the lack of comprehension in Judith's face. 'I gather that your mama has not told you of this.'

'No. Nothing.'

'Forgive me. Perhaps I should not have presumed.'

'No, no—I am delighted that you did.' Judith thought that the lady did not look particularly sorry. 'Come and sit.' She waved an expansive hand towards a chair. 'I was only a moment ago thinking that I was in need of a distraction.' And this, she thought, after an equally brief moment of being in the lady's company, might be exactly the diversion she needed.

As the lady settled herself on the cream-and-gold striped chair, shaking out her skirts and removing her gloves, Judith took stock of her visitor.

'I am Theodora Wooton-Devereux. We—my parents and I— have just arrived in town. My mother is set to launch me into society, you should understand.' The lady's opinion of this intent was signalled by the faintest of curls to her beautiful lips.

'Indeed.'

The lady who sat before Judith in her withdrawing room, and somehow seemed to fill it with her personality was, well, striking, Judith supposed. Perhaps not classically beautiful exactly. Stunning might be a better word. She would certainly draw all eyes when she entered a room. She did not wear a bonnet. Her fair hair shone and—oh, my—it was cut quite short into the neck with curls that lay softly, without artifice, against her cheeks and forehead. When it was all the rage to wear ringlets falling to the shoulder from a high crown, Judith could but stare. It was quite outrageous. But quite—charming, if one had the courage to wear it so. Judith knew that she would never dare. As Miss Wooton-Devereux turned her head, there was a touch of burnished copper amongst the gold where the sun caressed it. And those dark lashes and brows—an interesting combination with the deep blue of her eyes. Were her lashes actually dyed? And was there just a hint, the faintest brush of cosmetics on that flawless skin? Judith feared so—and was entranced. Her gown was both expensive and tasteful, but definitely not that of a débutante, shimmering as it did in pure silk of deepest amethyst, trimmed with knots of ribbon and a profusion of tiny silk flowers, in the same hue, around the hem and low-cut neckline.

Definitely *not* a débutante! Judith decided.

Nor did she wear the single strand of pearls so appropriate to a young girl on the brink of her presentation to society. Instead, a golden necklace of tiny entwined flowers and leaves lay against

her throat, coloured stones winking in their depths, and matching earrings dripped exotically from her delicate ears. A stole was
draped in artistic folds over her arms, of distinctly eastern pattern with just the hint of sparkle in the weave and the long
fringes. Her hands, now revealed as she placed her gloves and
reticule on the occasional table beside her, were long-fingered,
slender, with a number of intricately worked rings that gleamed
gold and silver in the sunlight.

The vision immediately stirred Judith's jaded appetite. It was
as if some exotic butterfly had taken it into its head to land in
her withdrawing room and bring it to life.

'You said that your name was Theodora?' Judith enquired
when she had completed her survey as tactfully as she might.

'Yes. My mama, Lady Drusilla, called me for the Empress of
the Roman Empire, the wife of the Emperor Justinian. She admired her, I believe. But do call me Thea.'

'Thea. Yes, of course. An unusual name.'

'Unfortunately. We do not choose our own and my mama has
eclectic tastes.' A glinting smile touched Thea's face. 'I have to
be grateful that she did not name me Cleopatra. Or Dido.'

'No, indeed! That would be most unfortunate!' The Countess
of Painscastle had no idea who Dido might be but decided that
it did not matter. 'Ah—you must call me Judith. You say that you
are to have a London Season?'

'Yes.'

'Forgive me, but…'

'I know what you are thinking.' Thea smiled with cheerful
composure. 'You think that I am too old to be a débutante. My
mama warned me that it must be so.'

'Well… That is to say… You are very forthright!'

'I was brought up to be so. And your comment is certainly
accurate. It is not my choice to have a Season at all. I wish to go
to Russia instead. But my mother insists. She wants an Earl for
me, you see.'

'Really.' Judith blinked. 'Well—that is to say…I expect she
might…'

'Yes. So my father has taken a house in Upper Brook Street and we are set to entertain. Your mama is acquainted with mine—and so suggested that you might give me some advice—how to go on here. I know the protocol in Paris and Constantinople. Even Vienna. But I have never lived in London before.'

'I see.' Judith didn't, but she was sure that this fascinating creature would soon explain.

'And so I thought I should come and see if you are willing—or if you would rather not. I hope that you would tell me what you truly feel. Parents can be so thoughtless and inconsiderate when they compromise their offspring—particularly when that offspring has no inclination for it at all!'

'Very true.' Judith found herself returning the smile in astonishment—and total agreement.

'Perhaps I should have not come here before we were introduced. Perhaps it is not *comme il faut?*'

Judith found herself sitting on the very edge of her seat. 'Perhaps not—well, no, it is definitely not the done thing, but I am delighted that you did. I was suffering from such a megrim before you arrived.'

'I have never suffered from a megrim in my life, but it pleases me that I can restore your spirits.' Miss Wooton-Devereux laughed gently, showing perfect teeth, her eyes gleaming with amusement. What an odd creature she was, to be sure.

'Tell me—' Judith had to satisfy her curiosity and decided that she felt no compunction in asking '—why have you not been presented before?'

Thea was perfectly willing to explain. 'My father, Sir Hector, is in the diplomatic service. He has been Ambassador to the Court of Constantinople of late. And we have travelled extensively so I have never had the opportunity to stay long in London or enjoy a Season. But now he is between posts. He expects to be sent to St Petersburg later in the year, but for the present we are to remain in London.'

The simple explanation was interrupted by Matthews, who brought in a tray bearing a decanter of ratafia, two glasses and a plate of little biscuits. He arranged them on the table beside Judith's chair and left, but not before directing another disapproving glance in the direction of their guest.

'I can not think what is wrong with Matthews.' Judith watched him as he left the room, shoulders rigid.

Thea laughed again, an infectious low chuckle that instantly encouraged Judith to smile in response. 'I believe that I have the answer. *I* am the cause of your butler's disapproval.'

'Why? What can you have done?'

'I came unchaperoned. Without my maid. He appears to disapprove.'

'Yes. I imagine that he would.'

'But it is only a step,' Thea explained. 'Hardly a stroll. Why should I need a maid with me? I am hardly likely to be set on by footpads in Mayfair in broad daylight, I presume.'

'No. Of course not. But it is most unconventional. It is not considered…seemly for an unmarried lady to venture on the streets unaccompanied.'

'I do not see—' She broke off as Judith handed her a glass of ratafia. She sipped it reluctantly, but with a practised pretence at enjoyment.

'It would not be good for you to be seen as *fast,*' Judith explained after taking a sip from her own glass, 'if you are to be accepted by the *haut ton*. You are not in Constantinople now— or Vienna.'

'I suppose not. I think your mama had the right of it. I need advice. Are you indeed willing to give me your support, Judith?'

'I think it would be the most delightful thing.' Judith put down her glass and all but clapped her hands with pleasure. 'It is just that you must be careful not to offend. You will wish to acquire tickets for Almack's, I suppose. And the patronesses are so strict, unpleasant even. The slightest whiff of scandal and they could refuse—and that would be fatal for anyone wishing to cut a dash in London.'

'Oh, there is no problem there.' Thea wafted away the problem with an elegant sweep of her hand. 'My mother is thick as thieves with Princess Esterhazy. They have known each other for ever—in diplomatic circles, you understand.'

'Oh dear. I did not mean to imply…' Instant colour rose in Judith's cheeks to clash with her hair.

'No matter. I know that she is not liked. But she can be very informative when she is not lecturing or finding fault. Perhaps you would be so kind as to drive or ride with me in the Park and point out some of the people I should know. And *not* know, of course, for I have not the least idea. Unless they are *very* entertaining. Have you noticed that those who are most scandalous and shunned by polite society are the most pleasurable to know?'

'I suppose so. I had not thought.' Judith's eyes grew round with astonishment.

'One has only to look at Lord Byron. Most unacceptable, but totally fascinating.'

'Well—yes. I agree. I suppose… Are you acquainted with my Lord Byron?'

'I know of him—all the scandals and the notoriety that he enjoys. And read his works of course. I thoroughly enjoyed *The Corsair*, but I think my mother would not welcome his lordship as a visitor to her withdrawing room. However free thinking she might claim to be, she disapproves of unbridled volatility above all things.'

Judith could think of no reply to this revelation.

'So will you help, Judith?' Thea returned to her original plea. 'I think we should deal well together.'

'I should be delighted.' Judith found her voice at last. And felt as if she had just been swept along by a positive whirlwind!

'On first acquaintance, I think that London could offer me a deal of pleasure.' Thea took another sip of ratafia with remarkably smooth features and looked hopeful.

'Oh, yes.' Judith gave a sigh of satisfaction and silently thanked her mama. Theodora Wooton-Devereux could just be a gift from heaven. But what polite society would make of Miss Wooton-Devereux, Judith could not imagine. It would be just too fascinating to discover. She decided to take the matter in hand immediately.

'If I might say, Thea—that is a very pretty stole. Quite eye-catching.'

'Yes. I like it.' Thea rearranged the folds of the scarf. 'I bought it in Palmyra. It is considered to be very typical of the delicate work produced in that city.' She caught a look in Judith's eye. 'Is there perhaps a problem with it? You must tell me, for I have not the slightest inclination.'

'Well—yes, it is certainly very attractive—but perhaps not for morning wear, you understand, as it is rather…decorative! For an afternoon visit it would be unexceptional. Or an evening at home. I hope that you do not mind me mentioning it?'

'Why, no.' Thea held up the luxurious fringing for inspection. 'Really? I would not have known. And I would dislike above all things to be considered lacking in taste. There! I said that we might deal well together, dear Judith.'

'I do hope so.' The Countess nodded with satisfaction.

'Now, enough of me. Tell me about yourself and your family.' Thea folded her hands in her lap and set herself to be sociable. 'Is your husband at home?'

'No, he is not. Simon has gone to Newmarket! I am quite vexed about it.'

'Ah! I understand that you have a young son.'

'Oh, yes. Giles. Now he is quite adorable. Come and see.'

Thea sighed a little, but was determined to fulfil her social duties. After all, she owed Judith much for her unaffected welcome of an unknown lady to her home, and suspected that she would owe her more before her sojourn in London came to an end. With a not quite enthusiastic smile, but a sharp relief at being able to abandon the much disliked ratafia, she followed Judith up the sweep of the staircase to the nursery to meet the heir to the Painscastle inheritance, prepared to admire and be charmed as was required.

Why her mother thought she needed a husband and children of her own, she could not imagine!

Thea returned to the smart rented property in Upper Brook Street, worthy of one of his Majesty's Ambassadors, to find a chaotic scene of boxes and packages littering the generous entrance hall. Their luggage, it appeared, had finally caught up with them. Servants, hired with the house, were in evidence and in the centre of it all, directing operations with imperious manner and a list in her hand, was Lady Drusilla. As wife to the Ambassador, she had successfully moved homes—and countries—many times. Sir Hector was, sensibly, nowhere to be seen. There was no hope, Thea realised, of her making an entrance undetected, so she did not try.

'Theodora! Where have you been? And without your maid—do not even try to deny it! Agnes informed me of your *sneaking* off within minutes of your leaving the house! As you must know she would!'

Thea bridled at the onslaught, even if it was expected. It was simply one more nail in the coffin of her much-prized freedom. 'If you had wished me to follow every social convention, you should have brought me up differently, Mama.' Her eyes snapped with irritation. She would have a few well-chosen words with Agnes Drew, her childhood nurse and now her maid—or perhaps more of a companion and confidante—whose loyalty seemed to be as much to Lady Drusilla as to herself.

'True. I myself have no time for many of them. That one. And that.' The lady pointed at two boxes and crossed them off her list as they were carried away. 'But here in London—it is important to have a care.'

'I have been out of the house barely two hours—and done nothing to draw attention to myself.' Thea narrowed her eyes at her mother's back. 'How should you think otherwise! Your opinion of me is not flattering, Mama.'

'Nonsense! My opinion of you is of the highest as you are very well aware. But by the end of the Season I hope to have acquired a rich and titled husband for you.' She announced her intentions with supreme disregard for the interested audience of maids and footmen around her.

'I know. An Earl. Any one of them will do, however old and ill favoured. As long as he is titled and rich! And available!'

'Now, Theodora! I have it on the best authority—from your father, no less—that the Earl of Moreton is in town. He is neither old nor ill favoured and has, I am given to understand, considerable address. Since he also has the advantage of being unmarried, he sounds to be just the thing. I have every hope.' For the first time, Lady Drusilla gave her daughter her full attention and noted the heightened colour in her cheeks, hardly engendered by a gentle stroll along Upper Brook Street, plus the sparkle in her eyes, which denoted a flash of temper. 'What have you been doing to put yourself so out of countenance?'

'Nothing. I am *not* out of countenance.' Except that she was after listening for an hour—was it only an hour?—to Judith singing the praises of a husband who seemed pleasant enough, but dull in the extreme. An equally tedious lifestyle of trivial pursuits and pastimes in London, of visits and conversations with the same set of acquaintance day after day, week after week. Winter spent incarcerated in the depths of the country, trapped by bad weather and worse roads. Was that the life for which she was destined? She shuddered at the prospect. There was no point telling her mama, who had quite made up her mind, of her fears, her depressing thoughts. But she did not have to like it. Or the unknown Earl of Moreton!

'So, where have you been?'

'To pay a morning call on Lady Painscastle.'

'I see. I am quite sure that you should not have done that without an invitation, Thea.' Lady Drusilla frowned her disapproval, but kept her tone light.

'Oh, she did not mind. I liked her. And she did not turn me from the door—although her butler would have dearly liked to.' A faint smile illuminated Thea's face at the memory.

'It is all your own fault if you allow servants the opportunity to patronise you, my dear.' Thea had to admire her mother's worldly wisdom expressed so casually. 'Take your maid in future! And wear a hat. I expect it is not at all the thing to go about with your head uncovered. At least you had the sense to wear gloves.'

'Yes, Mama.'

'So?' Lady Drusilla raised her brows. 'What has ruffled your feathers?'

Thea sighed a little. 'Do I really need a husband?'

'Yes. We have had this conversation before. You know my reasons—and your father's, of course.'

'But I have enjoyed independence for all my twenty-one years. Travel. Culture. Pleasing myself. Why can I not continue to do so?'

'You cannot travel for the rest of your life, Theodora. It is not suitable.'

'But you have.' Thea sat herself down on one of the unopened wooden packing cases, swinging her reticule carelessly by its silken strings.

'I had the felicity to meet and marry your father. Such opportunities as wife to a royal Ambassador are not given to everyone. You need a husband who will admire you for your qualities and allow you freedom to express yourself. As Sir Hector allowed me. I hope you will not *break* anything in that case on which you are sitting!'

Thea hid a smile. Secretly she doubted that Sir Hector had had any choice in his wife's chosen lifestyle. 'Does such a husband exist for me, do you suppose?'

'Of course.'

Thea pursed her pretty lips, looking sceptical, but made no reply.

'It is merely a matter of learning a few rules, knowing how to go on. And if you could pretend to be demure and biddable for a few weeks—'

'Ha!'

'And converse in a genteel and respectful manner, without interruption—'

'About fashion and embroidery, the latest dance and the latest *on dit*.'

'Exactly.'

'Oh, Mama. What have you committed me to!'

'It is not purgatory, my love.'

'And growing my hair into curls and ringlets again, if the glances I received today are anything to say to the matter.'

'I told you that you should not have been so extravagant! But you would do it!' Lady Drusilla stepped round a pair of leather travelling cases and leaned to kiss her daughter lightly on the cheek. She understood and sympathised with her concerns very well. 'You are a lovely young woman of whom I am very proud. Whether you grow your hair again, my love, is purely a matter of your own personal choice.'

'I have no intention of doing so.' Thea returned the salute and rose to her feet. 'By the by, I arranged for us to pay an afternoon call on Lady Beatrice Faringdon tomorrow if that suits.'

'Certainly. An excellent idea. My acquaintance with Lady Beatrice is from the very distant past, when we were still girls, but she is, I think, knowledgeable and accommodating. And, most important, has entrée to the best families in London. So begins our first step in the campaign.' Lady Drusilla crossed off two more items on her list. 'Did you learn anything other of import?'

'No. Except that this stole is pretty enough, but far more suitable for evening wear than for a morning visit.' The lady raised her brows, her mouth curling into a mischievous smile, as she lifted the delicate scarf from her shoulders.

'Oh.' Lady Drusilla inspected the garment with sudden interest. 'Perhaps we shall need a new wardrobe. It would not do to be regarded as *provincial*. Or oriental in our case! What is suitable in Constantinople is quite plainly not suitable here.'

The two ladies exchanged smiles, their differences reconciled.

'Let us go and discuss the matter with your father. Who, you will notice, has absented himself from all this.' She waved her hand in an expansive gesture at the chaos around her feet, then handed her list with great willingness to one of the footmen. 'And then, dear Thea, when we have some funds at our disposal, perhaps a stroll down Bond Street would be in order.'

* * *

On the following afternoon Lady Drusilla Wooton-Devereux and her daughter, with Agnes Drew discreetly, if a trifle smugly, in attendance, applied the knocker to Lady Beatrice Faringdon's imposing establishment in Berkeley Square. Expected, they were admitted and ushered into the lady's withdrawing room.

'Drusilla. My dear.' Lady Beatrice surged to her feet with a rustle of the puce damask that shrouded her opulent figure and clashed uncomfortably with her fading red hair. 'And this must be your daughter. Theodora.' She held out a hand in greeting, then halted, the hand falling to her side, and raised her lorgnette to deadly effect. She did not need to apply the lens as her eyesight was perfect. But the gesture was guaranteed to make an impression. She levelled the glass at her friend's daughter, surveyed her with a critical thoroughness from head to foot, and drew in a breath.

'Well. Caro Lamb, as I live and breathe!'

Which unwise comment was guaranteed to bring about a distinct pause in the proceedings. Lady Caroline Ponsonby, as she was before her marriage to William Lamb, Viscount Melbourne, was a spoiled capricious beauty whose appearance, behaviour and wild, tempestuous affair with Lord Byron some years previously had scandalised a notoriously decadent society.

Theodora took it upon herself to reply, with the politest of smiles, before her mother could intervene. But there was a noticeable edge to her voice and a glint in her eye, which might be interpreted as a challenge to their hostess. 'I hope that my upbringing has been more respectable than that of Lady Melbourne. It is certainly not my intention to distress my relatives by my outrageous behaviour or to take the town by storm in quite the same manner as that unfortunate lady. I would consider it exceptionally bad *ton* either to fly into a fit of rage in public, or to attempt to slash my wrists with broken glass.'

Lady Beatrice actually coloured at the implied set-down.

'Forgive me, my dear girl! Drusilla! It was not my intention to be so ill mannered. It is just… The hair, you understand. So fair…and so short. And so slender a figure. A mere fleeting impression, I do assure you.' She thought for a moment and raised her glass again. 'You have not been *ill*, have you?'

'Of course she has not.' Lady Drusilla stepped into the breach with calming words, a gracious smile for Lady Beatrice and a narrowed glance toward her daughter. 'We have travelled extensively in recent months in Arabia to see some of the archaeological sites. Theodora found it expedient to cut her hair. The sand is a great trial, you understand, and not kind to long hair. Theodora is always excessively healthy!'

'Of course. Forgive me, dear Drusilla…' Lady Beatrice almost gushed.

'And is nothing like poor Caro Lamb.'

'Indeed no. My wits must have abandoned me.' Lady Beatrice managed to recover her air of self-assurance and smiled with a trifle more warmth at the young lady who still regarded her with the coolest of expressions. 'And so charmingly dressed. I remember seeing Lady Melbourne in the most inappropriate gowns—if you could call them that—with not a stitch on beneath them, I warrant. Little wonder that she always looked as if a brisk breeze would demolish her. Some of the young girls today…' Lady Beatrice shook her head and brought her thoughts in line. 'But that is of no account. I am so delighted to see you again. Come and sit. And you, Theodora. How long is it since we last met, Drusilla?'

'Far too long to contemplate!'

The difficulties over, the three ladies sat, the two older ones intent on catching up over a dish of tea. Their paths had not crossed since school girls at Miss Felton's Academy for Young Ladies in Bath. Drusilla Hatton, as a daughter of wealthy parents, had even then nursed ambitions to travel and experience for herself what life could offer. Beatrice had been destined for a Season in London and as advantageous a marriage as she could achieve. The two girls had parted with many tears and protestations of undying loyalty. They would keep in touch. But they had not. And so of necessity the ladies had grown apart.

As the two ladies set to reminisce, Thea let her thoughts wonder, listening with only half an ear to the less than exciting doings of her parent at the Academy in Bath. What could they find to talk about that was of interest after all these years? It all sounded desperately dull and hedged about with restriction and parental expectations. She hid a yawn with considerable expertise. It reminded her of the worst of formal diplomatic receptions where nothing happened to relieve the tedium and no one had anything of moment to say after the introductions had been made. Thea fervently wished that she had found another occupation for the afternoon—until a stray comment from Lady Beatrice caught her attention.

'You had a sister, I remember. A year or so older, at school with us. Mary, I think.'

Thea's eyes snapped to her mother's face.

'Yes. You have a good memory.'

I did not know that my mother had a sister! Why did I not know? Lady Drusilla's reply was smooth enough, and yet Thea sensed the slightest of hesitations, a hint of reserve in her voice. She turned her attention fully.

'Does she live in London?' Lady Beatrice went on to enquire.

'No. Mary lived her whole life in the country. And is now dead. Some years ago.'

'I am sorry. Did she perhaps have family?'

'Yes. Two…two children. But we had not kept in touch. There was… an estrangement. Her marriage was not an easy one. I was not made welcome in her house.'

'You need not tell me about difficult marriages…'

The conversation moved on, leaving Thea to wonder about this branch of the family of which she was completely unaware.

The visit drew to a natural close when the ladies ran out of events and people to recall, criticise and chuckle over.

'As you know, we do not expect to remain long in London.' Lady Drusilla drew on her gloves in preparation to making her departure. 'But it is my wish to see my daughter married. You were kind enough to offer to ease our entrée into London society. I cannot express my gratitude sufficiently, Beatrice.'

'It will be my pleasure. At the end of the week I have an invitation to Lady Aston's drum. All the world and his wife will be there, I expect. It has been my intention to get up a small party—just family and close friends, you understand. I am expecting my nephew Nicholas to arrive here from the country any day—that is, if his recent correspondence rings true. But he is a difficult boy to pin down, with a mind of his own, and getting him to put in an appearance in town is more aggravating than you could possibly believe...' Lady Beatrice shook her head and huffed in indulgent irritation at the vagaries of her wiful relative. 'But that aside—you, my dear Drusilla, must come as my guest. It will be the perfect opportunity for you. And for Theodora to make some acquaintances.'

'We shall be delighted.' Lady Drusilla rose to her feet. 'It is my intention to entertain from Upper Brook Street, but we are not yet fully settled, as you might imagine.'

'Perhaps I might suggest—' Lady Beatrice cast another assessing glance towards Thea, who stood demurely beside her mother as if the visit had provided her with nothing but delight '—the matter of suitable dresses for dear Theodora. Not that she does not look charming. But...'

They both eyed the lady in question as if she were a strange object from antiquity.

'I thought she looked particularly fetching this afternoon.' Lady Drusilla stood back to take in the overall impression created by a high-waisted walking dress with long tight sleeves and a ruched hem in an eye-catching emerald and cream stripe.

'Yes. There is no question of that...' Beatrice was quick to soothe. 'But not quite in the way of a débutante.'

Lady Drusilla gave a little sigh. 'I have to admit that my daughter is not perhaps quite in the way of the usual débutante! I fear that it is my fault.'

'How old are you, my dear?' Lady Beatrice asked.

'I am twenty-one, Lady Beatrice.' Then, after a moment's hesitation, Thea could not prevent herself from adding, 'I fear that I have no control over that unfortunate situation.'

'Mmm.' The lorgnette came into play again. Lady Beatrice came to a rapid and sensible decision. 'Well. We will not allow it to be a problem. Perhaps we should say that Theodora made her curtsy to the Polite World in Constantinople. I am sure there were any number of official functions there which she attended.'

'Indeed she did. She helped me entertain on numerous occasions. She is perfectly versed in how to go on in such circles, so I have no fears on that account.'

Thea set her teeth against being talked over and around in such a fashion but, more amused than discomfited, allowed the ladies to continue their plans.

'She will need some suitable dresses. With a less—shall we say, *exotic* flavour. I am not sure what it is, but... Such a vibrant shade with such intricate decoration is not quite *suitable* for a young girl...'

'Very well. I bow to your judgement. Perhaps tomorrow morning we should visit the modistes in Bond Street. If you could recommend...?'

'I shall do more than recommend, dear Drusilla. I shall be delighted to accompany you...'

And so it was all settled. Theodora would make her curtsey at Lady Aston's drum, tastefully dressed, as far a possible, *à la jeune fille*.

The ladies parted in complete accord and satisfaction.

'Why did I not know of your sister? That I have cousins?' The two Wooton-Devereux ladies strolled home along Park Lane, parasols angled to shield their skin from the rays of the sun.

'The subject never came up.' Thea detected the slightest of shrugs as her mother replied. Nor was she fooled by the bland expression on her face.

'Mama!'

'We—Mary and I—were estranged,' Lady Drusilla explained further. 'I found it...painful. As I told Beatrice, we had had no contact for many years.'

'But you knew that she had died.'

'Yes. It was reported in the *Morning Post*. When we were in Paris.'

'I just thought you would have mentioned it—the fact that there were members of the family whom I had never met.'

'I suppose that I did not see any reason to do so. I had no intention of picking up the connection with that side of the family. There was nothing more sinister than that, I do assure you, Thea. Such estrangements happen in families. You have only to look at your father's cousin. He has not spoken to his own son for the best part of a decade.'

'I see.'

'Mary and I simply did not get on.'

Thea let the matter drop, but did not forget it. And it struck her some time later that during the whole of Lady Drusilla's explanation her eyes, usually so direct and forthright, had never once met those of her daughter.

Chapter Three

Lady Beatrice finally gave up on appearances, closed Miss Austen's *Emma*, which she had been assured was most refined and enjoyable, but over which she had been yawning, and allowed her eyes to close. After an exhausting morning spent choosing a new pair of evening gloves to wear at Lady Aston's drum, Lady Beatrice desired nothing more than to settle on to a comfortable sofa in a quiet parlour with the shades drawn and rest her eyes. She certainly had no intention of being at home to visitors. Instead, within minutes, she found herself playing hostess to Judith, who arrived in a flurry of energy to discuss with her mama their new friends. And then, following quickly on her heels, Lord Nicholas Faringdon.

'Nicholas. I had quite given up hope of seeing you this week. When did you arrive?' Lady Beatrice stretched out her hands in sincere pleasure, but did not bother to struggle to her feet. 'Ring the bell, Judith, for tea.'

'Would I dare ignore your summons, Aunt? I came yesterday evening.' Nicholas strode across the room to where his aunt was seated, raised her hands and kissed her fingers with rare grace. 'You look in excellent health, as ever.'

'Never mind my health! Let me look at you.' But she smiled almost girlishly at her nephew's elegant gesture as she surveyed him from head to foot. It was a relief to see him in town rig. For although he was no dandy and might have rusticated at Burford for over a year, there was nothing of the unfashionable country squire in the gentleman who graced her withdrawing room. The close-fitting coat of dark blue superfine, with all the hallmark of Weston's exquisite tailoring, was unexceptional. As were the pale biscuit pantaloons, polished Hessians and the sober but tasteful waistcoat. His neckcloth had been arranged with meticulous attention to detail. Altogether, a Man of Fashion.

'Very fine!' was the only comment she made. 'My letter was not in any way a summons. Merely a request. And, yes, you have been ignoring my advice for any number of years. Ever since you attained your majority, I shouldn't wonder.'

'I was not aware that I was so disobliging.' Nicholas turned to drop a light kiss on his cousin's cheek. 'Judith—and how is the heir to the Painscastle acres?'

'Giles is in excellent form. You must come to visit us, of course.' She patted the seat next to her. 'It is good to have you here Nick. We had thought you were becoming buried alive at Burford. Don't tell me that you have a young lady there who lures you into rural seclusion.'

'I shall tell you no such thing.' He showed his teeth in a quick smile, refusing to be baited.

'So you don't have a lady who is the object of your gallantry to while away the winter evenings?' She laughed, slanted him an arch look, glinting with mischief. 'I cannot believe that the ladies of Herefordshire are so blind to your charms. No cosy armful tucked away in the depths of Aymestry?'

'Judith! Such levity! It does not become you.' Beatrice frowned, rescued Nicholas and steered the conversation into the area of her own choosing. An area no less full of subtle—or not so subtle—suggestion.

'Now, tell us—how is Henry? And Eleanor. We have not heard for some months.'

'Hal is very well.' Nicholas leaned back and prepared to do his bit for family news and deflect any personal comments from either his aunt or his cousin. 'And he is now in possession of a thriving business, it seems. They have moved into the house. Eleanor said she was delighted to have her own front door at last. Her letter was full of furnishings and decorations as I recall. Hal's pockets will have to be bottomless if she is to have her way.'

'Eleanor is in an *interesting condition*, I believe.'

'Yes. She is. They are very happy.'

'As they deserve to be.' Beatrice nodded. 'What a blessing it was that they escaped the toils of that truly appalling man Edward Baxendale.'

Baxendale!

The name would have twisted Lord Nicholas's lips into a snarl if he had not been sitting in the civilised surroundings of Lady Beatrice's withdrawing room. Even now, after two years or more, it had the power to heat his blood and fill him with immoderate fury.

Sir Edward Baxendale had claimed that the marriage of Eleanor to Nicholas's eldest brother Thomas was illegal, and thus her baby son not, as all believed, the Marquis of Burford, but stained with the stigma of illegitimacy. He'd presented his own wife Octavia, with diabolical cunning, as Thomas's true wife, the true Marchioness of Burford. Since Thomas had died in a tragic accident, the shocking tale had cast the family into instant scandal, only salvaged by the efforts of Nicholas and his brother Hal proving that Eleanor's marriage to Thomas had indeed been valid and Baxendale nothing but a malevolent trickster. Hal had then declared his love for Eleanor and, with typical highhandedness, taken her and the baby off to New York. But all could so easily have been a disaster if Baxendale had triumphed. So much pain deliberately inflicted by the greed of one man. No wonder Nicholas detested Sir Edward with every sinew in his body, every drop of blood.

By sheer effort of will, Nicholas forced his muscles to relax, his hands to unclench, as Lady Beatrice continued with her social catechism, unaware of the impact of her chance comment.

'And Tom. He will be more than three years old now.'

'Four more like. Time passes. Eleanor said that Hal was teaching him to ride.'

'Do you think they will ever return?' Judith asked a little wistfully.

'No. I do not. I think Hal's life is there in America.'

'And the estate?' Disapproval was clear in Beatrice's tight-lipped mouth. She simply could not accept that the young Marquis of Burford should be allowed to live in America, far from his family, his land and his responsibilities. It was beyond anything. 'What will happen to it? It is all very well—'

'I don't know,' Nicholas broke in before she could get into full flow. This was not a new situation over which they disagreed. 'That is for the future. For the present it is carefully administered. I shall not permit anything other. What Hal will choose to do is entirely his own concern. And nothing to do with me—or, with respect, with you, Aunt Beatrice!'

Which statement, Lady Beatrice decided with something akin to shock, was certainly guaranteed to put her in her place!

'No. And of course you will act in the best interests of the family. I would expect no less and I intended no criticism of your trusteeship.' Beatrice controlled her concerns, leaned over to pat his arm. 'There is no point in discussing it further. Forgive me, Nicholas.' With respect, indeed! Now here was a novelty! 'Now, since you are here at last, perhaps you can escort us to Almack's one evening.' She hesitated only momentarily before launching in. 'There are some very pretty débutantes this Season.'

'I am sure there are.'

'One or two are quite exceptional. Sir John Carver's daughter, for instance.'

Nicholas raised his hand, turning a stern gaze on his aunt. His eyes, often so friendly and full of laughter, had the quality of ice. As had his voice. He may as well, he decided, nip this in the bud immediately. 'Aunt Beatrice, I wish that you would not. I am perfectly capable of selecting a wife for myself without any help from you, *when* I decide that I wish to marry. I agree with you that I should consider it, but it will be in the time of my choosing, as will be the identity of the lady who I eventually ask to become my bride. Do we have an understanding?'

There it was, laid out for her. Beatrice stiffened at the snub, taken aback for the second time since Nicholas had entered the room. She had forgotten that her nephew was no longer a young and impressionable boy. It was so easy to forget when he was the youngest in the family. But the years had moved on and he had put her firmly in her place twice within as many minutes with a perfect exhibition of suave, cool—and implacable—good manners. Beatrice took in the stern mouth, the austere features, and wisely retreated.

'Of course. I would not dream of interfering in your affairs, my boy—'

'Yes, you would. But I ask that you do not. I would not wish to feel obliged to refuse your kind invitations. And I will if necessary.' He was clearly not prepared to compromise over this. 'I am sure that you take my meaning?'

Oh, yes. She took his meaning very well—and realised that she must reassess Lord Nicholas Faringdon. She raised her hands and let them fall in her lap. 'Of course. I will do nothing that you do not wish for, Nicholas.'

'I should be grateful, Aunt.' He deliberately changed the subject. 'So, how is Sher? I have not seen or heard from him for well over a year.'

Lord Joshua Sherbourne Faringdon. Undoubtedly the black sheep of the otherwise impeccable Faringdon family. And the bane of Lady Beatrice's life.

'My son Joshua is still in Paris.'

'Is he well?'

'I presume.' The response from the less than doting mama was tight-lipped. 'All we hear is scandal and gossip.'

'He has a new mistress,' Judith added with an irrepressible twinkle. 'An actress, we understand.'

'I think that is not a subject for my withdrawing room, Judith. Joshua will go to the devil in his own way. There is no need for us to show interest in it. Now…did you know that Simon has been to Newmarket? One of his horses is expected to do particularly well on the Turf this year...'

The conversation passed into calmer waters, Nicholas turning to Judith for news of Simon and the promising stallion.

Beatrice watched the pair as they sat at ease, reliving old times, discussing friends in common. It was time Nicholas married. He needed a family. Not merely the responsibility of the estate—God knew he had enough of that!—but responsibility for a wife and children. He had been too long pleasing himself. He needed someone to ruffle his equilibrium, to shake his self-confidence. It appeared that he could be as difficult and opinionated as all male Faringdons. Look at Henry. A law unto himself, taking himself and Eleanor and the child off to New York without a word to anyone! And as for her own dearest husband, now long deceased, and her son...whom she did not even wish to contemplate. They were all the same—excessively handsome with all the charm and address in the world, but all with that fatal streak of arrogance and self-worth. And Nicholas, to make matters more difficult, had that cool reserve which was difficult to shake. When *that* had developed she did not know, but the aura of cold detachment and control coated him with a hard brilliance.

At least Judith was easy to deal with—she was like an open book! Beatrice watched with affection her daughter's expressive face as she laughed at some comment from Nicholas. That was from *her* side of the family, of course, just as much as the red hair and green eyes. Nicholas was a Faringdon from his dark hair and equally dark brows to his toes of his polished boots. And he needed someone who would challenge his intellect and keep him on those toes—give him something to think about other than farming and cattle and such.

She watched, tapping her lorgnette against her lips as she studied him, the lad whom she had known from birth and had watched grow into this spectacularly handsome young man. Even tempered, easy to converse with, but underneath...Well, they said still waters... She was quite sure that he could acquire a bride with an arch of those expressive brows or a crook of his finger. But not *any* débutante would do. He needed someone to stir him out of his complacence. He was too much in the habit of going his own way with no one to question his decisions or his opinion.

Lady Beatrice blinked as the thought slid so simply, so effortlessly into her mind, the image as clear as an etching on crystal. Now *there* was an interesting prospect. Beauty. Money. Excellent breeding. But also strong-willed, independent, outspoken and… Well! What could be better?

'Nicholas…' She interrupted the exchange of news between her nephew and her daughter. 'Will you be very busy during your stay in town?'

'Nothing out of the way. I have an appointment to see Hoskins. My tailor will no doubt see me. Friends, of course. I have no definite plans. Why?'

'No reason.' Her smile was pure innocence. 'Perhaps you would care to attend a number of social engagements with us? An extra gentleman is always valuable in a party. And you dance so well.'

'Why not? Since you are concerned to flatter me…' His tone and demeanour had reclaimed their habitual warmth, the chill forgotten. He saw nothing suspicious in Beatrice's bland smile and innocuous request, believing that he had made his opinions on the matter of marriage quite clear. Why should he harbour suspicions? And it would be good to circulate in society again.

'Tomorrow we are engaged to attend Lady Aston's drum. A large affair, totally lacking in exclusivity as such things usually are, but entertaining enough. I have got up a small party. Perhaps you would care to join us? We have some new acquaintance in town. One of them is to be our Royal Ambassador to the Russian Court. I am sure you will find him interesting company.'

'I am sure that I shall.'

Beatrice glanced over at Judith, smiled, her eyes guileless. And Judith, in spite of no words being spoken between them, was in no doubt as to exactly what her mama's plan might be.

'Do come.' Judith turned her persuasive gaze on her cousin. 'It should be a most entertaining evening.'

Unaware of the machinations of his female relatives, ignorant of the trap about to close over his head, Lord Nicholas bowed his agreement.

In Grosvenor Square on the following morning, very early, it was brought home to Nicholas how long it had been since his last visit to town. His body and mind were not in tune with town hours where it was customary to sleep and rise late. A combination of rural habits and the early sun through his bedroom window over and above the array of noises of a large city awakening to a new day—all assaulted his senses to ensure that he was wide awake. So he rose, dressed and headed for the stables behind Faringdon House. He might as well make the most of the opportunity to ride in Hyde Park so early as it would be mostly deserted; since he had no particular desire to converse with those who wished to parade and make a fashionable statement, it was the ideal time. There was a young horse that would benefit from a confidence-boosting outing without the habitual bustle and racket of London streets.

It was a perfect morning. He breathed deeply, encouraging the mare into a brisk walk through the light traffic. Through the ornamental gates and there, with an easing of the reins, he allowed the horse to break into a sedate canter along the grassy edge to the walk. And smiled his satisfaction. She was just as fluid and easy in her action as he had hoped.

In Upper Brook Street, Theodora woke from a restless sleep, certain that she would positively burst if she did not escape from the house and take some exercise, unwatched by either her mama or the ever-vigilant Agnes Drew. London was noisy, exciting, fascinating, all that she had hoped. But the restrictions irked. She was never alone. If she set foot outside the front door, Agnes had been instructed to be in attendance, even if all she did was step out to Hookham's Circulating Library, no further than Bond Street. She found it difficult to accept this necessity. She was hardly likely to be accosted by armed tribesmen or bands of fearsome robbers as might have been expected anywhere on their perambulations through Arabia. She closed her mind against that thought with a little shake of her head. She would not think about it…not now.

Therefore, driven by a need for open space and not a little adventure, Thea rose early before even the servants were afoot. No one would know if she rode in Hyde Park. She would be home long before one of the maids brought her morning cup of hot chocolate, long before anyone else—Agnes!—had the opportunity to miss her. And there would be no one in the park at this hour who would even take note of her, much less recognise her in the future. Perfect!

Thea stood before the doors of her closet. Then her face lit with mischief on a sudden thought. Of course. Why not? No one would ever know. She closed the door on her riding habit and, in a moment of delicious rebellion, turned from the closet and unearthed her travelling clothes from the chest in her dressing room. Without another moment to consider the impropriety of what she was about to do, she donned a long-sleeved shirt, a striped loose-weave waistcoat, loose breeches and boots, covering all with the light cloak she had worn in the desert, finally wrapping the long scarf round her hair. There. Her disguise was complete. She postured before the mirror. She would defy anyone to recognise her in future, at some social event, even if they did catch a glimpse of her that morning. Had she not been so very good and accommodating of her parents' plans for so long? Days at least! She deserved a treat, a moment of freedom.

Even the stables were deserted. She saddled her own mount, The Zephyr, one of the grey Arabs that they had shipped to London who was also in need of a good run, tossing her head and snatching at the bit with anticipation. It took no time at all to negotiate the empty streets, and if the shrouded figure earned some surprised glances and muttered comments, Thea was either unaware or simply did not care. The magnificent gateway opposite Apsley House beckoned. Once through Thea took a deep breath. She had been right to come. This was just what she needed. She eased into a canter, and then, the breeze tugging at her robes, she pushed the horse on into a gallop. The Arab responded with alacrity, leaping forward against the bit, its neat hooves skimming the ground as it fought for its head. Thea leaned into the movement with a little crow of pleasure, revelling in the speed and excitement. Exhilaration sang in her blood, rich as red wine, just as intoxicating. She gave herself over to the splendour of the moment, oblivious to everything around her but the pound of the hooves, the whip of the soft air on her face, the satin-smooth ripple of the horse's muscles beneath her.

Nicholas's mind was filled with nothing very much, apart from the excellent confirmation of his young mare as she answered the demands of heel and thigh. Nothing to disturb the placid tenor of the morning until he heard the sharp beat of hooves on grass, at speed coming from his left. He turned his head, his attention immediately caught. At considerable speed, he realised. He reined in the mare to look, squinting against the early rays of the sun, and saw a figure approaching at an angle, surely at full gallop, the rider crouched low in the saddle as the animal extended until it flew across the ground. Surely it was out of control. No one galloped in Hyde Park as though it was the hunting field. Or more like the Turf at Newmarket, given the speed of the animal. No one would choose to ride hell for leather here.

For the briefest moment Nicholas allowed himself to admire the fluid lines of the grey, the excellent conformation, the sheer beauty of the sight, but for a moment only. On a rapid decision, he kicked his mare on to intercept as the prospect of danger touched his spine with a shiver of unease. If the rider fell at that speed, there could be serious consequences. The animal could stumble, shy—and it seemed that the rider had no chance of drawing it to a standstill. Nor would intercepting be an easy matter on an untried young horse. But he must try.

Since the galloping animal kept up its headlong flight, Nicholas was forced to extend to head it off. His mare responded readily. The grey became aware of his approach, her ears twitching, even if her rider did not appear to react. She veered as he drew abreast but did not check her stride. If anything, she increased her momentum.

For what seemed like minutes—but was more likely seconds only—the two horses galloped side by side, the enforced rivalry adding an edge to the grey's speed, until Nicholas moved close enough that he could lean across the gap between them and grasp the bridle just above the bit, trusting his own animal to remain on course. She did, allowing him to tighten his muscles in arm, shoulder and thigh, grimacing at the strain as he drew both horses to a more seemly speed and finally to a trembling halt, their sides heaving with effort, nostrils wide, eyes rolling. At the same time he grasped the wrist of the rider in a firm hold, in case the grey jinked in sudden panic.

'You are quite safe. You are in no danger now.'

Nicholas's breathing was a little unsteady as he continued to control the reins of both horses. He looked down at the rider— a young boy, he thought, at closer inspection—to see if his reassurances were necessary, only to be struck by a pair of furious blue eyes turned on him, blazing with…what? Anger? Shock? But also more than a hint of fear.

'You are quite safe,' he repeated. Of course, the rider would be unnerved after such an uncontrolled bolt across the Park.

Before he could say or do more, the boy raised a riding crop and brought it down in a deliberate and painful blow across Nicholas's hand where he still had hold of the rider's wrist. Nicholas flinched, hissed, took a sharp intake of breath, perhaps more in amazement than pain, as a red welt appeared across the width of his fingers.

'What the devil…!'

'How dare you! Take your hands off me!' The rider pushed back the scarf—and Nicholas looked down into the face of a woman.

'How dare you interfere!' Her blue eyes were dark, almost black with emotion.

'I thought, madam, that your horse was out of control.' It was difficult to know what other to say. The last thing Nicholas had expected was to be under attack for his gallant, and supremely successful, attempt to rescue a damsel in distress. The absurdity of the situation might have amused him. It might if the blow on his hand was not so searingly painful!

'No, I was not out of control.' There was now the hint of a tremble in the angry voice. 'You had no right.' He watched as a range of emotions flitted across her face. Uppermost it seemed to him was a determination to regain control of a fear that threatened to overwhelm her.

He discovered that he was still grasping her wrist.

'I said, let go!'

Their eyes met and held for a long moment which seemed to stretch on and on. They remained frozen in the little tableau as the air positively sizzled between them, around them, as when lightning strikes in a summer storm—rapid, without warning, and possibly devastating. Nicholas was the first to break the contact.

'Forgive me.' He released her, cold now, all humour banished under the lash of her words and the shock of his reaction to her. 'I thought you were in distress.'

'No, I was not.'

'My mistake.' Reserve infiltrated his voice, but he still watched her carefully. There was some problem here of which he was unaware. 'Next time I will allow you to fall and break your neck.'

'Do so. There will not be a next time. I do not need your help. How dare you put your hands on a lady in this manner!'

Any latent sympathy Nicholas might have felt promptly vanished. 'You must excuse my concern, madam.' He looked her over from head to foot, taking in the whole of her appearance. 'I did not realise. I would not expect to see a *lady* galloping in Hyde Park. Please accept my apologies.' The emphasis in his words was unmistakable and made Thea flush, angrier than ever.

'Let go of my reins.'

He did with alacrity and reined his own animal away from her. In that one moment he thought, although perhaps he was mistaken, that there was a hint of tears in those eyes, which still snapped with temper.

The lady, if such she was, gathered up her own reins, kicked the still lively grey into action and set off in a canter towards the distant gate without a backward look.

Leaving Nicholas to sit and stare after her.

Thea arrived home, delivered The Zephyr into the hands of a sleepy groom who gazed at her in wordless astonishment, fled to her room and locked the door. There she stripped off her incriminating garments, folded them back into the chest and tied a ruffled, feminine muslin wrapper around her. Then, as the furious energy drained away, she sank on to the bed and covered her face with her hands.

What had she done? Not the gallop in the park. She could never regret that. How the grey had flown, fast as a desert hawk towards its prey. But she had struck him. The man who had come to her rescue. However unnecessary it might have been, he had thought she had been in danger and had ridden to her rescue. And what had she done? She had marked him with her riding whip. And then she had been so rude. Unforgivably so. She could not remember her exact words, uttered in the heat and confusion of the moment, but knew that they had been ungracious. Vicious, even. What would he think of her? How could she have allowed herself to do that?

But she knew why. And whatever the extenuating circumstances, she blamed herself totally.

She relived the events in her mind as she curled on to the bed in that sunny room. She had been unaware of his approach, so lost in the unity of horse and rider, in the glorious speed. But then, in that moment when his horse had stretched beside hers, when he had leaned and grasped her reins, his strong hands forcing her to come to a halt, the past had rushed back with all its pain and fear. She had thought it was forgotten, or mostly so, pushed away, buried deep within her subconscious, only to emerge with infrequent intensity when nightmares troubled her sleep.

She had been very young, hardly more than a child. On one of their journeys they had been beset by robbers in spite of the size and strength of their entourage. Forced to halt, to dismount, to stand and watch as her mother's jewellery was stripped from her, as her father was threatened at the point of a knife. The fear had been intense. They had been allowed to go free at the end, but the terror of that moment when they were held captive and in fear for their lives had not quite gone away.

Thea shook her head, scrubbed her hands over her face as if to dislodge the thoughts. She should not be so fearful now—but she had been only a little girl, after all. And her arm had been broken when she had been pulled from her horse. She rubbed her forearm as if the pain, inflicted so long ago, still lingered, as the image still lingered in her mind.

So when he had forced her to halt, had grasped her wrist in such a strong hold, the memory of the robbers, of being constrained and hurt and frightened, had rushed back and she had struck out blindly. At an innocent victim.

And he had reacted with disgust at her bad manners, her lack of gratitude. Her face flushed again with humiliation as she remembered the look of astonishment on his face. And what a face. Strikingly handsome. Heart-stoppingly so. But how he had looked down that high-bred nose at her, with such chilling hauteur. Eyes as glacial as chips of ice. Lips thinned in distaste— and probably pain, she was forced to admit. And she remembered his voice. Warm, reassuring at first when he had thought to comfort her, then cold and flat when she had actually accused him of trying to harm her.

She groaned aloud and twisted to bury her face into the coverlet. If she tried to put the blame squarely on her unknown rescuer for daring to interfere, her innate fairness quickly stopped her. Her behaviour towards him had been despicable. He had suffered for his quixotic actions because she had used enough force to mark his skin and inflict pain.

And then there was that strangest of moments. A little shiver ran over her skin as she felt again the force of it. She had no experience of such things. But as her eyes had met his, she could not look away, her breath had foundered in her lungs. She could still feel the hard imprint of his fingers around her wrist. What was it that had united them in that one moment of uncontrolled emotions, had robbed her of words, of actions? All she had seen was the beauty of his face, the run of emotions across it. And in that one fleeting moment she had wondered what it would be like if those firm lips had moved a little closer and actually touched hers.

Thea stood up, astounded at the direction of her thoughts.

All she could hope for was that she would never have to meet him again! In her usual forthright manner, Thea knew that she could not worry over what she could not undo. She must compose herself or her mother would ask far too many questions.

But she could not forget him, and her heart was sore.

Lord Nicholas Faringdon rode back to Grosvenor Square deep in thought, allowing the mare to choose her own pace. All he could think about was that lovely face when she had removed the enveloping scarf, and her hair—short and shining like a golden halo round her head. But she was no angel. He smiled a trifle grimly at the thought. Those furious eyes. Imperious as she lashed at him with whip and words. And there had been fear there. And at the end—distress? Had she actually flinched from him, cowered even for that one moment when he grasped her wrist? And whereas he might have expected her to be flushed from her exertions, her face had been white, all the blood drained from her cheeks as she had looked up into his face, until she had recovered and wielded her riding whip with considerable force and accuracy.

He was not sure, but her violent response seemed to be as much from fear as from anger. But why? Apart from bringing her horse to a halt, he had done nothing to threaten her. Could she really have believed that he was attempting to molest her, to force himself on her in so public a place? Or anywhere for that matter!

Take your hands off me!

Her tone and words were clearly imprinted on his mind. She had been terrified. Furthermore her whole appearance was—unusual, to say the least. Remarkable clothes, enveloped in some sort of eastern robe. And alone. No sign of a maid—not surprising in the circumstances—but neither was there an accompanying groom, not even in the distance. And—of course! Something else that now struck him: she had been riding astride. And if he had not been mistaken, there had been no sign of cumbersome skirts and petticoats. She had been wearing breeches and boots! Well, now!

Perhaps, then, she was merely some less-than-respectable woman to indulge in behaviour so particular—yet he did not think so. The impression was that she was undoubtedly a lady. Certainly not in the style of the notorious Letty Lade, who might have been an excellent horsewoman but who also had claims to being a highwayman's mistress before her advantageous marriage. No—there was a distinct air of class and style attached to this mysterious horsewoman who had just crossed his path. Moreover, the grey Arab had taken his eye. Now there was an example of superior horseflesh and breeding. And whoever she might be, he had to admit that the lady could ride!

Nicholas turned out of the park and allowed himself to think of that instant of—of connection, he supposed. He had not imagined it. It had held them both in thrall as the world continued round them. Shrugging his shoulders against a slight chill of discomfort, he pushed the memory away of the sudden heat that had spread through his blood as he had tightened his fingers around her wrist and felt the beat of her heart through her pulse. It had taken him aback. But it did not matter since they were unlikely ever to meet again. And what did he want with a woman who galloped her horse across Hyde Park, clad in unseemly garments, and responded to kindness with rude and insulting words? Yet a tinge of admiration crept under his skin, recognition of her courage and spirit, until he deliberately, ruthlessly thrust it away.

Lifting his hand from the reins, he stretched it, then made a fist with a grimace. The welt was red, a little swollen where the blow had broken the skin. He swore at the sting of pain.

Of one thing he was quite certain, he decided, as he turned into the entrance of Grosvenor Square. He had never met the woman before. And he would not be sorry if he never saw her again.

'It is a very pretty dress,' Thea acknowledged with what could be interpreted as a most accommodating smile, if one did not know the lady. 'And I am sure that the colour is most suitable and flattering to any young girl. But I will not wear pale pink.'

'But it is *Maiden's Blush*, miss.'

The four ladies all surveyed the gown being displayed in the arms of the assistant at Madame Therese's in New Bond Street with varying degrees of appreciation. The assistant frowned, impervious to the débutante's smile. As Madame Therese's senior assistant, she was used to dealing with their noble customers with superior and knowledgeable condescension. Dealing with this exacting, although exceedingly polite young lady, she felt her temper was beginning to fray.

'*Maiden's Blush* it may be, but it is still pale pink. It is entirely inappropriate for my colouring, either my hair or my skin. I will not wear it.' Thea's opinion was expressed in the gentlest of tones, almost apologetic in its denial, but her refusal could not be in doubt. The assistant's frown had no effect.

'Perhaps this would be better suited to you, miss.' The harassed lady laid the offending gown with its delightfully ruffled skirt and pearl-buttoned sleeves—the epitome of the art of dressmaking and one of their finest designs—across a chair and lifted another with tender care. 'This is *Evening's Kiss*. A most fashionable colour this year. A most exclusive garment, as you can see.'

'That is pale blue.'

'Indeed, it is very attractive, Thea. Such precise but delicate embroidery, don't you think? Will you not try it?' Lady Drusilla saw the set of her daughter's lovely mouth, despite the smile, and her heart sank. Not stubborn exactly, just…well, *decided*. Dressing Thea was never easy.

'I do not wish to wear pale anything, Mama. How can you ask it of me? You know that I look far better in something with a little—intensity, with depth.'

'But it is most becoming for a débutante.' The assistant appeared close to tears. This was the sixth gown that had been rejected out of hand and one of them had been *Damsel's Dreams*. How could any young lady reject such a confection of white organdie sprinkled with knots of forget-me-nots?

'No.'

'Jonquil?' suggested Judith. 'It is such a soothing colour, I always think, and unexceptional for morning wear.' The Countess of Painscastle had joined them at Madame Therese's with apologies for her late arrival. Simon had returned home earlier than she had expected, she explained, with a becoming flush to her cheeks. She had been detained.

Thea turned unbelieving eyes on Judith. 'Pale yellow? It will rob my hair of any colour at all! I shall look even more sallow. How I wish that I had been born a brunette with dark eyes! Or a redhead like you.' She turned her gaze back to the blue creation, determined that she would not grace Almack's, or any other occasion, in such an insipid dress, however fine the embroidered hem.

Lady Beatrice sighed and shuffled on her chair. This was going to be just as difficult as she had expected. Theodora had a most unfortunate strength of will. And her mama had apparently encouraged her to exert it with flair and confidence at every possible opportunity. The *Evening's Kiss* had been so pretty…

They were interrupted from any further discussion over the maligned gown by a slight, dark lady coming into the room. Her face was thin, her features narrow and prematurely lined, but her eyes were quick and assessing of the situation.

'Madame Therese.' Lady Beatrice hailed her in the light of a saviour. 'Yours is just the advice we need. Here we have Miss Wooton-Devereux who is to go about in society. She is reluctant to wear the dresses we have seen that are suitable for a young girl who is to make her début. Perhaps *you* can persuade her where *we* have failed.'

Madame Therese smiled a greeting. 'I will try. Let us consider what we might achieve for the lady.' Her accented voice was genuine. A French *emigrée* who had fled from her home in Paris, she had been forced to sell her skills. She had a decided air of fashion and an excellent eye for what would suit, so she was soon in demand when she opened her select little establishment in the heart of Mayfair. Rumour said that she had been a countess in her past life. It added a cachet so she did not disabuse her customers.

'Come, *mademoiselle*.' She took Thea's hand to draw her to her feet. 'If you would stand. And turn a little. You have an excellent figure, if I might venture. And such a slender neck. It will show to good advantage in the low necklines that are so fashionable this year. And with your hair so short—*c'est magnifique*. You are tall enough to carry the slender skirts with style. I think we shall manage very well. Tell me what *you* would choose to wear.'

The result was a comfortable and detailed conversation between Madame Therese and Miss Wooton-Devereux, which resulted in the hovering assistant being dispatched to collect a number of garments from the workroom at the back.

'You are not the traditional débutante, not the shy *ingénue*. I agree.' Madame Therese spoke her thoughts. 'I think we should—ah, experiment a little. I believe that we should try for a little restrained sophistication. For youth, of course, but with a layer of confidence. We will keep it simple but add a little gloss—how you say—town bronze.' She nodded, pleased with the direction of her thoughts. 'What a challenge it will be to promote a new style for a young lady who is not merely a child. I think that we might take the town by storm. I vow that you will wear any of my creations with panache, *mademoiselle*.'

'I do not think that we wish to draw too much attention...' Lady Drusilla was quietly horrified. It would take little to encourage Thea. Taking anything by storm was not a careful mama's intention. A quiet, demure introduction would be much more the thing and far more likely to attract the titled gentleman she had in mind.

'No, no, Mama.' Thea's eyes sparkled with enthusiasm for the first time since they had set foot inside the establishment. 'Madame Therese understands perfectly.'

'I do indeed.' The dark eyes reflected the sparkle. 'There is no need for concern, my lady,' she was quick to reassure Lady Drusilla. 'We shall consider nothing outrageous or unseemly. All will be tasteful and elegant. Now. Might I suggest...'

The next hour passed rapidly. An array of dresses appeared as if by magic for *mademoiselle* to try. Dresses for morning wear, for afternoon visits, for walking or driving in Hyde Park. Silk spencers for when the day was inclement. Gowns for an informal soirée at home, or an evening at Almack's. Even for a formal ball with a matching cloak and satin slippers. The prevailing style suited Thea to perfection, Judith had to admit with only a hint of jealousy, as she watched her new friend execute a sedate twirl in a high-waisted, low-necked column of shimmering gold with a transparent gauze overskirt. She was as tall and stately, as coolly elegant, as a *regale* lily until you saw the flash of fire, of sheer enjoyment in those dark blue eyes.

The gowns were, as Madame Therese had promised, simply constructed, with little decoration except for some silk lace to trim, a row of scallops or a neat ruche of ruffles. Perhaps a little satin ribbon or tiny pearl buttons, but nothing *outré*. But what an air. What style. And in such colours. Celestial blue, as deep as a robin's egg. A rich, clear pink, nothing like *Maiden's Blush*, but one which glowed like a newly unfurled rose in morning sunshine.

Thea was even talked into the palest of *eau de nil* silk, *Breath of the Sea*, she was assured—deliciously enhanced by an overskirt of spangled lace. It glittered as the light caught the spangles, gleamed as if under water where the light refracted into a million facets, turning her into a veritable mermaid. Who could resist such gowns?

Finally Madame Therese stood back, hands folded in complete satisfaction.

'*Enchanté!* It has been a pleasure to dress you, *mademoiselle*.'

If she knew the fashion world, as she undoubtedly did, she would wager the cost of the deep blue gown, which, at this moment, was turning Thea into the breathtaking image of a stately but delicate delphinium, that there would be any number of mamas wearing a path to her door to demand that she dress their daughters in such understated but sophisticated glory. But not all would carry off such simplicity as superbly as Mademoiselle Wooton-Devereux.

And as Sir Hector was generous to a fault where his daughter was concerned, Thea had no compunction in giving in to overwhelming temptation and purchasing a number of gowns for immediate delivery to Upper Brook Street.

There was relief on all sides. Not least Lady Beatrice, who responded to the final decisions as if she herself had achieved the unachievable. Miss Wooton-Devereux was now presentable. She raised the lorgnette, admiring a delectable cream and gold creation, most discreet, with a ruched satin border and a neckline enhanced by tiny satin pleats. And if it was made known— the quietest of whispers, in confidence, would do the trick—that the lady was set to inherit a considerable fortune from her beloved papa, Lady Drusilla might just achieve her heart's desire. Theodora might prove to be quite irresistible.

'I think that you are now ready to be presented, Theodora.' Lady Beatrice inclined her head in approval, the ostrich plumes in her bonnet nodding.

'So do I.' Thea surveyed herself in the long mirror. Her lips curved. Her mother had been right. London had much to recommend it.

Lady Aston's drum was everything that Lady Beatrice Faringdon anticipated it to be and more.

Dazzling. Crowded. Humming with gossip, intrigue and comment. Attended by every member of the *haut ton* who happened to be in London. Lady Aston would be able to crow with delight to the discomfiture of other hostesses who had enjoyed far less success since the beginning of the Season. It provided an excellent opportunity to bring Miss Theodora Wooton-Devereux to the combined and critical attention of the Polite World and launch her into society.

'Are you nervous?' Judith asked. 'You don't appear to be so.

How lowering!' Thea and Judith waited in a little anteroom as a flock of servants descended to relieve the party of their evening wraps. 'I remember some of my first balls and soirées. I was horribly nervous, almost so much that I did not enjoy them. Once I spilt a whole glass of lemonade, all down the front of a new gown. It was very expensive with Brussels lace over the bodice and—' She caught the amused glint in Thea's eyes. Short though their acquaintance might be, Judith's obsession with pretty clothes was an open secret. 'Well! Anyway, Mama was furious and threatened not to let me out of the schoolroom again until I could behave with more elegance.' She smiled at the memory. 'I suppose I was too naïve for words, but I was only seventeen.'

Thea nodded in sympathy as she arranged her stole and unfurled her fan. 'No. I am not nervous. But then I have an advantage over your position. I have attended any number of such events as this. I presume that I am suitably got up for this momentous occasion?' She arched her brows in gentle mockery, held out her arms for Judith's inspection. 'My mama considered me to be in relatively good looks and Sir Hector huffed at the bills, but did not object.'

Judith could not help but laugh. 'I think that Lady Drusilla had the right of it. You look quite the thing!'

Thea was in her guise of mermaid in the deliciously spangled *eau de nil* body with the delicate lace overskirt. She had competed her *toilette* with long silk gloves, a pretty beaded reticule and the ivory-and-feather fan. The spangled scarf from Madame Therese matched the overskirt. A pearl necklet and pearl drops in her ears completed the ensemble with the exact touch of sophistication. Judith was left to contemplate that in relatively good looks did not quite do justice to this apparition, but she had already come to the conclusion that the relationship between Thea and her mother was not of the common order.

'Good. Now I can enjoy myself.' Then the two young women turned to follow Lady Beatrice into the ballroom where their hostess was in the process of receiving a steady stream of guests, the majority of whom she had no idea she had invited.

The Faringdon party found itself absorbed happily into the throng and it was soon abundantly clear that Theodora was in her element in such surroundings. It was also abundantly clear that she would not lack for partners. She was introduced to so many gentlemen, all eager to salute the fingers of the willowy golden-haired beauty who would one day inherit a fortune, that she all but lost count. She chatted, sipped champagne and promised herself for any number of dances, with grace and aplomb and all the assurance of having acted as her mama's deputy in formal and diplomatic circles.

Lady Beatrice subjected her to more than one sharp glance, but soon was forced to accept that there was no cause here for anxiety that the girl might not know how to conduct herself. Her upbringing might be unusual, she might be of a forthright disposition, but her social skills were excellent and she would do nothing to bring a blush of mortification to her hostess's face. True, there might have been some concern over whether she should grace the ballroom in the waltz or not. But Lady Drusilla approved. If Theodora could waltz in Paris, she could waltz in London. So waltz she should, and most competently, thus Beatrice shrugged off all responsibility. After which decision, there was nothing to spoil the night.

For her part, Thea took her place in one country dance after another, never flagging. Sufficiently experienced, she did not lack for conversation, but could mind her feet and her tongue at the same time as she twirled and stepped with precision and elegance. Nor was she averse to a little light-hearted flirtation. She could use her fan most adeptly to draw attention to her glorious eyes, whose sparkle rivalled the crystal drops above her pretty head. Laughter and a bright spirit flowed from her. Who would not desire to dance with such an enchanting young lady? No fear that she would ever be a wallflower, destined to sit and watch as others trod the stately or lively measures. And if no unwed earl was present so far to ask for Miss Wooton-Devereux's hand in the next waltz, not even the Earl of Moreton, still Lady Drusilla could not be disappointed with the proceedings.

As for those who observed and assessed and might have stared in cold and stuffy disapproval, they came to the conclusion that Miss Wooton-Devereux was indeed something out of the way, but not unbecomingly so. And her mama. Well, perhaps Lady Drusilla was a little eccentric with the draped turban on her grey-ing curls, all hung about with jewels and feathers, rather in the manner of an eastern potentate. And the quantity of gold chains on her bosom. Rather strange but…interesting. And Sir Hector—of course—so distinguished and responsible. If the Princess Es-terhazy herself greeted Lady Drusilla with warm condescension and a light kiss on the cheek, then there was no matter for con-cern. And if the girl had been brought up in the courts of Europe, then that would account for any oddity in her manner. But her breeding and her appearance, it was decided, were beyond ques-tion. Of course, the prospect of money would win over even those who might still look askance at a girl who was one and twenty before making her formal curtsy.

At some point towards the hour when a light supper would be served, Thea returned from a sprightly reel with Simon, Earl of Painscastle, an enthusiastic if inexact exponent of the art of dancing, somewhat heavy on his own feet and those of his part-ner, to find Lady Beatrice, Sir Hector and Lady Drusilla in deep conversation with a newcomer to their party. He stood with his back to her. And laughed at something that had been said as they approached.

'Ah!' Simon pressed Thea's hand as it rested on his sleeve. 'Now here is a man I am pleased to see. And so will you be, I wager. Come—I will introduce you.'

He struck the gentleman on the shoulder, a light punch to draw his attention.

'Better late than never, Nick. We had quite given up on you. Your dancing skills are needed here by the ladies—and I can re-tire for a hand or two of whist.'

The gentleman turned, his face still alight from the previous laughter.

'Simon. Good to see you. Judith says that you are well.'

'Of course. Burford Hall keeping you busy?'

'A little. I have been told that I must visit you and admire your son.'

'Without doubt. Judith invites everyone to admire him!' But there was no mistaking the pride in his voice. 'You should try it yourself, my boy!'

'Not you as well!' Nicholas smiled, a quick and devastating grin. 'I am assaulted from all sides.'

'I'm sorry.' Simon risked a glance towards Lady Beatrice. 'I can imagine.'

'Never mind that. I hear you have a stallion for sale!'

'For sale? Not at all. Unless you can tempt me with gold!'

'I might, if he is superior to my own animals. Which I doubt!'

At which descent into purely masculine topics of conversation, which threatened to occupy them for the rest of the evening, Lady Beatrice grasped her son-in-law's arm with one hand and tapped her nephew's with her fan to remind them of their surroundings.

'Don't start talking horseflesh, for the Lord's sake.' But her tone was indulgent enough. 'Nicholas. I must introduce you…'

During the whole of this interchange, Thea had been standing a little to the side, out of direct line of sight. Out of neither cowardice nor shyness, but standing rooted to the spot, her heart beating rapidly, her mouth dry, for here was the gentleman of the Park. And, she realised in that one moment, the length of a heartbeat, that any memory she had of him bore no comparison with the reality that now stood before her. He took her breath away. Splendidly handsome, as she had realized, but now she had the opportunity to study him in the dark severity and elegance of formal evening clothes, at the same time horribly aware that he could reveal her unmaidenly behaviour to all. She had hoped never to see him again, but there was no escaping this introduction.

'Theodora, my dear.' Lady Beatrice drew her forward. 'This is my nephew, Lord Nicholas Faringdon. Nicholas, allow me to introduce Miss Theodora Wooton-Devereux, Sir Hector and Lady Drusilla's daughter. This is her first Season in London.'

Nicholas turned to the lady presented to him—and found himself looking into the eyes—those deep blue eyes fringed with the darkest of lashes—that had last flashed with anger and fear as his hand closed around her wrist. But here any similarity ended. Here was wealth, understated taste, elegance. Yet he felt the strange affinity again, rippling over his skin as if brushed by a chill draught of air.

Good manners prevailed, of course. Theodora curtsied in her best court manner, eyes demurely downcast, a smile pinned to her lips, her pretty hand extended to the gentleman. Just as she ought. Nicholas took the offered hand in his own and bowed, a formal inclination of the head, just touching his lips to her fingers. The epitome of the well-bred gentleman of fashion. They straightened, disengaged, the tension between them invisible to all, but palpable none the less.

Thea waited, swallowing against her panic. Was this the moment when he would acknowledge that he had met her before? Would he announce to one and all that she had been galloping in Hyde Park—and wearing boots and breeches? She could not prevent her eyes dropping to his right hand where the whip mark was clearly visible, still a vivid red scar. When he did not and the moment passed, relief surged through her blood, but she did not enjoy the sensation. Her previous behaviour had effectively thrown her into his hands, at his mercy. Resentment quickly overpowered the relief.

Meanwhile Nicholas fought against an equally strong torrent of anger. So this was his aunt's plan, in spite of his warning. It had all the hallmark of Beatrice Faringdon about it: devious, persistent, interfering. Introduce him to a débutante, wait for the knot to be tied and, in the event of any harm befalling Hal and the young boy in America, the Faringdon succession would be secured to her satisfaction. Furthermore, a débutante whose behaviour had been indecorous in the extreme. Well, he would not. He would not give Lady Beatrice the satisfaction of falling in with her plans. He might keep his face politely bland, his eyes flat, but inside he fumed.

Never had a meeting between lady and gentleman in a ballroom been so fraught with overtones and supposition.

'Why don't you invite Thea to dance, my dear Nicholas?' Beatrice remained oblivious to the passions seething around her.

'Of course, Aunt. It would be my pleasure.' His lips curved into a semblance of a smile, but there was no warmth in it. He fixed his gaze on Theodora. 'Although I presume that you do not waltz, madam,' he remarked as the musicians struck up.

'I do indeed, my lord.' Equally cool.

'Ah.' His raised brows were not quite a criticism.

'I have waltzed in Paris and Vienna, my lord. My mama sees no objection and I have every reason to believe that I have the blessing of the Princess Esterhazy. So I will willingly accept your invitation.'

'Then I shall be honoured.' Nicholas bowed in acknowledgement, led Thea on to the dance floor without further comment, where he turned her with one arm around her waist and began to circle to the music. She fit perfectly against him and moved smoothly, gracefully, through the simple demands of the dance. And as in Hyde Park he was stunned by his physical reaction to her. It was a body blow, like a fist to his gut, a tingle along his veins, an outrageous desire to lift her face and cover that enchanting mouth with his own. To kiss her slender fingers in a formal salute was simply not enough. No matter that the whole world might be watching—in that moment he did not care.

And then: *I do not want this!* His expression as he glanced down at her was almost fierce. Together with the overwhelming wave of lust came the knowledge that this girl was dangerous and his reaction to her was too extreme for comfort. He set himself to resist. He knew that her conduct could be far outside the acceptable and he could not afford to tolerate that. There had been enough scandal in the Faringdon family of late to last a lifetime. He must resist at all costs!

And Theodora? She was aware of none of these thoughts. Aware of nothing but the weight and strength of his arms around her, the clasp of his hand on hers, cool skin against cool skin, the slightest pressure of his body as it brushed hers in the demands of the dance. The memory of the touch of his lips on her hand still burned as a brand. She had waltzed with other partners with mild pleasure. But never anything like this. Lord Nicholas Faringdon quite simply caused her heart to beat against the confines of her bodice like a wild bird in a cage, until she was sure that he would feel the force of it against his chest when he held her close. Just as he had destroyed her composure when his hand had closed around her wrist with such mastery in Hyde Park.

This was no good! Thea knew that she could not remain silent.

'I have to thank you, my lord.' Thea raised her eyes to his as they settled into the rhythm of the music. Her colour was a trifle heightened, he noted as dispassionately as he was able, tinting her cheeks a delicious rose, but she was not shy. All he could think about was the sensation of holding her in his arms. He did not want this attraction.

'Why?'

She was taken aback by this somewhat curt response. And were not his eyes unsettlingly, chillingly grey rather than blue? Perhaps she had simply mistaken it and struggled to find the right words. 'I am not unaware of the debt I owe you. It would have been most uncomfortable for me if you had revealed the…the circumstances of our previous meeting. You deserve my gratitude, my lord.'

'It is not necessary.'

'And…and I should apologise for my…behaviour towards you,' she persisted. 'It was most regrettable.'

'There is no need.'

'But I hurt you!' Her eyes snapped up to his in some confusion. She could not read his expression behind the bland mask. No, she realised, it was not bland but icy with controlled temper. 'I see the evidence of it on your hand—you cannot deny it.'

'Very well, then. Yes. You did. Unnecessarily, as it happened. I had no intention of either harming or molesting you, Miss Wooton-Devereux.'

'I realise that… I should explain.' She was getting nowhere here. 'There were circumstances…' What should she say? She did not wish to bare her soul over the matter of her past experiences, her innermost fears, and certainly not in the centre of a ballroom with a partner who had an amazing effect on her senses and who was less than accommodating to her attempts to make remission. She had apologised and he was totally insensitive to the fact. What could she say? How could she explain? In the event she did not have to.

'I need no explanation, madam.' If his eyes froze her, his voice would reduce her to an icicle if she allowed it. 'You reacted as you saw fit.' Why did those words have all the air of a snub rather than a soothing offer of forgiveness? She could not be mistaken. There was a cold condemnation in that smooth voice and she did not know what she had done to deserve quite so harsh a judgement. 'I do not need to know,' Lord Nicholas continued in preparation for launching the final deadly arrow. 'But at least you are more conventionally dressed tonight than when we last had the misfortune to meet.'

Any number of sharp replies coming into her mind, Theodora opened her mouth to utter them. Then closed her lips. *Since when are you free to comment on what I might or might not wear, my lord?* She could not say that aloud, of course—or not here! This was not the time or place to create a scene. The fact that she had indeed been in the wrong ruffled her temper further but she kept a firm hold on it. She smiled, a miracle of control, and chose her words with deadly precision. 'Yes, I believe that I am, my lord. Everyone who has danced with me has complimented me on my stylish dress *à la mode* and the appropriateness of this particular creation. Madame Therese is a true *artiste*, is she not?'

He could not deny the delicate gloss of sarcasm over her words and had the grace to wince a little. But only inwardly.

'I am delighted that you approve my appearance, my lord. It gives me so much confidence. Without your approval I should be desolate indeed.' Thea did not let up. But *why* was he so cold? Perhaps she must accept that, in all truth, being struck by a rid-

ing whip would make him so. She had read the contempt in his
eyes as their first meeting drew to its unfortunate ending—an infinite quality of disdain—and there was no difference now. But
she denied his right to taunt her!

'I think that you do not lack for confidence, madam.'

A flash of anger darkened her eyes at this lethal sniping. She
bit down on any further sharp response. She could not understand
the reason for it, but gathered all her social skills about her.

'Perhaps we should talk of something less controversial, my
lord? A ballroom is no place for such a frank exchange of views.'
The smile was still in place. She would keep it there if it killed her!

'Of course, Miss Wooton-Devereux.' Nicholas, too, bared his
teeth in what could have passed for pleasure if anyone was ob-
serving the handsome couple. 'What do you suggest that we
might have in common to discuss?'

Before she could think of anything polite to reply to this challenge, the waltz had drawn to an end and he escorted her with
frigid good manners back to where her parents and the Faringdons were ensconced. He bowed to her, and with equal chill to
Lady Beatrice. Thea's hand was soon claimed. She saw Lord
Nicholas treading the measure of a country dance further down
the set with Judith.

Nicholas made no attempt to approach Thea for the rest of the
evening. Theodora made sure that her eyes did not follow him
as he danced with other ladies of his acquaintance.

'Nicholas is quite my favourite cousin,' Judith observed in a
deceptively neutral voice in an interval between dances.

'Is he?' Thea studied her dance list intently.

'And he is so handsome. Do you not agree?'

'Certainly. I doubt any woman here tonight would disagree.'

Judith gave up, not a little surprised at the lack of interest between them. Nicholas had not set foot near Thea since that one
first waltz. But there would be time and enough for them to get
to know each other. She would see to it that they did.

Nicholas returned to Faringdon House in a thoroughly bad mood. He was furious with Beatrice. Even after he had warned her off, his aunt had produced a beautiful débutante—he could not deny her lovely face and figure—whom she considered suitable. *Suitable?* She had no idea! He was also furious with himself for taking out his ill temper on the girl. He might have kept the semblance of good manners, but his comments had been unwarrantable. And he was equally furious with Theodora Wooton-Devereux, whose presence in his arms had left a lasting and most uncomfortable impression on him. He resigned himself to an uneasy night.

Theodora returned to Upper Brook Street equally angry and confused, despite the success of her first public occasion in London. How dare he treat her so! She did not deserve his damning opinions of her or his icy set-downs. And why should he react quite so violently against her? Was he so dull and hidebound that he should condemn her for one social solecism? Well—she did not care! But she determined as she removed the pearl drops from her ears that she would get the better of Lord Nicholas Faringdon!

Chapter Four

Since both Lord Nicholas Faringdon and Miss Theodora WootonDevereux moved in the first circles in London society, it was to be expected that their paths would cross with frequency. And they did. If they had not done so by accident, they would certainly have done so by design. For both Lady Beatrice and the Countess of Painscastle considered Theodora to be a most suitable and enlivening match for their uncooperative relative, and Nicholas an equally desirable husband for so delectable a débutante. The opinion of neither lady nor gentleman was sought.

So they came quite naturally within each other's orbit at the social events of the Season, whether it be alfresco breakfasts, riverboat parties on the Thames or the more conventional soirées and balls. Unfortunately for those most interested in the match, who watched the pair with keen eyes, it appeared that there would be little chance of his lordship fixing his interest with the lady. For there was a decided edge to their meetings from the very beginning.

'Lord Nicholas.' Theodora curtsied and smiled politely upon meeting his lordship as she descended the steps from the Painscastle Town House in Grosvenor Square, closely followed by Judith, two days after Lady Aston's drum. 'I had thought you might have returned to the country.'

'My estate will survive a day or two without my presence.' He bowed his head unsmilingly.

'I expect it will.' She unfurled her parasol with graceful expertise and only mild interest. 'I understand that the land belongs to your nephew?'

'Yes. He is the Marquis of Burford.'

'Tom is hardly more than a baby and lives in New York.' Judith added the explanation, struck by the unexpectedly stark confrontation.

'And you administer it, my lord.'

'I do.'

'I see. A worthwhile occupation, I expect.'

Lord Nicholas inclined his head. Now, why did he get the impression that she disapproved, that she had judged him as some variety of noxious parasite to live off the wealth and achievement of others? It ruffled him more than he cared to admit. But he strove with perfect success to preserve a courteous and faintly amused expression.

'Does it not meet with your liking, madam?'

'I am sure that it is no concern of mine, my lord, how you choose to live your life.'

'Very true. It is not.'

Accepting the put-down with raised brows, Miss Wooton-Devereux persisted. Of course he was ruffled. She would teach him to look at her with such arrogant superiority! 'I would have thought a man would want to develop his own land, my lord. Not that of another, however close the relationship with the owner.'

His voice became positively glacial, his eyes a distinct quality of arctic grey. 'It is a responsibility to my family, and so it is my duty. I am trustee for the estate's well-being.' So, she would have the temerity to hold his lifestyle up for criticism, would she? And why was he actually explaining his views to the woman…?

'Of course.' Theodora simply angled her head and smiled.

Nicholas felt the muscles in his jaw clench. Was she deliberately baiting him? Surely she was!

Judith leapt into the breach. 'You should know, Theodora, that Nicholas has his own estate at Aymestry Manor.'

'Ah.'

'He breeds horses.'

'How interesting.'

And although Theodora would have dearly loved to have entered into a discussion of the rival merits of English thorough-breds against Arab bloodlines, she restrained herself. She would not admit to any similarity of interest with his lordship.

Damn her! Nicholas watched as the two ladies made their way out of the Square. Why should it matter what Miss Wooton-Devereux thought of him?

But it did.

And became increasingly important as the days passed. Although he would have been the first to deny it, Nicholas could not help but be aware of the lady. Not that he approved of her to any degree! Her behaviour was always within the bounds of acceptance—yet not the demure and decorous demeanour to be expected of a débutante. Her appearance was noticeably unconventional with her short hair and striking gowns. She flirted outrageously, showing particular skill in the use of her fan and those miraculously long and thick eyelashes. Not that he had noticed them, of course! She was outspoken to a fault on all manner of subjects, from the politics of the day to the unfortunately corpulent and badly dressed figure presented by the Prince Regent.

When she danced with the highly eligible and extremely rich Earl of Moreton, her mother's chosen favourite in her plan to find a wealthy, titled husband for her daughter, Nicholas could do nothing but turn his back and invite another lady to partner him. He would not give her the pleasure of seeing him watch her circle the ballroom, however graceful and elegant she might be. He would not. And when his aunt once more invited him to take dear Thea into supper, or partner her in a country dance, he would bow and comply with firm composure as if it were a matter of no possible consequence to take that long-fingered hand in his—or else he would discover an instant excuse for his attendance elsewhere. But he would not single the lady out. He would not give the lady or Lady Beatrice the opportunity to gloat!

But if that were so, why was he still in town? Nicholas refused to consider the implication of such perverse behaviour.

Meanwhile, Thea refused to notice or to be disappointed when his lordship led another pretty débutante into a country dance set. Or failed to put in an appearance at Almack's when she had chosen to wear a particularly flattering gown of emerald silk overlaid with silver-grey lace. Instead, she took every opportunity to be deliberately provocative—a task that she found surprisingly easy. Quite as effortless as Lord Nicholas in taking her to task for her somewhat slighting remark on the overbearing tactics of the Duke of Wellington in the government of the day.

'Is that your own opinion, madam? Or that of Sir Hector?' Unable to ignore her in so small a gathering, Nicholas handed her a glass of champagne at Lady Beatrice's small soirée, his expression one of distinct disapproval.

'My own, of course.' Thea sipped the golden bubbles with a little smile.

'I did not realise that your interests stretched to politics, Miss Wooton-Devereux.'

'And should they not?'

'It is not always to be expected in a débutante.'

'It is important to be well informed, I believe.'

Lord Nicholas merely observed her without reply, one brow lifted a fraction of an inch.

Well! She could not allow so negative and *patronising* a response go unanswered!

'Can it be that you are criticising my upbringing and education, my lord?' Thea's brows rose in delicate arcs. She watched him over the rim of her glass.

'I would not be so bold, ma'am.'

'My upbringing has been impeccable,' the lady informed him, 'according to the advanced ideas of the philosopher Rousseau.

And as advocated by Maria Edgeworth, no less, in her *Practical Education*.'

'I can well believe it.'

'It is essential,' continued the lady, 'that every child and thus every adult be treated as an individual to develop his or her innate talents and abilities.'

'Most estimable, to be sure.'

'Thus I would consider it necessary that every intelligent woman be aware of the policies of our government and the political figures who influence them. Which makes me free to be critical if I find the Duke's approach not to my taste.'

'As I would agree.' Nicholas smiled with all the friendliness of a kestrel eyeing a tasty mouse. 'But even Rousseau considered the opinions of the female sex to be far inferior to those of the male.' He raised his glass in a little toast and drank from it. 'I am certain that, educated as you are, you see the force of my argument.'

'No! I do not, my lord!' Thea felt a warmth of colour touch her cheek at his underhand tactics.

'Now, why did I think that would be your answer?'

Which left Theodora without a parting shot.

And gave Lord Nicholas a degree of satisfaction.

But within the third week of their distinctly uneasy acquaintance, there was a particular development in the nature of their relationship, a strange little event that gave both lady and gentleman much to consider. As Nicholas drove his curricle through the city, having visited his bank, he spied a familiar female figure. There, standing on the pavement, on the corner of Chancery Lane and Fleet Street, was a lady whom he could not possibly mistake. She held her reticule, gloves and parasol in one hand, and a guide book, compiled for those travellers who might wish to enjoy the sights of London, open in the other. She was clearly oblivious to the small crowd of urchins and undesirables who had gathered, attracted by her obvious wealth and her unaccompanied state.

He drew in his horses beside her, a heavy frown apparent.

She looked up, a delightful picture in a gauze and satin straw bonnet, but her words did not hold the same charm.

'Do not say anything, my lord!'

So he obligingly did not, but made no attempt to hide his disapproval of her unchaperoned situation in the City as he held his matched chestnuts under firm control. What was she thinking! The fact that her presence here had caused him a ripple of concern for her safety was rapidly discarded.

'I am lost,' Thea snapped. Of all people, why did it have to be Lord Nicholas Faringdon to drive past, to look down his arrogant—if beautiful—nose at her as if she were a beetle in his path? 'I should not be here—and certainly not unchaperoned. I should have a maid with me. I should not be drawing attention to myself. Anything else, my lord?'

She had read him to perfection. He suppressed any sign of wry amusement, so his reply was cold and curt.

'I cannot think of anything at the moment. You appear to have covered every aspect of this unfortunate situation.'

He dismounted, handing the reins to the groom, his expression not pleasant at the inconvenience. 'I think I should return you to your family, ma'am.'

'Why should you? I would much rather go to St Paul's.'

Without a word he held out his hand and, when she complied—she could hardly do other in this busy street—helped her up into the curricle.

'And why *are* you without your maid?' Nicholas took his seat and the reins again, and the chestnuts stepped out with well-bred conformation.

'Agnes is not well. A cold. It would be more than cruel of me to drag her on a sightseeing expedition.' Theodora set her teeth, determined to remain composed. How like him to question her behaviour!

'Would not my cousin accompany you if you were intent on exploring?'

'Judith had other engagements.' Her tone became noticeably more clipped.

'You are too cavalier, ma'am. Do you have no regard for convention? What will people think? You cannot afford to set up the backs of those who are too quick to damn a lady's reputation. The town tabbies are quick to gossip.'

'Really?' With his concentration on the traffic, he did not see the angry glint in that lady's eyes. 'I know you disapprove of me, my lord.' She had given up any pretence at mild conversation. 'How can I spend my life worrying about what people think?'

'That may be all very well in the deserts of Syria or wherever you spent your formative years, with females such as Hester Stanhope setting herself up as the Queen of the Desert or some such nonsensical thing, but I fear it will not do here.'

'This is not Syria!'

'I am aware. But walking alone through the city? It is not appropriate, Miss Wooton-Devereux. As you well know.'

And she did—more than aware of the stark comments of Lady Drusilla if it ever came to her ears, which stirred her wrath even further. Without considering her words, she directed that wrath at Lord Nicholas. 'How dull life would be if I worried constantly about the possibility of getting lost.' She was soon in her stride, his reprimand a light to dry tinder. 'How restricting and tedious if I did nothing in the chance that I became the object of social condemnation. If I stayed at home because I feared to suffer an injury, or was captured by a band of robbers who...' Her words dried up. A stricken look on her face, Thea closed her mouth firmly and looked away so that he might not see her heightened colour.

Ah! So that was it!

Nicholas waited in silence, steering the chestnuts around a large wagon that had come to a halt in the street. He would give her time to regain her composure. He had heard the note of distress, hastily suppressed.

It worked. As the chestnuts settled again into an easy trot, Thea did not return to the dangerous topic, choosing something mildly innocuous, but continued placidly enough. 'It was such a lovely morning, it was impossible not to take advantage of it...'

So she will not talk of it. But it distressed her considerably.
Nicholas immediately pulled his horses to a standstill against the
curb, to her surprise.

'Thea…' He touched her hand, which held tightly to her
parasol, her fingers white against the ivory of the handle. 'Is that
what happened to you?' If it drew their attention to hear her
given name on his lips, neither of them gave any sign.

'I should not have spoken.'

'Why not? Is that why you reacted as you did in the Park, the
day you struck out at me? Had you been accosted by robbers?'

'I do not wish to speak of it.' She shook her head, would not
look at him.

'Will you not tell me what happened?'

'I cannot. I won't talk about it.' There was real distress now,
in her voice and in her face.

'Very well. I cannot force you. And would not wish to give
you more cause for pain.' His voice was low, soothing. 'But if
you ever wish to, I will listen.'

Ignoring their very public surroundings, Lord Nicholas took
possession of her hand, to lift it to his lips.

'I am grateful.' Her hand was as cold as ice and just as rigid
as it lay in his. A strained silence developed that Thea would
not—or could not—break. She had not expected such compassion from him. Just as he had not expected such an admission
from her.

Eventually she risked a glance at him, seeing nothing but
warmth and sympathy replacing the harsh condemnation in his
eyes. It drew from her an instant need to apologise. 'I am nothing like Lady Stanhope!'

'No.' He could not stop the smile.

'I would never do anything so outrageous as to wear male
clothing and take a lover in the desert! Well, not often—the
clothing, that is!'

'Of course not.'

'I am sorry if I was impolite.'

'I must admit that you were under extreme provocation.'

'Are you laughing at me?' She sighed as she saw the telltale curve of his lips. 'Yes, I was provoked—but I am grateful for the rescue. I knew that I was in the wrong.'

'Such an admission makes me think that you are more distressed than I had believed!' It roused a chuckle from her, which pleased him. 'It gave me pleasure to be of service to you on so beautiful a day.'

There was a tone in his voice that Thea could not quite interpret, forcing her to look up. And then she could not look away. Equally held in the moment, Lord Nicholas raised her hand again to press his lips to her fingers, a distinct pressure, far more than a formal salute. And lingered a little until a polite cough from his groom caught his attention.

'Some interested parties around, m'lord.'

Which brought him back to the fact that they were indeed in a very public street, which was no place to be drowning in the depths of a pair of sparkling sapphire eyes. Or enjoying the touch of silken skin. He laughed softly, perhaps to dispel his astonishment in being driven to such indecorous behaviour. But he did not let go of her hand.

'Will you take me home then, my lord?' Thea was as much held by the moment as he.

'Why, no.' He released her to pick up the reins again. 'I think that we go on to St Paul's. What do you say, Theodora?'

He was rewarded with the faintest hint of a smile, as if the lady had come to a momentous decision. As perhaps she had. 'I should like that above all things. How kind you are.'

It warmed his heart.

Which little episode led to a subtle change in their response towards each other. Theodora was nothing at all like the lady whom Lord Nicholas might consider setting up as his latest flirt. He was uneasy about his reactions to her, whereas Theodora still smarted under his stern gaze and disapproving demeanour.

But each was drawn to the other as a moth to a fatal flame.

It became an accustomed sight, giving Lady Beatrice a blaze

of triumph, to see the beautiful Miss Wooton-Devereux partnering the splendid Lord Nicholas Faringdon in the waltz. He was seen to invite the lady to drive with him in Hyde Park at five o'clock, the hour of the fashionable promenade. He even volunteered his services to squire the ladies to Almack's, giving the Earl of Painscastle reason to comment that he must be a lost cause indeed. But Lord Nicholas shook his head, admitting to himself that he was in a serious state of indecision. Yes, the lady was beautiful, interesting, intelligent—but equally outspoken, argumentative and opinionated. Not to mention given to unreliable quirks of behaviour that might make her the talk of the drawing rooms. But there again, when she walked into the room, the very quality of the air that he breathed seemed to change. He found himself entirely captivated...

Theodora was equally preoccupied, her eyes quickly scanning any room to note if he were present. And if she saw his tall figure, his dark hair, her evening took on a glow of its own. If he did not put in an appearance, the event, no matter how entertaining, was distinctly flat. She took to noticing his strong but fine-fingered hands as they controlled the reins of his high-spirited horses. The firm strength of his arm when he held her close against him in the waltz. The elegant grace when he presented her with a posy of flowers or held her reticule as she unfurled her parasol. The power of his body when he took her hand to help her take her place in the high-perch phaeton that he sometimes drove with such masterly skill. The sheer magnetism of his presence when their eyes met and neither could look away. A sad case, she decided, as delicious shivers fluttered over her skin. They were drawn to each other whether she wished it or not. She found him kind, generous, with a depth of compassion—despite his somewhat over-bearing personality and his liking to get his own way!

And if it was becoming clear to Theodora, it was becoming equally evident to Lady Drusilla that Lord Nicholas was winning a place in her daughter's usually sensible heart. When Drusilla frowned her disapproval at Thea's standing up with his lordship for the second time in an evening, it had absolutely no effect on her wayward offspring. And when Drusilla smiled her agreement to Thea's accepting an innocent invitation to drive in Hyde Park with Judith, there was little she could do when she discovered that Lord Nicholas was also to be included in the invitation. Furthermore, it was patently clear that the undoubted charms of the wealthy Earl of Moreton were no competition at all against the dark good looks and dashing grace of Lord Nicholas Faringdon.

Had Lady Drusilla but known it, the matter had progressed much further than even she had believed. Lord Nicholas had organised an evening of entertainment and pleasure at Vauxhall Gardens in the form of a masked supper for family and close friends. There would be music and dancing, of course, with an orchestra to play works by Handel in the concert hall during supper. A simple enough meal with champagne and punch and the specialities of the Gardens—cold chicken and wafer-thin slices of ham, all partaken in a private supper box, hired for the occasion. A most tasteful and unexceptional occasion.

Thea was both amused and entranced, never before having visited Vauxhall with its exotic attractions. She declared the enticing groves, the maze of secluded alleys and the secret arbours and grottoes to have great charm.

'The darkness lends enchantment, I fear.' Lord Nicholas smiled at her obvious enjoyment. And her delectable appearance. Her gown was covered by a shimmering domino of silver silk tissue, a matching silver mask covering her face, but with no pretence at disguise. Nor for Lord Nicholas, his evening rig cloaked in severe and elegant black.

'You are too cynical, sir. And superior. I like it very well. It reminds me of one of Mrs Radcliffe's Gothic novels. All the caves and waterfalls. I have never seen so many temples and pavilions and rotundas, all in one place, in my life. Even you must admit to the lamps in the trees being very pretty, my lord.'

'I will admit nothing.'

'I suppose that you prefer the rustic and natural delights of your manor at Aymestry.' Thea angled a glance in arched enquiry, having heard something of the delights of Lord Nicholas's home.

'Perhaps I do.'

'I would wish to see it.' Her gaze within its silver frame remained steady on his.

'And I would wish to show it to you.' A little silence lengthened between them, until Nicholas took himself in hand. 'But that aside, the lights here hide a multitude of sins.'

'Perhaps. But I will not allow you to spoil the evening by drawing attention to it!'

He hesitated again, the length of a breath. 'I would not wish to do so. That would never be my intent.'

'I know it.' And although she spread her fan with a flirtatious turn of her wrist, he could not mistake the solemn appraisal in her eyes, before she turned to answer a query from Lady Beatrice, formidable if incongruous in her deep purple domino.

After supper the younger members of the party dispersed to stroll down the lamp-lit walks, assuring Lady Beatrice and a reluctant Lady Drusilla that they would most certainly remain within sight and sound of Agnes Drew, their designated chaperon for the occasion. But it was clearly destined for Lord Nicholas to draw Miss Wooton-Devereux's hand through his arm, just as it was astonishingly easy for them to lose their companions in the deeply shadowed pathways.

'Which do you prefer, lady. Dark Walk or Druids Walk?' he enquired as they came to a parting of the ways.

'Definitely Druids. Do you think we might see some after all these hundreds of years? Lurking in the groves of Vauxhall with their oak leaves and mistletoe.'

'I doubt it—but let us try.' He guided her along the appropriate path.

'But we may hear nightingales, I expect.' She slanted a look.

'I have arranged it specially for you, lady.'

He sensed her smile in the darkness. They strolled in silence for some little way.

'It appears that we have lost our companions,' Theodora commented.

'So it would seem.' Nicholas came to a halt and turned to face her. 'Your mama would not approve.'

'No. She would not.' It did not seem to trouble Theodora unduly.

The night enclosed them in deep silence, the scents of earth and flowers, soft but intense. Every sense was heightened. Nicholas could catch the perfume that Theodora wore, was supremely aware of the light touch of her fingers on his arm. When he raised a hand to loosen the strings of her mask she made no resistance.

'Well, Miss Wooton-Devereux. I should never have known it to be you.' He removed his own mask.

'Your disguise was perfect, my lord.'

He bent his head and kissed her. A brush of lips against lips, soft as a sigh. Then he raised his head to look at her. 'I should not have done that.' A sardonic smile touched his austere features.

'Did you not wish to do so, my lord?'

'Why… Yes. I did. Very much.' It was an admission to himself as much as to the lady.

'And I should not have allowed it.' Obviously a night for admissions.

He kissed her again, savouring the warm softness of her lips as he increased the pressure. She was quite irresistible.

And Theodora was breathless. 'I am very glad that you did. How forward I am tonight! There is no hope for me. My reputation will be quite ruined.'

'Do you often allow gentlemen to kiss you?' Nicholas found himself asking. Part humour, part unease at her flippancy. Her answer suddenly mattered very much.

Serious, deadly serious, Theodora raise a hand to touch his lips 'Oh, no. Not at all. Do you often kiss ladies in Vauxhall Gardens, my lord?'

Well, he had deserved that, had he not?

'Certainly not! So, since neither of us is in the general way of kissing other people…I will kiss you again, Theodora, if it pleases you.'

'Yes, Nicholas, it does.'

So he did. His hands tightened over the silk at her shoulders, to draw her closer so that his arms could enfold, his lips take possession. Still persuasive against her soft mouth, still gentle, a promise rather than a demand. But he felt her shiver against him. And Theodora could think of nothing but the incredible sensation of being kissed until sparkling bubbles raced through her blood, as fine as any of the champagne she had drunk that night. Was aware of nothing but the heat that spread its fingers from the region of her heart to every extremity. Her experience of life had never prepared her for anything such as this. If she were breathless before, now she was positively light-headed.

Much as Lord Nicholas was stunned by his reaction to this delightful creature who melted into his embrace and returned his kisses with such sweetness. He wanted her. Wanted to touch her. Wanted her for his own. He thought it would be the easiest thing in the world to fall in love with her.

Which exactly mirrored Theodora's thoughts.

Her mother would indeed have been horrified.

Chapter Five

'We need to talk, Hector.'

Because his wife, always an exemplary diplomat's wife, rarely interrupted him when he had urgent business to complete, Sir Hector put down his pen and held out his hand in welcome to Lady Drusilla. She had come to a halt just inside the door of the library in Upper Brook Street.

'What is it, my love? I thought you were already gone—I forget where, but somewhere with Thea.'

'No. I have sent Thea off with Lady Beatrice and Judith. I need to talk with you and it would be better if Thea were not here.'

'Very well.' Sir Hector now saw the strain on his wife's face, so immediately rose to his feet and approached to draw her into the room. 'What has happened to put such a heavy line between your brows.' He rubbed at it with his thumb in a quaint gesture of deep affection. 'Is it Thea? What has she done now?'

'No, it is not Thea—well, yes, it is, in a way.' Drusilla caught her bottom lip with her teeth and sighed as if at the culmination of much painful thought. 'We have to tell her, Hector.'

'Hmm!' Hector drew his wife to sit beside him on the sofa before the empty fire grate. 'But why?' It was clear that he knew beyond question the cause of her distress and the meaning behind her enigmatic statement. 'We have kept it close for so long—all of twenty-one years. As you wished. Why stir up the mud in that particular pond now?'

'I know I wanted it,' Drusilla admitted. She looked down at their clasped hands and held tight. 'Because she is *our* daughter. She is ours—yours and mine—in upbringing, in character, in education—and in love. What does blood matter? I love her so much, Hector.' Tears began to track their path down her cheeks and she was unable to stifle a sob.

Hector sought in his pockets and began to apply his handkerchief with great tenderness. 'I know that you love her, Drusilla. As do I. No one could have been a better mother than you—and no daughter could be such a credit to our love and care. So, as I said—why has it become so imperative to break silence now?' His voice was all gentleness, but she was not soothed.

'Because it is becoming too dangerous *not* to tell her.'

'I don't see…'

'I think… I believe that Thea is falling in love with him. And he with her.'

Sir Hector frowned a little at what was obviously news to him. 'I thought your preference was fixed on the Earl of Moreton.'

'It is what I might prefer—all that wealth and consequence rather than a younger son—but Thea thinks only of Lord Nicholas Faringdon. I fear that the Earl does not compare favourably. And, in truth, I cannot blame her. Lord Nicholas has such address, such style. And is so very handsome. What young woman would not lose her heart to him—particularly when he has clearly set himself out to attract.'

'Drusilla! Are you as captivated as our daughter?'

'If I were twenty years younger, you would have serious competition, sir!' She managed a wan smile through her tears. 'You must acknowledge—he has considerable charm.'

'Mmm.' Sir Hector smiled in reply, quite sure of Drusilla's heart. 'And you think that it is more than a superficial attraction? Surely not, my dear. She has known him less than a month, after all.'

'What does that signify? *I* fell in love with *you* in less than twenty-four hours after I met you at the Pakenhams' ball. But that is of no consequence. I think that Thea is fast losing her heart. Whether she acknowledges it fully to herself, I am not sure. But she is very like me.' Drusilla took the damp square of linen from her husband and wiped away more tears. 'When she gives her heart, it will be without reserve. And I am very much afraid that her heart could be broken as a result.' She looked up at her husband. 'I don't want that for her. I would do anything to spare her pain. I had hoped to deflect this friendship—to stop it developing beyond a mere acquaintance—but I failed. There is a…a feeling between them—it is so strong that you can sometimes feel it when they are in the same room together. I see it in his eyes when he looks at her—and in hers, too.'

Sir Hector looked skeptical, but did not demur. Then, 'It may not come to anything, of course,' he considered after a moment's thought.

'Oh, Hector. He sends her posies of flowers. He takes her driving in the Park. He brought her a copy of Dr Clark's *Russia,* which apparently she expressed a desire to read, and yesterday he took her to the British Museum because she declared an interest in seeing the Parthenon Marbles. Does that not sound like a man in love to you?'

'He must be, by God!'

'*You* took *me* to an exhibition of minerals and fossils when you were trying to fix your interest with me!' she recalled with some asperity. 'And you loved me!'

'So I did. And have loved you ever since!' He kissed her damp cheeks. 'But look, Drusilla—would it really matter if we did not tell her? Would the truth ever have to come out? It was never a secret as such, but it has been of interest to no one but ourselves for more than twenty years. If no one has bothered to make the issue, why in Heaven's name should they do so now?'

'Because, until now, nothing has brought it to mind. But if there was an understanding to grow between Thea and Lord Nicholas, it might bring old memories to life. What if someone who knows the truth—and there must be members of the family who do—what if they make the connection and speak out?'

Drusilla's lips thinned into a bitter line. 'It would not have mattered at all, of course, if it had not been for that terrible scandal here in London when we were in Constantinople. Hector—you must see what could now occur if tongues start to wag.'

'It is always possible,' he agreed, but still not convinced. 'Did you not think of that possibility when you engaged the help of Beatrice Faringdon?'

'No. I did not. Perhaps I should—but when Beatrice offered her kind auspices to introduce Thea into society, I did not expect Thea to fall in love with her nephew!'

'Well, Faringdon is a man of sense from my reading of him. And if he loves Theodora I do not see the problem. She would be merely an innocent party in all this.'

'Are you prepared to take that chance?'

'I just don't see that he could blame her for anything other than a blood connection. And one of which she knew nothing.'

'But if the hatred were strong enough, and sufficiently long-lasting, Nicholas could equally condemn Thea. Can you imagine if he were driven to turn from her in disgust? It would break her heart! We dare not risk it, Hector.'

'We could, of course, just forbid her to develop the connection further.' The experienced diplomat, ever willing to consider all angles in an area of difficult negotiation, raised his brows in some speculation.

'Ha!' Drusilla was not impressed. Her husband sometimes thought that his reputation was as dust beneath her feet. 'Sometimes, Hector, I do believe that you have no knowledge or understanding of your daughter. To forbid would be fatal in these circumstances. And to reason with her... She is always open to reason, as I know—but when does reason carry weight if love is in the balance?'

He took her in his arms as tears threatened once more. 'There now, Drusilla. Don't cry again.' He held her close, his heart troubled as his mind mulled over the possible repercussions for Theodora. 'Then I suppose that we must tell her.'

'Yes.' She nodded against his chest. 'It will allow her to end this understanding between them before further damage is done. Before her heart is engaged irrevocably.'

Drusilla stood with a final brisk application of Sir Hector's handkerchief and walked to the door, her habitual composure once more in place. There she halted and turned on a final thought.

'Because there is one fact in this whole sorry mess of which we are certain,' he informed her husband. 'After Sir Edward Baxendale's devious and despicable behaviour, Lord Nicholas Faringdon will have nothing good to say about anyone with the name of Baxendale.'

Had her parents but known it, Thea's heart was already lost. Lord Nicholas Faringdon had fixed his interest with her with considerable success. From that very first moment when their eyes had locked as he forced her mount to a standstill, Thea had been aware of Nicholas Faringdon with disturbing intensity. His proximity, the mere anticipation of seeing him at some point during the day, of perhaps feeling the brush of his lips against her fingers, all spread a warm tingle of longing through her bloodstream. And what if he were tempted to repeat that more intimate touch of mouth against mouth. Her breath shortened. How scandalous! How delicious! The longing tightened as a band around her heart.

When, later that morning on her return to the house, Thea was requested by a footman to attend her parents in the library, she found nothing out of the way. They had always been a family who had talked together. But the serious and solemn expressions on their faces, their unified stance before the window, brought her up short. They had not been admiring the view.

'What is it? Have you had bad news?' Thea stepped forward, casting aside reticule and parasol, untying the satin ribbons of her bonnet.

'No. Dear Thea.' Her mother immediately came to take her hands and draw her towards the sofa. 'Come and sit down. We have something that we…that we have decided we must tell you.'

Thea was not in any way put at ease by these words, but she sat and looked from one to the other, aware that Sir Hector and Lady Drusilla also exchanged glances with considerable unease.

'Please don't keep me in suspense.' She tried a little laugh, but it dried in her throat. 'I cannot imagine what should make you so stern.'

Her father took his seat behind his desk, fixed her with a direct stare and began. 'Theodora, your mother and I have decided that we should put you in possession of a number of important facts.'

'Hector—for Heaven's sake!—you are not addressing a meeting of the crowned heads of Europe.' Drusilla took her daughter's hands. 'Listen, Thea, first I need to say that we love you dearly. And nothing can or will ever change that.'

'I know that—but what can it be that—?'

Lady Drusilla took a breath, determined to step into the raging torrent. 'You have to understand—' there was no easy way to put it '—you are not our daughter, dearest Thea. We are not your parents.'

Thea blinked. Looked from one to the other. Could find no words. 'Not my parents? I do not understand. How should you not be?'

'Your mother is—your *true* mother was my elder sister Mary.'

'Oh.' Thea simply could not *think*. 'Forgive me. I find it difficult…' Her hands tightened on those of the woman whom she had always known as her mother as if in a death grip. 'Please… will you tell me?'

'Of course.' Lady Drusilla leaned forward to place a light kiss on Thea's forehead. There was the suspicion of tears in her eyes, in spite of all her intentions to remain calm and composed as she explained. 'Two weeks after you were born, your father died. Mostly from a dissolute life and too much alcohol—I hesitate to say, but it is true. Your mother—my sister—fell into a decline and took to her bed with smelling salts and laudanum. We—Sir Hector and I—were informed. In those days I still had some contact with my sister, although we had found her husband beyond bearing. When we arrived at the Great House—her home—she was in a state of collapse, incoherent and hardly aware of her surroundings. And we found you, in your crib, not to put too fine a point on it, neglected and unwanted. You were hungry, I recall, not over-clean, and you were crying. A poor little scrap. At that moment my heart went out to you. I could not leave you like that and Mary certainly could not deal with you. There were serious money problems, we were to discover. The other two children were in the care of a governess of sorts, but there was no nurse to take charge of you. It was decided that we should take you and bring you up as our own. Mary was in full agreement, as much as she could agree to anything considering her tears and vapours. Sir Hector and I had no children.' She met his eyes again for support and smiled a little as he nodded. 'And so we took you. You were just a month old. We gave you a name of our own choosing. And from that day we brought you up as if you were our daughter.'

'I cannot think what to say. I had no idea.' Thea struggled to come to terms with the shattering revelation, her mind repeating over and over her mother's words.

For a little while they sat in silence to give Thea time to take it all in.

Finally she turned to Drusilla. 'And you said that your sister— my mother—agreed to this?'

'Yes, she did. I would not willingly choose to speak ill of the dead, and not of my own sister, but she did not want you.'

'Did she never ask after me, not in all the years when I was growing up?'

'No.' Drusilla lifted an unsteady hand to stroke her daughter's bright hair in sympathy. 'I could lie to you and tell you that she did. But I will not. I can make excuses for her, of course—she was unwell and even as a girl had never had the strongest of minds. And now she was alone with two young children, a new baby and a dead husband. I do not think that she wanted the responsibility of your upbringing. And perhaps you reminded her of her husband's death. Not that *he* was any loss to her. But, no, she never did. She told us that she never wanted to see you—or us—again. I think that she was perhaps more than a little deranged.'

'I see.'

'We occasionally sent money—so that she should not be completely without funds. But she never replied to my letters. They were returned unopened, although the money was always accepted. Perhaps she was ashamed. I never saw my sister again after the day I left her house with you in my arms—and she never saw you.'

'But her loss was our gain, Thea,' Sir Hector added. 'We could not have had a more loving daughter if you were our own child. We are and always have been very proud of you and it delights me that you will be my heir. You must never think otherwise.'

Thea managed a smile as this simple declaration began to thaw just a little the crystals of ice in her blood.

'But she—your sister—' she turned to Lady Drusilla again 'she is now dead, as you told Lady Beatrice.'

'Yes.'

'And I have a brother and a sister?'

'Yes. Edward and Sarah.'

'Do they know about me?'

Again that look passed between Sir Hector and Lady Drusilla.

'We do not know. Your birth must have been recorded within the family and that record was never altered to our knowledge. You were certainly baptised. As head of the family Edward is probably aware. And perhaps he was old enough at the time to understand the sudden absence of his baby sister. Other than that, I think that Mary would not have seen fit to discuss the matter with her other children. Why should she? It would not reflect well on her, after all.'

'So I was not always Theodora.' A genuine smile touched her mouth.

'No. That was a name of our choosing. Your baptismal name was Sophia Mary Baxendale.'

'I like Theodora better!' Thea sat and thought. And then spoke in her usual clear manner, although her mother saw the depth of sadness in her eyes and there was the slightest hitch in her voice before she steadied. 'It is very strange. But I find that I can feel little emotion towards either a father who did not know me or an unknown mother who effectively disowned me. Neither love nor contempt. Regret, perhaps.' She looked up at the two people who had taken her as their own, loved her and cared for her, showered her with every family blessing. How hard it must have been for them to tell her. How painful it must be to wait—as they were waiting now in silent anguish—to know what her reaction would be towards them.

Thea's heart swelled with sudden love for them. 'You are the mother and father whom I have always known and whom I love,' she explained. 'What you have told me—it makes no difference to my love for you. But...' a frown touched her brow '...why tell me now? I do not understand why you should have found a need to tell me, if you have kept the secret for so many years.'

Her parents once more looked at each other, as if to draw strength.

'It could have a bearing on your future,' Sir Hector began. 'On your happiness. We thought that you should know. It is not an edifying tale. I think your mother will tell it better than I.'

So she did, and throughout the telling of it, with all its implications, Thea's blood ran cold. 'A little over three years ago, Edward Baxendale, your brother, attempted to discredit the good name and the validity of the marriage of the Marchioness of Burford and her recently dead husband, the Marquis.'

'Nicholas's eldest brother?'

'Yes. We do not know the full facts. We were not in England and, although rumour and scandal were rife, the Faringdon family kept the matter close to protect the Marchioness and her young son. But we understand that there were accusations of a bigamous marriage and a vital claim on the Faringdon estates was made. Edward's wife, Octavia, too was involved in the charade. We believe that the motive was money—which would not be beyond belief. More than that we cannot say.'

'So how does this…?' But light began to dawn in Thea's mind. It was searingly bright and struck her with a wrenching dread.

'Whatever the content of the deceit, the result was the breaking of a scandal in London. The private affairs of the Faringdon family were held up to public scrutiny, stripped bare for all to pick over and speculate. They were the latest *on dit* during that Season, discussed as a matter for open conjecture in every drawing room and every club—until Lord Henry and Lord Nicholas apparently unmasked Edward for the villain that he undoubtedly was. Your brother could have done irreparable harm to the family. He must certainly have caused the young Marchioness great distress.'

'That would be Eleanor, who went to New York with Lord Henry.' Thea nodded as she put her knowledge of the family into place.

'Yes. What I need to ask you, Thea, is this—what are your feelings towards Lord Nicholas?'

'I…' Thea flushed as she considered her reply. 'I…' She lifted her hands in a hopeless little gesture.

Her father came to the rescue.

'Your mother thought that perhaps you were not…uninterested where Nicholas Faringdon is concerned. One thing we do know, dear girl, is that the outcome of the scandal must have left a residue of deep hatred between Faringdons and Baxendales.'

'If Nicholas learns from some interested source that you are the sister of Sir Edward Baxendale,' Drusilla continued, watching her daughter's reaction anxiously, 'we fear his reaction towards you.'

'I see.' Amazingly, Thea discovered that she could keep her voice cool and controlled when her inclination was to cry out in the sudden intolerable pain from the wound inflicted by the knowledge of her past. 'That he would condemn me by association, I suppose.'

'Yes. Because you, too, are a Baxendale. As much as Edward is.'

'I understand. The lees in that particular cup must be bitter indeed. But…' She sought for a way through the terrible morass of grief that appeared to be building within her chest, hampering her breathing. 'Why should anyone speak out after all this time? Why would it be of interest to anyone now after all these years? Would anyone even remember that I am a Baxendale by birth?'

'They may not, of course.' Sir Hector would have given the world to be able to offer a vestige of hope, to wipe away the distress that his daughter covered so admirably. He could not do it. 'But it is a risk, a serious risk, now that you are well known in London circles. And if gossip begins to unite your name with that of Lord Nicholas, however loosely… We did not think it wise for you to base a relationship with Nicholas on a lie.'

'Oh, Thea.' Drusilla swallowed against the imminent threat of tears. 'We did not want him to break your heart if you fell in love with him, you see.'

'I do see.' And perhaps, as of this moment, her heart was broken anyway.

'You do understand why we had to tell you, don't you?'

'Of course. Such information could destroy any relationship between us.'

'I fear it.'

'So, what do you advise?' Thea straightened her shoulders, took a deep breath, and tried to still her fingers, which plucked at a satin ribbon on her morning gown.

'I think you know. You have always been open to sense—to reason.' Overflowing with admiration for her spirit, Drusilla worked hard to put on as brave a face as her daughter. She could do no less. 'We think it would be best if you kept your distance from Lord Nicholas. You should do everything possible to discourage any connection between you. It should not be difficult.'

Difficult? It would be well nigh impossible! Perhaps the hardest thing she had ever been asked to do in her life.

'And if I don't?' But in her heart she already knew the answer.

'Maybe nothing. Perhaps you would fall in love. If he offered for you, then you would marry. But if he discovered the truth of your birth, that you are in truth Edward Baxendale's sister, would Lord Nicholas continue to look on you with love—or would he turn his back with condemnation and contempt?'

'I could not bear that.' A tear stole unnoticed down Thea's cheek to soak into the little satin ruff of her gown.

'No. It would be beyond anything. You must end it, Thea. I knew you would be sensible if we explained the situation to you.'

'Sensible? No—it is not that.' Thea wiped away another tear with an impatient hand. 'It is simply that I find I have no choice.'

Leaving the library almost in flight, Thea took herself, with the long-suffering and loudly-complaining Agnes Drew, for a brisk walk in Hyde Park. The sun had vanished behind a thickening layer of high cloud and a sharp little breeze had sprung up to shiver the new leaves. The grey light and the hint of rain exactly suited her mood, so she strode out, taking no thought to the possible threat to her new French straw bonnet with ribbon and flower trim. What did a bonnet matter, however fetching, when placed in the balance against the disturbing developments of the past hour?

She needed the space in which to think, without the tortured presence of Sir Hector and Lady Drusilla both watching her with loving but anxious eyes. How she would have loved to gallop across the grass, she thought, as she saw others on horseback along the rides, although at a more seemly canter. To gallop without restraint, to allow the speed and exhilaration to cleanse her mind of the weight of knowledge that had been laid upon her. And the wave of despair that threatened to engulf her as she recalled that first fateful meeting with Lord Nicholas when their eyes had met and held, his hand clasped so firmly around her wrist. How she wished that she could experience his touch, his closeness, again. And yet, if her mother's fears held weight, it appeared that any future together, any blossoming of love between them, could never be.

Her parentage, Thea quickly discovered, interested her very little—apart from a mild curiosity. This shocked her. Surely it should have some meaning for her to know more of her blood relatives—that her father had been a dissolute gambler who had drunk himself into an early grave, her mother apparently a weak, pathetic creature who had withdrawn into a laudanum-created haze rather than face up to the responsibilities of her family. Thea frowned at the image painted by Lady Drusilla's words. There appeared to be absolutely no connection between these two shadowy people and herself.

She found herself heartily thanking God for Sir Hector and Lady Drusilla, who had moulded her by example and loving care into much sterner stuff. She should be grateful indeed that her mother—Mary Baxendale—had seen fit to give her away! So, after worrying at the matter for a bare five minutes, she simply discarded it as something of no real importance and no bearing on her life. Sir Hector and Lady Drusilla were her parents. The Baxendale family was nothing to her. There was nothing other to consider.

But the repercussions... Ah, now there was an intricate weave of possible consequences that would threaten her happiness, would effectively shatter the new sensations which she had just begun to experience. Even now, these consequences kept her mind occupied until she felt the beginnings of a headache build behind her eyes. Theodora never suffered from the headache! But she did now, exacerbated when she could find no simple solution. Only one path presented itself to her and she cringed from it. But the fear that she had no choice weighed on her soul.

The true state of her heart with regard to Lord Nicholas Faringdon she hastily pushed aside. She could not think of that now. But what exactly had Sir Edward Baxendale—her brother!—done? Had it been so *very* bad that Nicholas could harbour an undying hatred for anyone of the name of Baxendale? Would he indeed consign her to the fiery pit of hell in company with Sir Edward simply because of their shared parentage? Even though she had not even been aware of it until an hour ago? Was it possible that her parents had got it wrong—had read too much into the gossip that they must have heard at least second-, if not third-, hand? It was not difficult for gossip to embroider and exaggerate the true state of affairs. Perhaps it was all a terrible mistake, over which she might laugh in glorious relief when she knew the truth of it. But if what Lady Drusilla had intimated was indeed true, how the family must have suffered, particularly Eleanor on behalf of her child who would have been disinherited. Yet it all sounded highly far-fetched.

The morass of conflicting thoughts and fears in her head brought Thea to an abrupt halt in the centre of the path, causing Mistress Drew to hastily side-step with more muttered comments on inconsiderate young ladies who had no concern for those with ageing bones and with no wish to take long and energetic walks when a downpour was imminent. In quick sympathy and apology, Thea closed her hand on her maid's arm, but quickly turned her face away to disguise the emotions that she could not hide.

She stared across the vibrant spring grass towards the distant stand of trees, knowing that if she closed her eyes she would be faced with a stark image of Nicholas. She would read his reaction to her if the facts of the Faringdon scandal were true—the icy hauteur in his eyes, the thinned lips, the disdainful inclination of his head when pride and self-control took command, as in their first introduction in Lady Aston's ballroom when other influences were allowed to stand between them. How far they had progressed since that cold meeting. Now Lord Nicholas's face lit with a subtle glow when his eyes made contact with hers, when he turned and saw her across a room, his smile…

No! She could not think about the contempt that would surely colour Nicholas's vision of her if Sir Edward were the evil villain of her parents' fears. Thea tightened her hold on her parasol, ignored the shiver brought on by the sudden chill, and stepped out again. Agnes sighed and followed.

So, rather than being emotional, she would be practical. She was good at that. Considering the practical, then, how should she discover the truth?

The obvious source was Nicholas, but that was not a path which she could take. She shuddered at the prospect. So, the next alternative? Judith, of course. Judith, who would know the full truth of Faringdon family affairs and was never reluctant to indulge in a little gossip.

How could she go about it? Simply ask, of course. Thea nodded to herself. It should be perfectly straightforward. She had heard a whisper of an old rumour. What could it have been about? This would give Judith the perfect opening to reminisce and inform her in more, and doubtless accurate, detail, without any fear that her own unfortunate connection with the Faringdon family history would be detected.

Because, whatever the outcome of her uncharacteristic subterfuge, however unpleasant and unpalatable the outcome, she must discover the truth. She was not prepared to live with less. But, oh, how she prayed that it would all be false. Her mother had feared that she might lose her heart to Nicholas, that it might be broken. Thea, with typical self-analysis and painful honesty, feared that *that* particular part of her anatomy was already in serious danger of being lost to her. Whether he was aware or not, Nicholas held the key to her happiness. To lose him now was a sharp sword of pure distress of which she had no previous experience.

So, she must ask Judith in the most innocent manner to divulge the family secrets. On which decision, Thea turned around and retraced her path home at an equally brisk pace. Surely it was all a terrible mistake. And Judith would be able to put her mind at ease.

Miss Theodora Wooton-Devereux discovered that, perhaps as a diplomat's daughter, she had a talent for devious and cunning manipulation. And an equally well-developed one for hiding her true thoughts and feelings.

'Judith. I heard such a strange thing yesterday.' The two ladies were taking the air in Lady Painscastle's smart new barouche. Thea's mind was far from the delightful picture they made, or the admiring glances that might be turned their way. The deep blue afternoon gown with the darker velvet spencer and matching flowers on her rakish little hat did nothing to raise her spirits. This was the best opportunity that she would be given and so took it with hardly a qualm. 'I know it is none of my affair—but I would not wish to do or say anything inadvertently that would disturb Lord Nicholas.'

'What on earth could you have heard?' Judith raised her kid-gloved hand in recognition of the occupants of a passing landau-let, but turned humorous and enquiring eyes toward her companion. 'I may of course have been mistaken, but I had thought that you *did* wish to disturb Nicholas!'

Thea flushed with discomfort. How cheap it made her feel, to be using the situation to lure her unsuspecting friend into innocent gossip! But there was no help for it.

Judith misinterpreted the rose tint. 'There! I knew I was not wrong, as I told dear Simon only this morning!'

Thea managed an ingenuous smile, a slight flutter of lashes. 'I am sure that I do not know what you mean! But as I was saying—yesterday I overheard, when I was taking tea with Mama in Gunter's, a mention of a…of a *Faringdon scandal*. And the name—Baxendale, I think? Could that have been so? I trust that it was nothing of a serious nature!'

'So *that* unfortunate affair has resurfaced. We had hoped that it would die a permanent death.' The bright interest in Judith's face disappeared behind a thin cloud of anxiety. 'I wish it had not—it can bring nothing but distress to all involved.'

Thea felt her throat tighten as she swallowed against a moment of pure panic. 'Was it very bad?'

'A disaster. Poor Eleanor—you cannot imagine!'

Worse and worse! 'The Marchioness?'

'Yes. It could have ruined her life and that of Tom, her son. If it had not been for Hal and Nicholas, I fear that it would have succeeded.'

'Oh! Was the outcome—was the final outcome satisfactory?' Thea felt her heart grow cold within her, a leaden weight that seemed to fill her chest. It could not be!

'Forgive me, Thea.' Judith's face was now emotionless, her expression closed. 'The secret, the terrible scandal—is not mine to tell and I would not wish to dredge it up again. Suffice to say Edward Baxendale was a rogue, a villain who would have destroyed the honour and integrity of our family. I will not say more.' Which was so unlike Judith as to speak volumes in itself.

'Oh. I had no idea…' Thea sought for something to say. 'It must have been when Sir Hector was still resident in Constantinople.'

'Yes. More than two years now. We shall never forgive him— Edward Baxendale. The name is not mentioned. His wife was also part of the tissue of lies. Even his sister Sarah was involved. You have no idea—it was a terrible thing.'

'I see.' But, of course, Thea did not. Only that it must have been terrible indeed if the effect was to close Judith up like an oyster over its pearl. Both Edward Baxendale and his sister. There was no hope for her.

'I know that you will understand.' Judith folded one hand in neat precision over the other as if that finished the matter. As it did. 'Baxendale is a black name in our family.'

Despair crawled along Thea's veins from head to toe And with it not a little anger at the twists and turns of unfeeling Fate—that the sins of a brother should be visited on a sister, even when that sister had not even known of his existence until two days ago.

'Of course. I understand.' Thea continued with the charade, her composure quite remarkable in the circumstances. 'I am sorry that I should cause you to remember something that obviously resurrects so much pain.'

The rest of the afternoon passed in something of a haze for the lady. She managed to chatter and gossip, wave and exchange greetings as if she had no care in the world. But when she arrived back in Upper Brook Street her emotions felt as if they had been completely wrung out. She neatly avoided Lady Drusilla to shut herself in her bedchamber, to look out over toward the Park where she had first met Nicholas. But she did not see the view from the window. Finally she turned from it, straightened her spine and rubbed her hands over her face where the muscles felt strained and stiff with the pretence of smiling and being happy. Now she felt that she would never be truly happy again.

But she knew what she had to do. Thea looked at herself in the mirror of her dressing table. She must set herself to destroy any vestige of the relationship that might have begun to blossom between herself and Lord Nicholas. It should not be too difficult, should it, to give him a disgust of her if she really tried? To make him wonder what he had ever seen in her to attract. To turn his attention to other fortunate débutantes who would not fear the outcome of falling in love with him.

And for herself? There might even be hope for her mama's Earl yet. Thea found that she could not smile at the prospect.

She wiped tears from her cheeks surreptitiously. She never cried. Just as she never had the headache. There was absolutely no purpose in either. She must be *sensible*—that was the word—hiding her shattered hopes and damaged heart from everyone. No one must guess. Not Lord Nicholas. Not ever Nicholas. And certainly not her mother, who would blame herself for the rest of her life if she were allowed to sense her daughter's despair.

And whilst his love found herself reduced to the blackness of utter misery, Lord Nicholas Faringdon was equally prey to extreme emotions. Against all the odds, against all his inclination to thwart the plotting of Lady Beatrice, against every vestige of will-power, he had fallen in love. Although his acquaintance with Theodora could be measured in weeks—days, even—there was no room for doubt in his mind. He wanted nothing more than to ask for the lady's hand in marriage and carry her back to Aymestry. Could think of nothing better than to make a life with her, create children with her. She fired his blood. She intrigued him. She entranced him. If he had his way, Miss Theodora Wooton-Devereux would become Lady Nicholas Faringdon in the shortest possible time. And a smile of satisfaction touched his mouth—there was nothing in the manner of that lady towards him that might indicate that she would not welcome his addresses.

Chapter Six

So Theodora set out to destroy any warmer feelings that Lord Nicholas Faringdon might enjoy towards her, to build a barrier that he would not care to scale. She considered it all very carefully through a sleepless night. As dawn light touched the trees in the Park with gold, she had decided that she could not bear that he hold her in total contempt. The thought of that almost drove her to abandon her planning and simply allow fate to take its course, to allow love to develop between them and risk the chance of cruel revelations of her past. But she dare not. Therefore, she would allow herself to be just sufficiently undisciplined, just sufficiently outrageous, perhaps even a little *fast,* so as to drive a wedge between them. Just enough to persuade Lord Nicholas that he did not wish to squire so volatile a lady to supper. He would not choose to be seen in company with so outré a débutante in Hyde Park. He would not feel obliged to solicit her hand to partner him in the waltz on even *one* occasion in an evening if he considered her upbringing and behaviour not quite *the thing*. And he certainly would not desire to take her pretty lips in a kiss, the memory of which still had the effect of bringing a heated flush to her face when she was foolish enough to remember. Or even to brush his smiling mouth across the tips of her fingers. And if she could achieve all that, the distance between them would be vast and there would be no danger of either of them falling in love with each other. And no reason for anyone to remember the old scandal and the secrets behind Thea's own lineage. Thea would never have to experience the horror of the man whom she…whom she…*liked* a little…turning from her in contempt and harsh judgement. A little chilly distance was all she needed to achieve.

Therefore Thea applied herself to it with all the attention to detail of a battle campaign. She would rejoice when he bowed over the hand of other damsels, or held them within the circle of his arm in a waltz. And she would weep bitterly when she saw the depths of hurt in his eyes before pride came to his rescue and swiftly masked it. Anything was better than allowing a declared love to be blighted by the revelation that she was really Sophia Mary Baxendale.

She set herself two weeks in which to change the course of her life. And discovered that even within one week her irreverent and cavalier behaviour had achieved a splendid success.

Astonished at her skill, Thea slipped into the role of outrageous débutante with ease. Flirting irresponsibly with the Earl of Moreton, she repressed the sharp twinge of guilt when that gentleman responded with some surprise, but apparent delight. She made great play with her lashes and her fan, practising a coquettish turn of her shoulder, a particular angle of her head that might encourage intimacy, an unspoken encouragement to the Earl—*Frederick*—to invite her to dance. She made sure to accept his invitations on sufficient occasions that would rouse comment from those who watched the developing relationship. And a heavy sigh from Lady Drusilla, who knew just what her daughter was about. If her new gown was cut slightly too low across the bosom for modesty, Thea smiled brightly and dared anyone to comment. When Nicholas approached and requested a dance, it was amazing how frequently Thea discovered that her dance card was already full. Even for the country dances. She would have loved to partner him, but…she explained with an arch look. She was never in need of a gentleman to escort her in to supper.

Well—so much for the evenings!

With her mother's wincing and critical collaboration, Thea purchased a satin straw bonnet. It resembled to a remarkable degree a coal scuttle with a large crown and a deep, enclosing and unflattering brim lined with pleated satin. The ribbons and flowers were in varying shades of purple, the daisies sporting large yellow centres.

'I have rarely seen anything quite so ugly—or so common!' Lady Drusilla frowned at the monstrosity. 'Are you sure about this, Thea?'

'I know it is—but think of its effect.' Thea closed her eyes as she did indeed think of it. But she could not retreat now. 'Think how disagreeable it will be when it comes into lurid proximity with my hair.'

'I am! Indeed, I am thinking about that very thing!' Thea's mama shuddered visibly. 'It is unbelievably dreadful. Never would I have thought a daughter of mine, with a nice degree of taste…'

Agnes was even more outspoken. 'Are you trying to set yourself up as a joke, Miss Thea?'

No! There was nothing amusing at all about this. Thea set her lips in a determined line as she tied the offending ribbons. Nicholas could not possibly admire either her appearance or her taste in fashion when he caught sight of her in this impossible creation!

So, when she wore it to a shopping outing with Judith and Lady Beatrice, it drew all eyes. And not a few unkind comments with hastily suppressed giggles. Lady Beatrice found a need to use her lorgnette once more and failed to hide her displeasure. And Nicholas, whom they just happened to meet in New Bond Street? Although not so well versed in ladies' fashions, Thea could not mistake the faint hint of shock in his eyes.

But two wearings for the detested bonnet were quite enough. She could not bring herself to don it again and, when her mama positively forbade it, consigned it to the rear of her closet.

So far, so good.

With what she considered a brilliant ruse, Thea next arranged the loan of a high-perch phaeton from an acquaintance of Sir Hector. A remarkable vehicle with its height and huge wheels, not frequently seen as a vehicle for a lady, in itself it would have drawn all eyes. But Thea chose to drive it in the Park, at the optimum time of day, without either her maid or an attendant groom. And, far worse, insisted on wrapping herself in her desert robes with the scarf around her hair. The strangest sight! With enough comment to satisfy her, some raised brows—even better. Thea set her teeth and bowed to a startled pair of ladies in a passing landau as she applied her long-handled whip with considerable expertise. Definitely fast! She would have worn the boots and breeches if she had the nerve. But even Thea did not dare.

Now for a more personal encounter with Lord Nicholas. It tore her heart in two!

On the day of the Sefton ball, Thea accepted the delivery of a tasteful posy of flowers in a filigree holder. It was delightfully delicate, white and cream blooms bound with silver ribbons. From Nicholas. She had not yet managed to drive him away and the little confection would be perfect with her dress. Regretfully, she stroked the dewy petals, then laid them aside. She must not carry them. It might proclaim the message of her heart, but she must be prepared to take a stronger stand. She had never been closer to weakening as at that moment, but no. She sent Agnes to purchase a less-than-tasteful cluster of yellow roses, far too large for a lady to carry to a ball. She positively flinched when she saw them with her glowing, delphinium blue gown, but carry them she would. And it would not be difficult to hint that they had been given to her by another admirer. Which should effectively destroy any desire on Nicholas's part to single her out!

And as Nicholas, on seeing the golden bouquet, bowed and withdrew to lead a sprightly dark-haired damsel into a waltz, his face coldly stern, Thea knew the glorious heights of success. And the abyss of black despair.

Thea's talent for deception continued to grow. Taking Agnes into her confidence, she arranged a cruel little scene, knowing that Nicholas would be present to witness it, and would not enjoy the experience of seeing the superior Miss Theodora Wooton-Devereux at her most callous. Emerging from Gunter's with Judith and Nicholas, it had begun to rain. Thea immediately dispatched Agnes to find a cab to take them home in some degree of comfort. When Nicholas would have objected and stepped out himself, Thea demurred.

'But it is now raining heavily.' She could not ignore the sharp criticism in his tone or the hardness in his gaze. 'Mistress Drew will be wet. That should not be.'

Thea shrugged, a nasty, selfish little gesture that she had practised before her mirror. 'But she is my maid. She will find a cab. It would not do for you to get wet, my lord.' She tried not to be wounded by the narrowed glances of both Judith and Nicholas.

The outcome was painful but satisfactory. Nicholas, with a firm gesture of his hand to Agnes to remain where she was, stepped out into the rain to summon a cab. Then handed Thea and Agnes up into the vehicle—but both he and Judith, somewhat stiffly, declined an invitation to accompany the ladies. So they did not see Thea enfold Agnes into a quick hug with a kiss for her cheek. Or the tears that she was forced to brush away from her lashes with an impatient hand when her nurse, who had always been there to comfort her since she was a child, returned the kiss.

'I trust that you are satisfied, Miss Theodora.' Agnes looked skeptical, but patted her charge's hand.

'I must be, dear Agnes. I think he now has a disgust of me, do you not?'

'I would certainly expect so!'

Perhaps just one more little event was needed to hammer the final nail into the coffin of their relationship. Ordering Agnes to remain at home, Thea donned an eye-catching gown of rich rose pink, tilted her silk and lace parasol at an elegant angle and proceeded to walk—to *saunter*, in effect—down St James's Street. She could feel the eyes of the dandy crowd from the Bow Window set at White's follow her every movement. They raised quizzing-glasses. Leers and smirks. The only blessing was that she was unable to hear any of the comments the gentlemen might make. But with a smile pinned to her lovely face, she completed her promenade—and prayed that she would never have to accomplish anything quite so obnoxious again. But, as she had intended, the gossips would undoubtedly tattle.

'What are you about, Thea?' Judith accosted her at a little soirée that they both attended that night. Her expression, for Judith, was austere, and there was a noticeable reserve in her demeanour. 'Are you deliberately wishing to make yourself the talk of the town? You are certainly succeeding. Why would you do something so particular? I must say, I had not thought it of you. If you do not take care, people will not wish to acknowledge you. And then where will you be?'

From which troubled comment, Thea presumed that her plan had achieved its ends.

She knew for sure when approached by Nicholas at Almack's on the following evening.

With a formal bow, Lord Nicholas Faringdon requested the honour of a dance.

With a bright smile, Miss Theodora Wooton-Devereux made her excuses.

'You appear to have developed a sudden aversion to my company, madam.'

'An aversion?' She laughed with a distinct toss of her head. She found that she could not read his thoughts behind the cool demeanour. 'Nothing so melodramatic, my lord.'

'I had hoped that we had an understanding.' Again that dangerous calm.

'An understanding? I am not sure of your meaning.' *Oh, Nicholas, forgive me!* 'We have certainly flirted. And most successfully. But an understanding? Why, no, my lord!'

'No. Forgive me for imposing on your time. I was clearly mistaken. I will relieve you of my presence.'

'If you wish it, of course.' And again that brittle little laugh.

For a long moment he looked at her, from her golden hair to the toes of her satin dancing slippers. 'I believe that I do, madam. I fear that I misread you in many ways. But you will not be without a host of suitors to your hand.'

'Why, no.' Thea was forced to take a breath against the lance of pain that struck at her heart, but her words were flippantly light-hearted. 'As you know, I am very rich. Of course I am most sought after. I would expect it. All I need is a title. My mama is very keen to see me settled and I agree with her.'

'I wish you well in your search.'

He bowed with glacial elegance and economy of movement and turned on his heel. He did not look again in her direction for the whole of the evening.

In their carriage on Thea's return to Upper Brook Street after one of the most miserable evenings of her life, tears fell. She could not stop them. Her mother put her arms around her in the darkness, struggling against the wave of guilt that swept through her at her daughter's distress. If she had not divulged her fears, the secrets of the past, this would never have happened. But what use now with regrets?

'It is very hard.'

'Yes.'

'It is for the best, Thea. You will meet someone whom you can love. Where there is no past to stand barrier. You will be happy again and your heart will mend.'

'If you say so, Mama. I cannot see it.' Theodora tried for a smile when she saw her mother's worried expression as they passed a lighted flambeau on Park Lane. 'At least if he has taken me in dislike, he will go home to Burford Hall and I can stop being quite so outrageous. It is far too exhausting.'

She rested her head against her mother's shoulder and prayed that he would go, whilst Lady Drusilla's heart was sore indeed that her advice had caused her daughter so much pain. She prayed that her daughter's strength of will would prevail, but how her heart went out to her child in her sufferings as her tears fell undetected on to Theodora's bright hair.

'I thought you liked Nicholas.'

'Nicholas?'

'Yes. My cousin.' With a sharpness quite alien to Judith, she pinned her companion with an accusing stare. 'With whom you have danced and dined and walked and driven…'

'I do not dislike him.'

'You know what I mean. He no longer seeks you out. You turn away from him. You refuse to dance. Have you quarrelled?'

'No.'

'And all that strange behaviour. I thought I would die when I saw you in that purple-flowered monstrosity! And as for St James's Street! Don't tell me there is nothing wrong!' Which was very percipient, Thea decided, for Judith. And also too close to the truth for comfort.

'I cannot say. Forgive me, Judith. I cannot say. I only hope that I have not hurt him.'

'I expect you have—although you would not know it. Nicholas always was good at hiding his feelings. But it seemed to me that you deliberately set out to do so.'

Thea found that she could not look at her friend. 'I…I hope that it will not matter to him—that he will soon forget…'

'I would never have believed that you could be so cruel and hard, Thea.'

'Forgive me.' Thea fled from the room.

She wept bitter tears.

Not only had she destroyed the promise of any love between herself and Nicholas, she had also damaged her friendship with Judith.

Was it worth it? Would it not have been better to let events take their course? How many times had she asked herself that question?

Judith had the right of it. She had indeed been cruel and hard. But into her mind crept another image. Of her standing before Nicholas. And in his eyes a fervent hatred that she was the sister of Edward Baxendale, the man who had deliberately set out to destroy the integrity of the Faringdon family for his own ends.

Oh, yes. It was worth it. She could not bear that. Nor could she bring such lasting pain to Nicholas. A little present discomfort, even heartache, would soon fade and would be forgotten as his life continued without her.

But her tears, privately shed, were bitter indeed.

And Lord Nicholas?

Nicholas found himself in an unusual and unpalatable state of mental upheaval. How could he have been so mistaken in his reading of the character of the lady? In the past week, such a short time, he had discovered her to be any number of things that he actively disliked. It was, he decided, like a nightmare from which he could not wake. He had seen her to be thoughtlessly unkind, lacking in all aspects of both good manners and breeding, and with a wilful rejection of acceptable standards of behaviour and taste. She was both spoiled and selfish. And an accomplished and heartless flirt. Surely he could not have read her so wrongly? A lovely face, he realised, had little to recommend it when overshadowed by the faults of character that he had the misfortune to encounter in the past seven days.

And he had come perilously close to allowing his heart to slip from his control and into those undoubtedly pretty but careless hands.

The thought angered him as he leafed through the pile of invitations that had arrived at Faringdon House, leaving him with a ridiculous sense of betrayal. He cast the gilt edged cards on to a side-table and shrugged. Better to discover now before he was entirely caught up in her sticky spinnings. It was not a web to his liking. He simply had to accept that she was nothing but a rather common flirt who had been allowed far too lax an education and now had her sights set on as elevated a title and as well-lined a pocket as she should achieve. He would have no further part in the scheming of this particular spider. He would not be made a fool of by a delicious smile or a pair of entrancingly blue eyes.

As for her attention-seeking perambulation around the Park in unacceptably exotic costume, and her scandalous flouting of convention by daring to walk down St James's Street, leaving herself open to being ogled by any man on the strut—she must have known that such behaviour would ruin her reputation. No. He wanted no more breath of scandal in his life. She was welcome to the Earl of Moreton, if that was what she wanted. And the Earl was welcome to her!

It struck him as he descended the stairs on his way to Brooks's that he had had quite enough of London. There was nothing to keep him here but pride—which would ensure that he remain for a little longer. He would not be seen to run from a connection that he had deliberately sought. But pride and self-control would keep him well out of Miss Theodora Wooton-Devereux's manipulative orbit. There was no need for him to consider her ever again.

So Nicholas stayed on for a few days. Keeping his mind closed to his motives, he made sure that he was seen squiring other eligible débutantes in his curricle in Hyde Park, at private parties and at Almack's. He even went so far as to organise another small party for an evening among the pleasures at Vauxhall Gardens, but deliberately did not invite Miss Theodora Wooton-Devereux, who would find out about it eventually from Judith, of course. And be hurt.

He found no interest in kissing anyone in the shadowed groves of Druids Walk!

After which superb show of indifference, Nicholas would go home to Aymestry Manor, and Burford Hall. But all he could see was a tall, slender, fair-haired lady who had enticed and then rejected him, leaving an ache in the region of his heart. Love? Of course not. Simply a mild interest, which would pass and the ache with it!

It had before.

It would again.

* * *

Theodora saw the results of her campaigning all too clearly. Nicholas was rigidly, freezingly polite when they met. He bowed in stern acknowledgement, but took care not to touch her. Not even her hand. He certainly did not seek her out. In fact, he remained as little time in her company as was politely possible. He did not smile at her or allow his eyes to meet with hers. They might have been mere distant acquaintances who did not like each other overmuch. Occasionally she surprised a quizzical look on his face as if he could not quite understand her. And he never flirted with her!

So why was she so unhappy? She had achieved exactly what she had set out to achieve. And in so short a time as to be almost miraculous. Perhaps she had missed her calling and should go on the stage!

At night she turned her face into her pillow, as if to block out the image of his face that haunted her waking and sleeping hours, and longed to feel the strength of his arms around her again.

'You are sadly out of countenance, my love.' Lady Drusilla eyed her daughter over the breakfast table and decided that the time had come not to mince words.

'It was late when I arrived home last night,' Thea explained in a somewhat colourless manner. 'The musical evening at the Southcotts', if you recall. I think you made an excellent choice not to attend, Mama. I have rarely spent a more tedious evening.'

'It is not lack of sleep that makes you so pale. I have known you to dance until dawn without ill effects. So, listening to music…' She paused. 'He has gone, Theodora. It is over. You know it was the best decision to make and you must accept it.' Her tone was bracing, but not without compassion.

It was three weeks since Lord Nicholas Faringdon had made his perfunctory excuses to his family, closed up Faringdon House and returned to Burford Hall. He had obviously made no attempt to see Theodora.

'I know.' Thea managed a smile as she reduced the warm roll to crumbs on her plate. 'You will note that I am making every attempt to fulfil your wishes for me. Frederick is becoming quite hopeful.'

'Unless he is driven away by your fading looks! I think you need a change of air, my dear. To leave London.'

'Will you let me accompany you to St Petersburg?' Thea looked up hopefully from the crumby disaster. *At least in Russia I would be as far from Nicholas as it would be possible to be!*

'No!'

'But why should I leave London now? In the middle of the Season?'

'Only for a short time. A few days. Until you have regained your looks. And I anticipate that the Earl will miss you—and be even keener to fix his interest with you on your return.'

'Or take up with another débutante in my absence. A sad case of out of sight, out of mind.' Not that she cared! 'Miss Walworth is very pretty, do you not think?'

'You need some colour in your cheeks.' Lady Drusilla recognised the diversionary tactics and refused to co-operate. 'And I think that you have lost weight. Furthermore, there are distinct shadows under your eyes this morning. It really will not do, Thea.'

Thea sighed and gave in, even as she took herself to task for lack of spirit. 'So, where are you sending me?' Perhaps a change of scene would restore her energies. She was simply not used to feeling so *down.*

Since Lord Nicholas's departure, Thea's errant behaviour had been transformed almost overnight, the unfortunate hitches forgotten, her social solecisms glossed over. Judith had apparently forgiven her, although she still expressed disquiet over her treatment of poor Nicholas. Lady Beatrice frowned and was inclined to refer to *that incident in St James's Street,* but was prepared to accept that perhaps Theodora had not realised the enormity of her transgression. Frederick was attentive. Smitten, Judith suggested with a suppressed chuckle. So all was comfortable again.

The only problem was with Thea's heart, which refused to return to its previously unawakened state and its normal steady rhythm.

'I have had an idea,' Lady Drusilla announced. 'I have an ancient cousin, Jennifer Hatton. She is mostly housebound and very deaf, but she is my only close relative. I have no wish to visit her in her rural solitude, but should enquire after her before we leave for St Petersburg. *You* could go, instead. With Agnes, of course. It would be the perfect solution. You will enjoy the freedom from London restrictions and a visit into the country will do you good.'

'Very well.' Thea abandoned her attempt at breakfast. She felt no great enthusiasm, but perhaps it would be better than allowing her eyes to search every soirée, every ballroom, every street, for a glimpse of Nicholas, when she knew for certain that he was no longer in town. And certainly better than suffering a severe attack of the nerves when she saw a dark-haired, broad shouldered gentleman. It was hopeless! She *never* suffered from nerves!

'There is one problem.'

She tuned her mind back into her mother's words.

'Cousin Jennifer lives in Tenbury Wells. In Herefordshire.'

'Oh!' *Burford Hall is in Herefordshire!*

Lady Drusilla caught the interested gleam in Thea's eyes. 'I expect you to be sensible, Theodora,' she declaimed in firm accents. 'On no account are you to make contact with Lord Nicholas. Not after all your hard work to distance yourself from him—it would be foolish in the extreme to put yourself in his way. It is an advantage that you will not be called upon to socialise while you are there in Tenbury Wells. My cousin is too elderly to visit or to keep open house.' She surveyed her daughter and wondered if her suggestion had been quite wise. There was a distinct return of colour to Thea's pale cheeks. 'You will do nothing to draw attention to yourself. You will go nowhere near Burford Hall. Fresh air, new surroundings, and back here at the end of the week. Do I make myself clear?'

'Yes, Mama. Very clear.' Thea smiled in perfect serenity. 'I will do just as you say.'

'You do not visit Burford Hall!'

'Of course not, Mama.' Of course she would go nowhere near Burford Hall.

But Aymestry Manor, Nicholas's own property, which her mama appeared to have overlooked, was not so very far from Tenbury Wells. Would she be able to resist going to see Nicholas's own home? If she were sensible, she would remain as distant as possible from it. How foolish it would be to even risk a chance meeting. But the temptation to see his home for herself was well-nigh irresistible…

Her spirits lifted as she left the breakfast parlour, informing her mama that she would go and supervise the packing for a visit into the country. She could not quite quell the little surge of— what? Hope? Anticipation? How foolish she was, but energy once more sang in her blood.

Lady Drusilla frowned at her daughter. 'Are you humming, Theodora?' she asked, her suspicions aroused, as the lady walked to the door with a lively flounce to her skirts?

'Humming? Certainly not, Mama. I never hum!'

And with that Lady Drusilla had to be content.

Chapter Seven

Thea discovered her mother's brief description of Cousin Jennifer to be exact to a point. Of advanced age, she lived retired from society, profoundly deaf and intolerant of those around her except for the equally elderly servants who ministered to her needs. Her days were spent in reading, tending her beloved garden and drinking a quantity of vintage port. She made Thea welcome in a casual manner, but, although friendly enough, made no alteration in her own itinerary beyond giving instructions for Thea's comfort in the house as long as she cared to remain there. She had clearly expected no visit from Lady Drusilla. Thea decided that it had all been a ruse on her mother's part to remove her from town for a little while, but accepted the cunning but obvious subterfuge with equanimity. She had enjoyed the journey in the company of Mistress Drew and her groom of long standing, Edward Dacre. Sir Hector had also insisted that a servant accompany her to handle her luggage, arrange her accommodation at hotels and inns *en route*. So they had made quite an entourage and Thea had found nothing demanded of her but to relax and enjoy the experience. Sir Hector had provided a light travelling coach for her comfort so she travelled in style and also had her grey Arab mare, The Zephyr, with her.

At Tenbury House, on the outskirts of the little town, Thea settled in. Nothing was required of her by her hostess, which gave Thea the opportunity to enjoy as much fresh air and freedom as her mother had recommended. She explored the little town, a minor spa graced with a parade of shops, an ancient church and a swiftly flowing river with swans and ducks. But, attractive as it was, its pleasures were soon exhausted.

So, now what should she do with her time? Thea discovered a little pamphlet describing the local sights worthy of admiration. She riffled through the pages with eyes that did not quite focus on the words and illustrations on the page. Because in the back of Thea's mind lurked the prospect of Aymestry Manor. It glowed like a jewel on black velvet. It lured her, enticed her, wearing down her good intentions. It was so close, after all. Surely a brief visit, just to *look*—from a distance, of course— would be acceptable? Conscience and common sense warned her of the dangers of such an escapade. Her own inclination was reluctant to listen. Her common sense took on the tone and accents of Lady Drusilla at her most imposing.

You must not go there, Theodora!

But why not?

What good would it do to meet Nicholas again? You know all the arguments, all the dangers, only too well.

He would not be there!

It would be wrong to see him. You care for him too much.

I have no intention of seeing him!

So what is the point of going?

Because…because I want to see the house that is his very own, which he cares for, which is close to his heart.

And what good would that do, pray?

I don't know. I simply want to see something that matters to him. There is no danger in that, is there?

So you are merely inquisitive? Really, Theodora!

Yes! And what is wrong with that?

Her common sense (and Lady Drusilla) gave up and lost the argument.

* * *

As a result, on a bright morning, the lady took Agnes Drew, Edward Dacre and their servant on a mounted expedition to Aymestry, a journey that could easily be managed in a day. A pleasant journey where they were free to admire the gentle rounded hills, wooded valleys, the flash of the deep and secret River Teme as it emerged from the undergrowth. Wild flowers cloaked verges with buttercups and ox-eye daisies. The apple trees were laden with blossom, promise of a good harvest.

Asking directions, they turned on to a little track that wound between high grass and old hedgerows. And there it was, in an open valley, surrounded by pasture and stands of oak and beech. Thea reined in The Zephyr on a rounded knoll to get a better view. Nicholas had spoken of Aymestry Manor often, not in any great detail, but with deep affection. Now she understood why, knowing that it had been willed to him from the family estate, originally part of a dowry from his mother's family.

The first impression to strike her was that it was not classically beautiful. No clean lines or porticoes, no symmetrical windows, no pillars or imposing steps. It was a hotchpotch of old construction over the centuries, with the addition of more recent wings and storeys. A mellow stone wing from the seventeenth century butted against wood and plaster half-timbered walls and gables. A carved entrance porch led to an arched doorway that smacked of medieval origins. One recent addition with a little tower rose above a double-hipped roof-line. Beside it, around a paved central courtyard, were half-timbered barns, a red-brick dove cote, a pair of oast houses with their tilted stone roofs and a range of stone and plaster stabling. It was not classical, but it was charming, offering an immediate warmth and welcome.

It was, she thought, on a sudden impulse, a *home*. But she knew that Nicholas, by necessity, spent little time there.

Around the house she could see evidence of gardens, both informal and formal, a ha-ha protecting them from the predations of animals that grazed in the open pastures beyond. Thea sighed and tried to ignore the little tug at her heart as the sun encouraged the roses along one gable-end to unfurl their petals and the doves flew in a flurry of white wings, to settle once more on their perches.

Yes. It looked like home. And had been over the centuries. A settled place, something of which she had no experience in her short life.

Agnes, seated beside her on a stolid gelding, interrupted her reverie. 'I think we should go back, Miss Thea.'

'No. I want to go closer.'

'It is not wise. His lordship might be here. And then where shall we be?'

'No.' Thea was certain. 'He visits only rarely, when business permits.'

Before Agnes could object further, she kicked the little mare into a descent from their vantage spot. All she wanted was to see what lay so close to Nicholas's heart. To know a little more about him, even if it would increase the pain, even if they were destined to live apart. She nodded in quick decision. It was worth the risk.

At close quarters the house was just as entrancing. Gardens carefully tended without being fussy, perhaps lacking the hand of a woman, Thea found herself thinking before she stopped herself. Voices from the further side of the house drew her to approach a small paddock where two mares with their new foals grazed, watched by a pair of grooms who leaned on the fence. But no sign of Nicholas.

Well, she was here. She would see what enthralled him about this place. She walked The Zephyr up to the paddock, leaving Agnes and their escort some way behind, and brought her to a halt.

An elderly man with grizzled hair and weatherbeaten face, with some authority on his shoulders, emerged from one of the barns at her approach. Touched his hand to his hat as he took in the quality of the visitors, and, more importantly, their horseflesh. Thea dismounted.

'Good day, miss.' He came over to hold her reins, a little bent with age. 'Can I be of help?' His voice held the soft Marches' burr.

'No. I was passing…visiting in the area…a cousin lives near

Tenbury. I am a little acquainted with Lord Nicholas Faringdon. Is he perhaps here?'

'No. Expect he's over at Burford. I'm Furness, his lordship's head groom 'ere at Aymestry.'

A curious mix of relief and disappointment flooded through her. Deciding that relief was the more apt of the two, she smiled at the groom. 'It is lovely here, Master Furness.'

'It is that.'

'Lord Nicholas has spoken often of his horses.'

'Prime beasts, miss.' He turned back to admire his charges, pride clear on his lined face. 'We hope to do well on the turf. Good lines in this breeding, y'see. These little 'uns are both thoroughbred. Much in demand in the hunting field too.'

'I can see.' She smiled at his enthusiasm and stretched out her fingers to scratch the forehead of an inquisitive mare.

'His lordship—he doesn't get enough time to concentrate on 'em. Not as much as he'd like. Too much business over at the big house and estate.'

'It takes a lot of his time?' The mare pushed at her hand, perhaps hoping for an apple. She laughed and shook her head.

'Too much, I'd say. His're the only shoulders to bear it, y'see—the Marquis being only a little lad and in foreign parts an' all.' Furness searched his pockets to find a wizened fruit, which the mare promptly crunched.

'Yes. I see. He is a conscientious landlord?' Thea discovered that she had no pride when it came to questioning the groom about his master. She flushed a little at the realisation. Thank God her mama was not within hearing distance!

'Aye. No hard feelings round here. Or none to speak of.'

'No. I suppose not. Is there much unrest?'

'Some. We hear rumour of it on Lord Westbourne's estates, which run between here and Tenbury. And in Leominster, o' course. But not at Aymestry. Or Burford. Even when we've had hard times—harvest bad and famine at hand—he cares for his own, does Lord Nicholas. Puts money from his own pocket back into the land. Keeps rents down, d'you see. Not like some I could name round 'ere. Lord Westbourne, for one. Them as thinks of nothing but their own comfort and pleasures.' Furness spat on the ground. 'Beggin' your pardon, miss.'

'You are fortunate indeed, Master Furness.'

He nodded. 'Not all agree. The markets are bad, but we do well enough. The cattle and sheep are sturdy breeds. Ryelands over there—see.' He pointed with gnarled fingers. 'And Herefords in the far pasture. New blood brought in to improve the stock. Lord Nicholas keeps up with the trends—always reading some pamphlet or other. Different from in my dad's day—when he was groom 'ere.' The old groom, it seemed, needed no encouragement from Thea to express his admiration. 'His lordship now—he's done it since he was nobbut a young lad, as well, his brother dying so young and Lord Henry being in New York.'

'Yes. Of course.' Thea found words difficult. Her heart swelled within her breast and emotion tightened its hold on her throat, surprising her with its intensity. To hear such praise from Master Furness. And she had to admit to the sly finger of guilt that touched her spine. She had been more than ready to condemn Nicholas as a frivolous, self-serving landlord with no thought for his tenants. And living on his nephew's inheritance too! How far, it seemed, she had been from the truth.

'I must go,' she decided eventually, giving the mare a final caress on her soft nose. 'I have enjoyed our meeting, Master Furness.'

'A nice horse you have there, miss.' He cast his eye over the grey, then leaned down to run his hands down her forelegs. 'His lordship could make good use of some swift Arab blood in the breeding. I reckon she runs well.'

'Yes. Like the wind. Sometimes she is difficult to stop.' Memories were suddenly stark in her mind. She had stayed long enough. It would not do to tempt fate further.

'I must go,' she repeated.

'Who shall I say that called, miss?'

'No matter. Goodbye, Master Furness.' She turned to go, suddenly aware of a hiss of expression from Agnes Drew.

And there he was.

* * *

On his return from London, Nicholas had found himself seamlessly absorbed into estate matters. It was not difficult. Lambing and calving continued apace at Burford and he was readily involved. Riding the family acres, a small glow of satisfaction touched him that he had thwarted Beatrice's less than subtle plans. He fervently hoped that she was feeling put out that he had escaped her clutches. Without doubt, he had enjoyed the pace and glamour of the London scene, but he was not sorry to be back. The stern lines of his face relaxed into a smile as he watched a pair of swans with their fluffy if unmanageable brood take to the water on the mere.

But the smile faded.

Theodora.

He would not think of her! She meant nothing to him. He looked down, a line developing between his brows as he rubbed at the skin on his hand where the mark of her whip had just faded to the slightest discoloration. A woman who was volatile and unreliable, spoilt, privileged and indulged from childhood. A lucky escape indeed to see her in her true colours when he might have been in danger of allowing himself to enjoy her company too much.

So why did the thought of her, the memory of her laughter, the sparkle in her magnificent eyes, still heat his blood? And trouble his sleep? Unwise enough to recall the softness of her mouth against his in those few stolen kisses in Vauxhall Gardens, the muscles in his loins tightened uncomfortably. Desire ran hot through his veins. He bared his teeth and kicked his horse into a canter. But the speed of the animal did nothing to distance him from the apparent hold Miss Wooton-Devereux continued to exert over his very masculine reaction to her. Against all logic, all good sense, he continued to be driven by the thought of taking Theodora to his bed, of claiming her lips in a furious possession that did not include gentleness. Igniting all that fire and energy in his arms. If only she hadn't been so irresponsible and wayward. Frustration made him groan and set his teeth. It could, he decided, be the death of him!

When matters at Burford allowed, Nicholas decided on impulse to spend some time at Aymestry Manor. It was a fine day and an easy ride through undemanding country. He did not need an excuse, but if he did, some of his mares would be ready to drop their foals. Furness would deal with it, of course—he had worked with horses all his life, and his father before him—but Nicholas wanted to see the fruition of his long-term planning for himself. He dropped down through the woods behind the little Manor, remembering boyhood adventures there with his brothers, and so was perhaps, a trifle melancholy, only to see a little group of visitors with their horses standing beside one of the paddocks. This was nothing out of the way. Most likely lost travellers stopped to ask direction. A lady was in conversation with his groom, another female companion and an escort in attendance. His first thought was that the lady held the reins of a prime piece of horseflesh. He cast an experienced eye over the short arched neck and glossy, deep-chested body, the powerful, glossy flanks. A pretty animal—and perhaps not unfamiliar? Then the lady turned, gathering up the reins and taking hold of the saddle to mount. At the same moment, as if on cue, the sun emerged from behind a little cloud to illuminate the scene.

Nicholas reined in his horse sharply, with a less-than-smooth gesture, causing his mount to toss its head in immediate resistance to the unusual treatment. Then he simply sat and stared through narrowed eyes.

Golden hair, curling neatly into her neck, a rakish little hat trimmed with a soft feather that curled to brush her cheek. A deep blue riding habit in some soft material that draped and clung to her tall, elegant figure. A heart-lifting smile as she turned her head to reply to some comment from Furness.

Oh, God! No!

Nicholas closed his eyes against the vivid scene. It was bad enough seeing her in his dreams, imagining her dancing in London in some other man's arms. Probably the damned Earl of Moreton! But not here! Not now!

But when he opened them, the vision was still there. The sun felt too hot on his skin, the light around him too bright to bear. Everything was in sharp focus as he heard her soft, infectious laugh, as his heart beat heavily against his ribs. Then, with a touch of his heel, he urged his horse forward.

Thea had no presentiment of his approach until the sharp hiss of warning from Agnes Drew caused her to turn her head. A figure mounted on a magnificent dark bay thoroughbred rode toward her, came to a halt, the sun behind him gilding his outline, casting his face into shadow. But she knew immediately—and froze, hands tight on her reins. He dismounted.

They simply stood and looked at each other. As if they were alone in the universe.

It was almost a month since they had set eyes on each other. Thea felt that it could have been yesterday as her gaze searched his familiar features.

Tension held them silent in its grip. Eyes locked as emotion arced between them. Attraction or latent hostility? A nameless desire? Neither could or would have named it, but it held them captive, unaware of either their surroundings or the more-than-interested audience. Until it was suddenly brought to Nicholas's mind, the recollection of the almost physical charge between his brother Henry and Eleanor, the love of his life, when they were in the same room together. No. There was nothing similar here. It could not be! And Thea found herself dissecting her motives in proposing this visit. Had she wanted this meeting all along? In honesty, she did not know. But her heart seemed to be lodged somewhere in the region of her throat. She could find no words to say.

Furness coughed respectfully. 'There now, miss. Here's his lordship. Timely come, I reckon. Just as you was about to leave, an' all.'

It broke the spell. The focus softened and the actors in the little scene fell back into accustomed responses. Lord Nicholas stepped forward, handing his horse over to Furness. Bowed formally in acknowledgement of Thea's presence. Inclined his head to Mistress Drew. Thea curtsied. Neither smiled.

'Miss Wooton-Devereux. Mistress Drew.' His bow was impeccable, worthy of a town withdrawing room, no indication of the churning surge of emotions through his body. They might have been the casual travellers he had first thought them to be. 'Welcome to Aymestry Manor. I would not have expected to see you here in this part of the country.' *Why are you here?*

Thea determined not to show her discomfiture. She could be just as cool as he. 'I am visiting an elderly relative, my lord—a cousin of my mama—in Tenbury Wells.' *I should not be here. What a terrible faux pas.* 'I remembered your description of your home here, and since it was so near... Master Furness has been telling me about your horses.'

'We are proud of them.' *It is too painful you being here. I wish you had not—and yet...*

'And rightly so. I have been admiring the foals...' *He is so cold, so stern. As if my sudden appearance at his door holds no significance for him. So what do I read in his eyes when he looks at me, when I am unable to look away or hide my own feelings?*

'Ah, yes. We have a new stallion. We are breeding for speed as well as endurance...' *She is so polite and composed. As if it is nothing to her that I have discovered her at my home. And that there is a passion which runs between us, almost visible as a shimmer in the air, which cannot be gainsaid, however much I would deny it.*

He was just as she remembered. Tall, imposing, his dark hair lifted by the light breeze. The straight nose and fine brows of all the Faringdons. Absurdly handsome in a distinctly masculine fashion, features dramatically sculpted with light and shadow. She had been used to seeing him elegant in town clothing. Now he wore the double-breasted riding coat, breeches and riding boots of the country gentleman, just as becoming, the dark green cloth of the coat emphasising his lithe, well-muscled build and broad shoulders. But his mouth was stern, his eyes cold, blue fire that held no warmth. Whatever flashed between them, shattering in their mutual awareness, was not a welcome—but of course she had destroyed the possibility of that, had not she?

'Perhaps you will stay for some refreshment, Miss Wooton-Devereux? Before your return to Tenbury.' *It would be better if you did not!*

'Why no. Thank you, my lord, but we must go back. My cousin…' *Once he would have called me Thea.*

'I am sure Mistress Drew and your groom would appreciate the opportunity to rest and refresh themselves.' The arch to his brows became more pronounced.

'Very well, my lord.' She accepted the inevitable with a gracious but chilling smile. 'It will be my pleasure.' She had noted the hint—the merest hint of arrogant criticism. How dare he make her aware of her responsibilities!

Lord Nicholas nodded as if he had no doubts of her acquiescence. 'I will go on up to the house. Furness here will take your animals and direct you. Mrs Grant, my housekeeper, will see to your comfort.' He turned on his heel and strode off towards the main wing of the house, leaving the ladies to follow at their leisure and Dacre to remain to discuss the finer points of horseflesh and enjoy a tankard of ale with Furness.

'I told you we should not have come!' Agnes's voice took on the tone of Thea's childhood nursemaid. 'Why would you not take my advice?'

'I know, I know! But we did and we have met him. Don't tell my mother!'

'Hmm!' Agnes huffed, but beyond glaring at her wilful mistress, she knew there was no ground to be made in saying more. At least she could rely on Lord Nicholas to behave as a gentleman should. His manners, in the circumstances, had been impeccable. She could not but admire him.

They were welcomed into the Manor by an elderly lady, clearly a family retainer, clad in black silk with the keys of the household secured by a silver chatelaine to her waist. She curtsied with placid composure, smiled in welcome and showed them into a sunny parlour where she invited them to sit at their ease. 'We do not see many visitors these days at Aymestry. Master Nicholas does not stay here often,' she explained, with the familiarity of long service to the family. 'It is good to have people about the place. Sometimes it is too quiet. His lordship said to bring you whatever you required. I shall bring tea, perhaps?'

'If you would be so kind, Mrs Grant. It is a beautiful old house.' Thea cast her eyes in admiration round the cosily panelled room, in the Tudor wing of the house, with its polished furniture and rich deep-red drapes.

'Indeed it is. I wish… But there. Master Nicholas will do just as he wishes! I shall bring the tea tray.' Leaving Thea to contemplate the knowledge that *Master Nicholas* probably always did *exactly* as he wished. Only to be interrupted by the return of the gentleman himself with Mrs Grant and the tea tray hard on his heels.

Without a hostess, Thea was called upon to preside over the little ceremony of brewing the tea which she did with consummate skill, calling on all her social skills to remain serenely at ease. As she poured the fragrant brew into delicate china cups, Lord Nicholas and Miss Wooton-Devereux indulged in polite and meaningless conversation about the scenery, the condition of the roads, the prospect of the harvest, the horses. Both lady and gentleman found themselves most adept at exchanging a number of opinions, in which neither had any particular interest at that moment, and in the coolest manner possible. And between them Agnes for the most part sat and listened. When called upon to give an opinion, she did so in brusque but not unfriendly manner, intent on watching the skilled thrust and parry that disguised far deeper emotions, emotions which had the edge of a honed duelling blade.

It was a relief for everyone when conversation was interrupted by a distant rumble of thunder.

'We should be going, Miss Thea,' Agnes interrupted with a glance at the thunder clouds now clear through the window. 'It may be nothing, just a summer shower, but we should not wish to be drenched.'

'Too late, I fear.' Nicholas stood as a flash of lightning pierced the shadows. They had failed to see the growing gloom in the room. 'I will ask Mrs Grant to prepare rooms. You will stay here for the night.'

Again the presumption that they would do as he said! Well, she would not. 'No, my lord. There is no need. I am sure it will soon blow over—and we will be home before dusk.'

'That would be a foolish decision. You will be quite safe here, Miss Wooton-Devereux.' Nicholas's lips curled in what might have been reassurance—or more likely a touch of derision. Thea was in no doubt. 'Mistress Drew is chaperon enough for you, I believe. Your reputation will not suffer under my roof. Do I need to send a message so that your cousin will be at ease?'

'I doubt she will notice our absence. She is somewhat cut off from the world.' Thea resented the sharp cut at her previous immoderate behaviour but had little choice except to let it go, even if she had to clench her hands into fists within the folds of the dark velvet to achieve it. The rain began to beat against the window, heralding an imminent downpour. It prompted her decision even as she hated the necessity. 'It seems that we must accept your kind invitation, my lord. We are most grateful.'

'Very well.' His lordship gave no indication that he had heard anything in her reply but the gratitude she professed. He inclined his head. 'Perhaps you will dine with me later? Mrs Grant will arrange all. Now…if you will excuse me, I need to conduct some business before the rain gets any heavier.'

And that was it. All icy good manners. *Damn him!*

'I told you—' Agnes began as soon as the door had closed after him.

'I know! Don't fuss.' Thea allowed her ruffled sensibilities to show. Why did she feel that she had been outmanoeuvred? 'I freely admit I was in the wrong. Does that make you feel any better?'

'No. It does not! We should not be staying here.'

'I know that too, Agnes.' She allowed herself a wry smile as the absurdity and potential discomfort of the situation struck her. 'You can sleep across the threshold of my room if it makes you feel any better.'

'No, it won't. Not that I would need to. I don't know what it is between you two—but I don't think his lordship likes you very much.'

'Good. Neither do I like him. And that is exactly how it should be, if you recall.' Thea stood, carefully replaced the china teacup on the tray and shook out her skirts. What was the use of regret? She must deal with what she could not change. 'We will leave Aymestry tomorrow morning and we can forget we were ever here. All I have to do is survive an evening of dining with him.'

'Hmm!'

'I trust the food will be warmer than his manners!'

'And perhaps sweeter and more palatable than yours, Miss Thea!'

On which tart word of warning, and ignoring the lady's answering flounce, Mistress Drew stalked from the room to discover the whereabouts of Mrs Grant.

Thea was shown into a bedroom in one of the more recent additions to the house where the panelling had been replaced with papered walls in white and cream stripes. Small and intimate, full of light, she had the impression that it had once been the room of a Faringdon lady. There were no personal touches now, but a pair of delicate watercolour paintings of country scenes hung beside the fireplace, a small dressing table with a mirror graced the window embrasure and there was a lingering smell of herbs— of lavender and perhaps rosemary. The bed hangings and window drapes were old, but distinctly feminine, in pale blue embroidered silk, well cared for, and had once been very fine.

She took off the close-fitting coat of her riding habit, shook out the lace ruffles on her cuffs and brushed her heavy skirts of any lingering dust from her ride. It was the best she could do. Hot water had been provided for her, so she washed her face and combed her hair with the ivory comb thoughtfully placed for her use on the dressing table.

Then she sat and looked out of the window at the new green leaves giving shape to the herbaceous border where it bloomed against the warm stone of the kitchen garden wall.

Now what? It was all very simple, she decided. As she had told Agnes, they would dine, she would try for sweetness and a

soft response to every topic of conversation—if it killed her!—
and she would leave tomorrow. There need be no complications
here. But Lord Nicholas's proximity brought a shiver of anticipation along her skin, as if a gentle breeze had got up with the
onset of evening to caress her arms and throat. A heightened colour touched her cheeks with rose. Recognising it, accepting it,
Thea warned herself to have a care, and believed that she could
rely on Nicholas to treat her with such icy indifference and formality that she would feel no inclination to behave in a less-than-
maidenly manner. She knew exactly how to conduct herself with
sufficient social skills to grace any occasion.

As the light began to fade, a footman came to lead her to the
dining room, again one of the old panelled rooms. Everything
had been made ready, with a fire lit against the chill of the early
summer evening and the dining table formally set, but with only
two places. Agnes was probably tucked up in a cosy gossip with
Mrs Grant, Thea decided with some envy.

Nicholas bowed Thea into the room and held her chair as she
sat, before taking his own place at the opposite end. So they were
to dine formally. She considered this decision on Nicholas's part.
Perhaps it was for the best.

A simple meal was served to them by two self-effacing footmen. The polished surface of the table stretched between them,
weighty with silver and crystal, discouraging conversation on a
personal level. The wide expanse exactly mirrored the distance
between the two who shared the meal.

It was the strangest meal, Thea decided, that she had ever
eaten in her life. The tension in the air robbed her of any real appetite but she did her best to do justice to Mrs Grant's kind preparations. The conversation that flowed so easily—cool, practised,
trivial, uncontroversial conversation—hid the charged undercurrent that wound the tension to snapping point, as taut as a watch
spring. His face was calm, expression enigmatic. She presumed
that hers was the same. Their manners could not be faulted.

But all the time that same undercurrent curled, as strong as the lethal drag below the surface of a placid millpond, spelling disaster to the unwary. Whenever their eyes met across the expanse of china and glassware, it held them, until one of them deliberately broke the contact by sheer effort of will. It was almost a courtship, held suspended in icy restraint. Thea found that her breathing was shallow and, despite an excellent wine, her mouth was dry. The words that they addressed to each other did not express what was in their hearts. And both knew it. It was almost as if the air around them held its breath for the outcome.

Eventually the footmen withdrew, leaving fruit, sweetmeats, a decanter of port. Candles were lit against the shadows, the drapes closed, enclosing Nicholas and Theodora in a small personal world of heightened emotion. The flickering lights glowed on the soft velvet of her gown and on the bright curls of her hair. It sparked fire from the diamond pin in his cravat. Her beauty struck him once again, rare as the jewel at his throat, as she looked up from the apple that she had begun to pare. An urge to push the situation on—to some sort of conclusion—gripped him. Indeed, he realised that he had no choice.

'Do you wish to withdraw to one of the parlours, madam? Or retire?' His voice was low, as if deliberately controlled. It made her shiver. Here was the ideal chance to escape his dominating presence and she knew that she should take it. Then tomorrow she could leave—and the visit would be over with no lasting repercussions for either. She had made a mistake in coming here, but it would soon be rectified.

She should say yes, should return to the restful solitude of her bedchamber, where she could breathe again.

'No. I would stay here,' she heard herself say. Her pulse began to beat, an insistent throb in the tender hollow at the base of her throat.

'Of course.' He appeared to accept her decision with equanimity and poured a glass of port for both of them.

She accepted it. Raised it to her lips, took a little sip. 'It is a beautiful house. You are very fortunate, my lord.'

He watched her, caught up by the trace of wistfulness here.

All he could think was that here was no vestige of the flighty débutante who had played fast and loose with his emotions and then deliberately driven him away, as carelessly as she might discard a dress that no longer became her. She sat at the end of the table, the candlelight in her eyes and gilding her skin, composed, beautiful and most desirable. Neither flighty nor frivolous.

'I like it,' he replied. 'But it seems that I am not destined to spend much time here.'

'So Master Furness told me. You have loyal people around you.'

'I suppose. I inherited most of them. Perhaps I am fortunate.' He hesitated. Then, for the first time, he introduced a personal note into the dialogue between them. 'Where do you call home?'

'I have never had a settled home,' she replied willingly enough, but looked down at the rings of apple peel. 'We have a small estate in Yorkshire, but we have tenants who occupy it because of our long absences. All I recall from when I was a young girl is living in embassies and rented town houses. Always very comfortable, some of them luxurious even. The one in Paris was so splendid as to be positively intimidating.' She laughed a little at the memory of the overpowering grandeur. 'But it was not home, you understand…' Again that breath of regret, of which she was perhaps unaware.

Silence stretched between them, broken only by a faint crackle from the fire and the soft ticking of a long case clock.

Then, 'Why did you come here today, Thea?'

She looked at him down the length of the table, astonished that he should ask so direct a question, thinking quickly. The truth could be dangerous. It could indicate the state of her heart. It could destroy all her careful and painful strategy. And she would have no one to blame but herself if she showed her vulnerability to him. Yet she found that she had no compulsion to lie.

'Because I wanted to see your home.'

Nicholas sat for a long moment, fingers holding the stem of his glass, considering her reply.

'Why did you deliberately reject me in London, Thea?' Thea was not the only one driven by honesty, it seemed.

'I did not!' A wash of shame brought guilty colour to her face and made her dissemble, which made the guilt even stronger.

'You did. I would suggest that it was a carefully constructed little charade to drive me away.' His voice remained low, soft, but there was an implacable quality about it. 'I did not see it at the time. But I do now. The girl I saw in London who went out of her way to ruffle so many feathers—and with remarkable success—was so out of character, I think, as to be ludicrous. I should have seen it, but did not. Perhaps because it touched me so personally.' He watched her every move, every expression that flitted over her lovely features, his eyes demanding that she tell him the truth. 'Why did you do it, Thea? You cannot deny what is between us, however uncomfortable it might be. However much we might wish that we could.'

She raised the tips of her fingers to her lips as if to stop incriminating words. For once she did not know what to say.

He rose to his feet with fluid grace and came towards her. Held out his hand. For a moment she looked at it and then up into his face. Finding that she had no will of her own against such silent insistence, she closed her fingers over his. Stood and moved away from her chair, where they faced each other in the centre of the room, both her hands clasped in his.

'Tell me the truth, Thea. You are attracted to me as much as I am attracted to you. Don't tell me that you do not feel it.'

'Yes.' It was hardly more than a whisper, but she did not hesitate. 'I feel it every time that you look at me.'

'So what was all that about, when you resisted every attempt of mine to spend time with you? When you tried to give me a disgust of you?'

'I cannot say.' She swallowed against the dryness in her throat, but kept her eyes on his. It was suddenly imperative that he did not doubt her. 'But however it might have seemed, my lord, I did not deliberately intend to hurt you.' She sighed a little. 'I would never do that.'

'Very well.' He could press her for more, knew that he needed to do so. But intuition told him that it was not the time. He would leave it for now.

Time stretched out as they looked at each other—a minute, an hour…it could have been a lifetime. Then he drew her slowly forward into his arms. Giving her the chance to refuse if that was her inclination. His intention was clear.

'Tell me no, if you do not wish for this, Thea.'

'I cannot, my lord.'

'Call me by my name.'

'Nicholas.' A sigh, as soft as a caress, skin against skin. This was fatal! But she could not resist. She wanted more than anything to feel the strength of his arms around her, the demand of his mouth on hers. So she stood as Nicholas ran his hands in one long caress from wrist to shoulder and then on to frame her face. With gentle fingers, a little callused, he traced along the line of her eyebrows, across her delicate cheek-bones. Then to follow the same path, equally gently, with his lips. She held her breath at the featherlight touch, closed her eyes at the sensation of his fingers and mouth, his own breath a whisper against her hair.

'Open your eyes, Thea.'

As she did so, obedient to his every demand, he lowered his head, holding her in submission. Not that he needed to do so. She could not have moved, drawn into the enchantment of the occasion. Aware only of his lips, firm and cool. Seeking and exploring, without haste. Yet it was not the chaste kiss that they had shared in London—far from it, as he changed the angle for his own pleasure, increased the pressure, until her lips parted beneath his. He allowed his tongue to caress the soft skin, outlining her lips. Still gentle, as if he, too, were holding his breath against the promise of passion.

She was soft and responsive and willing. He knew that he should be filled with exhilaration at holding her in his arms at last. And yet… It was not a straightforward matter at all. He determined to close his mind against the sharp edge of doubt, almost in the way of a premonition, which refused to let him rest, and concentrated on enjoying the awakening of her responses to him. On keeping his own demands light and uncomplicated, mindful of her inexperience. But it became increasingly difficult when she sighed against his mouth, when her fingers dug into the hard flesh of his shoulders as if to anchor her in the present, when she took a little step, moulding her body against his, hip and thigh and breast.

She was everything he could ever want in a woman. And he was afraid—of her and of the emotions that she aroused in him.

With a low growl in his throat, Nicholas was the one to end the kiss, lifting his head as he put her away from him. Dropping his hands from around her slender body, he stepped back, his breathing as heightened as hers. When Thea lifted her hands to stop him, he took another careful step in retreat, his face austere as if he had just made an almost impossible decision.

'Why?'

He knew her meaning. 'I must not.'

'I am not resisting you, Nicholas.'

'I know. And that is part of the issue! If we are into honesty, which we appear to be...' a touch of humour deepened the colour of his eyes '...it is my inclination at this moment to take you to my room—to my bed. I doubt that you are aware of how much I want you. Your innocence would be no shield against the passion that fires my blood when your lips open beneath mine.'

Her breathing caught at his outspoken intent. But she was not shocked. 'And if I agreed?'

'No.' Another step away. 'You must not. And I will not.'

'I see. I have no experience of this. So you will not.' A little smile curved her mouth, but her face was sad. 'Because, in spite of your...your desire, you do not like me enough?'

'Because it would be unworthy of me to take advantage of that innocence.'

'And if I am willing?' She tilted her chin, a hint of challenge in the gesture. The sapphire glint in her eyes bridged the gulf between them. Unmaidenly indeed!

'No. You do not understand. How could I risk your reputation? As a gentleman my honour is at stake. And of course there must be no breath of scandal around your name that is of my making.' He suddenly turned on his heel, presenting his back to her, so that he could not see the invitation in her face. 'I wish you had not come here today, Thea. It compromises my control where you are concerned.'

'And you would not risk scandal.' A statement rather than a question. Perhaps she knew why. Of course she knew why!

'Never. For scandal can wound beyond bearing. Can destroy.'

'For you or for myself?'

'Thea…' He sighed 'You do not know what you ask of me.'

'I do. And now I am the one to be rejected.' She stepped forward across the space that he had deliberately created. 'Is this a punishment? Because I hurt you?'

At first he did not respond, nor did he turn towards her. Instead he picked up the neglected glass of port and drank it in one swallow, then twisted to face her again and answered, a hint of weariness in his voice, 'No. Such a suggestion would dishonour me.'

'Forgive me. I know that it was unworthy. It is just that…it hurts.'

She looked so desolate as she turned her face from him and, in so doing, destroyed all his honourable intentions to preserve the distance between them.

'Theodora…' He reached for her, encircling her once more into his arms. The gentle encouragement of his previous kisses deserted him. Possession. Demand. His need for her swept through him as his mouth ravaged hers, the glorious curve of her throat, the lovely slope of her shoulders to the lace edging of her garment. His arms banded round her as steel, preventing any escape. But in Thea, under the onslaught of new emotions and sensations, there was no desire to escape and he sensed it as she allowed him to take her mouth in a searing possession. Her innocence was a delight, but her willingness fanned the flames to a raging fire. For Thea, the searing kisses forced her to acknowledge finally and without question the ultimate loss of her heart to Lord Nicholas Faringdon.

At last he released her, but not before he pressed a final salute to her hair, to the tender skin at her temples, deliberately gentling the touch of his hands at her shoulders. 'It is better that you go to bed alone.' He smiled to reassure her, just the slightest curve to his mouth, then took her hand as if she were a child and led her from the room to the foot of the staircase. There he lit a candle for her, then bowed low and lifted her hand as if to kiss it in a formal leave-taking. Instead he turned it, cupping her hand in his and pressing his lips to her palm in the most intimate of caresses, then closed her fingers over it before he released her.

'Nicholas…'

He shook his head to stop her. 'Go up, Thea. There are limits to my control. I would not wish to regret my actions tomorrow in the cold grey light of dawn.'

Her lips parted, as if to argue, to beg even. Where were all her good intentions now? Destroyed to ashes, consumed in the fire of passion, ignited by his lips. She had all but thrown herself at him. And he had refused. And she knew why—and could hardly blame him. She could ask nothing from him that he was not prepared to give. She allowed her lashes to veil the sense of hurt and loss that assailed her as she realised that there was no possibility of a future for them together. So be it. With a deep breath she called on all her pride and dignity. Now she was cool and calm again.

'Of course. Forgive me, if I have made your situation difficult.'

'There is no need for forgiveness. Perhaps neither of us has shown wisdom this night.'

She trod the stairs, aware of his tall figure standing quietly. How foolish she had been to press him—and how forward. Her mother, however liberal Lady Drusilla might be, would be horrified if she had seen and heard her daughter this night. But the touch of his mouth, the power of his body, the timbre of his voice, every quality of Lord Nicholas Faringdon was imprinted on her soul. She must leave as soon as she could. It would be unfair of her to do any other.

Nicholas stood and watched her until she turned the bend in the stairs and vanished into the gloom of the corridor, only the faint glow from her candle marking her passage. He pushed his fingers through his hair. What an incredible complication this was. And one that he did not fully understand. Theodora—a complicated weave of contradictions. He liked her—more than liked her. Oh, God, he wanted her! Imagined stripping the soft velvet from her body, lifting her in his arms to lay her on the cool sheets of his bed and to cover her body with his own. To possess those elegant, slender limbs with hot caresses and wild kisses, giving her no choice but to shiver beneath him with a passion of her own. She had no knowledge of such things, as she had said. It would delight him to give her that knowledge, to take that innocence for himself until she cried out with uncontrollable longing. And he would bury himself in her, possess her utterly. The thought, the taste of her lips, her skin, heated his blood beyond bearing. He returned to the dining room to pour another glass of port and pace a track between window and fireplace.

Perhaps he had seen the true Theodora tonight. A little vulnerable. Haunted, surprisingly, by a longing for a home of her own. And perhaps he had seen himself. His own desires, rather than those demanded by his family. He wanted her. Her kisses had roused him beyond sense; her honesty, her openness, her intelligence, had touched a chord within him. But there was something between them, something to cloud the brilliance of her eyes, to draw a faint line between her brows. Something which, in London, had driven her to put a distance between them. He did not know what—and she had refused to explain her deliberate wilfulness. Perhaps it would be wiser to keep his distance after all. He had without doubt made the best decision possible.

At this moment, wisdom was far from his thoughts.

Chapter Eight

On the following morning over breakfast in a sunny parlour, Thea, with the brightest of smiles, assured Agnes that she had slept perfectly well, not stirring until a maid brought her a cup of hot chocolate. Agnes, on seeing the rather strained expression on Thea's face and even the hint of a shadow beneath her lovely eyes, could have argued the point, but realised that there was nothing to be gained and so remained silent on the subject. Nor did she ask about Lord Nicholas, who had already broken his fast and was, they were given to understand by Mrs Grant, somewhere about the stables and had been since dawn.

'I see that you survived the ordeal,' Agnes ventured, watching carefully to see Thea's response.

'Yes, indeed.' Thea smiled brightly. 'You would have been proud of me. We did not discover one topic to disagree over throughout the whole of the meal.'

'Remarkable. A miracle, some would say.'

Thea might have replied with some acerbity, but a footman entered the room to inform them that their horses were ready and awaited their convenience, which silenced her as she finished the meal, understanding Nicholas's decision to make the parting as public and as impersonal as possible.

* * *

So their final meeting, as he had planned, was in the court-yard beside the stables. He smiled at their approach, inclined his head in greeting, wished the ladies a good morning. But his eyes were flat, not reflecting his smile. And he did not touch her, allowing Dacre to hand her up into the saddle of The Zephyr as he himself aided Agnes. But the memory of that shared moment of passion when he had kissed and held her, as if he wanted nothing more in life than to keep her with him, lingered around them, an almost visible swirl of emotion, like smoke on an autumn day.

'You should make good time.' He spoke to Edward Dacre as the groom and the servant mounted. 'Take care of them. Any problems on the road, don't stop. You should be safe enough on the Aymestry and Burford estates.' He thought that he should provide the little group with an escort, but understood that the lady would be more than likely to refuse. There were ways around that which he was prepared to take.

He approached the shoulder of the little mare for a final leave-taking.

'Goodbye, Miss Wooton-Devereux.' Not farewell or adieu. Or Godspeed. Thea noted and understood the deliberate choice of words and followed suit.

'Goodbye, my lord. We are grateful for your hospitality.' Her voice as light and uninvolved as his. And her eyes just as carefully guarded.

But now, as if it were beyond him to resist, he took her hand from where it lay loosely on her reins and raised it to his lips, first turning it, as he had the previous night, to press his mouth to her palm, then released her. She raised that hand for just a moment, tempted to bend and touch the dark hair where it lay at his temple. But did not, of course, could not prolong the pain of this brief and dispassionate farewell for either of them. But she pressed her palm with its burning imprint against the bosom of her velvet jacket, against her heart.

He watched her go. If Furness thought his expression a little bleak, he decided that it had more to do with a colicky mare than the departure of the guests.

'Jed.' Lord Nicholas beckoned one of the stable boys, a likely lad, who was emerging from the stable. 'Follow them. Take someone with you—George Abbot, perhaps. And keep your eyes open on Lord Westbourne's acres.'

'Afraid of trouble, my lord?' Furness frowned, not liking the possibility.

'No. But I would not wish harm to come to them. I have heard that the Maidens have been active this fortnight.'

Stepping forward to hold Jed's mount steady, Furness grunted his disgust. 'Men dressed as women!'

'Disguised they may be, but they are a rough crowd with little respect for the law when their wages are low and their children starving.' Lord Nicholas turned back to the lad as he mounted. 'Stay with them until Tenbury is in sight, Jed. Anything that worries you, anything at all, one of you ride to get help.'

Some little time later Nicholas, sleeves rolled up, was inspecting a newly arrived foal, all long legged and satin smooth, as it lay and dozed in the sunshine beside its protective mother. He looked up and rose to his feet, a finger of disquiet touching his spine, as Jed galloped into the courtyard with a hasty clatter of hooves, the horse in a lather.

'What?' Nicholas strode over.

'The Maidens're out, m'lord.'

'Are they on the road?' Nicholas grabbed the bridle in an urgent hand, muscles suddenly tense at the news.

'Aye, my lord. Met Nol Price from the Westbourne estate by the packhorse bridge,' Jed gasped, not bothering to dismount. 'The word is out. Riots, m'lord. Labourers have gathered—most like the Maidens—decked out in skirts and shawls and such. Nol said a big group, out for trouble against my lord Westbourne. Burning ricks. And I saw black smoke in the distance.' He ran a hand over his face, which was red from his efforts. 'I didn't know…I thought I should come back here for help. George went on to warn them…or lead them to safety. But if the Maidens're out in force and it's mischief they're after…'

Nicholas did not linger. The relaxed country gentleman underwent an instant transformation. 'You did the right thing, Jed. Get a fresh horse and tell Mat to join us.' He was already grabbing saddle and bridle and opening the door of the bay stallion's stall. 'Come with me, Furness. We'll take the pistols—better safe than sorry. And move it!'

The scenery on that bright morning, which had so captivated Thea when she rode to Aymestry on the previous day, now meant nothing to her. She travelled in silence, lost in her own thoughts, blind to the beauty around her. Sensing her abstraction, Agnes, too, kept her own council and any comments she might make were directed at Dacre. She was aware of the new level of tension between her mistress and Lord Nicholas—who could not be? Yesterday, the atmosphere in the stable yard and when they had take tea had been strained, even uncomfortable. But now? Agnes would have given her best kid gloves to know what passed between them the previous evening when they had dined together. But whatever it was, it had brought neither of them happiness. She could have cut the atmosphere this morning with the silver scissors in her reticule.

Thea was oblivious to Agnes's speculations, to everything but the àche that was almost physical around her heart. It gnawed at her, intensified by the anguish of the knowledge that, however much she might love him, however much he might be drawn to her, fate had determined that she would never see him again. Or be allowed to love him as she wished.

Thea deliberately straightened her shoulders, shortened her reins as The Zephyr tossed her head. There was nothing she could do about it, she lectured herself. She must forget Lord Nicholas Faringdon and turn her thoughts to the future. But she could not. The memory of the possessive touch of his mouth on hers remained a tangible presence, his rejection of her an impenetrable mist of sorrow.

Dacre's voice jolted her out of her preoccupation.

'Look to the left, Miss Thea. Smoke over by those barns. Looks like a large fire.'

Thea blinked, realised that they had already left the Burford estate and were crossing the arable fields of a neighbouring landowner. And, yes, there was a large fire, dark smoke billowing, flames clear as they leapt into the sky from the dry timber and straw.

She pulled the grey mare to a halt. 'Does the road go near? I don't remember.'

'No, Miss Thea. It curves to the east. It should not be a problem.' But Dacre, although unwilling to voice it, kept Lord Faringdon's warning in mind.

The little party continued, more cautiously now and with closed ranks, keeping a watch on the road ahead. It dipped towards a small copse and they could see a crossroads where a wider track, obviously a drove road, came in from Ludlow to the west. The fire was now closer, with the dense smoke beginning to drift across their path in the still air, but did not necessarily give any cause for concern.

'Only some old hay ricks.' There was relief in Dacre's voice. 'No danger, I think.'

'But look at the crossroads.' Thea raised her hand to point to the meeting of the tracks.

A little crowd of people, perhaps a dozen or more, had gathered. Still too far away for any detail, they could hear raised voices and the movement of the bodies suggested some agitation. Thea squinted against the sun and then it struck her.

'Why, look. They are women.' She could see the heavy skirts and bright shawls habitually worn by countrywomen in the fields, their heads covered by scarves or white cotton bonnets. 'What can it be?'

'I mislike it.' Dacre pushed his horse parallel with Thea's and motioned the servant to take closer order behind him next to Agnes Drew. For indeed there was a tension about the little group, despite their distance.

'It may be that someone has been hurt in the fire,' Agnes suggested. 'A child perhaps.'

They continued to approach with some caution, too conscious of the harsh tone in the voices that now carried to them. Women they might be, but something had occurred to reduce them to stark anger.

'But they are not women.' Thea's sudden and surprised statement brought the travellers to a halt again, for, despite the swirl of skirts, the layers of scarves and shawls, the forms beneath were now clearly masculine, long limbed and broad shouldered, as were the harsh voices that shouted and demanded attention. Now it could be seen that their skirts, hitched up from the ground for ease of movement, covered breeches, rough stockings and heavy work boots. And they carried a range of sticks and scythes and even an old shotgun, all being wielded with evidence of high-running emotions.

The Maidens!

Dacre immediately, acting on pure instinct, stretched out his hand to snatch at Thea's bridle, whether she would approve or no. Emotions were indeed running high. One of the group had swung himself up on to a tree stump and was haranguing the rest, emphasising his points with fierce gestures. There could be danger here for the well-born travellers.

'We have no quarrel with them, nor they with us.' Thea glanced at her groom with raised brows and not a little anxiety. 'Why should they harm us?' She twitched her bridle free and applied her heels to the grey's flanks. Better to get past the danger as quickly as possible. Nothing could be gained by sitting here in the road, simply waiting for God knew what outcome. But as they walked their mounts forward, confidently enough in appearance, shouts broke out. They were able to hear, one overlapping another, as the men addressed their leader who had taken up a stance on the fallen oak, his skirts flapping round his legs in his agitation.

'We'll starve if he has his way...'

'The bastard cares nought for us, now that...'

'He's told us we'll be laid off come summer...'

'Wages be so low...'

A litany of rural complaint that had been given a sharp edge by some local crisis.

Thea refused to halt, determined to press forward. She might sympathise, but the responsibility was not hers to remedy. Rather her need and her duty was to ensure the safety of Agnes and her servants. She found herself praying that the volatile gathering would accept their ignorance of local affairs and allow them to pass with nothing more than harsh words and accusations. Besides, there was no help to be sought in the circumstances. They must brazen it out.

Then a shawl-draped head in the crowd turned at the beat of the hooves and saw them.

'What have we here? Fine feathers on even finer horseflesh.' He laughed derisively at the prospect of such wealthy prey.

The crowd turned, harsh, masculine faces ridiculously framed by scarves and shawls and bonnets. But there was nothing ridiculous in the scene. The faces turned towards them were twisted in anger and despair. There would be no sympathy here for their innocence.

'They're not from round 'ere.' One voice, perhaps of reason, drifted on the charged air. 'They've nothing to do with Lord Westbourne and his damnable machines...'

It was only one voice, easily swamped by the rest.

'They do well from our labour by the looks of 'em...'

'Look at those horses—we can sell 'em...'

A stone was thrown. Then another. And, as one, the crowd rushed towards them, intent on stealing anything of value from the hated landlord class.

For Thea, everything afterwards happened in a mad rush of uncontrolled and confused aggression. A well-aimed stone struck Agnes on the side of her head, causing her horse to shy, and she fell heavily on to the road. Thea cried out in alarm and tried to reach her. Dacre's bridle and that of their servant were both seized, preventing them from either going to the rescue or riding to secure help. Thea also found herself surrounded by a sea of bodies, ungentle hands grasping at her bridle, her saddlebags, her long skirts. She could do nothing but fight to prevent herself being pulled from the saddle as The Zephyr stamped and fidgeted, head tossing in increasing unease at the harsh treatment.

'She'll 'ave something of value 'ere... And this animal's worth a pretty penny...'

Suddenly the outcome, or any sense of the present outrage, was taken out of Thea's hands. She simply froze in a blind, unreasoning panic. Memories flooded back, vivid and intense, to rob her of all sense. She knew in her mind, clear as faceted crystal, that she should ride for help. She should go to the aid of Agnes, who lay on the ground amidst the stamping hooves and the swarm of attackers. As if from a distance, she watched herself in mounting horror. She could not move, could not force her body to follow the dictates of her brain. Her whip was snatched from her unresponsive hand. She was unable to breathe, her ribs constricted by sheer irrational terror. Pulled from the saddle, she landed on her knees on the stony ground. She did not even feel the sharp edges that cut into her flesh, only felt the hands that grasped her arms, and urged her to stand. She could see where Agnes was trying to sit up and knew that she should go to her— but could not. Dacre attempted to push his horse between the rabble and his stricken mistress, but to no avail. They were outnumbered and in the violent control of their attackers.

'Let's make an example of 'em...show his bloody lordship that we mean business... He'll 'ave to listen to us...'

Again it was only one voice. But it was enough. Shouts of enthusiasm and encouragement exploded round them.

Thus the outcome for the travellers was fraught with more than the danger of being robbed. And yet for Thea, dragged to her feet, dishevelled, skirts covered with dust, it had no meaning. Terror continued to hold her, cold and immobile in its grip.

The sound of a single shot brought the furious rabble to a halt, caught in a strange moment of silent stillness. Even the birds were shocked into silence.

Lord Nicholas Faringdon, accompanied by Furness and his two grooms, had come to a halt on the little rise above the crossroads, just long enough to assess the situation. It took no more than a moment to see the intent, if not the detail of it. And it was clear that one pistol shot fired over their heads would not disperse this enraged gathering. Nor could Nicholas risk firing again. It would be impossible to ensure the safety of Thea and her escort in the seething mass before him.

'What the hell in going on here?'

'They're Lord Westbourne's tenants, m'lord.' Furness pulled up beside him, pistol in hand.

'So I see.' It explained all.

Lord Nicholas could see Dacre still trying to escape the attentions of three skirt-clad individuals. He could not see Agnes at all. And Thea? There was a flash of blue velvet in the very heart of the group. And he glimpsed her plumed hat being whirled aloft by a shawl-swathed arm. His blood ran cold in spite of the heat of the day and the sweat which trickled between his shoulder blades after their hard ride.

'Ride on!' His voice was urgent but betrayed none of his fear. 'But don't risk firing.'

Without another thought, even though desperately outnumbered, they kicked their mounts into action, relying on fists, the power of their horses and any remaining vestige of authority that Lord Nicholas might have with the Maidens.

The rioters gave way at the initial charge, but were not to be overawed or intimidated by a mere four men and surged forward again. Using his riding whip and the force of his horse, Furness managed to thrust his way to Agnes's side where she still half-lay in the dirt. Nicholas aimed his horse towards Thea. A heavy blow on his shoulder from an accurately wielded length of wood caused him to wince and snarl though his teeth, but did not deter him. He turned his body to use his booted foot to push aside a man with a pitchfork. A sharp right jab deterred another from attempting to pull him from the saddle. He pressed on.

And recognised a face amidst the mêlée. Lewis Bates, Lord Westbourne's head groom. A man who had always impressed Lord Nicholas with his good sense and calm demeanour—or at least in his dealings with Westbourne's well-bred and highly strung hunters. Nicholas found himself praying that the same

good sense and moderation might be prevailed upon in this cru-
cially dangerous situation.

'Bates!' he shouted. 'Lewis Bates!' He pressed his horse
against the tide of violent humanity, over to the man's side.
'What in God's name are you doing? What are you about?'
Nicholas took hold of a fistful of woollen shawl and shook the
man, dragging him closer. 'Two unarmed women? They're no
danger or threat to your livelihoods. You do your cause more
harm than good, man.'

'You don't know the half of it, m'lord.' Bates snarled his answer.

'Perhaps not. But this is no way to gain a sympathetic ear.
Have sense, man. What will it bring you if they are injured? Only
condemnation and a bad name. Who'll listen to you then?'

Bates squinted up with narrowed eyes, whiskers and a weatherbeaten complexion incongruous beneath the grubby cotton
bonnet.

'Lord Westbourne, damn him to hell, is laying 'em off.
They're out for blood, m'lord.'

'I can see that. And a liberal helping of ale has removed any
sense they may have had. But they'll listen to you. For God's
sake, Bates…'

The man looked at his lordship, considering his words. The
outcome of the ugly incident hung in the balance.

'Your quarrel is with Westbourne, Lewis. Not with chance
travellers who have been my guests.'

It tipped the balance.

'Aye. Reckon you're right. As a landlord, you're better'n
most.' Bates raised the shotgun and fired into the air, then leapt
back on to the oak stump, agile in spite of the hampering skirts.
The loud explosion at close quarters once more brought the proceedings to a halt, just as The Zephyr, her composure finally de-
serting her, pulled free from her captor and bolted down the
road, back in the direction of Aymestry.

'It's my lord Faringdon, lads.' Bates's voice rolled over the
restive gathering. 'We have no quarrel with him.'

'They're all landlords. They're all rich on our backs.' A short, stocky man, younger that most, pushed back his shawl and glowered up at Bates. 'Why should we treat him any different? Or them?' He swung his arm to indicate their erstwhile captives.

'Not all are as bad as Westbourne, Sam.'

'Are you in league with them, then? Are the landlords paying you?' Sensing defeat, Sam's features registered thwarted anger. He spat his disgust into the dust at his feet. 'And who says you're our spokesman?'

'I do. As for being in league with the landlords—don't be a damned fool, Sam Dyer.'

'I don't like it!' Dyer would not let go, like a terrier with a rat.

'Neither do I. But you'll do as I say.'

Their eyes met, a challenge until the younger man backed down with a snarl and a muttered oath.

'As his lordship says,' Bates addressed the men who now waited uncertainly, 'better that we don't antagonise the whole countryside, lads.'

'Why not? What have we to lose? We've nothing left as it is.' A voice from behind Sam Dyer expressed the desperation of all present.

'We may need friends. Them as'll stand up and speak for us.'

'It'll not look good if you harm two women.' Lord Nicholas added the weight of his argument, his eyes fixed on Thea where she stood, completely unmoving and apparently unaware in the centre of the group.

'Keep out of this, my lord, and go while you still can,' Bates hissed in a low voice. 'Not your concern.'

'As JP it is my concern.' Nicholas would not turn and run from the confrontation. He allowed his eyes to travel the crowd before him, the expressions ranging from fury to drunken exhilaration to careworn despair. 'And you can be sure that I will see justice done. For the landlords. And also for you.' His firm gaze, which took in the throng, holding every pair of eyes that stared back, was both a challenge and a promise. Would they resist his authority? Or would they accept his word for honest dealings with the law? 'But it is not justice to rob and hinder innocent travellers.'

'Not now, my lord.' Bates's quiet voice came from behind him. 'Not now. I suggest you leave. We'll not hinder you. And you should forget what you've seen here this day.'

Nicholas saw the sense of it. They were outnumbered and the mutterings were still ugly with suppressed violence. Bates might have deflected their anger, but for how long? He nodded in recognition of his debt. 'I owe you, Lewis.'

'I'll remind you of it, my lord.'

The crowd withdrew into a little group. Still sullen. Still angry and silently threatening, but willing to accept the logic of Bates's argument as Lord Nicholas and the travellers made their preparations for departure. The grey, severely lame from an uncontrolled stumble on the boulder-strewn path, was rescued by Mat and led gently back. Dacre, suffering the after-effects of a number of hard blows to his back and shoulders, regained his composure with gruff thanks to his lordship, and went to help Mistress Drew. She was lifted to her feet with a damaged arm and painful temple where the stone had struck. It might have broken the skin, but not her spirit. Having been lifted on to her horse, she insisted that she was quite all right and could ride on without aid. Better to look to Mistress Thea. She glowered at the band of *women* who, she announced in loud accents, should know better than to attack helpless females. She would have gone to Thea's side, but Nicholas shook his head. Furness looped her reins with his and led her away before she could say more to antagonise the still-hostile labourers.

And Thea? When Lord Nicholas finally made his way to her side, she simply stood in the road in a paralysed state of shock. Eyes glassy and unfocused, skin pale and clammy, she appeared not to recognise her rescuer when he took her arm and gently led her toward his horse. He mounted.

'I'll take her. She is not fit to ride alone. If you will lift her…'

Dacre steadied his mistress in his arms and lifted her, allowing his lordship to take her and settle her in the saddle before him. She made no response other than a little sigh as she allowed her head to rest against his shoulder. But her whole body was tense and rigid, as if held in check against some unseen enemy. And although he spoke, soft words of comfort and reassurance, she made no response. In the end he simply held her, one arm firm about her waist, aware of nothing but the rapid beat of her heart against him, as a helpless bird would flutter for its freedom from a trap.

And on that journey back to Aymestry Manor, in a blinding revelation, Lord Nicholas Faringdon knew that all he had ever wanted in life, all he had dreamed of, lay at that moment in his arms, held tight and safe against the world, her hands clutched in the material of his riding coat. He could do nothing but take her back to Aymestry. He had persuaded himself that Theodora should have no place in his life. He had made that decision. But now, for better or worse, fate had determined that he have no choice in the matter.

At Aymestry Manor, Lord Nicholas sent servants scurrying with brisk and practical instructions that hid the depth of anger and fear which still rode him. Jed was ordered into the house at a run to warn Mrs Grant of the urgent needs of their guests. The little grey, limping and distressed from a severely strained fetlock, was dispatched to a vacant stall in the stables with orders to one of the stable lads to prepare and apply a hot poultice to reduce the swelling in the injured leg.

Mistress Drew was helped from her horse by Furness, who took it upon himself to escort her into the house. There she was immediately taken under the wing of Mrs Grant, ushered up to her bedchamber with promises of tea and a sympathetic ear. A housemaid was sent for hot water and bandages. A bottle of spirits. And Mrs Grant assured the lady that Furness could set a broken limb as well as any doctor, as she would soon see for herself. In a little while, the pain would be eased and then all Mistress Drew would have to do would be to rest and allow the bone to knit. There was no need for her to concern herself over Miss Thea's well-being. They would take good care of her. Just the shock of the events. The young lady would soon feel more the thing and Mistress Drew could visit her as soon as she wished. What was the world coming to, that law-abiding citizens were not free to travel the king's highway without fear for their property and their lives from men who should know better…The Maidens, indeed! The sound of Mrs Grant's soothing voice disappeared into the echoes of the upper landing.

Meanwhile Lord Nicholas carried Thea into the entrance hall where he gently stood her on her feet and allowed his arms to fall from around her. She still appeared strangely disoriented and clung to his arm with rigid fingers. Her face was unduly pale with a slight sheen of sweat on her brow and upper lip. The pulse at the base of her throat fluttered light and fast. When she raised her head to take in her surroundings, her eyes still lacked focus and she appeared not to recognise where she was.

'I…I'm sorry. I don't…' She gazed at him as if unsure of his identity. 'I don't quite remember…'

Nicholas frowned. Shock at the attack, yes. But this was more than could be expected. What had happened to cause her such distress? He made a rapid decision. 'Elspeth.' He summoned one of the hovering maids. 'Fetch tea and a bottle of brandy. Hot water and towels. Bring them up to Miss Thea's room. She needs to rest.'

'No…' Thea's reply was strained, hesitant, quite unlike her usual firm voice and manner. 'I shall be quite well if I can just sit… Poor Agnes needs more care than I… I must see her…'

'You will rest.'

'But I…'

Ignoring her reluctance, and with a suppressed oath at his inability to deal effectively with this situation, Nicholas simply swept her up into his arms again, up the staircase and into the room that she had previously occupied. There he lowered her feet to the floor, noting that any resistance had disappeared. She frowned a little as if unsure what she should do next, so, with a typical masterful demonstration, he made the decision for her and began to unbutton the velvet jacket of her riding habit and ease it down her arms. She allowed him to do so, standing before him as lifeless as a doll. Eyeing the lace ruff at the high neckline, he contemplated dealing with the tiny pearl buttons. No. He would not. But he unpinned the diamond-and-sapphire brooch at her neck and laid it on the dressing table. Then, with gentle sensitivity, he took her by the hand and led her to the bed where he pushed her to sit. When she obeyed, he knelt before her to pull off her soft riding boots, all the while keeping up a steady stream of comment in a calm voice, notwithstanding her wordless acceptance of all his actions, however intimate they might be. The little grey would soon recover — it was a sprain only and she would be sound enough. Furness was a worker of miracles. Mistress Drew would no doubt find cause to complain, but Furness would have her put to rights. A man of great skill, with horses and humans. They could stay comfortably at Aymestry under Mrs Grant's care. He would dispatch a message to her cousin in Tenbury that very hour, that she would not worry, and perhaps send clothes and other necessities back for the ladies. The dangers were over. She was quite safe here.

Thea did not answer, but sat and watched him with utmost concentration.

As soon as Nicholas had removed her boots, he sat beside her and lifted her inert hands from her lap. He found them cold, shockingly so in the warmth of the room and despite the perspiration on her face, as if all the blood had retreated from the surface of her skin. He enfolded them to warm them between his own.

At that she looked up at him. Bloodless lips parted, eyes wide and anxious.

'I have to thank you.' Her voice caught. 'I think…I think that you saved our lives.'

'Nothing so momentous.' He tried to reassure with a smile and a gentle pressure on her fingers. 'But it was a timely intervention. You were unlucky to be there at the moment that the Maidens fired the ricks.' Despite the lack of comprehension in her gaze, he continued to explain, hoping that the sound of his voice and the calm that enveloped them in the sunny room would help to restore her composure. 'I had your little party followed—to be certain of your safe-passage to Tenbury. When one of my grooms saw the dangers he rode back. So I was able to be there before more damage could be done.'

'Yes…' Her eyes continued to search his face as if for enlightenment. 'I am sorry to be such a trouble to you. To return here when you did not wish me to do so…'

And Theodora promptly startled both of them when she pulled her hands free of him, covered her face with her hands and disintegrated into tearful sobs.

Nicholas had no choice. He did the only thing any man could do faced with such distress. He drew her into his arms and let her cry against his chest, holding her close, his cheek resting gently against the crown of her head. Saying nothing, but just holding her and allowing her to sob out all the fear. She seemed so fragile, so vulnerable. All he wanted to do was protect her, hold her, keep her unknown fears, whatever they might be, at bay. There was nothing that he could find to say to her in this situation as, without doubt, she was not receptive to any words of comfort. So he simply kept silence, submerging an urgent need to pour out his own love and his desire to protect her for ever. That was not what she would wish to hear.

Gradually her sobs quietened. Only then did he ease her away. With a hand beneath her chin, he made her lift her face and used his handkerchief to wipe away her tears, when Elspeth arrived with another of the Aymestry maids and a loaded tray.

Nicholas stood, admitting to some relief. Oh, he would have stayed and held her in his arms for ever if she had need of him. But she needed a woman's ministrations more and would not thank him for lingering. It would be too humiliating for her when she came to her senses, realising that he had seen her when her distress had overcome her pride and reduced her to such desolation in his arms.

'Elspeth.' He stepped away from the bed, putting a distance between them. 'I will leave Miss Thea in your care for now. She needs to eat and drink. Then let her sleep. But leave one of the maids with her.' He did not want her to awake alone and be afraid.

'Of course, my lord. The young lady will do very well.'

'Let me know if there is any problem—if the lady needs anything.'

'Of course, my lord.' Elspeth almost swept him from the room. Clearly in her eyes, this situation held no role for a man.

With a final glance towards Theodora, who had raised her hands again to hide the ravages of her tears from him, Lord Nicholas took his leave.

He took himself to his own rooms where he proceeded to strip off his soiled and damaged coat and shirt, to flinch as the movement put pressure on his arm and shoulder. There were already signs of livid bruising, as he could see, although the skin was not broken. As he shrugged carefully into his clean linen, he let his thoughts roam over the past few hours. A serious affair, perhaps more serious than he had first believed. It had been diffused of course, thanks to Lewis Bates, and he was not the target of the violent hatred, but it was not a situation he could ignore when he and his guests came under attack. There were troublemakers amongst that little gathering who might not be willing to listen to the dictates of reason and the law again in the future. Samuel Dyer was a name to remember, perhaps. And the deliberate disguise of women's clothing showed a depth of organisation that he would not previously have considered. Perhaps he should talk with Lord Westbourne to find out the background. But Westbourne was known as a harsh landlord, with little sympathy for those who might stand in the way of what he saw as progress. Nicholas grimaced as he worked his arm back into a coat. Whatever the cause of today's disturbance, he did not want such discontent to spread to the Faringdon estates.

But such matters, serious as they might be, did not retain his attention beyond the changing of his clothes.

For there was Theodora. The complications and contradictions of that beautiful girl swamped his thoughts. There was so much that he did not understand.

As he headed towards the stables to check on the progress of The Zephyr, he remembered Thea's first reaction to him when he had intercepted her horse in Hyde Park. Not as extreme as this, of course, but the same uncontrollable panic that robbed her of thought, the same inordinate amount of fear. When he had asked her before, she had refused to explain further than that one obscure statement. Shrugged it off as of no account. Obviously it was not.

Well, if Thea would not tell him, he must use other means to discover the truth. He would have an honest and direct conversation with Mistress Drew. Because he was forced to acknowledge the fear in his own heart at the thought that she might have been injured, a fear that had been sharp and lethal when he saw her at the mercy of that rabble of a drunken mob. His blood still ran cold as the scene replayed itself in his mind, when he had been helpless and outnumbered against their hostility. He could no longer deny the strength of his feelings for Theodora. It would be foolish to even try.

Thea woke from a restless sleep where dreams had chased her relentlessly. Of faceless riders who shouted orders at her. Forced her to rein in her horse and dismount. To stand under the beating desert sun. Riders wrapped in the loose robes of the desert meshed into men who wore skirts and shawls, men with hard, merciless hands and cruel smiles. It was a relief to escape into reality, into the still quietness of the familiar room. She lay for a little while, allowing her fears to subside, her breathing to quieten, enjoying the rays of sunshine through the window. She could not remember where she was at first, but it did not seem to matter. The bed was soft, the air warm and comfortable, the atmosphere still. She lay and drifted, making no attempt to draw her thoughts back to the present. Until she heard a little movement. Turning her head, she saw a maidservant sitting beside her, with sewing in her lap. The young girl smiled as she waited for Thea to speak.

'Hello.'

'There, mistress. You look so much better.'

'I don't remember very much.' Did not wish to remember!

'You fell in with some of the rioters from Lord Westbourne's estate. The Maidens, Mr Furness said.' The word had spread around the household with the rapidity of a heath fire. 'Lord Nicholas came to rescue you. You were a bit shocked, that's all. You fell from your horse. But now you are safe.'

'Oh.' She thought for a moment. 'Am I at Aymestry Manor?'

'Yes, miss. Don't you recognise the room?' The girl smiled with gentle encouragement.

Of course. She remembered everything, allowing the vivid pictures to slide back into her mind. And how frightened she had been, how useless when Agnes had been struck, incapable of doing anything of any value to help herself or her escort. The humiliation and shame ran deep. What on earth would Nicholas think of her? And had she really wept in his arms? She feared that it was so.

'I must get up.'

'No need.' The maid's voice soothed with its Marches' burr. 'You did not sleep for very long, miss. His lordship says you need rest. There is nothing to get up for. Lord Nicholas will take care of everything, you'll see.'

'I suppose he will.'

Which she accepted, and allowed herself to sink once more into sleep. Deep and dreamless and healing. For some strange reason that she could not comprehend with her tired mind, she felt totally reassured that Lord Nicholas would indeed take care of everything.

'Mistress Drew. Are you sufficiently restored to talk to me?'

Agnes Drew sat in Mistress Grant's little parlour, that lady having taken herself off to overlook preparations for the evening meal, giving his lordship the opportunity for a private conversation as he had requested. Agnes's wrist was bandaged and immobilised against her flat chest. The wound in her hairline had been bathed, but she had refused a bandage. The headache was unimportant, she would simply ignore it. A restorative glass of claret stood at her elbow, a book lay open on her lap. Perhaps there were lines of strain around eyes and mouth, and a faint frown between her brows, but, considering her ordeal, she was remarkably composed.

'Of course, my lord.' She would have struggled to her feet, but Lord Nicholas restrained her with a gentle hand to her undamaged wrist. 'It will take more than that rabble to see me off. I have to thank you. And for Miss Thea. If any harm had come to her…' For the first time there was fear in Agnes Drew's eyes.

'It is no matter, Mistress Drew.'

'It is. I know the dangers we were in today. I have been to see my mistress. She is resting well.'

'It is about Thea—your mistress—that I wish to speak.'

Agnes's brows rose a little in some surprise at his direct approach, his use of Thea's name, but she waited for him to speak.

He did, without preamble. 'Will you tell me what happened to her, Mistress Drew? Some time in the past. Something that causes her to react with such withdrawal, such extreme shock, when faced with certain situations.'

'I don't—'

'I have seen it twice. I know that I have not imagined it. Please do not denigrate my intelligence by denying the existence of any problem. Thea herself once hinted at it.'

Mistress Drew flushed at the gentle criticism. 'I think that Miss Thea would not wish me to say. It is not my story to tell. My loyalty is to her, my lord, not you.'

'But it causes her considerable distress. I would know what it is.'

Agnes pursed her lips, sharp eyes considering his lordship. Here was a man of strong will, as wilful as Theodora. And there was undoubtedly that *connection* between them. But should she tell?

'I will not tell her what you tell me, if you do not wish it.' Nicholas's lips twitched into a dry smile as he acknowledged Mistress Drew's silent and frank assessment of him. 'But I find that her well-being has become a concern for me.'

Such honesty! Perhaps he deserved to know. And there was no doubt that they owed him much.

'Very well. I will tell you what I know.' Agnes waited as his lordship pulled up a chair. 'I was not there when it happened. But I can tell you of the effects that I have seen for myself. As have you, my lord.' She took a sip of the claret as she marshalled her thoughts, then proceeded to tell him of Theodora's terrifying experience in the desert near Palmyra as a child. 'It was a frightening experience for a young girl and has left a lasting fear, a weakness if you will.' Agnes hesitated. 'Miss Thea is as brave as a lion, but not when surrounded by noisy yelling crowds who might be interpreted as a threat. In Constantinople she was caught up in a large family group who were celebrating a wedding. Her reaction was just the same, even when there was no threat at all to her, only noise and high spirits. She has no control over it, poor girl, but then recovers as if nothing was amiss. That is all I can say—but it explains her withdrawal from reality today.'

'Yes. It does.' It explained much. 'Thank you, Mistress Drew. I value your confidence.'

'I would rather you did not say that I told you.' Mistress Drew's face was stern even as she asked for Nicholas's silence. 'It embarrasses her— because she can not control it. She sees it as a *fault,* you understand—and would not have it known.'

'No.' He smiled at the lady, deliberately taking possession of her good hand and raising it to his lips. 'I will not tell her. Your secret is safe in my keeping.'

Agnes found herself blushing— as if she were a young girl, indeed!—at the unexpected and completely charming gesture, but her voice was firm, her gaze direct when she made her answer with deliberate honesty for her reading of the situation between her mistress and Lord Nicholas Faringdon. 'Take care of her, my lord.' Their eyes held, united in understanding and concern for Theodora. 'She is worthy of your love.'

'Of course.' He rose to his feet and bowed. 'It is my intention.'

He made his way down to the library, deep in thought. He had not thought himself to be so transparent, but perhaps where

Theodora was concerned, his emotions were clear to all. And now he knew. That was one of her secrets laid bare. Would she be willing to tell him herself? But there was, of course, a far deeper mystery. Would she ever be willing to tell him why she had worked so hard to end any relationship between them? Her explanation that it was too complicated to explain her aberrant behaviour was no answer at all.

And that, he knew with some disquiet, was no sound basis for any lasting relationship, no matter the undoubted attraction between them.

Yet after all that, did it matter? The connection between them, some basic inexplicable attraction, had not been severed in spite of all Theodora's amazing efforts to give him a disgust of her. His mind might say that it did, but his heart would deny it.

Thea awoke from a deep healing sleep and stretched luxuriously, at one with herself and the world. No dreams had troubled her, no memory of the horror of the Maidens' attack now assailed her. She pushed herself up on to her elbows, her spirits fully restored. It was late evening, as she could see by the quality of the light—she must have slept for hours. Shadows lurked in the corners of the room and encroached on to the edge of the bed, yet she felt alert and restored.

The little maid who still sat beside her smiled.

'Are you well, mistress?'

'Yes.' Thea returned the smile. 'I feel alive again.'

She got up, dismissed the maid with grateful thanks, and lifted the cover on a little tray that had been left for her, since it seemed that her appetite had been restored also. She drank a glass of wine, ate a little bread and cheese and fruit. Having no clothes other than the riding habit in which she had arrived the previous day, she donned her riding skirt—brushed clean of the dust of her adventures—and the long-sleeved blouse, pinning her sapphire and diamond brooch at the high neck.

She must see Agnes, of course.

One of the maids escorted her to Mistress Drew's room. Since she found that lady tucked comfortably into bed and sleeping, with no sign of fever or discomfort, her bound wrist resting easily on the coverlet, Thea withdrew. And then her courage wavered. She stood outside Agnes's room and thought as the somewhat hazy memories crowded in. She must now find Lord Nicholas. She must thank him for his timely rescue, apologise for her appalling weakness when she had lost all control over her senses and actions. Overcome the embarrassment which even now brought colour to her cheeks as she recalled how she had wept in his arms and, with so little will of her own, had allowed him to carry her to her room. Not that she remembered much of that. What must he think of her? She must explain somehow. It was not a task she relished.

So first she would see how her mare had fared.

It was an easy matter for her to find her way to the stables. They were now deserted of the grooms and Master Furness, dim and warm at the end of a sun-filled day. Silent except for the shifting of hooves on straw, the occasional snort and wicker of a restless horse. Stray beams of sun, the final gleams, still lanced through the windows, layers of brightness in the gloom, the dust motes dancing. But the shadows were deep and calming, the scents of straw and leather and horses familiar and welcoming. What a restful place it was at the end of a day.

Thea looked in on a mare and foal, who looked back at her with large unblinking eyes. A chestnut mare stretched her nose over the stall door for her visitor to scratch. And then there was The Zephyr. The mare turned her gleaming body, the faint dapples in her neck glowing in the light, and limped towards her as Thea softly called her name. And leaned against her hand, allowing Thea to scratch along the soft line of her jaw.

'Poor Zephyr! You are safe now. How frightened you must have been. I was afraid too.'

But now there appeared to be no residue of that fear. The Zephyr returned to pulling strands from a hay net, tossing her head. If she were well enough to eat, there could be little wrong. Somewhat like herself, Thea mused. She leaned her arms along the top of the door and watched, content simply to be still and quiet.

'Theodora.'

The soft voice from the open door made her fingers tighten their grip on the wooden ledge, her heart make a leap into her throat. She turned her head—and was stunned by the sight of him. And immediately wished that she had been given longer to decide what she could possibly say to him, how she could possibly respond in his presence.

Lord Nicholas stood in the shadows, just inside the door, making no movement towards her, his coat removed and slung negligently over his shoulder so that the white of his shirt glimmered. She could see neither his face, nor gauge the expression in his single word of greeting, so she made no reply. Simply waited.

'Theodora. You look better—rested. Have you eaten?' He walked towards her, his boots making little sound on the straw-strewn surface, to stop a few feet away from her. A breathing space. Now she could see him and allowed her eyes to search his face. His eyes were dark, deep blue and still as shaded pools. His mouth firm-lipped, unsmiling, as if he, too, awaited some desired outcome. She had no idea what he might be thinking. Why was the man so difficult to read? But how beautiful he was, the dark hair and well-formed features. That lithe, agile figure, which moved with such elegant assurance. Any woman would want him. She wanted him.

And when he saw her illuminated in that soft beam of dusty sunshine, all his doubts vanished, dry chaff in a breath of air. She was beautiful. She was safe and alive and free of danger. She was any man's dream of perfection. But she could be his. It was all as simple as that. He would willingly sink for ever into the depths of those magnificent dark-lashed eyes, gleaming sapphire flecked with gold. Those slender-fingered hands, so capable, which had last clung to him in an agony of fearful anguish, held his heart. The thought might terrify him. He could not wish it any other way.

'Thea—'

'I need to apologise, my lord,' she interrupted, suddenly nervous. 'I reacted without sense or courage. I have no excuses. Sir Hector and Lady Drusilla would have been ashamed of me indeed. I did not intend to embarrass you…'

Lord Nicholas waited no longer. In one stride he covered the space between them, lifting his hand to touch her lips with a brush of fingers, to stop the flow of words.

'Hush, Thea. There is no need.' He smoothed the fullness of her lower lip with the pad of his thumb, a most sensuous caress that took her breath. And his. Would she tell him the cause of her unreasonable fears? Perhaps she would eventually, but this was the time for him to take her in his arms and show her what it could be like when a man desired a woman as much as he desired her. So he silenced her and, with the supreme confidence of a man lost in love, bared his own soul to her.

'Do you still not know? Are you still so unaware? I love you. I would do anything to protect you, to stand against the world for you. I love you Thea.' He hesitated, as if he feared to reveal all, but his eyes never left hers, blinding in their honesty. 'I have known it since the moment I first saw you, first heard your voice, but refused to acknowledge it. It is not in my nature to accept a sensation so overwhelming, or so extreme. It seemed to me that you took away my choices. But there it is.' Now he lifted a hand to tease the wisps of curl on her cheek. 'I think that you are meant to be here in my arms. You are the love of my life.'

'Nicholas…'

'Does it distress you?' His laugh was low and seductive to a lady who could have dreamed of no more splendid gift than this. 'You are free to reject me, of course.'

'No. Oh, no. I am so… I cannot find the words to say it.' Thea echoed his laugh. 'The events of the day appear to have robbed me of coherent thought.'

'I wish you would say them.' His answering smile was rueful as he took possession of her wrists, to lift them and press his mouth to the soft inner skin where her pulse beat with a feverish intensity that had nothing to do with her health. 'Unless it is your intent to kill me by cruel suspense.'

'Ah, Nicholas. Don't *you* know it? I love you.' She found her voice at last. It was easy to say the words that had been in her mind and heart for so many weeks. 'I thought that I had destroyed any chance of that love, and mourned it bitterly. I do not ever want us to be apart.'

'Then there is no need. Smile at me.'

She did. Her face was radiant. When he took her hands to lift them to his lips, she tightened her fingers around his as if she would never let him go.

'I am not an Earl,' he murmured against her palm.

'I do not want an Earl.'

'I am not as wealthy as the Earl of Moreton.' He kissed the soft swell of flesh at the base of her thumb.

'I am not interested in the Earl of Moreton's wealth.' Thea held her breath.

'Theodora…' With utmost delicacy, he applied his lips to her other palm. 'Will you marry me?'

'Yes.' There was no uncertainty here.

'I should ask Sir Hector for his permission to address you. But I think it more important that I discover your views on the matter.' His teeth nibbled along the ends of her fingers.

'Of course.' He could hear her smile in her voice. 'As any sensible man must. Yes and yes.'

Now he looked up, released her hands. 'Then my lips will seal the bond between us. For all time.'

'As will mine.'

And her fears? Theodora jettisoned them all. Her love for him was too great to consider any limitations against it. She would risk everything for the love and desire that she could read in that moment in his face. Her fears might never happen. She would marry her lord, her love, and consign those groundless terrors to some deep dark spot, never to be reborn.

So when Nicholas drew her forward, close into the circle of his arms, Thea accepted without regret. Drawing her firmly against him, he lowered his mouth to hers. She responded with all the delight that he could have hoped for, allowing her hands to smooth over the soft, warm linen of his shirt, savouring the play of firm muscle beneath, from wrist to shoulder. Until he flinched on a gasp and pulled away.

'What is it? What did I do?' She searched his face with anxious eyes.

'A bruise. Courtesy of our lady rioters.' He shrugged against the pull of muscle and sinew where the heavy blow from a cudgel had fallen.

'Oh, Nicholas. That you should have been hurt for my sake, when I could do nothing to help myself or you…'

'It is nothing. I would do anything for you, Thea. Anything to keep you from harm or distress.'

'Then kiss me again,' she invited, 'if it will help you to forget the pain.'

So he did. The tenderness of before was now overlaid by a hint of possession. A hunger. His kiss more demanding, his arms strongly banded around her to hold her in submission against the hard strength of his chest and thighs. Until the breathing of both was heightened. And he stepped away.

'You are too desirable.'

But Thea stepped forward, surprising him, reluctant to forgo the amazing needs that flooded through her body at the evidence of Nicholas's fierce desire for her. 'And you would reject that?'

'I must.'

'You did once before, as I recall.' Thea angled her head to watch him, allowing her hands to linger on the flat planes of his chest, her eyes alight. His concern for her touched her more than she would ever tell him.

'I know.' A sudden grin lifted the tension. 'It was one of the most uncomfortable nights of my life.'

'Then why repeat it?'

She took another step until her body almost brushed his and her hands could clasp together around her neck, more than a little startled at her own forwardness.

As was Nicholas. He choked on a laugh. 'Are you *fast*, madam? What would Mistress Drew say?' His heart beat with insistent rhythm. His command of his body and his senses appeared to be slipping from his grasp, second by second.

'It seems that I am where you are concerned, my lord.' A low husky chuckle was almost his undoing. 'And Agnes would not approve.'

'Thea—' He tried for sanity, taking a light hold of her shoulders to keep her at bay. 'I would not hurt you—or give cause for condemnation in the eyes of the world, no matter the provocation.' Without thought, he turned his face against her hair. 'Do you realise how impossible it is for me to resist you? You are delicious and desirable beyond imagination.'

'Why should you resist?' In her voice the temptation of Eve, in her hands, in the softness of her skin. Her lips were so close, the warmth of her breath so sweet, 'Are you going to break your promise—of only one minute ago—to marry me? And you a man of honour, my lord!'

He was lost. Completely. Utterly. Acknowledged it with a sigh against her temple. 'No. I want you. I will not renege.'

'Then kiss me again. Unless you do not wish to, of course.' Her lips formed a delicious—and tantalising—*moue* of disappointment.

'Do you know what you ask?' He held her lightly, torn between amusement and frustration. Virgin and temptress, innocent and wanton. How could he be expected to resist her? How could any man?

He could not, of course. 'My inclination is not in question. It is my self-control that has suddenly become compromised. But you, my love, must be quite certain.'

'Oh, yes. I told my mother that if I never married I would take a lover. It seems to me that if I can do both at the same time, I would have every advantage.'

He laughed, despite himself. 'I cannot imagine such a conversation.'

'I think that Lady Drusilla did not approve.'

'But I like the sentiment. And I like you.'

'I am relieved. How humiliating it would be for me if you decided that we would not suit. After showing such lack of delicacy.' She waited, for the long beat of her heart.

His reply was quite serious, stern even. 'There will be no humiliation. It will please me to worship you with my body. There can be no shame. Nothing but the new, bright splendour of our love.' Nicholas dropped his hands to her waist and lifted her, swung her in a circle to replace her on her feet. 'What a delight you are to me.' His kiss was swift and thorough, a promise of the pleasures that he could bring to her. Then he lifted her into his arms, as if her weight was nothing, carried her to an open stall, freshly swept with a bed of sweet straw and lowered her there to her feet in the middle. Covered the straw with his ill-used coat.

'Do you realise that this is the second time today that I have begun to undress you?' he asked conversationally, even though his fingers were not quite steady at the task. 'Last time I took the coward's way and retreated in disorder.'

'Why would you do that?' There was no mistaking the firtatiousness in her voice, but she awaited his reply with some anxiety.

'It was not seemly.' He applied himself to the intricate catch of the brooch at her throat. 'Why did you have to wear something so difficult!' But the catch sprang free beneath skilful fingers. 'You were distressed—not aware of me or your surroundings. When I undress you, I want you to be aware of my every movement, every touch. Every lingering caress.' He leaned to press his mouth to the exact place where the pulse beat above the high neck of her blouse.

His reply, his action, heated her blood. 'I am aware now.'

'Also, I did not think Mistress Drew would enjoy the sight of you unclothed in my arms.' His fingers sought the buttons at her lace cuffs.

'Mistress Drew is not here now.'

'No. She is not.' A wealth of meaning spoke in this low reply, in the fierce light in his eyes as they now found and held hers. Theodora knew that she was entirely at his mercy—and rejoiced in it.

'Don't stop this time, my lord.'

'No. Not unless you would wish it.' Her cuffs were loosened, allowing him to concentrate on the row of tiny buttons from nape to waist.

'I definitely would not wish it.' Tremors of anticipation raced across her skin. But also nerves. A little fear. A heady need for the experience drove her on, but her dependence on this man was not to be taken lightly.

Reading her fears, Nicholas abandoned his task to let his hands fall by his sides. He simply wanted her. He was hard and hot and ready, driven now by his body's desire to take and own her. The blood throbbed in his loins, yet he still had a care for her inexperience. He had felt the tremors that had shivered along her spine and would not willingly push her beyond what she was prepared to give.

'I think you have no idea of your effect on me.' His voice was low to soothe, the desire for her swiftly banked. 'But it is not too late. Tell me honestly, my dear love, that this is what you want. I would not distress you. You have my love, regardless of the outcome between us this night.'

At his words of understanding, a delicate warmth touched her, dispelling her doubts as mist lifts at the rising of the sun. She raised her hand to his cheek, to brush the fine cheekbone with soft finger tips. 'How considerate you are. I am yours, Nicholas. I would like very much to be held in your arms.'

Lord Nicholas bowed. A strangely formal gesture given the circumstances and the setting. But it calmed Thea's fears. 'I will take care of you.'

Once again, with something like a hiss of frustration, he applied himself to the tiny buttons.

'I should tell you, my lord—I have no experience of this, despite my somewhat unconventional upbringing.'

'I know it.' The linen and lace blouse fell in a delicate heap to the straw.

'Lady Drusilla has been informative, but I expect she omitted some salient facts.'

'I am sure that she did.' With a grunt of acknowledgement he bent his head to the fastenings of the skirt at her slim waist.

'I have some knowledge of the marriage customs of the Bedouin.'

'Interesting. But perhaps not helpful.' The skirt sank into velvet waves around her feet to leave the lady clad in a fine linen chemise. Nicholas sighed at the fragile beauty so revealed and bent his head to press little kisses along the satin of her exposed shoulder.

'In Constantinople—'

'Thea. Be quiet!' With a smile he took her by the hand to encourage her to step from the folds, then bent to kneel before her and remove her soft boots.

'I am nervous.' Her teeth sank into her lip at the admission. 'And most woefully ignorant.'

'I, fortunately, am neither of those things. Despite my lack of knowledge of the Bedouin.' Now he stood before her again, laughter in his face, but also an exquisite tenderness. 'Is there anything other that you think I should know?'

Laughter gurgled in Thea's throat. Then stopped as she drew in her breath, for there was no mistaking the blazing passion, the rampant need in his brilliant eyes.

'I am very willing to learn,' she managed to whisper.

'Thank God!'

Nicholas pulled her down to the straw. Sat beside her to remove his boots. The sun had finally sunk below Burford Edge, allowing the deeper shadows of encroaching night to envelop them and grant them some privacy. There was no moonlight to illuminate or embarrass an inexperienced lady with intrusive shimmer.

So Lord Nicholas began his seduction of the lady who had invaded his waking and dreaming hours. Soft kisses to encourage and soothe, discovering the most delicate, most enticing curves of her face. And then her lips, softer yet, which parted beneath his urgings, inviting his tongue to take such liberties as made the lady's breath catch and quicken. His breathing deepened as he determined to slow the tender development, one caress leading to another, each touch more intoxicating than the last. His tongue traced its path down the long sweep of her throat, tasting, savouring, until he reached the feverish beat of the pulse in that most sensitive of hollows. There he paused with open-mouthed kisses, before pushing the chemise from her shoulders so that he might know the satin slide of shoulders and breast.

Theodora allowed every intimacy, astonished at the sensitivity of her skin to his caresses, even the whisper of his warm breath, as delicious shivers rippled across her skin. Daringly she pushed her hands beneath the heavy linen of his shirt to trace the play of muscle and sinew, flesh on flesh. How smooth and well defined, how fine and utterly masculine.

Thea held her breath.

'My love. My dear one.' The merest whisper against the curve. 'It is permitted for you to breathe.' He felt her laugh softly—or perhaps it was a sob—as he pressed his lips to the shallow valley where her heart beat in hectic rhythm with his own.

Gradually, imperceptibly, he sensed her softening against him as she came to know and accept his touch. Only then did he allow his hands to move where they would, to follow the path of his tongue and mouth, and then on, a gentle moulding to smooth and slide. Swell of breast, dip of waist, curve of hip and thigh.

And under that tender assault, Thea held on. Until, as her nails dug deep into his shoulders, she felt him flinch on a sharp intake of breath.

'Did I hurt you?' A soft concern.

'No. Or no more than the Maidens.' Nicholas continued to press a line of feathery kisses along one fine-boned shoulder. 'You are allowed to draw blood in such circumstances as this. But only a very little.'

'I think I am afraid.'

'The courageous Theodora admitting to fear?' He raised his head to see her watching him, eyes a little wide.

'Yes. Have mercy.'

'Perhaps. Perhaps not.' Now he drew his hand over her breast, brushing her nipple with the pad of his thumb, gently, sensuously, until it hardened and she drew in her breath on a little cry. But rather than resist she wound her arms around his neck, an invitation, which he answered by reaching to smooth one hand slowly up the glorious length from knee to thigh to waist, bringing the fullness of her chemise with it. He did not wish to remove the garment, in recognition of her inexperience, but his hands could now discover the secret delights of her. With gentle pressure he parted her thighs, stroking her with knowing fingers until she gasped. Soft, so soft. So responsive as he felt her push, a mere flex of hips, in unspoken answer against the heel of his hand. But still tense. As he captured her lips once more with his own, Nicholas knew that there was no advantage to be gained for her in prolonging the deed. It was all too new and ridden with uncertainties, no matter how skilful and patient he might be. She would suffer—but very little, if he set himself to distract, to lure her into trusting him with her well-being.

'Look at me, Thea.' He took his weight on his forearms, demanding all her attention. 'You do not need to fear.'

'But I do. You may not like me.' Admitting her most secret fear.

'I may not, of course,' he agreed, dropping the lightest of kisses on the tip of her nose.

'What will you do then?'

'If I decide that we will not suit, I will simply send you back to Cousin Jennifer.'

'Oh.' The thought made her smile. He caught the quick flash of white in the shadow. 'Do you think there is any possibility of that?'

Now he kissed her with a passion, allowing his tongue to seek the silk and heat of her mouth, retreating, then claiming her once more, delighted when her tongue touched his in ready response.

'Do you think there is such a possibility?' A little breathless now, desire riding him hard, a hunting cat with sharp claws.

'Perhaps not.'

Moving a little, he allowed his erection to press urgently against her thigh.

'Do you think I do not want you?'

'No.' He felt her arms tighten around him at this clear evidence of his need for her.

'Nor do I. I want you, Thea. Feel how much I want you.'

So he pushed against her and into her, aware of her eyes fixed on him, wide and trusting. Slowly and carefully, when all his instincts were to take and possess, until he reached a natural resistance. And held back. All her muscles were tense around him. He felt her body flinch from his at the intrusion.

'Nicholas…! I can't…'

'Hush,' he murmured. 'Think about…' What? In the circumstances he had no ideas.

Neither had Theodora. 'I cannot think about anything but you.'

'Very well. Hold on to me. Remember that I am as much in your power as you are in mine.'

For he could hold back no longer. One firm thrust and she was his. As without doubt he was hers, buried deep.

She cried out in sudden shock and would have struggled against the weight and power of his body. He felt her muscles tense around him.

'Wait. Lie still a moment.' She was immediately obedient, anxiety plain in every fine line of her body. So he kissed her. Lightly, teasingly on face and shoulders, to remind her of the more gentle pleasures of love, holding himself perfectly still. And then began to rock gently until she was accustomed to the movement. Until he felt her sigh, relax and enfold him in the softest heat.

'Better?' he murmured against her temple, still controlling every muscle in his body. Resisting the almost overwhelming urge to drive on and on.

'Oh, yes!' A sigh.

'Then, lady, let us finish it together. Move with me.' He encouraged her to arch against him, to move and slide and flex, answering every thrust of his loins until he could resist no longer. Innocent as she was, unaware of the effect she had on him, she drove him to insanity just by being here in his arms. One final thrust brought him to ultimate completion.

Afterwards they lay still until their breathing settled, Thea's arms still entwined around Nicholas's shoulders, held tight, as if in disbelief at what had just passed between them. Until

Nicholas rolled from her, but not away, so that he might look down into her expressive eyes and read the truth of what she might feel. Except that the shadows would effectively hide all trace of emotion if she chose to dissemble.

He must know! It was suddenly too important to leave unsaid between them.

'Well, my Queen of the Desert?'

'I don't know what to say.' Unusually shy, Thea hid her face against his throat. The experience had taken over all her senses, leaving her drained with a strange lassitude, yet longing to know more at the hands of this most skilful lover.

'Well—let me see. What about: I hate you? It was the worst experience of my life?'

'No!'

'I will go back to Cousin Jennifer immediately?'

'Only if you insist!'

'Perhaps then that, to your expert knowledge, the Bedouin are far more sophisticated?' She caught the gleam of a quick grin.

'No. I cannot claim that.'

Suddenly all amusement left his voice, his eyes. To be replaced by a stern intensity. 'It will be better, Thea. I promise you that it will.'

'I said that I can learn.' Was there still a hint of uncertainty there?

'You need learn nothing.' Nicholas kissed her again. 'Only how to enjoy my body as much as I enjoy yours. You are beautiful and desirable, Theodora.'

The exquisite tenderness of his mouth, his enfolding arms as he pulled her close again, brought a rose-tinted blush from the neck of her disordered chemise to the roots of her hair.

'Was it very bad?' It mattered.

'No.' Thea sighed, her breath warm against his throat. 'It was wonderful.'

'Straw does not make for the most comfortable of bedding. Next time we will do better—with a mattress and pillows.'

Nicholas helped her to her feet, helped her to dress again with careful attention, applying himself to the tiny buttons and laces, pulling on her boots, then putting his own clothing to rights. The little brooch he slid into his coat pocket for safe-keeping, then simply stood and looked at her as if she were a miracle.

'What is it?'

'I remember, when they were still living at Burford—and in London—seeing Hal look at Eleanor. As if for him there was no other woman in the world. I think I envied him such a depth of passion and commitment, but I did not understand it. Now I do. You are my world, Theodora. You are my universe.'

'As you are mine.'

'I took your innocence.'

'Do you regret it?'

'No. How could I when you are here in my arms, as beautiful as you are. But you might. Tomorrow, in the full light of day. You might regret having given yourself to me.' He feathered his fingers through her hair, removing a stray wisp of hay. 'So willingly. So generously.' In his eyes, if she could have seen them in the heavy dusk, there was a plea that she should not hold any regrets.

Nor did she. She spoke from her heart so that he might not doubt her. 'No. I am yours to take. I think that it was always so. I have been waiting for you my whole life. Now that I am yours, I feel complete.'

His heart turned over in his chest. Such a strong woman admitting to such a dependence, such a depth of emotion that would effectively place one's future happiness into the hands of another. It would take courage indeed.

'We will go in,' he said, holding out his hand. 'Tomorrow will be a new day. A new life. When I can love you in the eyes of the whole world.'

'Can I say something?' She pulled back, resisting as he took her hand to lead her from the stable. When she lifted his hand to cup her cheek, he found it wet with tears.

'Thea. What is it? Did I indeed hurt you?' He caught the tears with gentle fingers, suddenly appalled that he might have pushed her further than she wished to go. 'Is it that you can not love me so soon? Forgive me, forgive me…'

'No. It is not that.'

'Then what is it, my heart? Nothing is worth your tears. If you can not find it in your heart to love me, then you must say it.' He fought to quell the sudden rush of panic at such an eventuality.

But there was no need. 'I think you do not understand me.' He heard a hesitation of breath, but Thea's voice was clear and confident. 'This is what I wished to say. I love you, Nicholas Faringdon. I love you.'

He found that he had been holding his breath. Now he could breathe and live again. 'What more could any man wish to hear from the woman who holds his heart in her hands?'

With an arm around her waist, so that she might lean on him, her head resting on his shoulder, he led her to the house.

Chapter Nine

New York

The house still smelt of new wood and paint, but at least it was complete with walls and roof intact. Or nearly so. Eleanor could still hear sounds of hammering somewhere in the distance, but not so insistently or loudly enough to annoy. Probably the stables, she thought. The room was warm with early summer heat, despite lowered blinds and a light breeze through the opened windows. It was a boudoir, although still lacking more than basic furniture, and Eleanor was at ease. Or she would have been, she thought, if ease was possible for a lady in her condition. She shuffled on the satin day bed, trying to find a more comfortable position. She had been instructed, on pain of death, to rest her swollen ankles and, for a lady who had remained distressingly active throughout her pregnancy until the eighth month, was finding the enforced leisure difficult.

But it was merely a matter of waiting, she consoled herself. And not long now. A smile touched her lips. Pregnancy had done nothing to rob Eleanor Faringdon, once Marchioness of Burford, of her beauty. Her rich auburn hair, only loosely restrained and allowed to fall in waves onto her shoulders, shone with health, her skin glowed. And those deep amethyst eyes, eyes that had captivated Lord Henry Faringdon when she had been a young débutante making her first curtsy to polite society, shone with love and anticipation. The years between that first meeting and the present, in this new home in New York, had been long and fraught with difficulties. But now Eleanor was united with the one who held her heart and would remain so until the day of her death. If she were certain of nothing in life, it was that one incontrovertible fact.

If only she were not so hot. And so...*large*!

The dark shadows of those distant weeks in London had finally melted away. In New York, free from gossip and sly comment, critical or knowing glances, wrapped around by Henry's love and constant care, Eleanor had grown into her full maturity, content and confident in their future together. Nothing would ever separate them again. And now she awaited the birth of her second child. Henry's second child.

It was all so different, she mused, from Tom's birth, when she had been racked by guilt and anger, the child's father far distant on the other side of the world, ignorant of her situation. Now Henry was no further away than the warehouse or the stables—and refused to be lured much further until this child had arrived safely. Her thoughts naturally moved on to Thomas, her first husband, lapping her in a well of tenderness. How generous and understanding he had been, how incredibly honourable to give his name to his brother's illegitimate child. He had loved her, supported her and kept her safe through all the difficulties. Eleanor sighed a little at the sad memories, but they no longer hurt her. Her son Tom was a constant delight. And she believed that in some way Thomas knew and approved of her present happiness.

So, clad in a loose-fitting silk-and-lace robe, Eleanor sat and waited for someone to come and entertain her. Sarah had said that she would call. She would bring patterns for furnishings. And news of any local events or interesting gossip. They would pass a pleasant hour or so.

But until then—a letter lay unopened in Eleanor's lap. Her mother's astringent comments were always guaranteed to entertain. Mrs Stamford was in London for a few weeks of the Season, before going to Bath to drink the waters. She had been complaining of the rheumatics in her shoulders and hoped for a miracle at the fashionable spa. Eleanor opened the letter with pleasure at the number of closely written sheets and read for a short while.

A clatter on the stairs heralded an interruption. Eleanor smiled and folded the sheets away There would be no further quiet reading of a letter yet.

'Mama!' A sturdy child, tall for his age of almost four years, bounded into the room, with a small black dog of indeterminate origin at his heels, to slide to a halt before the day bed, the dog flopping beside him and panting loudly in the heat.

'You must come and see, Mama. We have a new horse. Papa says he is for me. That I can feed and groom him—and ride him all by myself.'

Eleanor saw the Faringdon inheritance in her son and her heart turned over in her breast. Her own eyes sparkled out of the youthful face, to be sure. But the rest was pure Faringdon. Dark hair, dense and glossy as a crow's wing. Straight nose, firm chin, the curves of babyhood beginning to disappear to reveal aristocratic cheekbones. Splendidly arched brows. And a remarkable curled lip, uncannily reminiscent of his father, at the silent reference to the despised leading rein. He was very like his father. All energy and determination, at present overflowing and uncontrolled in youth, but she had seen the adult version in her husband, combined with a certain self-assurance, arrogance even. Tom would ride the horse alone and would pester until allowed to do so. She could not help hoping that her imminent child would be a daughter with a little more of her own softer characteristics in evidence.

'I will come,' she assured her son. 'A little later in the day when it is cooler. You can show me everything then.' She stretched out her hand to touch his untidy hair, chuckling as he tossed his head with impatience. Another Faringdon trait.

'He has a black mane and tail and has no name. Papa says I can choose.'

'And so you shall. What have you been doing?' His clothes were distinctly the worse for wear and his hair had a faint sheen of dust. 'At breakfast, as I recall, you were very clean and tidy.'

'Helping Nat in the warehouse.'

Mr Bridges, she considered, deserved a gold medallion for patience. Tom was at the stage where everything must be investigated and questioned.

'You should call him Mr Bridges. Have you been a nuisance?'

'He says to call him Nat. So I do. He does not mind if I help him. He says I talk a lot for someone my size. Are you sure you'll not come now to see the new horse, Mama?' Tom hopped from one foot to the other.

Before she could reply, more footsteps approached the room. Eleanor turned her face to the door, her eyes alight with joy.

Hal. Her adored Hal.

He stepped into the room. 'I see that you are being propositioned.' And smiled. Devastatingly. Causing the colour in Eleanor's cheeks to deepen at the realisation that he was here and that he was hers.

'Yes.'

'Mama says that she will come later,' Tom explained, hoping for a change of plan now that his father, who could achieve all things, was present.

'I will bring her down to the stables when the temperature drops.'

'Promise?'

'Of course.' He grinned in understanding of the boy's enthusiasms. 'Now, why don't you go and look at the pony again—and think of a name before your mama sees him. There is a new bridle for you to use, as well.'

Tom opened his mouth as if to say more, but when Henry shook his head, his face broke into a replica grin before he clapped his hands over his mouth and giggled through his fingers.

'I didn't say, Papa. It's a secret.'

'I know. So go before you do.'

At that, boy and dog left at speed.

Which left them together.

'What was all that about?' Eleanor stretched out her hand in invitation.

'Nothing for you to worry about.' He removed his riding coat, casting it carelessly over a chairback, and covered the ground between them in easy strides.

'You can keep a secret better than your son! He'll tell me, you know.' Her eyes told him all the secrets of her heart.

'I know it. It will not matter.' Henry bent to kiss her, gently, little more than a brush of lips, but with the low heat of passion that was always there. 'Nell. You look wonderful.'

She sniffed. 'You, my love, smell of wood and…spices?'

'I have been in the warehouse. Do you object?'

'No. Better than the stables! Come and sit with me.'

He sat beside her, easing her body so that she could lay back comfortably against his shoulder and side, his arms supporting her. 'I am pleased to see that you are following orders.'

'Have I any choice?' She tilted her chin to look up at him, her lips in a little pout of mock displeasure. 'You threatened to lock me in my bedchamber and to tie my ankle to the bed if I came down to see what you and Tom were doing once more.'

He laughed. 'It will not be long.' Was there perhaps a hint of anxiety in his reassurance? Eleanor thought there was and understood.

'No. Not long.' She lifted his hand and laid it on her belly where the child kicked.

'Lively?'

'Oh, yes!' She could feel his smile against her hair.

'You are more beautiful now than the day I met you.'

'I shall be even more so when I have something resembling a waist again.'

He turned his face into her hair, kissing the elegant curve of her ear and then all the way to her temple, featherlight caresses where the curls lay damply.

'I see that you have a letter from your dear mama.' There was a dry edge to his voice. The relationship between Henry and Mrs Stamford had always had an edge. 'Now, can I guess—gossip?

Who is wearing what? Who is speaking to whom? She wishes you were not so far away—and for preference not with me?' He lifted the weight of pages. 'How can anyone write so much about so little?'

'As ever, my love—you have it in a nutshell. Although she has forgiven you, I think. She wishes that she could see the new baby, of course. It is understandable that she regrets the distance. By the by, did any news come from Nicholas in the business packet?'

'No. Why? Were we expecting some?'

'Aha! Then I have news for you, Hal. Nicholas is in London. The social thing. Probably encouraged by Beatrice.'

'Summoned more like, knowing my aunt. Very noble of him. I doubt he'll stay the pace long. Almack's was never his scene.'

'Nor yours, I remember! But he might surprise you. Mama says that he is dancing attendance on a very handsome débutante.'

Hal raised his brows. 'Well, he has done that before. He is hardly immune to the fair sex.'

'But this time he seems to be very taken. She is very handsome. With a fortune. Her father is one of our foreign ambassadors, so she is well connected. Although a trifle unconventional, according to my mama. Perhaps even a touch fast.' Eleanor's eyes twinkled at the prospect of such a lady engaging Nicholas's affections.

'That does not sound like Nicholas.'

'Mama says that she *reads*. And dances the waltz even though it is her first Season. She rides a grey Arab in the Park with considerable dash and has been seen in a high-perch phaeton—driving *alone* without a groom or maid in attendance! She is quite sophisticated—has travelled somewhere in the deserts, although exactly where Mama is unsure. I do not think that she approves.'

'Well, that is hardly surprising!' Henry considered the news. 'Apart from the grey Arab, it sounds even less like Nicholas. But perhaps he will marry at last. I wish him well if he has found a lady who can win his heart.'

'Is that all you have to say?'

'Nicholas has kissed the pretty fingers of any number of débutantes to my knowledge. Why should this one be any different?'

'Well, as long as he does not marry Amelia Hawkes!'

'Who?'

'Sir William Hawkes's daughter. Surely you recall—your neighbour's daughter at Burford Hall. Although perhaps you don't… Anyway, the poor girl has been sighing over Nicholas and his horses for as long as I can remember! And, in my opinion, without the least hope of success. I hope that I am not to be proved wrong.'

'Perhaps you had better write and tell him so! But Nicholas will do just what he likes. As always.'

'Just like you.'

'Exactly. A Faringdon failing.' He linked his fingers with hers, a symbol of unity. 'I wanted you. And look what happened. Despite all the hurdles.'

'And it took no persuasion on my part?'

'A little,' he had the grace to admit, remembering her determined occupation of his cabin on the *Sea Emerald* before he sailed back to America, her refusal to leave. Her sheer determination to ride roughshod over any principles he might have over the affair.

'And look how grateful you are.' Eleanor's fingers tightened on his.

'You do not know the half of it.' Suddenly sober, he held her and their unborn child close, unbearably moved by the memory of how close they had come to losing each other and the possibility of a future together.

Where Sarah found them some half an hour later.

Life in New York suited Mrs Sarah Russell very well. Her restrained manner, her nervous pallor, which Eleanor and Henry remembered from those anxious days in London when she had been forced by her brother to pose against her will as nursemaid to her own child, had completely vanished. She was no longer permanently ridden by guilt and shame at the despicable actions of Sir Edward Baxendale, and also of herself by his manipulation of her. The unqualified love and acceptance from the Faringdons had done much to help her heal and regain some small degree of self-respect. Now twenty-five years old, widowed and mother to an overwhelming five-year-old, she was brisk, confident and capable, enjoying an independent life, far from the powerful influence of her brother. She never mentioned him. His sins, as far as she was concerned, were too great. Likewise her sister-in-law Octavia, so weak that she would obey Edward's commands to the letter. Whatever the ease of Sarah's relationship with Henry and Eleanor Faringdon, it was not appropriate to remind anyone in this household that her own name by birth had been Baxendale.

She had left her son John with Tom and Nathaniel Bridges in the warehouse and climbed the stairs to the newly furnished boudoir, knowing that she would find Eleanor there, and set herself to entertain in these final trying days. The door on to the wide corridor was open, to catch any passing current of air, so she simply entered. She did not stand on ceremony in this house.

But the domestic scene, so relaxed and yet so intimate, made her hesitate and blush a little at her intrusion, until she saw and answered Eleanor's smile of welcome and continued into the room.

'You look comfortable.'

'It is all relative,' Eleanor muttered darkly.

'And only until she shuffles and twitches again—in about ten seconds, I should imagine, on past experience.' Henry winced a little and laughed as a sharp elbow found his ribs.

'But I am so uncomfortable—the heat and the lack of air. When I carried Tom, it was England and in winter.' Eleanor slanted a look up into Henry's face. 'I do not know why I am apologising to you, Hal! Some would say that it is all your fault!'

'Then, my love, I must accept all the blame.'

'Well, you *look* exceptionally content.' Sarah took a seat and lowered the books of furnishings and patterns to the floor to hide the sharp stab of envy. The love between them was so tangible, so all-consuming, the glance between them exclusive, effectively shutting out all others. He might well have kissed her—as he was not averse to doing in public. As a sharp stab to her heart, it made

Sarah regret her own widowed state, long for strong arms to hold her against her fears when the nights were dark, someone as intense and passionate as Henry Faringdon. She took a deep breath. Better not, she told herself quickly. Better that she should rejoice in her freedom to make her own decisions, determine her own lifestyle. She had had enough of domineering men, however attractive they might be.

'Here is someone who will appreciate Mama's news.' Eleanor shuffled into a cooler spot, a mischievous smile for Sarah.

'What's that?' Sarah untied the ribbons of her bonnet, dropped it on the floor at her side with a sigh of relief.

'Nicholas and a débutante.'

'Ah. Some London gossip.' Her eyes shone. 'Do tell. Is it serious?'

'So Mama thinks.' Eleanor searched the pages in her hand for the name. 'A Miss Wooton-Devereux, indeed,' she finally announced. 'Rich *and* beautiful. What more could he want to bring him solace as he runs the Burford acres with such fiendish efficiency?'

There was no corresponding humour in Sarah's reply. 'Oh… Oh, no.' It was certainly not the response that Eleanor had expected. 'What…what was the name again?' Sarah had become quite still. Eleanor noticed that her hands had suddenly clenched into tight fists on the skirt of her gown.

'Miss Wooton-Devereux,' she repeated, a little frown between her brows. 'Do you know of her?'

Sarah passed her tongue over dry lips, conscious that the air seemed to press down on her with a great weight so that she felt a little dizzy. 'Do you…do you know the lady's first name?'

'Mama said that it was something out of the common way. Let me see… Ah, yes—Theodora. Why…what is it, Sarah? Are you unwell?'

Suddenly finding it difficult to breathe in the hot still air, the lady pressed her hands to her face. It seemed that the past, with all its burden of guilt and intrigue, had fallen once again at her feet, to harm and destroy. 'I don't believe it,' she managed to say.

'That a malicious fate should have brought her…' Her words ended on something suspiciously like a sob.

Eleanor tried to sit up, only to be restrained by Henry, who gently extricated himself from the sofa and went to pour a glass of brandy. He returned to the stricken lady and pressed it into her unresisting hand.

'Sarah.' She looked up into his face, her own blank with shock, her mind working furiously to remember all that she had been told of this particular débutante. 'Listen to me. Drink this.' He waited until she had complied, a few sips at least. 'Now tell me. What is it? Do you know the lady? Is there a problem?' He took the glass from her and crouched at her side, holding her hands comfortingly in his.

'Yes… No… That is…I never thought to hear that name in this house—in connection with one of your family.'

'Dear Sarah. Tell us,' Eleanor encouraged. The shimmer of distress around her friend was almost visible. 'It cannot surely be as bad as all that.'

Sarah looked from one to the other. They had been so kind to her, so supportive, when she had aided and abetted her brother in bringing them such pain. And now she must tell them… Of course, she must. 'Oh, yes,' she stated, her soft voice surprisingly harsh. 'There is a problem. And it may be as bad as we could ever imagine.' She looked at Henry with frightened eyes. 'Her name by birth is not Wooton-Devereux. It is Baxendale.'

Baxendale! There was a shattering silence in the room. It seemed to echo from every corner. Even the distant hammering was silent as they absorbed that one name.

'I don't understand.' Eleanor instantly swung her feet to the floor. Sarah's remarkable statement had effectively destroyed all her contentment.

'She is Sophia Mary Baxendale and she is my sister.' Sarah announced it in firmer accents. Whatever the outcome, she must face it. Her past had just come back to haunt her and, whatever she felt about the revelation, it had stunned her audience of two.

'Your sister? I did not know you even had a sister.'

'I have not thought of her for years.' Sarah's eyes were full of sympathy as she watched the emotions flit across Eleanor's face. 'How should I? But listen. I must tell you what I know.'

Henry, reading his wife's anxiety, went to sit beside her again and took her hands, soothing the soft skin on the inside of her wrists with his thumb. And Sarah, unearthing her family secrets, gleaned from her own reluctant mother and from Edward's memories when she was a child and thus fascinated by such things, explained all. A disorganised household, increasing debts, the difficult birth. Then the arrival of Drusilla, her mother's managing sister, followed by the removal of the baby to a new home, a new family.

'So she is Sophia Mary Baxendale,' Eleanor repeated.

'Yes. But I have never met her. Only know of her from family records.'

'But the crucial question now…' Henry said slowly, considering the implications of this potentially explosive news, 'is whether there is any recent connection, any communication, between your sister and Edward.'

'I don't know.' Sarah understood the implications all too well.

'What are you thinking, Hal?' Eleanor also knew well what he was thinking, believed her thoughts ran in the same direction, but she needed him to say it aloud.

'I am thinking—what do we have here? Another Baxendale plot? An attempt to strike once more at the Faringdon family—in a desire for revenge? Presumably a revenge made even more bitter by the past failures.' There it was, laid out in stark terms as cold and flat as Henry's eyes, dark with anger.

'To lure Nicholas into marriage with a Baxendale,' Sarah whispered.

'Is the coincidence too great?' Eleanor prayed that it was so.

'Nothing is beyond Edward.' Sarah fought to hide the shame as she outlined Edward Baxendale's past sins. Something that Henry had deliberately refrained from doing, out of respect for Sarah's unenviable position. 'He was willing to use me and my child. He was willing to destroy the good name of you, Eleanor, and Thomas. He would have made your position in society untenable. What would he not be capable of? Would he not use a young sister? Even if she were innocent of his intentions, she could still be a weapon for his revenge. He cannot touch you now, however much he might wish it, but he could harm Nicholas. Simply through the humiliation of luring him into marriage with a Baxendale without his knowledge. And if my brother could get money out of it…Edward is not beyond blackmail.'

'But would the girl agree to such a deception?' Eleanor asked in disbelief. 'To deliberately set out to fix Nicholas's interest, a cruel charade for a brother she hardly knows?'

'We don't know, Nell.' Henry's fingers tightened round her wrists, forcing her to look at him and consider the weight of his words. 'We know nothing about her. But what we do know is that Edward is quite capable of playing a role—of winning the lady's compliance with a heart-rending tale of the need for justice. The evil Faringdons and the innocent Baxendales.'

'Of course he would.' Eleanor nodded her agreement. 'So what do we do? Can we do anything?'

'It could be a completely false alarm, of course.' Henry frowned down at Eleanor's hands where they still rested, enclosed in his. 'Nick's interest might have moved on to someone else, another débutante. Or your mama might have misread his gallantry. But better that he knows.'

'I agree.' Sarah sighed. 'If nothing else, Lord Nicholas needs to know that Miss Theodora Wooton-Devereux is not who she seems.'

Chapter Ten

At Aymestry Manor, Nicholas and Theodora fell headlong and effortlessly into a love affair, watched closely but with indulgence and a wry acceptance by Agnes Drew and Mrs Grant. There was no doubting the happiness that wrapped the pair around, excluding all others, so that they might as well have been living on a deserted mountain top. It did a body good, Mrs Grant informed her interested guest, to see Lord Nicholas so taken up with a young lady who clearly returned his sentiments. It was high time he had something to occupy his mind, other than the state of the summer crop or the quality of wool from his prize Ryeland sheep! And a man as handsome and desirable as he in the marriage market—he should not be burying himself in the country. It was more than time he was wed and producing an heir for Aymestry. The Manor had been empty of children for far too long.

Agnes Drew listened, but made little comment, attempting without success to ignore the concern that would not let her be. A relationship built on a lie at worst—a deliberate falsehood at best—was flawed from the very beginning. But Miss Thea was past taking advice, as held fast in love as Lord Nicholas. So she listened and watched. And hoped that fate would not manipulate events in so cruel a fashion as to bring loss and heartbreak to either of the lovers. When her conscience dictated that she should advise Thea that a return to London was both expected and eminently sensible, Agnes for once threw good sense to the winds, considered it—and kept her counsel.

They rode the estate together. Nicholas lent her one of his well-bred horses, a compact chestnut mare with a mind of her own, to replace The Zephyr, who was still recovering. Across the pasture and open meadow, so unlike the confines of Hyde Park, Thea was free to gallop. And did so. Nicholas and his lady were quick to discover their equally competitive nature and revelled in the freedom to exercise it. Who might win did not seem to matter.

He showed her Aymestry, newly aware of the pride and affection in which he held this jewel of an estate. It pleased him to see it through her eyes, the pastures and mixed woodland, the mere where the swans were still in residence with their almost-fledged young. Not a large estate, but beautiful, a gleaming emerald, in a perfect setting of green hills and sparkling streams.

Then on to Burford—the vast house with its classical architecture and extensive estate, where herds of sheep and cattle grazed the pastures.

Thea was an interested and critical observer. She heard nothing but good of Lord Nicholas. He was well received, whether on the estate or in the small town of Kingshall. After her experience of the Maidens, it would not have surprised her to sense some animosity. But here there was no threat of danger. And Nicholas's manner was easy. He stopped to speak to those he passed, he knew their names, their families and their concerns.

Her admiration grew as she saw the extent of his responsibilities. However much he might be involved in his own property of Aymestry and his dreams of breeding desirable horseflesh, the estate at Burford was never to be neglected. He told her a little about his brothers. And his nephew Tom, Marquis of Burford. If—when—Tom took over the running of the estate in his own right, he would not find it wanting.

So Nicholas was a man quick to recognise obligation and stern duty. Yet he did not crow of his achievements. And Thea had actually accused him of living on the profit and possessions of others. How little she had known of him then! She had the grace to feel ashamed.

When it rained and discouraged their daily rides, they gravitated to the library at Burford Hall. To Thea's delight, amongst the dusty leather volumes there were novels to be read. Scott's *Waverley* and *Guy Mannering* were soon discovered. And *Ivanhoe*, which she declared she liked less well, the plot being more farfetched. She devoured *Glenarvon* by Caroline Lamb, with her sensational and outrageous dissection of members of society whom Thea was quick to recognise with wicked pleasure. Also a remarkable choice of Gothic novels, which made her laugh and groan at their absurdities. She gave up on Mrs Radcliffe's *Mysteries of Udolpho* and turned instead with something like relief to Lord Byron's *Childe Harold*.

A further source of surprise was the vast number of travel books, which it was impossible for her to ignore. Descriptions of far-flung lands all spoke to Thea's adventurous heart. But she had never been as happy as she was at that moment in the rural fastness of Herefordshire. And gloried in it.

And could discover another side to the man whom she was coming to know. For the library also contained treatises on estate improvement. She browsed through back copies of the *Farmers' Journal*, articles on making use of marls and clover and new grasses. Reports encouraged land drainage and the use of new implements for ploughing and threshing. Arthur Young's writings on his travels around the country were well thumbed, she noted, as were advice on improvements to cattle and sheep breeding. And, of course, horses.

For Nicholas cared. Thea's admiration grew, as did her love.

Nicholas, for his part, was totally captivated. Theodora was everything he could want, everything he had dreamed of. Released from the rigid convention of life in the judgmental eye of society, she relaxed, enabling him to see her true nature: an intelligent woman, well read, well traveled, which made her a delight to converse with. Energetic, full of life, she was eager to explore his home, to ask and discover. She was even interested in his plans for the estate, God help him! He was lost indeed! And she laughed. Whenever he thought of her it was to see her eyes sparkling, her lips curved to show her pretty teeth, her face alight. How could he not laugh with her? What more could any man desire in a wife?

As for the physical attraction—he had never wanted a woman as he wanted Theodora. Had never been aroused so readily by a mere glance, by a simple turn of a head, by a brush of feminine fingers against his. Sometimes he did not know how he kept his hands from seizing her shoulders and dragging her into his embrace, into his bed, capturing her mouth with his. He smiled with sardonic humour. She wore his self-control to breaking point— and was well aware of it. For Miss Wooton-Devereux was, without doubt, flirtatious when the mood took her.

And, if all that were not enough, a thick luxurious layer over all was the conviction that she was meant for him. He had simply been waiting for her all his life. He woke every morning, at ease with the knowledge that he could spend the day with her. The vague dissatisfaction and unease with the future vanished as soon as Thea came to stand with him, or sit or ride. As long as she was there, life could hold nothing more.

Sometimes he saw a shadow in her eyes. It concerned him, but perhaps it was simply a lingering memory of the terror of the Maidens' attack. It had pleased him that at last she trusted him enough to tell him the truth of that disturbing episode. It had not been easy for her. They had ridden to Dinmore Hill, where they had dismounted to stroll through the woods with their new brightness of leaves and the intense hue of the bluebells.

'I should tell you, Nicholas…' She had been quiet for a little time, lost in her thoughts or in the surrounding beauty, but now she took his hand and turned to face him. She did not smile.

'Hmm?' He watched the dappled sunlight play over her hair, her fair skin. How lovely she was.

'About…about my strange behaviour.'

His brows arched in silent enquiry.

'The Maidens—when I…when I…'

'Thea—I had not thought of it again.'

'But I have. I do. It was the same when I struck out at you with my whip. I should tell you—'

'Thea.' His fingers tightened on hers. 'There is no need.'

'I think I must. There should be no shadows between us.' *Except for the one, the darkest of dark shadows, which I dare not name!*

'No. Thea—I asked Agnes. After the incident with the Maidens. When you were so distressed—I thought I needed to know.' His voice was very gentle.

'Oh. Well, then…' It took Thea by surprise. She did not know how she felt about that.

'She was very loyal, but I pressed her.'

'And she told you.'

'Yes. Enough that I might understand.' He lifted a hand to run his fingers down her cheek, a soft brush of sympathy.

'I cannot control the fear. It is the overwhelming noise—the crush of people.'

'I know. I understand, darling Thea. It is not important.'

'I feel a coward.' She turned her face to press against his fingers.

'You are no coward. You are brave and resourceful. And I love you beyond reason.'

His kiss was a confirmation of the care, the depth of compassion that she heard in his voice. Gentle, lingering, a warmth of comfort for a damaged soul until her tense muscles softened and she clung to him in relief and gratitude. Until the gentle warmth of the kiss flared into heat and need, a desire that could not be denied, when the light around them became too bright, the colours too intense. Their senses were stripped naked before the onslaught of their love, leaving Nicholas in no doubt that she was as lost as he.

But he still did not know of the reason for her strange behaviour in London, when he had been so sure that she had deliberately set herself to put distance between them. In effect, to drive him away. He dare not ask her and closed his mind against it.

Nothing must be allowed to encroach on this summer idyll.

* * *

Time came to have no meaning for Nicholas and Theodora, measured only by the days and hours and minutes—seconds, even—which they spent in each other's presence. In each other's arms. It was a compulsion, an obsession, heightened by the brush of hands, the touch of lips. Nothing outside their two selves had any meaning.

So, riding on the edge of the estate, they were unaware of the changes round them as the clear light leached from the sky. Storm clouds banked to the west with a sultry heaviness. The first presentiment that they were far from home and the weather would break was a chilling ripple of wind. The sun disappeared behind encroaching high cloud, the far hill withdrawing into an enveloping mist and the first swirl of rain. Picking up the scent of the approaching storm, the horses danced in the freshening breeze, eager for their stable.

There was, of course, the temptation of a nearby barn.

'Well, my lady? Do we take the barn?'

'Or do we get wet?' Thea's face glowed with the sheer joy of life, of being in the presence of the man she loved. Of being able to reach out and touch him whenever the thought arose.

Nicholas turned his head, picking up her mood. 'Will you then gamble. Will we run the storm?' The wildness of the approaching elements was in his blood. There was a reckless challenge in his face that she loved and it seduced her utterly. She saw the challenge and loved it, allowed the seduction.

'Yes. And yes.'

'Come, then.' He stretched out a hand in imperious demand, manoeuvred his bay close, then leaned to allow an arm to steal around her waist. A kiss. Necessarily brief, a mere meeting of mouth on mouth. But hot and hard, a thrill of passion, of burning need.

For a moment her lips parted beneath his, her heart increasing its beat, a pulse that shook her and had nothing to do with the storm, but everything to do with the fever that engulfed her at his touch, the sheer sensuality as his tongue outlined the delicate shape of her lips.

Then he released her. 'Let us do the thing.'

And they fled before the storm, the rain and wind urging them on.

A crazy ride. At full, headlong gallop, control stretched to the limit. Sleek lines and straining power, horses and riders moving as one. They leapt small obstacles, ditches and hedges. Flew as if the hounds of hell pursued them in full cry as thunder rolled over the hills of Burford Edge behind them.

And the heavens opened, a deluge that drenched them to the skin in seconds. Thea failed to suppress a shriek as cold rain fell on her heated flesh. And laughed aloud with the exhilaration of it.

Nicholas slowed the pace. 'Do we shelter?' He had to raise his voice over the lash of wind and rain.

'No. Home.'

They picked up the pace and soared over the stream that bordered the home pasture. Extending again to thwart the worst of the relentless downpour. When they clattered into the stableyard and Nicholas lifted her down, the steaming horses were turned over to waiting hands and they ran for the house. Madness was in their blood, as elemental as the lightning that flashed across the sky.

In the entrance hall they stood on the worn slates and dripped. And looked at each other.

'I am drenched.' Thea tentatively lifted the clammy skirts of her velvet riding habit.

'And I.'

'We lost the gamble.'

'Did we?'

The shock of recognition between them was beyond experience, as electric as the storm that raged without. Breathing shallow, their eyes caught and held. It was impossible to look away, one held captive in the existence of the other. Chains of pure gold bound and held them—and neither resisted the gentle but inexorable tightening of the bond.

Nicholas smiled, both tender and a demand. Held out his hand, as he had at the onset of the storm. And Thea, breath caught in her throat, was compelled to respond, palm to palm, fingers interlocked. A remarkable seduction that tempted and beckoned them on into a depth of emotion and desire which neither could have envisaged. And both fell.

'My lord.' Mrs Grant had arrived unnoticed. 'I see you were caught in the storm. And Miss Thea.' She clucked indulgently at the puddles on the floor as she approached. They looked like children daring the power of the elements, she thought. Carefree. And Nicholas—as if a boy again, shedding the responsibilities that he had so willingly shouldered. Energy and vitality burned through him, his face alight with it.

'Can I be of help?'

'No.' Her question brought them back to the present. 'Thank you, Mrs Grant. No. I will deal with it.' His smile was preoccupied.

With Thea's hand in his, they climbed the stairs together, leaving the housekeeper to watch them.

No. Lord Nicholas was no longer a boy. The expression Mrs Grant had seen in his face and eyes had nothing to do with youth and immaturity. She hoped fate would be kind to him. And stepped back into the shadows.

This vibrant, laughing girl had brought him to life again.

No further words passed between them. They were beyond speech as they came to a halt at the head of the stairs where decisions had to be made. Nicholas tightened the clasp of his hand on hers, the slightest pressure, his gaze questioning. Theodora responded by moving to his side. Answering the unspoken, he led her along the corridor to his bedchamber.

Outside the storm raged on—capricious gusts of wind swirling the rain to lash unmercifully against the windows, distant thunder rumbling ever closer over woods and hills. Thea and Nicholas stood within his room, the door barred to all, oblivious to the onslaught. Within that wood-panelled room, safe and warm and offering every comfort, the elements were set to rage no less ferociously.

'I want you. I want you every minute in the day, from the moment that I wake until the second I fall into sleep. Even my dreams are tormented by your presence. Your perfume, your voice. You are in my blood, Thea.'

'I know it. I know it because my thought mirrors yours.' How could she not know it? Love washed over her, through her, a relentless tide. She felt the power of his eyes, fierce and intense, a dark midnight blue as they held her own. In response she felt the flush of heat over her skin, a flutter of nervous anticipation in her veins. For him, her smile was answer enough.

'Shall we ride this storm too, lady?' Nicholas drew her inexorably toward him, so that he could bend his head and kiss her hands, then take her lips with his own. Impossibly gentle, a mere sensuous brush of mouth against mouth, despite the raging fire in his blood.

'We can match the glory of anything in nature's creation.' Her lips parted beneath his in confident invitation. 'Love me, Nicholas.'

'It will be my pleasure and my delight, lady.'

Now their breathing was heightened. Their movements driven by unrestrained need, as wild and urgent as the summer storm. Soaked garments, boots were quickly stripped away until nothing existed between them except the charged quality of the air. Until he lifted her high in his arms, to fall with her to the bed where they rolled, a tangle of limbs, cool damp rapidly replaced by throbbing heat as skin slid seductively against skin. The lightning that speared across the sky was no more brilliant than the passion which consumed them. Diamond bright, it wrapped them around.

Both were already aroused, he hard as stone, she hot and slick with need, desiring nothing more than to be submerged one within the other as their hands united, palm to palm, fingers meshed. Nicholas pinned Theodora to the soft mattress, hands imprisoned above her head. She needed no instruction now, but opened for him, arching her body in silent demand.

'I love you.' She gasped the words as shivers ran along her skin at his dominant power. 'I love you.'

With one powerful thrust he possessed her. And again. Deep and deeper yet. Thea took him in.

'Thea.'

His name was also on her lips. Both held suspended in that one moment of glorious joining.

'Don't close your eyes.' His voice was low and harsh. She could not look away from the fierce wanting she could see in his face as he forced himself to hold back, a brief hiatus in the turbulence that threatened to overturn all control. 'Look at me.' She could do no other. 'I want you to see me when I am inside you. As I need to see myself in your eyes.'

'Yes.'

It was all the acceptance he needed. 'Then come with me.'

The storm struck with violent intensity, overwhelming them both as they had been enveloped by the rain on the hill. As his mouth took hers, swallowing her cries, he withdrew, thrust again. And again she arched and moved beneath him, as driven and demanding as her lover. All feminine elegance, all gentle curves and sleek planes, but yet wielding total power over his senses. When her nails seared his back, he was unaware. Nothing existed but this outrageous need to own, to achieve fulfilment—and still to pleasure. For even within the rough madness of it all, this furious craving to possess, was his care for her, woven through the tapestry as bright threads of silver throughout the silken texture of it all.

'Nicholas!' Thea answered every demand with intense joy. Never had her strong mind been taken over so completely by the commands of another. Her whole world was suddenly narrowed to this one sharp focus, the man who held her captive and governed her every action with such power. When he touched her, when he looked at her, compelling her with those amazing eyes, she no longer had a will of her own—and rejoiced in the knowledge, the absolute thrill of it.

Beyond any control, Nicholas now drove on, muscles screaming, tendons stretched to snapping point. Until the tight wet heat of her body brought him to his fulfilment.

'Did we survive the storm?' Thea managed to turn her face to press a kiss against the dark hair. They lay together in the ruins of the bed.

Beyond the room the storm had moved on. In the quietness the wind had dropped and the clouds began to break, allowing the first gleam of hesitant sunshine to brighten the corner of the room. But neither lover noticed the rich glow of linenfold or the return of birdsong, both too caught up in their own world.

'I think that we might.' Still buried deep within her, his weight still holding her, his face turned into the pillow. 'When my powers of thought and movement have returned. They appear to have deserted me.'

'Your powers were amazing.' The faintest chuckle.

'I might have hoped for more finesse. You robbed me of any skill I lay claim to.'

'You were magnificent.' Thea knew he was smiling in smug satisfaction, much as she was. Her hands smoothed over sweat-slicked muscle and hard flesh. She stretched luxuriously beneath him. 'Is it always like this?'

'Hmm?'

'Overwhelming. Devastating.' She nudged him when he did not reply. 'Are you sleeping, my lord? I shall flatter you no longer if your intent is to ignore me. Now that you no longer have need of me!' She carefully placed a row of kisses along his shoulder and back again. 'But is it always like this?'

'It can be.' Nicholas lifted his head now to reply with all seriousness. Had he ever known it like this? Where control was at its thinnest, stretched beyond bearing, beyond thought, until he had no choice but to empty himself into her glorious body? No. He thought that he had never known such an unleashed hunger. 'Perhaps it is not always so…mindless,' he offered. Because he knew that the craving had driven him to be careless with her. Selfish, if he admitted the truth. She had given herself to him, but he had not brought her to her own complete enjoyment. He felt himself harden again in sharp anticipation at the prospect of doing exactly that. 'It can be better—and you deserve that it should.'

'How can it be?' A little frown touched her smooth brow. 'You have given me such pleasure. Is the fault mine?'

'How foolish you are, my dear love.' He had to kiss her into silence. 'There is no fault with you. How could there be? But I can give you more.' He withdrew from her to stretch beside her, still hard. 'Hold me.' He took her hand. Both request and demand.

With growing confidence Thea enclosed him to explore the smooth hardness, enjoying his sharp intake of breath as she stroked and touched and heat built beneath her hand. She gave a soft purr, deep in her throat, as the heavy pulse began to beat.

He caught a glint of mischief in her eyes.

'Well?'

'It seems that I am not powerless here, my lord.'

'No.' He clenched his teeth on a groan. 'And *you* once begged *me* to have mercy! I believe that you did warn me that you learnt quickly.'

'So I do. Does it please you?'

'Yes. As I can please you.' Sensing the end of control under that alluring caress, he pushed her back on to the pillows. 'Like this.' With lips and a slow drift of hands he set himself to pleasure and to soothe, to awaken every nerve ending—and then to arouse again with tongue and teeth. 'Like this.' He closed his mouth over her breast, then the other, as the bright wedge of sunshine crept round to illuminate them in a wash of gold. 'And this and this.' A ruthlessly, exquisitely gentle campaign until he had driven her to the very edge of madness. But not quite beyond. Not yet. Slowly. So slowly. A steady relentless burn rather than a fiery heat, he built it layer upon layer, flame upon flame, until she was engulfed. Refusing to release her, even when she pleaded in desperation against the intensity of the sensations, until he knew that she could stand no more. Lifting her hips, he slid within her, so easily within that silken heat, now all gilded beauty, to finally drive her over that precipitate edge. When she cried out in shocked amazement, he followed, to fall with her into oblivion. Just as mindlessly, he realised, as before.

Much later awareness returned. Thea lay against him, content to allow her thoughts to drift, her heart to settle back to its usual steady beat. But perhaps it never would. It seemed to her at that moment that life would never be the same. Her heart was no longer in her possession, yet she was quite content that it should be in the keeping of the man whose arms still held her so securely. How splendid he was, how completely magnificent. She shuddered a little at the memory of his determination to reduce her to boneless delight. His ultimate and sensational triumph.

'Nicholas?'

'My lady?' His fingers drifted lazily along her spine, setting up little shivers along its length.

'I did not believe you. That I could experience more, that there were sensations and emotions to be explored more wonderful than I had ever imagined.' Her breathing still compromised, she rested her cheek on his chest, against his thundering heart. And smiled in utter contentment. 'But it is true.'

Lord Nicholas sat at his desk in the library at Aymestry, reluctant but resigned. However delightful, however necessary for his happiness it might have become to spend time with Theodora, duty and work called loudly this morning. Some documents pertaining to the Burford Estate had arrived for his attention from Mr Hoskins, the London-based lawyer, and needed a rapid reply. Furthermore, there was an unexpected packet of correspondence from New York. The one that caught his eye was in Nell's hand, which surprised him. He picked it up, tapped it thoughtfully on the desk. Now, why should Nell write to him? And, considering the thickness of the missive, at some length.

He spread the sheets on the desk and began to read, first letting his eye travel quickly down the pages. Until picking out one name. Halted. Nicholas's fingers tightened on the paper, much as invisible hands seemed to be tightening around his chest. Returning to the beginning, he began to read more slowly, perhaps hoping that there might be some mistake that could be remedied by careful perusal of Nell's neat script. It began with personal, family affairs. Normal and comforting, reassuring that all was well. But then she reached the bitter purpose of the letter and all Nicholas's comfort fled, to leave a gaping hole of pain and disillusion.

Eventually he finished it, taking only seconds to realise its import, not the endless hours it seemed. Pushed himself to his feet to go and stand by the window, as if the light flooding into the room would offer more illumination to the content.

Surely Nell's information was wrong. Surely it was all some dreadful mistake. But Nell had written of Sarah, who would undoubtedly know the truth... His eyes focused once again on the chilling words before him.

My mama has recently written that whilst in London you have made the acquaintance of a Miss Theodora Wooton-Devereux. That you have been attracted to her. I pray that you will forgive my interference in so personal a matter, dear Nick, but Sarah and I have decided—and Henry, too—that you must be told. Or perhaps by now the lady herself has told you the truth of her birth. Lady Drusilla Wooton-Devereux is sister to Lady Mary Baxendale, the now deceased mother of Sarah and Edward. The child whom you now know as Theodora was the child of Lady Mary and her husband, but was taken by Lady Drusilla soon after her birth and brought up as her own when the Baxendale circumstances became difficult. Thus Theodora's true name is Sophia Mary Baxendale. She is sister to Sarah and Edward.

We do not know if there is any understanding between you and the lady, but we believe that you should be made aware that the lady's name is Baxendale. We fear that it is not beyond belief that she is in touch with Edward. You should have a care, dear Nick. It may be that the Baxendale desire for revenge against the Faringdon family is not dead as we had believed, and that the lady is either a willing participant or a helpless pawn in Edward's vile games. I know the anguish and despair that this can cause. I would not wish for you to be dragged into a plot, leading to heartbreak and recrimination.

Miss Wooton-Devereux, I would advise you most strongly, may not be as innocent as she might appear.

I am sorry if this will cause problems between you. Perhaps I should pray that when this letter finally reaches you, your association with the lady has come to a natural end and she is looking elsewhere for a husband.

Nicholas simply stood, staring unseeingly at the dramatic prospect of open parkland and sunlit, mature oaks before him. For some reason his mind seemed unable to function with its usual sharp perception. Could not take in the full detail of Nell's warning words. Thea was a *Baxendale*. This was the only thought that hammered in his brain, over and over again. Sister of Edward Baxendale. No—it must not be so! But if Sarah had told Eleanor that Theodora was indeed her sister, then it must be so.

What in God's name did he feel about this?

Disbelief, primarily. Then a desperately piercing anxiety that it might just be true. And beneath that emotion, a terrible burning anger and an all-consuming fear that it might indeed be all part of a further plot as Nell had hinted, concocted in Edward Baxendale's corrupt mind, to hurt the Faringdons. To hurt *him*! Was it the plan to drag him into a marriage with Thea, the lure of a lovely face and pleasing manners, and then extort money by some means into Edward's greedy pockets? Or simply humiliate him when he discovered that he, Lord Nicholas Faringdon, had taken a Baxendale bride against either his knowledge or his wishes.

But the reasons behind the charade did not matter. Theodora's possible involvement was the weapon that sliced at his heart. He loved her. He had accepted without question that she loved him. He had taken her to his bed, asked her to marry him, believing that their love was a substantial thing, of mutual satisfaction and heart-wrenching beauty. Had he been so wrong? But he must accept that he was now faced with evidence of her perfidy, that such a beautiful face could hide such deceit. But of course he knew that she had been hiding something from him, had known it since the early days in London. Was this it? Her involvement, willing or otherwise, with her brother's scheming?

All he knew was that it was imperative that he talk to Theodora. And guard his emotions when doing so. Because if she was innocent of all involvement with her brother, as he hoped and prayed, why had she not told him that by birth she was a Baxendale?

Love? Ha! He crumpled Nell's letter in a furious fist. If love did exist, and he seriously doubted it after the revelations of the past hour, it must not be allowed to blind him to realities.

As Nicholas stalked to the library door, intent on running Theodora to ground and requesting—*demanding*—an explanation, it opened. Thea stood there. Her face immediately lit with an inner glow at the sight of her lover. Stretching out her hands, she would have covered the Aubusson carpet between them with the lightest of steps to kiss him in greeting, with no intimation of the disaster which awaited her in that pleasant, book-filled room. A lethal sword of Damocles, shrouded in the form of Edward Baxendale, to destroy all her new-found love and happiness.

But she immediately sensed the tension in Nicholas's body, saw his spine held rigid, his shoulders braced, hands clenched into fists at his sides. The lines between nose and mouth were starkly engraved. And his eyes? Usually so intensely blue and smiling when they lighted on her, or burning with passion and desire—now they were the dense, flat grey of glacial ice. Thea came to a halt as if a wall had been thrown up between them.

'What is it, Nicholas?' She saw the pages scattered on the desk. 'Have you had bad news? Is it your family in New York? Eleanor…?'

'Why did you not tell me, Thea?'

His voice was soft, apparently unthreatening, but held a quality that she had never before heard. It froze the very marrow in her bones.

'What is it that I should have told you? What can have disturbed you so?' She tried to keep her tone light, but a sharp finger of warning traced its insidious path along her backbone. She could think of only one cause for this latent hostility, and did not have long to wait to learn the truth.

'That your name is Baxendale. Sophia Mary Baxendale, to be exact. And that you are sister to Sir Edward Baxendale.'

'I—' She buried her teeth in her lip, as a bottomless crevasse opened before her unwary feet. Her worst fears had just been realised, announced in one brusque statement by the man whom she loved more than life itself, in a voice that cut with rapier sharpness to her heart. What could she say? A terrible premonition enfolded her as she read the condemnation in Nicholas's face.

'I see that you do not bother to deny it.'

She found, of necessity, her voice. 'No. For it is true.'

'Why did you not tell me? What can possibly have been your motive in not telling me?'

The simmering anger in his voice, the deadly repetition of the accusation stirred her into a response. Taking a deep breath, she willed the quivering nerves in her stomach to quieten. She *would not* feel guilt or shame over a situation that was not her fault, over which she had no control. She met his cold eyes squarely.

'I thought it would cause dissension between us. And I see that I was right.'

'So you would have kept the information from me for ever?' Now the softness was layered with a thick coating of derision. 'Even if we had married? An unlikely scenario, Thea, even you must accept.'

Which Thea silently had to admit the truth of. 'Who told you? Who told you the truth of my birth?'

'Eleanor. Who had the interesting details of your little masquerade from your sister, Sarah.'

'From *Sarah*?' Thea attempted to separate the strands of knowledge that were being hurled at her by the man she loved. 'I did not know that my sister was in communication with Eleanor. Is she then in New York?'

'What is the possible relevance of that? Suffice to say that Sarah informed Eleanor of your Baxendale connection.' Nicholas waited a brief, tense moment as Theodora remained silent. 'You have remarkably little to say about it, considering the depths of your deception.'

Which spurred her into reply. 'I do not see that my connection to the Baxendale family has any bearing on what lies between us.' *But I do. I should have told you. Forgive me, Nicholas, forgive me.* She kept her lips pressed firmly together, her head high.

'No? When you must be aware to some degree at least of the damaging scandal that struck my family nearly three years ago at the hands of Edward Baxendale. And yet you thought that it had *no bearing*?' His brows rose beautifully in arrogant disbelief. 'I cannot believe that you were not aware of the gossip. Certainly I cannot believe that Judith has been silent about it.'

Thea shook her head, panic rising at the unexpected viciousness of the attack. 'Judith refused to discuss the matter, claiming that it was not her secret to tell. She was very discreet.' She tried to keep calm, to breathe deeply. How could Nicholas, her love, accuse her of such perfidy?

'Then, if that is so, it must be for the first time in her life.' Nicholas was clearly sceptical of Judith's self-control. 'Tell me, then, Theodora, are you in communication with your brother?'

'I have never met Edward Baxendale.'

'Really? I find that also difficult to believe.' His lip curled in contempt and harsh mockery.

'I do not know him.' She resisted the urge to lift her hands, to plead her innocence. 'I do not lie.'

'Your brother was a past master at the art of deception. Perhaps you, too, have the skill. You were certainly able to take me in with your winning ways and your lovely face.'

'And so you would suspect me of similar sins to those of my brother, simply because we share a blood relationship?' Thea marvelled at her ability to reply with such care when all her instincts were to succumb to the intimations of disaster, which drew the colour from her fair skin.

Nicholas shrugged. The nasty little gesture was as wounding as his words. And Thea, who had been inclined to explain her total innocence, her ignorance of any family connection until only the previous month, decided that she would not. If Nicholas was not prepared to believe her, to accept her word, what point in dragging her family complications into the open? He would take her on trust or not at all.

'I have never met Edward or Sarah Baxendale,' was all that she would say in explanation.

'But you knew of the connection.'

'Yes.'

'Yet you saw fit not to break the interesting news to me. I wish you had told me. Why did you not—if you were innocent of all involvement with your brother?'

'I feared to do so.' Theodora discovered that her control of her emotions was slipping increasingly on a knife edge. 'For so many reasons. Not least that you would reject me if you knew the truth. I tried to end the…the growing closeness between us in London, if you remember. Indeed I did, when I realised that I might be falling in love with you. I thought it best if I could create a distance between us, so that love could never bloom. So that we should never find ourselves in this impossbile situation.' She found a need to dash a stray tear from her cheek with an impatient hand. 'I think I succeeded very well. But then fate brought us together again. I knew beyond doubt that I loved you… And I feared to tell you the truth.'

Nicholas swung away, to prowl to the sideboard, as dangerous and highly tuned as a hunting cat, to pour a glass of brandy, take a long swallow, presenting his back to Thea. The silence stretched between them until she could stand it no longer.

'What did Edward do, Nicholas? Was it so bad, so unforgivable, that it will stand between us for all time?'

'Yes.'

'Why? What happened? No one who knows the true facts will tell me.'

'It is in the past and not something I care to contemplate. Certainly not something I wish to discuss with you.'

'But not sufficiently in the past that it can be forgotten.'

'No. It can never be forgotten.'

So there was the barrier between them. Solid. Bitter. Impossible, Thea realised, to breach.

'So all that we meant to each other is worth nothing in the balance with Edward's sins.'

He turned his head to look at her now. 'Tell me this, Thea. Are you part of a new Baxendale plot? You and your brother working together against us?'

'Of course not.' Seeing the abyss at her feet widen even further, Thea whispered her reply. 'But you do not trust me, do you?'

'I do not know. Perhaps I do not know you as well as I believed.' Blazing anger suddenly sprang into life between them and engulfed the cold. 'If you are an innocent party to this, you would have not left me in ignorance. Have you and Edward rejoiced together over your successes?' The thought fed the flames of his anger with dry tinder. 'Have you and Edward exchanged to your mutual delight the methods by which you might have entrapped me into marriage? What did you hope for, Thea? A financial settlement for yourself, which would benefit your brother? Or merely the pleasure of seeing me wed unknowingly to a Baxendale, perhaps with a suitable and expensive settlement to allow me to escape from such an alliance?'

Before Theodora could react, Nicholas put down the glass, closed the distance between them and pounced with lethal intent. He seized her by her shoulders, wilfully ignoring her sharp cry of surprise and protest, and dragged her into an embrace that contained all the fury and frustrated desire which had built since his reading of the letter. His mouth was hard, ruthless against her soft lips, set to take and ravage, his harsh grasp imprinting the tender skin of her arms.

Thea could do nothing but submit. Simply waited, refusing to struggle.

When he raised his head, but did not release her, there was no softening in his face.

'Is this what you wanted from me? Kisses and commitment?' His eyes burned into hers with savage fire. 'Was this all pretence? Did you feel nothing in my arms but triumph that you had fooled me into believing that you loved me? Damn you, Thea! How could you do it?' He took her lips again, a wild gesture of desperate love and despair. Then let her go, so rapidly that she almost fell, as if he could no longer bear the contact. He stalked away to pick up the brandy once more, and drank.

Then he laughed, a harsh sound in the quiet room. 'The possibilities, it seems, are endless. And none of them pleasant or flattering to either of us.' He took a breath. His voice was now cold, so cold. 'Forgive me. I suppose I should ask your pardon for handling you with such insensitivity.'

Thea listened as if from a great distance, aware only of the desperate hatred that underpinned Nicholas's rage. 'You must hate my brother very much.'

'I do. By God, I do. If indeed you do not know, I suggest that you ask him yourself.' Lord Nicholas showed his teeth in a vicious snarl. 'I am sure that he will be delighted to tell you—but do not wager that very pretty pearl drop that you are wearing around your equally pretty neck on the truth of it.'

'I think I must indeed ask him. If only to see if his version of events tallies with yours. Or perhaps it will prove that you are as vindictive and vengeful as you claim Edward to be.'

'I care not what you discover. You are hardly likely to believe my words over his, are you?'

With which words, words that would effectively destroy any hope for a reconciliation between them, Lord Nicholas Faringdon, always a model of propriety and good manners, discovered that his fury could escape his control. He lifted his arm and flung the glass and the brandy at the wall, where it smashed in a shower of crystal to the floor. The brandy ran stickily down the wood panelling to puddle below.

Thea watched the shards of crystal glitter on the carpet, shocked to the core. But not as outraged as Nicholas himself at the violent reaction that had broken free of his determination to remain cold and calm to the last.

Thea was the one to speak. Her words were very simple and from the heart. They hit home as a more emotional response might not. 'I love you, Nicholas. I cannot believe that you would put your hatred for my brother before your love for me. How shallow your love must be. Perhaps it never existed. It certainly could not stand the test of time.'

'How can you possibly decry my love for you—' he rounded on her, eyes ablaze '—when our whole relationship was based on a deceit? If you had truly loved me, you would have trusted me with your family history. You would not have kept silent on a matter that touches me so personally.'

'And you would have believed in my innocence?' Guilt brought a slight flush to her cheeks, for his words contained a grain of truth—that she had known of the dangers of silence, but had chosen not to tell him. Now she was forced to accept that such reticence was not proof of true love.

'Of course.' A flash of uncertainty might have made him hesitate, but he quickly banished it.

'I think all is plain, my lord.' Thea took the only course that she could see open to her. A step away from him, at the same time taking refuge in rigid formality, very much Sir Hector's daughter. She was now shockingly pale, her skin as colourless as the fine wax candles in their chased silver candelabra on the table beside her. She raised her chin and spoke with chilling hauteur. 'You deem me to be without either honour or veracity, my lord, capable of tricking you into a relationship purely to humiliate and wreak revenge on you. Since you would destroy my character with such unfounded accusations, there is no place for me in your life. I am clearly no longer welcome here. You offered me marriage. I refuse your offer. What a fortunate escape we have both had, to be sure! Now—if you would be so good as to provide a horse for me to ride, I can be gone from your presence and your property within the hour.'

So she would leave, with no further explanation, no need for further association with Lord Nicholas Faringdon.

Nicholas watched her, suddenly struck by the magnitude of the gulf that had widened between them in so short a time. *What am I doing? What am I saying?* She looked shattered. So pale.

So sad. Admiration, albeit reluctant, surged through him that she could stand before him with pride and composure, regardless of his deliberately cruel words and the astounding violence that had reduced him to such a lack of control. He should be whipped for this, his conscience pricked with sharp insistence. What he *should* do was take her in his arms and kiss that desolate mouth into smiling joy. How could she possibly be guilty of the sins that he had laid before her? When she had sighed in his arms, when she had shivered in newly awakened desire beneath him, when she had allowed and welcomed such intimate possession of her body—surely he must be wrong. And deserve to be cursed to the fires of everlasting hell for such insensitive handling of her. But the vicious memories returned with vivid clarity. Edward Baxendale. Smug, self-satisfied, malicious, manipulative. If he could use his wife and his sister Sarah to feed his own ambitions, so he could use Theodora. And, ultimately, Theodora had lied to him. He must not weaken, must not allow his heart to rule his head.

'No. You will not ride.' His response exactly mirrored hers. 'I will provide you with a post chaise and postilions. I do not want your safety or comfort on the journey on my conscience.'

'There is no need for your conscience to be involved.' If Nicholas could be so cold and distant, so could she. 'My welfare is no longer your concern, my lord.'

'You have no choice in the matter, Miss Wooton-Devereux. The coach will be waiting at the front steps, for your convenience within the hour.'

The sooner the better! How dare he make her so indebted to him at the last! 'Then I shall be grateful, for Agnes's sake.' There was not the slightest hint of gratitude in her face or her voice.

Of which Lord Nicholas was made painfully aware.

Theodora turned on her heel and stalked from the room before she, too, was tempted into an action of mindless, uncontrolled violence. To sweep the candles, together with their elegant silver stand, to the carpet, with the flat of her hand.

* * *

As good as his word, Nicholas arranged for a post chaise and four to be ready before the door within the hour. Always the impeccable host and gentleman, he handed the two ladies into it, ordered a fur wrap for their knees, for their comfort from the chill wind. Promised the return of The Zephyr when her sprain had healed sufficiently for her to make the journey. Added two of his own grooms to Thea's two henchmen, to ensure their safe passage. They were instructed to keep their pistols primed and eyes alert for any sign of the Maidens.

Throughout the proceedings, Lord Nicholas was as remote as the chill air quality around them, his self-control held on a tight rein. He did not allow his eyes to meet Thea's, or even to dwell on the expression on her face, afraid of what he might see there. He did not take her hand or kiss her fingers in farewell. His expression remained closed and unemotional throughout the brief leave-taking as if the whole event was a matter of little importance or interest. Thea's remained pale and set. Agnes, painfully aware of every nuance, made all the suitable farewells and necessary statements of gratitude. She did not dare ask her mistress what had occurred to cause this shattering tension between them.

Finally Lord Nicholas bowed with superb grace as the coach departed—then stalked back into the Manor without a backward glance.

The occupants travelled in taut silence for the first half-hour, both ladies pretending to admire the passing scenery. Until Agnes was aware that silent tears had begun to track down Thea's cheeks. She was crying, silently and helplessly.

Agnes sighed. 'He is hurt, Miss Thea.'

'But so am I.' Thea tried to wipe the tears away with one finger. 'Are all men so stubborn and blinkered?'

'I imagine.'

'But not as stubborn as Nicholas Faringdon!' She sniffed and turned her face away. She did not see Agnes narrow her gaze at a particularly fine sweep of woodland carpeted with bluebells.

'It's not my place to say, Miss Thea.'

'Since when did that ever stop you giving an opinion!' The bitterness in Thea's voice was overlaid by a storm of suppressed grief.

'Very well. If you want honesty from me, you should have told him.'

'I know.' An audible sob escaped. 'And now he does not trust me. With no possible evidence of my guilt. Simply because my name is Baxendale.'

Silence.

'It is not fair! And I love him so.'

'I know.' Agnes could find no words of comfort, but her heart ached for the girl whom she had known and cared for since she had come into the family as an unwanted baby, a mere four weeks old. No, it was not fair, but life was not guaranteed to hand out fairness.

'I am sorry I snapped at you, Agnes.' Thea sniffed again and used her handkerchief to great effect. 'I must not weep. It does no good.'

'No.' Agnes hid a little smile. This was more like the Thea she knew.

'I have decided one thing. I need to know the truth.' The lady tucked away the damp linen square and, once composed, turned back to her maid. 'There is only one person who might tell me.'

'So you will go to Sir Edward. Is it wise? Will you get the truth from him?'

Theodora thought for a moment, weighing the possibilities in the balance. 'Why not? I am his sister, after all. Certainly no one else is prepared to tell me what happened between Faringdons and Baxendales. I shall visit Whitchurch on our route to London.'

Thea lapsed into silence again, her thoughts taken up with that final interview between herself and Nicholas. Her emotions tore at her and gave her no rest. Guilt that she had indeed embarked on their relationship on a lie, knowing that she had not told him the truth, even when she had been aware of the dangers in remaining silent. Anger that he should believe in her culpability rather than her innocence. And frustration that he would not tell her why he was so hostile, what it was that Edward had done that was so diabolical.

But mostly it was pain that stole her breath. She loved Nicholas—yet she had lost him. And feared that nothing she could do would ever win him back. All she could see was the condemnation in his face, his eyes dark and stormy as he surveyed her with arrogant disdain, and the desolation was a band around her heart. It was a relief when they arrived in Tenbury Wells, to the surprise but casual acceptance of Cousin Jennifer, where she could retire to her bedchamber and indulge in a private deluge of tears until she could weep no more—for herself, and for Nicholas, caught up in the complicated weavings of a net from which there was no escape.

At Aymestry, denied the luxury of a confidant, Nicholas strode directly from the house to the stables, ordered the saddling of a bay gelding and informed his silent and wary staff that he would be at Burford for the rest of the day. His tone denied the need for anyone to contact him there.

'Will Miss Thea return?' Furness enquired, risking the storm clouds.

'No.'

'Do we send The Zephyr on to London when she is sound?'

'Yes.'

'Do I continue the poultices or do I turn her out into a paddock?'

'Do what ever you wish, Furness. I am sure that you know as well as I how to deal with a lame animal.'

Thus ending any conversation about horses or more personal matters. Nicholas ignored the resulting exchange of knowing glances as he rode the gelding out of the stableyard on a tight rein.

He had, he realised, no intention of going to Burford. He simply rode, hard and fast, allowing his fresh mount its head as they hit the rising ground through the park. But there was no joy in it. Anything to rid his mind of Thea's face when she had finally walked from his library, pale as the most delicate of magnolia blossoms, her expressive eyes veiled by a deliberate downsweep of thick lashes. Was it anguish from a broken heart that had brought the tension to her face, or was it shame that she had tricked him into a fraudulent relationship? How could he possibly know!

At the brow of the hill, he finally drew the gelding to a halt to look out over the acres of Aymestry to where they marched with Burford, usually a scene to soothe his heart. But today he found no satisfaction in it. He had last ridden these lanes and pastures, the shady woodland rides and the path beside the lake, with Thea. Now she had destroyed all his enjoyment in it, the pleasure in its possession and his peace of mind. And he missed her. He wanted her. His loins and his heart ached with the loss of her.

Lord Nicholas cursed fluently and long. He had known that there was some secret, some matter that had presented a barrier between them. But never this. What a stupid fool he had been, to give his heart into the keeping of a woman who, with cruel hindsight, was so clearly not what she seemed and bent on mischief. So much for love! When he married it would be for convenience, a wife to run his household, entertain his guests and carry his heirs. No emotions involved, nothing beyond a mild affection and tolerance. Henry was free to enjoy his grand passion with Eleanor. A cool calm friendship would do very well for him.

Lord Nicholas fervently hoped that he would never again have the misfortune to set eyes on Sophia Mary Baxendale.

Chapter Eleven

Thea was bowed into the entrance hall of the Great House in Whitchurch by an elderly servant who shuffled off to discover the whereabouts of Sir Edward Baxendale, leaving the lady to look about her. It was a lovely old house with mellow stone and graciously symmetrical lines of Jacobean origin. The main staircase and the wooden panelling was imposing enough, but gave the impression of faded grandeur. The house had seen better days. There was heavy dust on the table and settle beside her and the fireplace had not been swept of the debris of any number of fires. Curtains at the windows were worn and faded from an assault by the sun over the years. Outside the ornamental hedges were untidy and unclipped and the hinges of the wrought-iron gates were in need of repair. It spoke of a lack of servants. Thea suspected a lack of money.

But for her the most important, the most astounding, thought was that this was the house where she had been born and spent the first four weeks of her life. How strange it was to return here—and under such circumstances. How strange it would be to meet her brother for the first time in her life that she could recall. Nerves raised a shiver of disquiet along her arms. If her brother was prepared to discuss the Faringdon scandal with her, what would it reveal? And could she trust him to speak the truth?

'I remember nothing of this.'

Agnes saw the nerves and touched her young mistress's hand with light fingers. 'You would not, of course. Don't fret, Miss Thea. You must use your own judgement—whether what you will hear in this house is true or false.'

Which did nothing to ease Theodora's anxieties.

The servant returned to show her into a room that looked out over a walled garden to the rear. She sat and waited, determined to retain her composure and her impartiality. Then the door opened and a gentleman entered with quiet dignity. The first impressions for Thea were undoubtedly pleasing. Not over tall, but compact and well muscled. Fair haired with clear, friendly blue eyes, he was clad in a double-breasted coat, breeches and boots suitable for any country gentlemen, of good quality but with no extremes of fashion. His figure was good, elegant even, as was his address.

Sir Edward Baxendale. Her brother.

Yes. An attractive man, but Thea kept her council, and her expression and greeting cool. She did not know him.

Sir Edward came to a halt before her and inclined his head in gracious welcome. So this was his sister. After all these years. He had almost forgotten her very existence. Lady Drusilla had seen to that!

'Sir Edward.'

'Miss Wooton-Devereux.' With a smile as warm as the sunshine that flooded the room, he raised her hand to his lips. 'Or may I call you Theodora? If I may say—you have the look of our mother. She, too, was acknowledged to be a beauty as a young girl.'

'I did not know that.' Thea allowed a light smile in response, but remained aloof and wary. There was much that she needed to learn about Sir Edward Baxendale.

'Please sit.' He motioned to the chair from which she had just risen. 'Allow me to give you a glass of claret. I am sure that refreshment after your journey will be acceptable.'

He poured and handed her a glass, but after thanking him she placed it untouched on the table.

Edward eyed her with mild curiosity as he lowered himself to a chair beside her, close enough for easy conversation, but not so as to be an imposition. 'To what do I owe the pleasure, Theodora? I had believed that our relationship was past mending and so have done nothing to make contact with you. My mother and Lady Drusilla had nothing to say to each other. I did not even know that you were aware of the connection between us. And now here you are in Whitchurch…'

'I was ignorant of our relationship until some weeks ago. Lady Drusilla saw no necessity to tell me.'

'Ah. But she did finally.'

'Yes.'

'May I be permitted to ask why?' Sir Edward's manner betrayed nothing but a mild interest—and perhaps a sensitivity for so difficult an occasion.

'That is of no consequence.'

'Very well.' He accepted her reluctance with apparent equanimity. 'So why *are* you here today?' He watched her. Thinking rapidly, he noted the sheen of wealth, of the confidence of the rich and privileged, of high fashion. It immediately caught his interest. Here was a lady who could be of use to him. A very useful weapon, although in what manner he was not yet sure. Why had he not thought of this connection before? It would be wise to be open to any opportunity that might present itself from this unlooked-for conversation.

Equally, Theodora took a keen assessment of her brother. A gentleman, certainly. With, according to the little she had heard, a vast catalogue of unidentified sins. He looked pleasant and affable, with open features and a ready smile. Nothing sly or untrustworthy to prick her instincts. But whether he would tell her the truth, she had no idea.

'I am given to understand, Sir Edward, that I also have a sister.'

'Why, yes, indeed. Sarah.'

'Does she live near? Can I meet her?'

'Forgive me, my dear.' He rose to refill his glass, looking back at her over his shoulder. There was true regret in his voice.

'I no longer know where she resides. Sarah married a naval man against the family wishes. Not an advantageous marriage or, I believe, a happy one for my sister. Unfortunately he lacked good family and connections. Sarah, I am loathe to admit, has chosen no longer to communicate with us—despite encouragement from me. She has a child, I think. But more than that…' He shrugged as he returned to his chair and lifted his glass to his lips.

Leaving Thea with little choice but to broach the subject that had brought her to Whitchurch.

'It has come to my knowledge, sir, that there was some…unpleasantness…between the Baxendales and the Marquis of Burford. I have come here hoping to discover the truth.'

'Ah!' *The Faringdons. So that was the issue! Now, how was his sister possibly linked with the Faringdons? It would be well to have a care.* 'So that old scandal has reared its head. I had hoped for Octavia's sake that it had died a death.' A tightening of the lips was the only emotion Sir Edward allowed himself to betray.

'Octavia?'

'My dear wife. You can meet her soon. She has gone into the village on an errand of mercy.'

'I would like that.' Thea could detect nothing but concern in her brother. 'Will you tell me?'

'What is it you wish to know?'

'I would know what the issue is between you and the Faringdons.'

'Very well. We never speak of it now, as you will soon understand—but I will tell you. As a close member of family, perhaps you should know the truth.' Sir Edward leaned back, crossing one elegantly booted leg over the other. 'Tell me, are you acquainted with any members of the Faringdon family? We rarely socialize, so I am not aware…'

'Yes. A little.'

So there was something here. Perhaps something that he could use to their detriment—and his satisfaction.

'Lord Nicholas, perhaps? Or the Countess of Painscastle? If

you have moved in the first circles in London—as I am sure you have—I expect that you will have been introduced.'

'We have been introduced.' Thea watched her brother. Again, nothing in his manner to disturb her, to make her aware of the direction of her brother's calculations, the sudden explosion of insight, the chance of a sharp thrust of revenge for past injuries. And if there happened to be an understanding between Lord Nicholas and his sister…well, it would please Sir Edward greatly to destroy any chance of happiness there. As for this sister who sat so confidingly before him, he had no feelings for her, did not know her. Envied her, of course. She had enjoyed an easy, wealthy life of luxury and comfort, whilst they at Whitchurch… He owed her nothing! It would not hurt him to apply a gentle twist to a knife buried to its hilt in her hopes and dreams of love. Miss Wooton-Devereux deserved nothing from him! He smiled at Thea, all warmth and brotherly concern. He would sow a few bitter seeds, then wait and see what the harvest would bring. All carefully masked behind those smiling blue eyes, guaranteed to ease Thea's doubts. So he began his tissue of lies, as skilfully woven as cloth of the finest quality.

'It is not a comfortable tale and I beg that you will not discuss it in the hearing of Octavia. You will soon appreciate why. But these are the bones of it. Thomas, Marquis of Burford, promised Octavia marriage in the year when she was presented for a Season in London. He courted her most assiduously. She was impressionable and young, overawed by his wealth and his title—and his handsome face, of course. He seduced her and left her carrying his child.'

Edward took a sip of claret as if to removed an unpleasant taste from his mouth.

'Forgive me. It still brings me pain. The Marquis then reneged on his promise, refused to recognise the child as his own and cast her off. He married Eleanor Stamford instead.' His lips sneered.

'I see. But why?' Thea felt her heart soften towards the unknown Octavia. 'Why did he not marry Octavia?'

'Simple enough. Because although she was gently born, he

claimed that her birth was not good enough, not *appropriate* for a Marchioness of Burford. She was good enough for him to seduce!' His bitterness on behalf of the lady won Thea's acceptance.

'So what happened to Octavia?'

'I knew Octavia—had known her from her girlhood.' His lips now curled a little in a smile at the memory. 'I married her to protect her name and give the child a home and a father. When the child was born I applied to the Marquis for financial recompense for Octavia's sufferings—and for the child, of course. We were refused and threatened with a court case against us if we persisted. I did persist.' Sir Edward shook his head in apparent disbelief. 'It seemed so wrong that the Faringdons should be able to reject so innocent a lady as Octavia. I took her to Burford Hall, with the child, to beg for restitution. By then the Marquis had died and matters were in the hands of his brother, Lord Henry. We were faced by the united Faringdons. Can you imagine the humiliation? Yes, they listened to what I had to say—and then promptly turned us from the door. Denied any involvement or proof of the child's paternity. Accused me of being a charlatan and Octavia—well, there is no need to explain what the implications were of her. It would be too shaming to resurrect such words as we heard that day from the lips of Lord Henry Faringdon. Enough to say, they would have destroyed our credibility in society if we had pursued the matter further.'

'I did not realise…' Theodora found her thoughts almost paralysed with shock at this appalling situation, concerning a lady who was, after all, her sister-in-law.

'It is not a flattering picture, I am afraid.' Edward's gaze was sharp and bright on his sister's face, but full of compassion.

'No, indeed. It is…it is a disaster!'

'I am sorry if it distresses you—' *now, how will she react!* '—if perhaps you had a…an understanding with Lord Nicholas?'

'No. I…'

Thea fought to bring her thoughts into some form of order. This dreadful tale of deliberate, wilful cruelty to an innocent young girl. Could Henry and Nicholas Faringdon have behaved with such callous insensitivity and selfishness? Surely she could not have been so mistaken in the man to whom she had so willingly and joyfully given her heart.

'Could I ask,' Sir Edward broke into her despair, 'what have the Faringdons said about the affair?'

She does not know the truth. She will accept anything I say!

'I could not discover the truth,' Thea confirmed to Edward's satisfaction. 'Neither Judith—nor Lord Nicholas—was willing to discuss it. I believed it was to shield the name and reputation of Eleanor, but perhaps…'

'What could they say that would not be shaming to themselves?' Edward gently increased the pain. 'They acted with complete ignominy. Octavia was better off out of their clutches.'

Thea drew in a deep breath. It all seemed so horribly possible. 'And the baby?'

'A son.' Edward acknowledged. 'Unfortunately it died. We—Octavia and I—have never had the felicity to have more children.' His lowered lashes hid any grief.

'I am very sorry, sir…'

'I, too, am sorry if it brings you pain, Theodora, but it is better that you know the truth. The Faringdons were arrogant and unfeeling, with no thought for a poor wronged girl who was preyed upon, who was robbed of her youth and innocence. I fear that Octavia has never recovered her spirit or her pure enjoyment of life. She lives in shadows, fearful and suspicious of all—other than myself.'

So there it was. Or Edward Baxendale's version of it. As Thea sat and studied her brother's face, the sorrow and concern that she could read there, it came to her that there was no reason for her not to believe the wretched tale she had just heard. But it was a terrible indictment of Nicholas and the whole Faringdon family. Anger simmered. If it were true, how humiliating it was that she had failed so completely in her judgement of human nature, had fallen in love with someone who in effect did not exist. The Nicholas she knew—caring, careful and concerned for the feelings and welfare of others—did not match this terrible portrait painted by her brother. How could she have been so wrong, have misjudged him so completely? How could she have given herself to a man who could treat a defenceless and needy woman with so little respect? *But was it all true?*

Edward watched the uncertainties flit across his sister's face and worked to preserve a bland appearance. So far, so good.

'Listen.' He stood and stretched out a hand to bring Thea to her feet. 'That will be Octavia. Now you can meet her—my very dear wife.'

So Theodora met the lady in question. A fair lady, slender almost to the point of thinness, with pale eyes that seemed reluctant to rest for long. Pretty enough, but the fine lines in the delicate skin of her face suggested a life touched with grief, perhaps nervous strain. Yet she responded to her husband with real affection and made Theodora welcome.

Thea did not stay long. She soon discovered that Octavia had little to say beyond a comment on the weather or the state of her rose arbours. Thea could well believe Octavia having been a victim. She was as insubstantial as a sunbeam on a winter's day. Yet her situation demanded sympathy. Her loss and her rejection by one whom she thought had loved her—a Faringdon—must have been hard indeed.

Thea made her farewells and felt the similarity of rejection with bitter pain.

'It would please me if you would keep in touch with us here in the country,' Sir Edward invited as Thea stood in the hall, preparing to depart. 'We do not go into society. Times are hard with us.' He hoped a slick of guilt would attack the lady's conscience. 'I congratulate you on your good fortune. Life has blessed you, with Sir Hector and Lady Drusilla.'

'It has. I must be grateful.' The comparisons between their lifestyles touched her with discomfort. As intended.

'Octavia would much enjoy your visits. To hear of events in London. We have few acquaintance who stay in town.' Sir Edward smiled again, the perfect host, the deadliest of enemies.

Thea made a non-committal reply as she curtsied her farewell. Edward kissed her hand and her cheek.

'Well?' Agnes Drew enquired as they were once more embarked on their journey and Thea showed little inclination to break the silence.

The lady sighed and turned her head. 'I do not know! I simply don't know.'

'Was it what you had hoped for?'

'No. It was worse than I could possibly have imagined.'

'Hmm. But can you trust Sir Edward? You do not know him.'

'I do not know that either.'

'And Lord Nicholas? After all, you *do* know him, Miss Thea.'

Yes. I thought I loved him. I still do. But is he a man worthy of my love? Sir Edward has cast all into doubt.

Life at Burford Hall and Aymestry Manor followed inexorably the demands of the changing seasons. Enough to occupy Nicholas, enough to fill his mind with the day-to-day affairs of running two estates and planning for the future. Enough to distract his thoughts from a blighted love affair, the final ending of which should have been a matter for rejoicing. But when he rode beneath the dripping beeches in a heavy shower, he sensed her beside him. When he rose from a troubled sleep at early light or took himself to bed—alone!—with dreams that teased and haunted him. Nicholas cursed and informed himself that Theodora WootonDevereux no longer had a niche in his life. Unfortunately he discovered, long forgotten in a coat pocket, a little diamond-and-sapphire brooch, which forced him to remember how he had removed it in the soft twilight of the stable and kissed its owner into shocked delight. For a moment he watched it catch the light with rare brilliance, then pushed it out of sight, too painful a talisman. There was no need for him to spend one second in a day in thinking of her. It would all get better with time.

It did not.

* * *

The most urgent business to confront him was the matter of the Maidens. Some days after Thea's departure, he rode into Leominster to meet with his fellow JPs at the Talbot, to discover with no surprise that the rural unrest was to be the main subject of discussion. The Maidens, with their skirts and scarves, their vociferous complaints, were extending their demands and their range of operation. Lewis Bates was still recognised as the leading voice, but the name of Samuel Dyer came often to the fore, particularly when the event involved more violence or threats of retribution than had emerged in the past. Almost every JP had some tale to tell of their activity. More old ricks had been burnt— not a great matter in itself, but a symptom of the disruption that they all understood. Two of the gentlemen making inroads into the port at the Talbot had received threatening letters, badly written but clear in their intent if the landlords did not answer their demands. Sir Thomas Clifford over towards Kingsland had suffered an actual attack on his house, forcing him to barricade his doors and windows to safeguard his wife and young family, until his neighbour could arrive and help drive the mob of drunken, swaggering labourers from their entrenched positions.

The demands were simple and clear, exacerbated by the poor harvest in the previous year and the cool spring, but there was no immediate remedy for the hunger sweeping the countryside beyond the setting up of soup kitchens, which most landlords were prepared to do. As for the desired lower rents and higher wages, it was an individual matter for each landlord. Lord Westbourne, as might have been expected, had no intention of giving in to the rabble at his doors. Nicholas winced at his lordship's forthright condemnation of his estate workers. Any attempts to ease the local suffering would receive no aid in that quarter. For himself, Nicholas arranged a meeting with his agent to see what could be done for those Faringdon tenants hardest hit. Meanwhile, the gentlemen of Herefordshire discussed the wisdom of calling out the local militia if news of further riots reached them.

For a short time, it gave considerable direction to Nicholas's thoughts.

* * *

'Well, Theodora. Sir Hector and I thought that you had abandoned us for good. I had no idea that you would find Cousin Jennifer's company so entertaining or Tenbury Wells so attractive.' Lady Drusilla regarded her daughter with close and critical attention on her eventual and belated return to Upper Brook Street.

'Cousin Jennifer liked to reminisce,' Thea informed her mother as she took a seat in that lady's boudoir and steeled herself to withstand the probing questions in the inevitable cross-examination. She had been dispatched to Herefordshire for a few days—which had mysteriously and inexplicably transformed themselves into weeks.

'She must have done. Apparently you were captivated.'

Thea ignored the dry comment, kept her lips curved into some semblance of pleasure and merely folding her hands in her lap expectantly. She must keep her wits sharp if her mother were to remain in ignorance.

'And The Zephyr. I understand that she is not with you. Why did you not bring her home?'

'A minor sprain. Some of the roads and tracks in the area of Tenbury Wells were very uneven. She will be sent on when fit again.'

'Did you enjoy the visit?'

'Yes.'

'Country life?'

'Very…ah, relaxing.'

So why do you give the impression that you are neither sleeping nor eating well? And avoiding my questions!

'And the scenery?'

'Very pretty.'

'Hmm.' Lady Drusilla clasped a chain of sapphires around her neck, watching her daughter through the mirror with narrowed eyes. 'What did you find to do in all this pretty scenery that gave you so much enjoyment?'

'What one does in the English countryside at this time of year, I expect—walk, ride, read a little on wet days, converse with Cousin Jennifer.' Thea studied her fingernails in rapt concentration.

'It sounds fascinating.'

'Yes.'

'I see.' Lady Drusilla tapped her fingers on the dressing table. Thea was as tight-lipped as an oyster, but something had occurred. Something momentous. She looked well enough, perhaps a little distracted. Tense also, by the evidence of her fingers, which she had now clenched into admirable fists as she tried to keep her mama at bay. In good health—although Thea was rarely otherwise—but with no bloom, no sparkle. And not sleeping well. The lady frowned at her daughter's image. Lady Drusilla would try again.

'Agnes had a fall, I understand.'

'Indeed. A broken bone in her wrist.' For the first time a little anxiety touched Thea's carefully bland expression. 'But it was set with great skill and now Agnes says that she suffers no pain, although it is still stiff, of course. She insisted that she was fit to travel and seems to have no lasting ill effects.'

'And the bruise to her temple? Was that acquired on the same occasion?'

'Yes.'

'So how did poor Agnes come by these unfortunate injuries?'

The reply came with the swiftness of truth—or a carefully-thought-out plan of evasion. Lady Drusilla had no doubt which of the two 'The paving stones in Cousin Jennifer's garden were uneven and slippery after a shower of rain. It was a most unexpected accident. Cousin Jennifer was quite anxious.'

I imagine! 'I see.' Lady Drusilla gave up on her daughter, but determined to have a detailed conversation with Agnes Drew.

But Agnes with an eye to her mistress's fine-drawn features, and her knowledge of the sleepless nights that caused Thea to prowl her bedchamber in the early hours, kept her own council. No point in worrying Lady Drusilla and drawing Thea into that lady's line of fire. And of course Agnes could say with all honesty that she herself had never been to Burford Hall in her life.

So Thea entered once more into the round of pleasure offered by the London Season with apparent enthusiasm and carefree enjoyment. She was soon seen riding in Hyde Park, early in the morning and also at the hour of the fashionable promenade, although not on her usual grey mare. Sometimes she could be met when tooling her mother along the open carriageways in a smart tilbury with a fine highstepping bay gelding between the shafts. The deluge of invitations for the returned débutante ensured that she graced any number of parties, soirées and drums. The Exhibition at the Royal Academy found her in attendance with Lady Beatrice Faringdon and the Countess of Painscastle, who had welcomed her back with easy affection and a deep concern. She danced until dawn and waltzed at Almack's with the Earl of Moreton, that particular gentleman both flattered and entranced by the return of the lady who had engaged his affections—Thea soon found herself the unwelcome recipient of flowers, books, a fine pair of gloves.

And could not but be overcome by a sharp guilt that she should be encouraging so honest a gentleman when her heart was in the keeping of another.

Lady Drusilla saw events moving in the exact direction that she had hoped and prayed for. Lord Nicholas Faringdon was fortunately no longer the object of Theodora's affections. He had not been seen in town for some time and there was no suggestion that he would return. Meanwhile Theodora's mama would wager any money that the Earl would declare himself within the month—in excellent time for them to arrange a most fashionable marriage before she and Sir Hector went on to St Petersburg. Thea would be well settled at last. Thus she informed Sir Hector of the delightful prospect, waving aside any objections when he expressed his undoubted satisfaction, but hoped that his wife would be kind enough to consider the state of his purse strings.

And Thea resigned herself. She liked the Earl well enough. Without doubt he would prove to be a most attractive and generous husband to satisfy the demands of all but the most exacting of young ladies. But the Earl's face was not the face that troubled her dreams and robbed her of her appetite. His voice was not the one to shiver over her skin when she remembered his words of love and desire. The sight of his distant figure in a ballroom or at a reception did not bring an instant flush of warm colour to her cheeks. And his presence was not the one to steal her breath—or reduce her to burning indignation against all self-opinionated, arrogant and impossible members of the male sex.

If the interested household at Aymestry Manor considered Lord Nicholas to be a man in torment, they would not have been in any way surprised to discover that *that* was exactly the opinion formed by the Countess of Painscastle when she met Nicholas later in the month in Grosvenor Square. Judith eyed him speculatively as he descended the steps of the Faringdon town house and approached where she stood on her own doorstep, having returned from a visit to Lady Beatrice. She sent her nursemaid on into the house with the baby and waited. Judith had not thought that Nicholas was back in town. Although no one could have faulted his bow or his general address when he halted before her, he did not look entranced by the prospect of a few days in London society—or the pleasure of her own company, for that matter. Indeed, his lips were set in an uncompromising line and his eyes did not smile. After a few weeks of Thea's brittle companionship, Judith believed that she knew the reason why.

What on earth is wrong with you two?

Since she knew that she would get a short answer if she asked the question of either of them, she decided to try a little cousinly manoeuvring.

'Nicholas. I did not know you were in town.' She gave him her kid-gloved hand to kiss and beamed at him, ignoring his lack of response. 'Does Mama know?'

'No. This is not a social visit.'

'Oh, business!' She wrinkled her nose. 'I am entertaining next week. Will you come?'

'No.'

'So what has happened to ruffle your feathers, Nick?'

'Nothing other than a trivial misunderstanding.'

'Oh.' *A trivial misunderstanding, indeed!* Judith was not getting far here. She would try another tack.

'Why are you here? What has dragged you away from Burford?' She tapped his arm before he could respond. 'Do try for more than a yes or no this time, dear Nicholas!'

At last he smiled. 'Forgive me, Judith. I am ill humoured, but you should not have to suffer the consequences. I have been to Tattersalls. Horses for sale, you understand.'

'Ah.' *Perfect!* 'Then you must come and talk to Simon. I believe he will part with his winning mare at last if the price is right.'

'I may just do that.'

'He's over at Painscastle at present'—and Nicholas was not to know that the Earl was probably sitting in the library here in Grosvenor Square with his feet comfortably propped on a footstool and a glass of burgundy in his hand—'but will be here tomorrow. Come in the afternoon. We will have tea and you can tell me what makes you such dismal company.'

Nicholas winced at the prospect. 'I believe that we can find something more entertaining to discuss. But, yes, I will be there.'

So now all Judith needed to do was to ensure that Simon be elsewhere (for there would be no opportunity for the discussion of horseflesh, if Judith had any say in the matter) and that Thea present herself for tea at exactly the same time as Nicholas arrived. Surely all the pair of them needed to do was to meet in relaxed surroundings where they could talk and sort out their differences. Two intelligent and attractive individuals who anyone could see were meant for each other. And once they had decided that the estrangement between them was not so serious as could not be remedied, then they would surely forgive her for interfering in their private affairs.

Besides, Judith decided as her worried gaze followed Nicholas to the entrance to the square, she was willing to risk all if it would wipe away the bleak unhappiness in their eyes when they thought no one was looking!

* * *

If they can only meet again.

Judith paced her withdrawing room on the afternoon of the following day, awaiting her two guests, who still lived in blissful ignorance of her devious intent.

I am certain all can be mended.

She was certain of no such thing. Theodora was undoubtedly enjoying the gratification of being one of the most sought-after débutantes of the Season. Her stamina was remarkable. But sometimes, when thinking herself unobserved, she was so sad. As if her heart was cold within her breast, untouched by the compliments and flattery, weighed down by its own secret sorrow. As for Nicholas! The expression on his face the previous day, before he noted his cousin watching him, had been both preoccupied and grave, austere even. Judith had never seen him look so *distant*.

She shook her head, refusing to accept the estrangement. All they needed was an opportunity to talk undisturbed. Which she had duly arranged. Now it was up to them. So why did she feel so uneasy? She had plotted the visit, in close discussion with her butler. Simon was instructed to be anywhere but Grosvenor Square for the duration of the afternoon. Thea was not to be announced, but instead allowed to come up alone as a close friend might, which would give Nicholas no chance to think of excuses to neither see nor speak to the lady. Unless he was prepared to forgo good manners and beat a retreat. Most unlikely!

What could possibly go wrong?

Nicholas arrived promptly as arranged. Relaxed, amiable, charming, somewhat more forthcoming than on the previous day, he put himself out to entertain and indulge Judith in her love of gossip. But the shadows were still present to add a gloss of maturity to his features. Judith found herself glancing towards the door, her fingers clasped tightly in her lap to still their fidgeting.

'Expecting someone, Ju?'

'Why, no.'

'Simon, perhaps? As that *was* the purpose of this visit, if you remember.' Nicholas smiled indulgently, having no confidence in his cousin's powers of recall.

'Simon should be here within the half-hour,' Judith assured him with a discreet lowering of lashes. 'I advised him most strictly.'

A light knock sounded. At last! Judith silently cursed the deep flush that rose to her cheeks, to contrast with her russet curls. The door opened.

'Your butler was very accommodating this afternoon, Judith. He told me to come up and announce myself. Perhaps he no longer disapproves quite so—'

Theodora came to an abrupt halt just inside the door. A delectable picture in a deep blue velvet spencer and silk bonnet trimmed with matching flowers and ribbons, her hands encased in a little sable muff against the chill breeze outside. It was nothing to the instant chill in the room. All the vivacity in her face fled, as if a bright candle had been snuffed out. The blood drained from her fair skin, leaving her pale, almost fragile.

'Why, Thea—' Judith jumped to her feet, her voice a little breathless '—is it not delightful? Look who has just come to town.'

Beside her, Nicholas, too, rose to his feet. It was impossible to read any expression there.

'My lord.' Thea inclined her head a very little. She did not smile. It was almost as if she were holding her breath.

'Miss Wooton-Devereux.' Nicholas executed a perfect bow, equally controlled. Equally severe.

And that was the end of their communication. Judith found herself standing between them, taken aback by the bleak divide.

'Thea…' Judith swallowed and launched in to her prepared speech '…Nicholas has just been telling me that he intended to call—'

'I am quite certain that Lord Nicholas told you no such thing.'

Judith stammered to a halt. 'But I know that—'

'No, Judith. I know for a fact that Lord Nicholas has no intention of renewing his acquaintance with me. He has made the decision, and kindly informed me of it, that I am quite beneath his notice—my birth, my morals and my family all conspire against me. How strange that I was not previously aware of it.'

Judith looked desperately to Nicholas for help. Surely this could not be true!

'I am amazed,' Thea continued, 'that Lord Nicholas has not apprised you of my many sins. I expect that he would not consider me fit to be your friend.'

'No, Miss Wooton-Devereux, I have not in any way broached the matter to which you refer.' Now Nicholas intervened in clipped tones, to come to Judith's rescue, but not in any manner likely to reassure her of a mere trivial misunderstanding that might be healed—or to soothe the decidedly angry lady before him. 'It would be beneath my dignity to discuss with anyone such an unfortunate situation as developed between us.' He bowed again with magnificent disdain.

'*Unfortunate situation?* If that is how you wish to continue to read it…' Thea raised her brows, hostility in every line of her body.

'I have no reason to read it differently. Our differences are plain. And nothing, as far as I am aware, has occurred since we last communicated to cast a more acceptable light on them.'

Thea concentrated on breathing. Could this be the lover who had held and kissed her? Who had declared his love and desire in so splendid a fashion that she would willingly cast all caution to the winds and lay naked in his arms?

'I have not lied to you, my lord.' All she could do was to repeat her previous assertions. 'I have done nought with the intention of causing you any harm.'

'So you say.'

'I do. And I took your ill-timed advice. I have been to Whitchurch. I now have reason to see the…the *unfortunate situation* between us very differently.'

There was a little pause in the room, the tension close to snapping point with Judith still looking from one to the other in unabashed horror. Was this really happening in her withdrawing room?

'So you have been to see him! It does not surprise me.' Nicholas's smile was cold and hard and bitter.

'Yes. I told you that I would.'

'And he told you *his* version of events.'

'He told me how he interpreted the events that occurred between you, between his family and yours. Since you will not discuss it, my lord, I have to take his word on trust. I have no evidence to prove him either a liar or a charlatan. I should tell you that his description of events does not flatter the actions taken by you or by your brother.'

She ignored the gasp from Judith.

'It would not, of course.' A sneer curled Nicholas's mouth. 'And you will believe it.'

It felt to Thea that she was struggling through deep, dark water, swirling weeds grasping at her limbs to drag her down even deeper. Was there no way out of this morass of accusation and counter-accusation, when her heart cried out for one word of love from him, one softened look of sympathy and acceptance? Yet she kept her spine straight, her chin raised. She would not weaken before him.

'Whatever happened in the past, does not involve me—has never involved me. I did nothing to bring harm to you or to those you love.'

'Your family name is harm enough.' There it was again. The simple statement of indisputable fact that would separate them irrevocably, whatever arguments Thea could find to use in her own defence. It was hopeless.

So be it. She forced her cold lips to form the words.

'Since you continue to distrust me, my lord, to misrepresent my actions, to reject all that was said and promised between us, there is little point in me remaining here.'

'Thea…' He almost stretched out a hand to her. For an instant Nicholas thought, although of course he must be mistaken, that there was a sheen of tears in Thea's beautiful eyes.

'No.' She blinked the forbidden moisture away. Definitely mistaken! 'You have explained your position with perfect clarity. I understand and accept.'

'Thea, listen…' Forcing herself into action at last, Judith

would have taken hold of her hand to pull her forward into the room. 'Don't go like this—let me—' Anything to prevent her leaving in this fashion. Judith had no doubt at all of the hastily disguised sparkle of tears.

'No. Forgive me, Judith, if I do not stay.' The composure was quickly back in place, grief sternly governed. 'Mama is expecting me. And then I have an engagement to visit Kew Gardens with Lord Moreton. I am sure you will accept my apologies. And for bringing so much unpleasantness into your home.'

'If you must, of course...' Judith frowned her distress.

'My lord.' A frigid little curtsy in his direction from Miss Theodora Wooton-Devereux, all formal protocol, gained by years of experience in the Royal Courts of Europe. It was a masterpiece. 'Perhaps you will explain to your cousin the futility in setting up any future meeting between us.'

She hesitated at the door, turned back. And looked at him once more, her clear gaze holding his. Her voice was low, but she spoke without hesitation. No one could doubt her sincerity. It shook Nicholas to the core as the words struck home. 'I loved you, Nicholas. You are the only man I ever loved. It hurts me—and my pride—to discover that you are just one of those arrogant Faringdons who will ride roughshod over any who do not measure up to your superior notions or opinions of your social rank and status. It is a damnable situation.' She did not even wince at borrowing from Sir Hector's vocabulary. 'You broke my heart, Nicholas. And I did not deserve it.'

And she left the room. Her firm footsteps echoed down the polished treads of the staircase, followed by the echo of soft voices as she addressed Agnes Drew in the entrance hall.

'What?' Judith found her voice at least and wheeled to face her cousin, accusation in every gesture. 'What did she mean—about her birth—her family? Surely there is no question over her birth. She would seem entirely suitable for a Faringdon bride.' She fisted her hands on her hips, looking remarkably like Lady Beatrice. 'I understood barely half of that! What have you done to her, Nicholas? And when? Surely you have not seen her since you left town last? What can you possibly have said to her?' She lifted her hands and let them fall in frustration. 'In fact, I don't understand *any* of this!' she amended.

Nicholas flung away to the window to see Theodora walk out of the Square, Agnes in attendance, no hint of the ravaged emotions that tore at her in her graceful deportment and proud carriage of her head. He remembered the words she had used, the deliberate tense. She had *loved* him. And he had destroyed that love. Deliberately and effectively. Because she was a Baxendale. He should have felt satisfied, relieved that he had escaped the clutches of that accursed family. But in so doing he had hurt her, which rent his own heart to rags. His fingers clenched round the delicate jewelled circle still in his pocket. He should have restored it to her. What possible reason had he to keep it from her? But he could not. It was the only reminder that he loved Theodora and had once believed that she loved him. He turned his head away from the sight of her, his reactions more than a little compromised.

And he turned on Judith, the nearest target on which to vent his anger. 'Why in God's name do you instantly consider me to be at fault?'

'She was so unhappy, Nicholas.'

'And I, I suppose, am rejoicing?' All the icy control was gone. Judith watched the stormy emotions. Oh, yes, he loved her. He wore his passion for Theodora like a dark cloak, all embracing, shrouding all other emotions.

'No. You are not,' she admitted in softer tones. 'But how could you bear to see her leave like that? Your words were so cruel. I would not have thought it of you, Nicholas.'

'It has to be. There are circumstances here of which you know nothing. Let it go, Judith. And learn from this distressing situation. It will be as well if you do not interfere—don't, for God's sake, try to bring us together again—for my sake and for Theodora's.'

'But I was so certain that you liked each other,' Judith persisted, guilt-ridden that she might have caused even more distress. 'More than liked—if you could only get over whatever separates you. Do let me talk to Thea. I thought you loved Thea, Nicholas. I still think it. I think that you have lost your heart to her completely.'

'Ha!' The laugh was harsh and brief, a mere baring of gritted teeth. 'Perhaps I have. But no—' as Judith's face lit with hope '—don't get involved. It is beyond healing. You must accept it— and allow us to have our secrets. What is there to be gained by going over the same rough ground again and again? I am tired of it all.' And indeed she saw the pale shade of exhaustion around his mouth, the disillusion and regret.

And on that bleak pronouncement, he left, for once no easy companionship between the two.

Judith was left to ponder the results of her meddling. So much hurt and anguish. And yet, when Thea had entered the room, such fire between them. It had leapt to bridge the space, burning all before it. If that were not love…! But then the flames had been extinguished, ground into ashes beneath, it would seem, Nicholas's careless and cruel heel. Judith was forced to consider that there was indeed no hope. No future. And she grieved for her cousin and her friend. Because without doubt there was a passion there that had been wilfully rejected, for what reason she did not know and could not guess.

Chapter Twelve

Some days later Judith woke to a familiar cloud of dark depression. She sat in her bed with her cup of hot chocolate, blind to the attractive picture she made against the pale green furnishings, finding no pleasure in her plans for the day ahead. The brief but explosive liaison between Nicholas and Thea was at an end. She had finally to accept it, still shocked by the anger and bitter recriminations that had assaulted her ears. Furthermore, Judith was now sworn never to interfere again. And even if she did, what possible hope was there?

She sighed at the collapse of all her planning. But Thea would become the Countess of Moreton in the fullness of time. And Nicholas would probably marry some hunting squire's daughter with no fashion sense or desire for town life.

How depressing!

As she placed her cup and saucer on her nightstand to pick up a sheaf of invitations, her depression was interrupted by her personal maid.

'My lady…'

'What is it, Martha?'

'There is a visitor, my lady. A lady…'

'At this time of day? Tell her I am not available. I am amazed that you would even consider—'

'It is a Mrs Russell,' Martha interrupted before her ladyship could get into full flow. 'She says it is of the utmost urgency that she speak with you.'

'Mrs Russell?' Judith's mind went blank. 'Do I know a Mrs Russell?'

'She is definitely a lady, madam. And most insistent.'

'Very well, I will get up. Show her into my boudoir, Martha. Ten minutes.'

Mrs Russell?

When Judith eventually emerged into her boudoir a little after half an hour, in a ruffled and lace-trimmed wrap, it was to see a fair, slight lady sitting on the edge of her day bed, certainly not at ease, and holding the hand of a robust lad of some five years who was barely containing his energies amidst such feminine surroundings.

Judith halted. Then surged forward with a little cry. 'Sarah. Oh, Sarah.'

'Judith. I know it is unforgivably early—I am so sorry…'

'No, no. I am delighted. I did not realise—I have never thought of you as Mrs Russell…' Judith flushed at the less than tactful admission. 'Oh, Sarah, I did not mean…'

'I know. The name of Baxendale has a terrible lasting quality, does it not, in the Faringdon household?'

'Nonsense! I am so pleased to see you. And John. Let me look at you! How you have grown. You were quite a baby when I saw you last.'

The two ladies embraced with a few sentimental tears. John squirmed away from the kisses. Judith laughed and told Sarah of her own entrancing infant whom she must see and admire in a little while. Another pot of hot chocolate was ordered and John was dispatched to the nursery with a willing nursemaid, who promised him a sugared biscuit if he were good.

'Now!' Judith sat herself down in a welter of ruffles beside her visitor. 'Tell me all. What on earth are you doing here? I had no idea of your return. Is Eleanor well? The baby?' Questions flooded out in typical Judith style. Knowing her hostess of old, Sarah decided to answer all the questions first.

Finally they were exhausted. 'So Why are you here? I had thought that you would remain in New York.' Judith angled her head. 'I believe you said that it is urgent—and here have I been gossiping on…'

'It might be. It seemed to me that you were the most suitable person to approach…' Sarah bit her bottom lip in a nervous little gesture which Judith remembered well. 'First I need some information. Does the…the relationship between Lord Nicholas and Theodora Wooton-Devereux still exist?'

'How did you know about that?'

'Mrs Stamford is a useful source of gossip.'

'Ah!' Judith returned Sarah's wry smile. 'But no, it does not. The attraction is at an end.'

'Thank God! If they never became deeply attracted, the damage can not be as great as I feared—'

'No…it is a tragedy!' Judith interrupted. 'You do not understand. They are made for each other. So in love—you would not believe unless you saw them together. But there has been some terrible disagreement. I cannot imagine—and Nicholas will not explain. There is no remedying it. They are both so unhappy—it is all very lowering—and Thea—she is my particular friend, you understand—is pretending that she is quite *happy*. And she is nothing of the sort! She is quite worn down by it, although she would be the last to admit it. Nicholas has taken himself back to Burford in total gloom and despondency. I despair, Sarah. It is not a relief at all!'

'So you say that Nicholas is back at Burford?'

'Yes. Or at Aymestry. He and Thea had a spectacular argument in this very house not a week ago.'

'And the lady? Is she still in London?'

'With her parents in Upper Brook Street. Allowing herself to be courted most assiduously by the Earl of Moreton.'

Sarah appeared to think rapidly over the news and with no degree of pleasure as she picked at the fingers of her kid gloves. Finally she looked up.

'Are you quite certain that they love each other?'

'Why, yes. Not a doubt in the world.'

Sarah nodded as if she had come to a decision. 'Judith. Will you help me?'

'Of course.' Judith waved aside any objections. 'Now, what is it that you wish me to do?'

'I need to meet Miss Wooton-Devereux.'

'You do?' Judith put down her cup and saucer in surprise.

'Yes. It is essential, especially if there is a serious rift. Can you arrange a meeting between us? Where I can talk to her?'

'Yes. No difficulty at all. I will invite her to come here this very afternoon.'

'It may be that I can put things right between her and Nicholas. Or at least warn her—'

'I doubt it.' Judith huffed her displeasure. 'Thea is flirting madly and Nicholas damning all women to perdition, I expect.'

'But I must try. I fear that I may have been the cause of their rift. And if Theodora is innocent... Well, Theodora needs to know.'

'Know what? What is she innocent of? I declare that you are as bad as Nicholas!' She leaned over to catch Sarah's hand in hers, concerned by the lady's distress. 'Why do you need to see her? How can you help?'

Sarah fixed Judith with her calm gaze, returning the clasp of her fingers. 'I need to see her because Theodora Wooton-Devereux is my sister.'

'What?' It was almost a squeak.

'Her name is Sophia Mary Baxendale. She is my sister.'

'Well!' Judith sat back, lips parted. 'I did not know you had a sister!'

'Nevertheless...'

'And so she is also sister to Edward. Well, now! So that explains...' Judith had picked up on the nuances of the relationship with remarkable speed.

'Yes, it does. Because if Theodora's relationship with Edward would not cause a rift between her and Nicholas, I do not know what would. And I, wrongly as it may be, informed Nicholas of the connection through Eleanor's letter to him. I need to discover from her…' Her words dried, her eyes dropped before Judith's inquisitive glance.

'What?'

'It shames me to admit it—but I need to discover if my brother has had any hand in these events, using Theodora as he once used me. Or if she is an innocent, caught up in a cruel twist of fate. Whatever I discover, my sister needs to know the truth about our brother. It is not beyond belief, is it?'

'No.' Judith rose to her feet to stride to the window and back with a stirring of ruffles, in some agitation. 'We know of what Edward is capable. But I would never suspect Thea of being involved in anything unseemly.'

'Unseemly? Edward's actions were far more than unseemly, if you recall. And very manipulative.'

'True.'

'And also, as you most assuredly recall, I too became involved! I became as guilty as Edward in that disgraceful deception. There is no guarantee that Theodora is blameless, that she has not been drawn into my brother's web of deceit.'

'Oh, Sarah.' Judith sank down beside Sarah again, hugged her in remorse at the unhappiness that had begun to resurface. 'You were never as guilty as Edward. How could you be? Oh, dear! How tangled it all is.'

'Yes. And I must do all I can to stop Thea falling into any mischief, now or in the future, dreamed up by my brother.'

'I think it may be too late.' Judith admitted with a rueful look. 'Thea said—now, what was it?—she said, "I have been to see him." I did not understand at the time. But it made Nicholas angrier than ever.'

'Oh. I imagine it would.' Sarah nodded. 'It is even more imperative that I speak with her.'

'Well! It is easy enough to arrange.' Judith rose again to pick up pen and paper. 'But how is it that she is your sister? Perhaps you would like to tell me a little more of these amazing events

while we have something stronger to drink than this chocolate.
Perhaps a little ratafia…'

Judith's depression had instantly lifted.

Later that morning Theodora received a little gilt-edged invitation, delivered by hand by a maid who, she informed the lady
in breathless haste, had been instructed by her mistress to await
a reply. Thea opened it.

*The Countess of Painscastle requests the pleasure of Miss
Theodora Wooton-Devereux's company this afternoon for tea
at 3 o'clock.*

Thea tapped the card thoughtfully against her hand. Sat at her
little escritoire in the morning room and dashed off a reply before she could change her mind.

*Thank you, Judith. But I will not come if Nicholas is to be there.
I am certain that it will be better if we do not meet again.
Your dear friend, Thea.*

She despatched it, only to receive another missive by the
same maid some little time later. The handwriting was hasty and
informal with one careless blot.

Thea—do not be difficult. Nicholas is back in the country. Imperative that you come at 3 o'clock. Do not disappoint. Judith.

So it was settled.

When Thea walked into Judith's withdrawing room, promptly
at three, it was to see her ladyship in deep conversation with another visitor unknown to Thea. They rose to their feet as Thea
entered. The lady was older than Thea, in her mid-twenties.
Slightly built, fair haired, but not as burnished as Thea's, blue
eyes, but not as deep a hue. An attractive woman, quietly dressed,

with a calm composure and confidence. She smiled at Thea as if she might know her.

'Thea.' Judith spoke. 'At last. Here is a lady come to see you. From New York. Mrs Russell.'

'I don't…' Thea glanced questioningly at her hostess, but the unknown lady kept her attention.

'I am Sarah,' the lady explained gently. 'Sarah Baxendale. Your sister. And you are Theodora. I am sorry that we have not met until now.'

'Sarah!' Astonishment flooded her cheeks with colour.

'I decided that I needed to come to see you,' Sarah continued, giving Thea time to gather her wits. 'To ensure that you learnt the truth about our family and our past involvement with the Faringdons, not some terrible mischievous version from Edward. And I think it may be that I need to ask your forgiveness.'

'Well!' Thea selected her most immediate thought. 'I asked Edward about you. He said that he did not know where you were.'

Sarah nodded complacently. 'Much as I would expect. Edward lied. He knew that I had gone to New York. We have much to talk about, Thea.'

'I think so.'

Judith went to the door with a quick smile and an encouraging pat on Thea's arm as she passed. 'I will leave you two ladies as I am not needed here. I will be in the nursery.'

'How tactful she is being.' Thea smiled, perhaps a little nervously.

'Yes. Judith has been a good friend to me.' Sarah now took the time to survey her new sister. Her lips curved into a genuine smile of pleasure at what she saw. 'How smart you are. And how beautiful. I think that you are very like our mother.'

'Ah…' Thea laughed lightly, shaking her head at her inability to take in what was happening. 'How difficult this is.'

'It is. And we have no shared memories to help us through it.' Sarah's composed maturity was soothing in itself. 'Come and sit and I will try to explain why I needed to come.'

Thea obeyed, but with a sudden frown between her brows as

her present predicament swept back into her mind. 'You warned Nicholas about me, didn't you?'

'I did. Eleanor wrote the letter.'

'You cannot imagine the extent of the damage it caused.' There was a chill in Thea's voice. Here it seemed, sitting in Judith's withdrawing room, was the source of all her ills.

'Perhaps I was wrong.' Sarah showed little remorse. 'But there were reasons. Good reasons. I was afraid.'

'Then tell me. Tell me about my family's connection with the Faringdons. Because it has broken my heart.' It was spoken quite matter of factly, but it could not hide the sadness in those glorious eyes or the brief flash of blame.

'Of course.' Sarah felt the urge to take Thea's hand as she sat beside her, but resisted. There was a need to build trust between them before this splendid sister would accept any intimacies from her. 'First tell me this—you have seen Edward?'

'Yes.'

'What did he say to you? I presume that you asked him the same question as you now ask me.'

Thea took a breath, bringing all the words to mind. And repeated them to her sister in all their bitter detail. Only coming to a halt, to run her tongue along dry lips, as she recalled the damning final condemnation of the man she loved. 'He said that Lord Henry and Lord Nicholas were content to consign Octavia and her young son to the gutter to safeguard the reputation of the Faringdon name.'

'Thea… What can I say?' Sarah's eyes had widened in distress.

'Is it true?'

'It is all lies. Every word of it.'

'But how can I know that?' It was Thea who stretched out a hand to Sarah for honesty and comfort. 'Judith and Lord Nicholas will not talk of it. And even if they did, their version would perhaps be quite as selective as Edward's. How am I to know what is truth and what is falsehood?'

'I will tell you the truth.' Now Sarah linked her fingers firmly with Thea's, as if the unity between them, of blood and the flesh, would prove her veracity.

'How do I know it? I have only known you for fifteen minutes!'

'You must be the judge, little sister. But what I have to tell you is painful and does not cast me in a good light. It shames me to tell you. But you need to know how Edward is skilled at subterfuge and manipulation. He must not be allowed to use you against the Faringdons. For that is what I feared most in New York, when it was impossible to know what had transpired.'

'That is certainly what Nicholas believes.' Thea huffed a little breath. 'But Edward has no part in this,' she assured. 'I have only met him the once. I did not even know of his—or your—existence until some few months ago when my mother—Lady Drusilla, that is—told me. My meeting Nicholas—that was a matter of pure chance. Or mayhap fate.'

And Sarah believed her as Theodora sat before her, her heart in her eyes. Without doubt, she loved Nicholas Faringdon. 'That is good.'

'But Nicholas would not believe me.'

'No. He was wrong, I know.'

'He would not listen. He was so intransigent. Nothing like the sensitive, compassionate man I thought I had come to know…'

'There are reasons, Theodora.'

So Sarah filled in the missing facts for Theodora. The truth that Edward had so skilfully manipulated. How Edward introduced Octavia as his sister, legally married to Thomas, with a child, at least a year before Thomas's fraudulent marriage to Eleanor. Thus Octavia should be presented to society as the Marchioness of Burford. Edward claimed the whole estate and title on her behalf and that of her son. Which would have disinherited Eleanor and her child, with all the attendant gossip and social ostracism when the *on dit* became public knowledge. Eleanor would be cast adrift with no appropriate settlement for her as party to a false marriage. Far from driving them from the door, Henry and Nicholas had agreed that Edward and Octavia take up residence in Faringdon House here in Grosvenor Square.

'Did Edward have proof of his accusation?' Thea had listened in silent astonishment at this version of events. How outrageous the plot had been!

'Oh, yes. He had all the necessary legal documents. They certainly fooled Mr Hoskins, the Faringdon lawyer. Octavia's brother, a clergyman of dubious habits, was easily bribed into producing the appropriate papers for the marriage and the birth.'

'I see. Octavia's baby—it died, did it not?' Thea still felt a sharp tug of sympathy for the frail figure in the garden at Whitchurch. She held on to it amongst all the turmoil in her brain as her preconceived ideas were destroyed one by one.

'No. It did not.' Sarah's voice had acquired an edge that made Thea note the faint lines of tension around her mouth. 'Octavia never had a child.'

'Then how? How did she claim to be the mother of Thomas's child?' Now she saw a stricken look on Sarah's face.

'Edward used me. And my son. He presented John—my little boy—as Octavia's son. And I...I played the role of nursemaid. As you see, I am not innocent in all this.'

'Oh, Sarah.'

Tears gathered in Sarah's eyes, to roll helplessly down her cheeks. 'I have no excuses. My husband had recently died... I was widowed and without resources. Edward offered me money and a home for my compliance. And, God forgive me, in a moment of despair and weakness, I agreed to go along with his nefarious plan.'

'And Edward could do that?'

'Oh, yes. He had the perfect scheme to feather his own nest from the Faringdon coffers. It was a very clever scheme. It almost succeeded.'

'So how was it foiled?' Thea found herself caught up in the incredible drama.

'Hal and Nick discovered the truth of Octavia's brother. And I...I turned evidence. I spoke out against Edward and told the truth. My conscience would not allow me to do other.'

'And you went to New York.'

'Yes.'

'With Henry and Eleanor.' There was the faintest question in Thea's voice that Sarah could not ignore. A smile lit her countenance as she replied.

'They understood and forgave me, you see. And gave me a home. Hal and Nell gave me a life and hope, with no recriminations or blame for the damage that I helped to bring them.' She held Thea's gaze with her own. 'I love them both. So I must repay them. I must not allow you to be used by Edward to hurt Nicholas.'

'No, Edward did nothing to hurt Nicholas.' Thea sighed. 'I think I have done that on my own without any assistance! I have done a dreadful thing, Sarah— because I did not fully understand. I accused Nicholas of overbearing arrogance and cruelty. Of putting too little value on our love. Of destroying it for a hatred that I could not accept. Now I understand why he detested Edward— the very name of Baxendale. And so he should.'

'Perhaps. But don't exonerate Nicholas too lightly. He should not have been so quick to judge—he should have listened to you.'

'I know. But *I* should have been honest with *him*. I did not tell him that I knew of my birth, so, when Eleanor's letter arrived…my denials did not carry much weight. Sarah—how I wish that we had met before.'

'And I. Do you believe me, Thea?'

'Yes. I do.' Thea realised that she had not one doubt that Sarah's heart-wrenching tale of ruthless and vindictive plotting by their brother was the truth, because, in so doing, she had heaped blame on her own head. On impulse she put her arms around Sarah's slight shoulders and hugged her. 'It must have brought you great pain to relive it all again.'

'I hoped never to have to refer to it again. But sins have a habit of returning to haunt. Now we must try to heal the wounds.'

'Dear Sarah. I think there is nothing to be done and your journey has been in vain. Nicholas will not talk to me—or I with him, I have to confess. Our lives will take different paths. We had our chance at love—and it was not to be. I fear that any hope of love between us is at an end. Can love survive such anguish? I do not know.' Her fingers curled into claws. 'Is it right to hate one's brother? I certainly hate Edward for all the lives he has touched.'

'You are not alone.'

'What will you do, Sarah?'

'Speak honestly to me. Do you love Nicholas still, after everything that has been between you?'

'Yes. For we were both at fault. He fills my sleeping and all my waking moments. Yes, I love him.'

'Then this is what I shall do. I shall go to Aymestry. Tell Nicholas what I know—of your innocence and of Edward's continuing lies.'

'Will he listen?' She looked doubtful.

'I think so. I think I have one argument that he would find impossible to refute. There is one thing I would ask.'

'Of course.'

'Will you come with me? To Aymestry.'

'Yes.' With typical courage Thea thrust aside all her doubts and grasped the one positive opportunity to salve her own conscience and perhaps bring some peace to Nicholas's troubled mind. Her love for him insisted on it. 'I will come with you. I think I must. Whether Nicholas wishes to see me or not, I have my own apologies to make, for I think I cannot live with myself or my lineage until I do. I will not allow Edward to continue to influence my life in any manner. I will come with you to Aymestry. I will ask Nicholas's forgiveness—and if it is his will that we part, then so be it.'

Thea walked slowly back to Upper Brook Street from Grosvenor Square, preparing to inform Lady Drusilla and Sir Hector that she had spent the past two hours in the company of her sister, learning unbelievable horrors about Edward, things no sister should ever have to learn about her brother. Sarah, with her years of knowledge, had recounted the events with calm acceptance of his culpability. For Thea it was all too shockingly new and painful.

Now she knew. All the secrets and tensions that had worked so effectively to destroy her relationship with Nicholas. The perfidy of her brother. The Faringdon pride in their family name and the protective instinct of Nicholas towards Eleanor and her child, the security of the estate in the absence of the Marquis. After a mere two hours in Sarah's company, all was clear.

Thea entertained no doubts concerning Sarah's revelations. On her return from the nursery with Sarah's little boy in tow, Judith had confirmed every word when she knew that Sarah had told Thea everything that was to be told. The Faringdon scandal was thus in Thea's domain. And with it came recognition, explaining Nicholas's intransigence and suspicion. Thea, her Baxendale birth disguised, was most probably implicated, a matter of terrible and inescapable logic. And because she had deliberately hidden the truth of her birth from him, it had provided the final bitter conviction for him.

Oh, Nicholas!

And now Thea found herself committed to going to Aymestry Manor with Sarah. What on earth would that achieve between her and Nicholas? Forgiveness, perhaps. Understanding, of course. Some sense of closure for the whole affair. But love? For a fleeting moment Thea wished that she had not made the impulsive promise to Sarah. Almost retraced her footsteps to tell her sister that she could not go. Really, she could not.

Did love not need deep and fertile soil in which to grow and flourish? All that lay between her and Nicholas was surely hard and stony ground. No sooner had they discovered each other, acknowledged the bright passion that stirred their blood and demanded that they be together, than they had been torn apart by the legacy of Edward's stirring of a deep, dangerous pot of envy and greed, indiscriminately selecting the Faringdons as his quarry. Would this provide sufficient soil for even the most robust shoot to survive?

No. Thea did not relish the prospect of this visit. But as she had told Sarah, she needed to make her peace with Nicholas. Only then could she look forward. And perhaps there could be a contented future for her with the Earl of Moreton—if she were able to banish Nicholas from her mind and her heart.

She really must not dwell on that.

Miss Wooton-Devereux arrived back in Upper Brook Street with no recollection of her journey, thoroughly damp from a persistent drizzle that had begun as she left Grosvenor Square. She winced in discomfort, realising that her little satin slippers were definitely the worse for wear, and untied the ribbons of her bonnet with clammy fingers. A vivid memory caused her to halt on the first step of the staircase, of that previous glorious occasion when she and Nicholas had been caught in the storm. Soaked to the skin, it had not seemed a matter for depression at all. She flushed a little at the intimate pictures in her mind. But now? Why, even the clouds wept in unity with her, she decided, as she surveyed the limp ostrich plumes of her bonnet with dismay.

Chapter Thirteen

Four days later Sarah and Theodora and also Agnes Drew, whom Lady Drusilla had insisted accompany them to stand guard against all unforeseen dangers on the journey, stood in the familiar entrance hall at Aymestry Manor before a surprised Mrs Grant. The housekeeper's face broke into an instant smile.

'Miss Thea. And Mistress Drew. What a pleasure.' She peered closely at the third lady. 'It's Mrs Russell, isn't it? Well, now. We were not expecting you. But come in, come in. How is your little boy, madam?' She remembered Sarah from her living at Burford Hall with Henry and Eleanor, when she had on occasion visited Aymestry Manor.

'John is well and growing. I have left him with the Countess of Painscastle in London since I anticipate this visit being very brief. He still talks of you, Mrs Grant.'

'Does he enjoy gingerbread pigs as he used to?'

'He does.' Sarah laughed. 'I will tell him that you remembered him.'

'Of course. Now, was it Lord Nicholas you wished to see?'

'Yes.'

Mrs Grant shook her head. 'His lordship must not have known. He's over at Burford. Been there all week. But come into the parlour where there is a fire and I will bring tea.'

They did, grateful for the warmth and comfort. It had been a relatively easy journey made in style, thanks to Sir Hector's post chaise, but for Thea fraught with anxieties. She had worked hard to keep her spirits and her confidence high. Soon all would be put to rights, with Sarah standing as her friend. And then… Well, she would wait and see. Her heart beat rapidly at the prospect of seeing Nicholas again, but her palms were damp with nerves. She pressed them surreptitiously against her muslin skirts, ashamed of her lack of composure as the end of the road—and Nicholas's presence—grew closer.

And now he was not here. Her spirits plummeted to the level of her little kid boots.

'Do you expect his lordship to return?' Sarah asked Mrs Grant when the housekeeper returned to usher in a maid carrying a large tray.

'Why, no, madam.' She busied herself with the china and tea caddy, selecting a key from the chain around her waist. 'Probably not until next week. There are horse sales in Hereford, I believe. And the assizes in Leominster in two days.'

The tea was made and the ladies left to drink it, Mrs Grant assuring them that his lordship would wish them to remain at Aymestry for as long as they desired.

'What do we do now?' Thea turned to her sister. She felt very much an interloper in this house where she had not been invited, where it was very possible that she would not be made welcome. Sarah had no such qualms about their taking up occupation.

'We follow Nicholas to Burford, of course.' Sarah's decisiveness sometimes sat at odds with her apparent but deceptive fragility. 'We cannot sit here and wait.'

'No.' In a moment of chicken-hearted weakness, as Thea castigated herself, the lady thought that she would rather do just that. And found herself forced to admit it with a deep sigh. 'Sarah— I fear the outcome. I have ridden across the deserts of Syria and explored the ruins of more ancient cities than you could imagine—but I fear a meeting with Nicholas. How can that be?' Her eyes flashed with something like annoyance or even anger at her shameful weakness. 'It is so frustrating and not a little humiliating. That one man should reduce me to such cowardice. I would rather face a whole band of desert robbers. Or even the Maidens—and they were frightening enough. As if the blame is all mine—which it certainly is not! Nicholas was overbearing and insensitive—and I have no idea why I should care what he thinks or says! Or even if he wishes to see me. Indeed, I think I should go home now!'

'I think it has something to do with the nature of love!' Sarah smiled, acknowledging her sister's dilemma with deep compassion. 'So here is my plan. Stay here with Agnes. I will take the coach, go on to Burford and attempt to talk some sense into his lordship! Tell him that you are waiting here with the best of intentions. How he could believe that you could be in league with Edward I will never understand! Then, when he is in possession of all the true facts, it will be up to him to make the grand gesture. You have come all the way from London to acknowledge your guilt, as you see it, although I cannot agree with you. The least he can do is travel the few miles from Burford to Aymestry. But do not yield too quickly, Theodora. In my opinion, it is good for a man who is used to wielding authority with ease and a high degree of success to be put under some pressure and be unsure of the outcome. And Nicholas is certainly more authoritarian than many!'

'How devious you are, dear Sarah.' Theodora chuckled, her perspective somewhat restored by her astute sister. 'I think you understand Nicholas very well.'

'Not devious. Determined.' Sarah raised her fair brows. The family resemblance was suddenly clear. 'And don't forget that I lived in the same house as Nicholas for a little time. He was younger then, but he has always had what might be described as a strong character and a flair for getting his own way. As do all the Faringdon men. But I have a strong affection for him. He was very kind to me when life was difficult and my self-esteem was at its lowest ebb, and he never once blamed me for—' She caught herself up on the unhappy thoughts. 'But that is long ago now. I want the best for both of you. I am of the opinion that it would be better if I see Nicholas when you are not present. Then I need not mince my words.' She took Thea's hand in both of hers and pressed it warmly. 'Don't worry so. Mrs Grant will look after you very well. I think you will not have long to wait.'

'Well!' As Sarah left the room to continue her journey, Agnes rose to her feet to enquire about a room for her mistress, a thoughtful expression on her face. 'A forceful lady—crafty, even—in spite of appearances to the contrary. I can well believe that she is your sister, miss!' She turned her head as she reached the door, a little smile deepening the lines on her face. 'I don't give much hope for Lord Nicholas if that one has her way. With both of you hunting him down, the man does not stand a chance.'

'Indeed, dear Agnes, I hope not.'

'I think there is no need for you to lose any more sleep over it, Miss Thea. It would not be good for it to affect you looks, now would it? I think we should expect Lord Nicholas before the night is much advanced. And then perhaps at last we can all get back to a more placid lifestyle!'

Ignoring the dark mutterings, but none the less accepting the sense of them, Theodora followed Agnes from the room, praying for the success of her sister in persuading Nicholas to see the light.

'I have come here, Nicholas, to illuminate a few basic misconceptions concerning my sister Theodora.' No sooner had she alighted from the coach than Sarah had stalked into the library at Burford Hall, not even waiting to remove her bonnet and gloves. She now stood defiantly in the centre of the room, the light of battle in her eye. The clear gaze that she fixed on Nicholas held a severity, a conviction, of which he had no recollection. New York, it seemed, had allowed the somewhat reticent and self-conscious Mrs Sarah Russell to blossom into a lady with a core of steel. He admired it.

Yet, on this matter he was not to be intimidated.

'Then I am afraid that you are doomed to be disappointed and your journey a wasted one. Sister or no, she is the last person of whom I wish to speak.'

'Nevertheless, I have travelled from New York for this sole purpose. Because I felt that I owed a debt to your family and to my sister. And unless you forbid me the house, I shall say what I feel I must.'

Nicholas discovered with not a little surprise that he had taken a stance behind his desk, as if to put the expanse of polished wood between himself and the lady who had arrived a mere few minutes ago, her impressive post chaise and escort pulling up on the gravel sweep with considerable dash. The last person he had expected to see was Sarah Russell, believing her to be comfortably established on the far side of the Atlantic, probably in domestic harmony with some worthy American gentleman. Yet here she was breathing fire, and, it appeared, hell-bent on taking him to task.

As he watched her with a degree of caution, his thoughts fell into the painful and familiar pattern that he had signally failed to banish. He did not want this…this *interview*. He had persuaded himself that the death of his liaison with Theodora with all its attendant suspicions was a matter for rejoicing. *Almost persuaded!* He felt his jaw clench. It continued to amaze and infuriate him, as every day passed, that his existence without Thea's warm smile and infectious laughter, the slide of her silken skin beneath his fingers, was disagreeable in the extreme. He could not stop thinking about her. Could not stop wanting her. A disease that had got a hold and would not let go! Would it be a lifelong ailment?

Oh, God!

And here was Sarah Russell to stir and reignite the banked sensations even further. From the beginning he set his mind and his will against her.

'Very well. Say what you must—and that can be the end of it. It is of little consequence.' He picked up a sealed document from the desk, one which he had been working on when Sarah arrived, as if this conversation was a mere interruption to his daily routine.

And it would not be an easy conversation, Sarah realised, as she took in the discouraging set of his jaw and his shuttered expression. She assessed him with some interest. Here was a power. Not dormant as in his youth, but tightly leashed. Here in the high-bridged nose, the elegantly carved cheekbones, the decided chin, was not the careless, smiling boy whom she remembered. Nor in the cold hauteur as he regarded her across the desk, brows raised, disapproval in every inch of him. Thea was right. Matters had become dangerously difficult between the two of them.

'I have left Thea at Aymestry, Nicholas,' she informed him before he could change his mind and be tempted to show her the door. And that nugget of information, she was delighted to note, forced him to focus on her and to concentrate on her words. The expression of supercilious boredom had vanished entirely. She took immediate advantage, embroidering the truth a little. 'The poor girl is waiting there, quaking in her kid slippers.'

At Aymestry. Theodora was at Aymestry. His pulse took a fast leap in response. She was at Aymestry, his own home. So close that he could be with her within the hour, could hold her in his arms and claim those smiling lips with his own. His heart would urge him to take a horse and ride through the growing dusk, to throw himself at her feet and ask forgiveness for any false accusation. He took a deep breath against that impulse. For there would lie disaster. His mind, proud and hurt, questioned why she had come, refused any spirit of compromise and so forbade it. But his willpower was severely tested. Nicholas turned his mind back to Sarah, who patiently awaited his response, no sympathy at all in her expression.

'Theodora is not a poor girl. Neither does she quake.' His words were brusque, voice cynical, eyes cold. 'She is the most headstrong female I have ever had the misfortune to meet. There is nothing between us.'

'Nevertheless, she is afraid. Of you primarily, although she would find it difficult to admit to such a weakness. Your possible reactions to her if she had accompanied me here to Burford. Of the depth of emotion that has taken over her life and will give her no peace. But she forced herself to come here because she believes that she wronged you. I cannot think why.' Sarah frowned at Lord Nicholas. 'It seems to me that *you* were far more to blame in all this.'

The document crumpled as his hand clenched. 'Your confidence in me and my judgement of a situation where you were not yourself present is most flattering. Thank you, Sarah!'

She ignored the bitter irony and pushed on, aware only of the controlled emotion in his face and the bleak grey of his eyes, a symptom of unhappiness if she knew anything about it. 'You should have believed her, Nicholas. Her integrity is beyond question. I have known her less than a week, but that is clear to me. She is no more Edward's tool against you than…than…' Suddenly Sarah could not find the words as the horror of the past and her own part in it rolled back to swamp her with regret and shame.

Nicholas sighed, the taut muscles in his face relaxing. 'Than you are now, dear Sarah.' He replaced the manuscript back on the desk, carefully, smoothing it with his hand. The softening of his expression and the deliberate kindness in his words were almost her undoing.

'Yes. That is what I would say.' She took a breath to steady herself again. 'Theodora is innocent, Nicholas. There was no plot between her and Edward. No deceit. The rift in the family a mere month after her birth was final, all connections between the Wooton-Devereux and the Baxendales cut. Even I had almost forgotten my sister's existence until Mrs Stamford wrote to Eleanor about your interest in the lady.'

'Eleanor's mama! I should have guessed.' Nicholas snorted in grim amusement at Mrs Stamford's involvement.

Sarah clenched her still-gloved hands before her, willing Nicholas to listen and believe. 'Thea did not know of her birth until after you had met in London. She was not aware until Lady Drusilla told her of it. Lady Drusilla did not know much of the old scandal, but warned Thea that nothing good would ever come of a relationship between Baxendale and Faringdon—and suggested that it would be best if it were ended before it could become a matter for pain and heartache between you.'

'Ah. Now I understand.' A faint line touched his brow. 'So that is why she tried to end it.'

'I know nothing of that—but it certainly explains why Thea decided no good would come of telling you that Edward Baxendale was her brother. Her mother—Lady Drusilla—had warned her well. You should have talked to her, Nicholas. Indeed you should.'

As Sarah's impassioned words bit, forcing his mind to reconsider, Nicholas prowled to the fireplace. Kicked a smouldering log into life. Returned again to face her, running fingers through his hair, an impatient gesture that almost made her smile. How often had she seen Henry do exactly that when assailed by frustrations and doubts.

'I know,' Nicholas admitted at last. 'I know it. I wish that she had told me. It made me think that…that she had a motive for her lack of openness. Then afterwards, when I had accused her of baiting a trap to lure me into marriage—then it was too late for explanations, for either of us.'

'So I understand.' At last. A hint of regret. Sarah felt for the first time a relaxing of the tense muscles in her shoulders, but still she did not cease her attack. 'You did not explain to her why you should hold the name of Baxendale in such hatred, which left her thinking you to be capricious and unreasonable.'

'No.' He raised his eyes to Sarah's. 'Neither of us was very wise, I think.' His lips curved in a bitter parody of a smile. 'The past casts a long shadow, Sarah, whether we wish it or not?'

'Yes. I too remember the torment Eleanor had to live through.' Sarah at last dropped her eyes from his fierce gaze.

'Forgive me, Sarah. I would not have resurrected all this for the world. I can see that it brings you pain.'

'Yes, it does. I hate the need to remember. I still feel the shame. But the legacy is here before us and we must deal with it.' She could no longer prevent a tear escaping to track down her cheek.

At which Nicholas abandoned his entrenched and distant position to stride round the desk, and took her in his arms as any brother might and kissed her damp cheeks. 'Don't think of it, Sarah. There is no blame attached to you. You have proved your loyalty to this family time and again. You know that you are loved and respected here.'

'Yes.'

He led her to a chair and sat beside her. Leaned forward to rest his forearms on his thighs, hands clasped loosely before him, and set himself to bare his soul.

'What should I say to you? I think—if I am honest—that the portrait you have painted of Thea's innocence is no stranger to me.' For a long moment he dropped his head into his hands. Tempting Sarah to reach out to touch his dark hair in compassion. But now was not the time to weaken. She must push the message home. As if picking up her thought pattern, he raised his head to look at Sarah. The longing in his eyes struck at her heart, even before he spoke. 'I have made such a mess of things, Sarah. You would not believe... When I received Eleanor's letter—it brought it all back. And then everything went wrong, layer upon agonising layer. We said things that would deliberately hurt and tear. Neither of us would step back and reconsider.'

'Headstrong! I knew it!' But there was a smile now in Sarah's voice and a sigh of relief. 'You are both the same.'

'Yes. I fear so. And pride. And the legacy of Baxendale is still too close to ignore. The name is still an anathema,' he admitted, 'however much I might wish to bury it.'

Sarah remained silent for a long moment. She knew exactly how to destroy these chains that still bound Nicholas to the past. And set herself to do it.

'Nicholas—do you love Theodora?'

'Yes. I cannot get her out of my mind. But is it now too late? I fear that I have killed her love for me.'

'Of course you have! That is why, foolish girl that she is, she was prepared to travel all the way across the country, simply to make her peace with you! Have a little sense!' She curbed her impatience at the blindness of men, and hid a triumphant little smile. 'She has so much courage Nicholas. It astounds me.'

'I know. I see the same courage in you.'

'Never! But Theodora… What are you going to do about her?'

'I think it is all beyond remedy.'

'You say the name stands between you. Think about this. Do you have any friendship for me?'

'Of course.' He looked puzzled. 'Do you need to ask?'

'No. Do you trust me?'

'Of course.'

'Then what is the problem?'

'I fear that you have left me wallowing in unrequited love!' At last she saw a glint of appreciation. 'You will have to explain.'

'It is very simple, Nicholas. How you have failed to work it out for yourself is beyond belief. You rejected Theodora, the love of your life by all accounts, because her name was Baxendale.'

'I…' A hint of colour flared along his cheek bones at the realisation of how empty and futile and ridiculous it sounded in Sarah's words.

'Of course you did. But I, too, am a Baxendale—or have you forgotten?' She slanted a surprisingly mischievous glance at him. 'If you can trust me and care for me a little, why is loving Thea any different? And you adore her! Her name should not stand between you. It cannot. As a man of logic, you must realise it.'

Nicholas searched Sarah's face as he absorbed her undoubted logic. Then he laughed, as if a weight had been lifted from his heart. 'Sarah… What have I been doing all these weeks? Perhaps I needed you to put it so simply that even a child would see it.'

'Or beat you over the head with it! I wager no one has had the temerity to do so, unless it be Lady Beatrice.' She watched him shrewdly, rewarded by Nicholas wincing in reluctant agreement. 'It *is* simple. You love her and she, for some reason which I cannot fathom, loves you. Her name is irrelevant. Besides, she is my sister and I love her and want her happiness. She has decided that she can find it only with you. Now if *I* were in need of a husband—' there was a distinct twinkle in her eye '—I would have given the Earl of Moreton more of a chance. He is so much easier to deal with. The Faringdons are never easy!'

She was relieved to see humour creeping back into the stern lines of Nicholas's face to dispel the bleak misery. 'You are a managing female, Sarah. I did not realise it. Moreton does not know of his lucky escape. So I must go to Aymestry, it seems.' He rubbed his hands over his face as if he had just awoken from a dire nightmare.

'Of course you must. What is taking you so long? You should have saddled a horse at least half an hour ago.'

'Will you come?'

'No. I have travelled enough in recent days. And I should most decidedly be in the way.'

'Perhaps.' He kissed Sarah's fingers, then her cheek. 'My thanks are beyond expression. It may be that you have just given me back my life.'

As she accompanied him to the door, Sarah gave him some parting advice. 'If you love her, Nick, don't lose this chance.' She touched his arm lightly, amazed at the courage she had shown this night in speaking so candidly to this most complex of Faringdon men. 'You know how it is between Henry and Nell. You have seen it for yourself. It is beyond magnificent. The affection and the caring—and the blazing passion that only grows with time. If you and Theodora achieve only half of the love that they have, it would be enough for a lifetime. Don't throw it away, Nicholas. You would regret it for the rest of your life.'

Nicholas bent his head, kissed her cheek again in heartfelt gratitude.

As he strode from the house toward the stables, Sarah's words echoed in his mind, clear and strong. So much advice, confirming what he had known all along and been too blind and proud, too bent on revenge, to accept. It was time that he faced the truth and old hatreds were buried. His future happiness depended on it.

At Aymestry Manor, whilst Sarah was taking Nicholas to task at Burford Hall and advising him, much as Lady Beatrice might, on the only course of action open to a man of common sense, Theodora brooded and awaited the outcome. The day gradually drew on into late afternoon as she watched the road with anxious eyes. She could not possibly expect him before dusk. Nevertheless she watched and waited impatiently. Clouds heralding oncoming rain began to gather on the horizon to the west. Time hung heavily. Thea's patience became thinly stretched.

She visited the stables where she became reacquainted with The Zephyr. The beautiful mare bloomed with health, her coat gleaming in the late sun, and seemed perfectly sound as she trotted across the paddock at Thea's voice. Furness was encouraging, already lamenting the loss of the little mare when she returned to Thea's possession. Thea admired the new foals. Played with an enthusiastic litter of spaniel puppies who at least made her laugh and forget her woes.

Still he did not come.

She strolled in the gardens with Agnes, mentally stocking them with her favourite flowers. Aquilegia and hearts' ease, honeysuckle and… and… But what was the purpose in such wishful thinking? She would like to grow herbs and…. No. She must not think of it. It would never come to that if Nicholas decided that her Baxendale connection created too great an obstacle.

And still no sound of hooves on the road or on the track that dropped down through the woods.

Of course he might reject everything that Sarah could lay before him in her sister's defence. Theodora cursed the name of Edward Baxendale in language that would have drawn her mama's deep disapproval.

She took herself to the kitchens out of interest to see Mrs Grant's kingdom. And spoke with the lady, who readily conversed about the running of such a household and the particular likes and dislikes of his lordship, whom she had known since a young boy. So Lord Nicholas disliked sweetbreads, did he? Well, so did she! Thea would have enjoyed the experience if nerves had not begun to flutter with persistent wings in her stomach.

Dusk shrouded the house and candles were lit. Still no Nicholas.

Thea and Agnes shared a meal, neither having much appetite. Then Agnes was sent off to her bed, leaving Thea to pace the library, without even a pretence at finding solace in one of the many volumes that hemmed her in. He would not come. Not now.

Then, at last, noises outside. Muted but just discernible. Hooves and voices. Thea stopped her pacing, gripped the back of a chair with her hands and watched the door.

But no Nicholas. On a hiss of frustration at what could possibly be detaining the man—probably a mare in foal!—she went to the window to peer out. It was dark with the now-heavy cloud covering the moon so she could see nothing. But that was not right! There were figures, black on black, on the carriage drive to the left. And there! A flash of light—and another from torches. And in the light from those torches, Thea was able to see the truth. Figures clad in skirts and shawls. The Maidens. Torches. Now they moved quietly as one led away a horse. Voices deliberately kept low, but there was no doubt in Thea's mind that their presence was a threat and their intent evil. As they disappeared from view towards the stables, Thea fled. First to the kitchens, where by chance Furness was lifting a jug of ale and enjoying a pipe as he exchanged opinions with Mrs Grant.

'Miss Thea?' Mrs Grant immediately rose to her feet. 'Is there a problem…?'

'Master Furness…'

He put down his ale in concern at the lady's wide eyes and breathless state.

'The Maidens are paying us a visit,' Thea gasped. 'I have seen them. Heading to the stables, I would say…with torches—' Before she had finished, Furness was on his feet with the agility of youth and out of the room at a run.

Without thought, Thea followed.

Nick rode to Aymestry, his mind full of Sarah's forthright words. And hope surged through his veins with every mile as he took the track through the woods, despite the falling light. Every instinct persuaded him to reach his manor with all speed. He knew Sarah well enough, had enough experience of the innate honesty that had troubled her conscience and driven her to expose the deceit of her brother. And so he had believed her every word. Thea would be waiting for him. She was entirely innocent, as he must assuredly have known. The shame of his lack of trust crawled beneath his skin, yet the prospect of his loved one quaking made him smile again. What a delight it would be to hold her and kiss her and calm any fears she might have. But he would have to ask forgiveness first, for indeed it was his fault that he had judged her without cause. Surely she would not reject him. If she had come all this way she could not be cold to his advances. He winced under Sarah's biting criticisms. But he could put it right.

Joy leapt in his blood as he rode out of the trees where the track began its descent to the manor. It was late, but not too late. She would be awake, watching for him. A light rain began to spatter on his shoulders, but he would soon be home. He kicked his horse into a controlled canter, making use of his intimate knowledge of the track. But then with an oath reined in, staring forward to where the house nestled in the shallow depression.

Lights. Too many lights. Indeed, they were flickering torches. And shouts. Some crisis had occurred. The possibilities jostled in his mind as the unease grew. And then the truth was clear, for the first tongues of fire climbed into the sky from the corner of the stables, the wing where the mares and foals were kept for their safety at night. The unease blossomed into desperate and fully-fledged panic.

Fire!

The stallions and mares would die if the alarm was not raised. And if the flames got a hold on the stables, they would spread to the house with its plaster and dry beams before anything could be done to save it. His home, where Theodora awaited him.

Nicholas applied his heels to his horse and galloped heedlessly towards the looming disaster.

The scene in the stableyard rushed towards her, swamping Thea with terror, every sensation in her body under instant attack, every instinct to freeze in abject fear or to run for her safety. It was a scene straight from the torments of hell. Flames were already licking along one side of the three wings of wood-timbered buildings, stonework already blackened. Within the enclosed space, illuminated by torches and fire, chaos reigned. Figures loomed and dispersed through the billowing smoke. Shouts and cries of anger and encouragement filled the air. There appeared to be few skirted figures—certainly not as many as when Thea had met them on the road—but in their midst, urging them on with wild, triumphant gestures, was Samuel Dyer.

Violence had broken out between the stablelads and the intruders. Blows falling, from fists and wooden staves and pitchforks, wielded on both sides with bloody intent. A firearm was discharged to her left with a flash of fire and a loud retort, causing her to retreat a step. By the stable door lay the deep and ominous shadow of a body on the floor, friend or foe impossible to tell. And over all, the shrill, heartrending cries of horses in a state of ultimate fear and panic as smoke and flames invaded the stalls.

Furness had already taken command, to set a line of men to bring buckets of water from the stream that tumbled down the slope from the distant woods, and struggle with a cumbersome water-pump. But it was so little and so ineffective compared with the blazing wood and plaster! Thea found herself watching in despair the meagre efforts to quench the flames, thwarted at every step by the Maidens.

Now Furness had turned his attention to the horses. It was imperative to get into the stables, to overcome their terror and liberate them into the paddocks where they would come to no harm.

'Open the doors!' His voice cracked as acrid smoke engulfed him.

The bolts were drawn, the huge doors dragged back.

'Get the mares out—the foals will follow! Turn the stallions loose.'

He and others plunged into the hell of noise and flame within, with little thought for their own safety. Smoke thickened as the dry timbers caught. Sparks flared and blew in the light wind, threatening the house itself. If the house took, there would be nothing they could do.

Thea stood on the edge. Familiar cold settled on her senses. Noise. Violence. Danger. A constant swirl of movement that seemed to draw her in and enclose her into its deadly centre. She knew it all, had experienced it all, and knew her probable reaction to it. It was as if she stood at a distance, outside herself, and watched as the rigid panic assailed her limbs, gripping her chest with iron-tipped claws. She struggled to breathe. She could not move.

Even when a terrified mare was led out, only yards from her, her offspring following, wide-eyed and distressed.

From that safe distance, trapped within her mind, Thea focused on the scene, forcing her conscious thoughts to stay in contact with the horrors she was witnessing. She could not let the horses die in such agony. Or Nicholas's men. Not when she had the power to move her limbs and help. She could not stand by in a fit of useless and selfish panic and let others take the risks.

A stallion was sent out with a hard slap to its neck and rump, with tossing head and rolling eyes, and turned loose to canter off into the darkness.

The Zephyr is in there. Do something! Don't think—just do something!

A group of bodies pushed and swayed between her and the stable, arms swinging. She could hear the grunts quite clearly as the blows made contact. They would not stop her. They must not stop her. She took a breath. Too much at stake. And pushed between, looking neither left nor right, dodging the blows, ignoring a pistol fired close by. She followed Furness into the stable.

'Get out, Miss Thea.' The head groom cast one horrified glance in her direction. 'Too dangerous. No place for you. What his lordship would say if you was harmed…' He coughed in the smoke, wiping a filthy hand over red-rimmed eyes. 'Get out and up to the house.' But he was too occupied to force her to obey.

'No. You need all the help you can get.' She seized a blanket, submerging it in a water trough. 'Wrap yourself in this.' She did likewise. And joined the men struggling to release the horses. Aware only of wildly lashing feet, wicked teeth. It was hot dangerous work. She did not once stop to think what she was doing.

Outside shouts went up from a dozen voices. Matters appeared to be coming to a head, which prompted Thea to make a detour to collect one of the coachman's pistols from the room that stored harness and saddles. She had no idea whether it was loaded or not and did not stop to look. It might serve its purpose and there was no time to do more, certainly not to prime a pistol in the dark. Back outside, the first sight that met her horrified gaze was Sam Dyer with a flaming torch, stooping to apply it to the inner wing.

'Stop.'

By some miracle her voice carried in a slight lull in the general pandemonium. Dyer looked up, torch held high, across the space that separated them.

'Do that and I fire.' The blanket falling from her shoulders to the floor, she held the pistol in both hands and aimed it at his chest.

Dyer halted. Looked at her in amazement. And laughed in terrible mockery—but he lowered the torch.

'A real woman, lads.' He waved to draw the attention of his associates. 'No false skirts here. Get her. Or she blows my head off!' Before Thea could respond or even be aware of those around her in the shifting shadows, the pistol was knocked from her hand to the ground and she was seized from both sides in a rough grasp.

The panic rose within her chest. She could hear her own heartbeat thundering in her ears. Her breathing became tight and difficult.

But surrender she would not.

She struggled furiously, resisted every effort to restrain her. Surprised her captors into letting her go free, with jeers and amused comment, now that they had possession of the pistol. A mere woman who could do no harm. Instantly she dashed across the courtyard toward Dyer, who still held the torch in close proximity to the walls and a pile of straw that would provide superior tinder. What she would do she had no idea. But she could not stand by and watch him burn down Nicholas's home. Dyer caught her by the arm.

'Oh, no, you don't.'

'Take your hands off me!'

'So his lordship is using women to defend his rights now, is he? And a pretty one too.' The grin was sly in the flickering light. 'How does he pay you? In kisses?' He ran his hand down her arm in a terrible intimacy and leered. 'Perhaps you would be willing to kiss me, my lady. If you want me to set you free.'

'Let go! You cannot stop me. I will not let those animals burn to death.' She fought furiously, digging her nails into his hands. 'You disgust me—you have no quarrel with the Faringdon estate. To stop me you will have to either kill me or tie me up!' She brought the edge of her heel down heavily on to his instep, so that he grunted with pain. And looked at her with reluctant admiration. The gilded hair impossibly ruffled. The stylish gown soiled and singed beyond recognition as a creation of Bond Street. Her face smeared with soot, but determination writ clearly on every feature.

'Well, now. A firebrand. Which shall it be then, my lady, a bullet or a rope? It matters little to me.'

'Neither.' The cool voice cut through the heat of the situation. 'I suggest that you take your filthy hands from the lady.'

There in the courtyard stood Lord Nicholas Faringdon, pistol raised and aimed, with far more precision than Thea's earlier attempt, most dangerously at Dyer's head.

'Well, my lord. We did not expect to see you here this night. Come to watch your pretty house burn?' Dyer grinned, gestured at the dire results of his work, full of confident bluster. 'We will be glad to accommodate you.' But he gripped the torch firmly as he kept a wary eye on the icy rage that emanated from the motionless figure before him. Lord Nicholas was never to be underestimated.

'Let her go!' Lord Nicholas snarled. Ignored the blatant threat to his property. 'Or, by God, you may be sure that I shall not miss if you give me cause to fire.'

Thea found herself instantly released. Without a glance at the two men she set about her self-imposed task, running back towards the stable door where a foal was engaged in a full panic, refusing to follow its mother. Grabbing its mane, she pulled and cajoled until it consented to escape into the safety of the darkness after the mare.

The two men faced each other. 'If you shoot me, my lord, it will not save your precious buildings. They'll still go up in flames. As all landlords should, damn their black souls to hell!'

'But you will be in hell first.'

'Would you shoot an unarmed man?' Dyer challenged. 'A man who is fighting for a wage to put bread into the mouths of his family?'

'Perhaps not.' Lord Faringdon seemed to give the matter some consideration. 'But you will pay for this night's work.'

A split-second decision, Nicholas leapt the distance between them, fast and sure, a short left jab to Dyer's ribs, followed by a powerful straight right to his jaw. The man fell to the floor, dropping the torch, as if struck by a blow from a heavy club. When he struggled to regain his feet, his lordship hauled him to his feet and hit him again.

This time he lay still. Until Nicholas, not wasting any further words, dragged him to his feet and summoned two of his lads to take him up to the house, with instructions to lock him in the cellar. Then he was free to turn back to the disaster unfolding before him. To assess the damage and the possibility that the manor house in its entirety would be nothing but a blackened shell by the morning.

The flames still leapt with crackling intensity. Horses were still being brought out. Nicholas strode forward to relieve one of the smaller lads of a recalcitrant stallion. Although the rest of the Maidens had suddenly melted away with the obvious defeat of their leader, their work had been done with terrible efficiency. The walls well lit, flames encroaching onto the roof. Water was still being ferried in a chain, but it was a desperate race against time. Surely the house would catch.

Then the rain began. The threat that had been evident throughout the evening came to their rescue when they least expected it, drenching everyone and everything. Damping down the flames. Nature achieving what they could never have done alone. They stood and watched, in mingled horror and relief, the results of the night's attack.

'Master Furness.' Nicholas turned to his head groom who emerged from the smoke-blackened inferno to stand beside him. 'Be so kind as to get those burning walls pulled down to stop the spread of the flames. Keep damping down those not yet burning. And pray that the rain continues.'

'Thea. Look at you. You should not have risked yourself.' Nicholas pulled her from the soaking mire of the stableyard into the shadows of the dovecote. The doves whirled in silent panic in the dark above their head. 'Are you hurt in any way? You should not—' He bit down on the terror and fury that had gripped him since he saw her in Samuel Dyer's ungentle grip, and drew an unsteady hand over her wet hair in a rough caress.

'We saved them.' Thea found herself holding on to the sleeve of his coat as if her life depended on it. 'The horses—they are all alive, I think. And The Zephyr. I don't know about your people.' Her eyes were wide, her breathing disordered, her clothing beyond repair. But there was no hint of panic about her. Only a wild sense of achievement that they had thwarted the Maidens.

'Thea…' The wet and soot and grime did not matter. His eyes sought her features as if he could not quite believe that she stood safe and unharmed before him. The dangers had been so great. Ignoring her squeak of surprise, he dragged her into his arms and captured her mouth with his in a kiss as hot and fierce as the flames themselves, marvelling at the strength and courage that she had shown. It was an insistent demand, pressing her close from breast to thigh, a unity against those who would threaten and destroy. Thea responded with equal fervour. Faced with possible death and certain destruction, with weakness and surrender, she had stood firm. Here in his arms was life and power—and, she was certain, forgiveness.

Nicholas could not get enough of her. He held on, oblivious to wet and discomfort.

Then sense reasserted itself, the demands and problems of the moment taking precedence, to release her from his close embrace, yet sliding his hands to encompass her wrists, unable to let her go.

'Thank God you are alive.' He touched his lips to her forehead, a tender blessing.

'And you.' Thea spread her hands, fingers wide, against his chest, needing the muscular solidity of him, the firm beat of his heart against her palms.

'The danger was yours. I saw you.'

'And you saved me.'

Their eyes held in the dark, their fingers linked at last.

'I did not panic.' As Thea realised her achievement, her breath caught on a sob. But there was no place for tears. 'I wanted to. I wanted to flee. But I did not.'

'I know. You have all my admiration. I cannot say it.' What a marvellous woman she was. How he loved her.

'I think the rain has saved us.' A soft laugh shook her when Thea became aware of the heavy drops pattering on her head and running down her smoke-smeared face.

'Yes. But now you must go.'

'No.' Her fingers tightened, preventing any separation. 'I will stay with you.'

Nicholas shook his head, gentle but firm. 'Go to Burford, Thea. There is little you can do here now and I have to know that you are safe. I will send someone with you. Take my horse.' When she would still have resisted, he made a plea from the heart. 'Go to Burford for my sake, if not for your own. I could not bear it if you were hurt now.'

'I don't—'

'Don't argue. It will be easier for me if you are not here in all this debris. You have done enough this day.'

'Very well.' She accepted the force of it. She would achieve nothing through dissension.

For a brief moment Nicholas held her close, to imprint her on his mind and body—then led her to his horse, suddenly aware of the shivers that began to attack her in her thin gown now that the dangers which had driven her were finally past. Taking off his own coat, he pushed her arms into the sleeves even as she objected. 'You are cold. You will need this on the journey.' The warmth from his body enveloped her, to soothe and comfort as if his arms were still around her. He helped her to mount before summoning two of the stable lads. His instructions were brief and plain.

'Take Miss Thea to Burford Hall, Sim. Take care of her. Do you understand? Any danger, anything at all that gives you cause for unease, don't fear to use the pistols. And shoot to kill.'

'Yes, my lord.' Sim was already mounted, the pistols stowed away. 'The lady will come to no harm.'

Nicholas watched her go. Watched her turn to look back once, her face a pale blur, before swallowed up in the rain-sodden darkness. So much to say. So little chance to say it. But tomorrow he would.

For now, he walked back into the stableyard to see how much of his property had survived the vicious attack of the Maidens.

Later, much later, once he was certain that all at Aymestry was secure, Nicholas arrived back at Burford Hall. Waiting for him in the entrance hall, in a borrowed lace bedrobe, was Theodora.

'You should have gone to bed.' He spoke softly, the great house silent around them.

'I could not—not until I knew that you were safe.'

He shrugged out of his coat, grimacing at the discomfort, to stand before her, grimy, smoke blackened, wet to the skin from the rain that was still falling. His clothes were in ruin, his hands and face hopelessly smeared. 'I am not fit, Thea—' He halted, as if words failed him.

'Is the house safe? And your people?'

'Yes. The rain was a blessing. Some cuts and bruises. A sore head or two. Singed hair and eyebrows, I expect. But no lives were lost.'

'And the horses?'

'Yes.'

Exhaustion was imprinted on every engraved line on his face.

'What of the Maidens?'

'Dispersed for the moment. Samuel Dyer is spending tonight locked in one of the store rooms off the stables here, with a guard!' The muscles along his jaw clenched. 'I will deal with him tomorrow.'

'And you, my lord?' Despite all that had passed between them, Thea found it impossible to reach out to touch him. Even though she needed to convince herself that he was here and he was safe.

He managed a smile. 'I took no harm.'

The gulf between them appeared to Thea to be as wide as ever. It was not the time to say the words in her mind, but she could wait no longer.

'I am so sorry. I did not mean to lie, but I did not tell you the truth. I never meant to hurt you. I had to come here to tell you that.'

'I know. You have an excellent champion in Sarah.' A weary smile touched his mouth. 'She argued your case most persuasively. And left me in no doubt of her opinion of me!'

'I do not know Edward Baxendale. But I now know the depths of which he is capable. I understand the pain and the hurt he brought to you.'

'Thea…' Nicholas ran his hands through his dishevelled hair with a sigh. 'I have my own apologies to make.'

'You are exhausted.' At last she touched his arm lightly.

'Yes. But I should thank you. You saved my home and the bloodstock from certain destruction. I cannot find the words to express my gratitude—or not tonight, in any event.'

'I could do no other.'

'I saw you face Sam Dyer. I shall not forget it.'

She shook her head. 'You need rest. Go to bed, my lord.'

'I will take your advice.' Yet he could still find the grace to take possession of her hand and raise it to his lips. Then walked slowly to the stairs.

'Good night, Thea. Tomorrow we will talk.'

Which left Thea curiously dissatisfied. But she held to that moment in the stableyard when he had snatched her away from the noise and the chaos for one long moment. Had held her and kissed her as if he would never let her go.

Chapter Fourteen

On the following morning Sarah sat at a leisurely breakfast in one of the parlours, allowing her mind to drift with possibilities for the future. Nicholas would claim the bride he so clearly needed. Soon—she rubbed the crumbs from her fingers with an inner delight—she could return to London and her darling John. A little frown settled to mar her brow. For then a decision would have to be made over what she should do next. Stay in London or return to New York. Sarah did not know. If she stayed, there would be the problem of where she would live and how she would find financial security for herself and her son... But she would not think of that yet.

Her thoughts were interrupted by Nicholas, who entered the room to take a seat at the opposite side of the table with a groan in acknowledgement of his aching muscles.

'I feel as if I have not slept this sennight.'

Sarah studied the faint prints of exhaustion beneath his eyes, the lines bracketing his mouth, but also saw the absence of tension in his arms and shoulders. Cleansed of all the soot and grime from the previous night, he looked remarkably at ease despite some evidence of singed hair at one temple. Sarah smiled across at him, her own anxieties dispersed, then rose to pour coffee when he sank into a chair, placing the cup before him, fighting a need to take him in her arms and offer comfort as she would her son. Instead she seated herself again, elbows on the table, chin propped on her hands to hear the news. 'I heard a brief account of the events, when Thea returned. Is the damage very great?'

'No.' Nicholas stretched and yawned. 'It could have been worse. Far worse, if Dyer had had his way. He has no personal quarrel with me, but in his eyes all landlords are tarred with the same brush.' A shrug, a tightening of the lips, the only comment he would make on the man who had threatened his livelihood. And, far greater in consequence, the life of the woman who was everything to him. At the thought, without his knowledge, Nicholas's fingers clenched around the cup to the imminent danger of the fragile porcelain. 'The house is intact apart from one corner of the roof on the south side, which caught before we could get the flames under control. Thank God for the rain. Without it the whole house would have been a charred ruin by this morning.' He rubbed his hands over his face as if to erase the memory of the hopeless battle against the fire. 'The stables have gone, of course.'

'But Thea said that the horses are safe.'

'Yes.' He shook his head to dislodge the tragic images of what might have happened. 'Thank God also for sympathetic neighbours. William Hawkes has agreed to take the mares and foals for as long as need be—we'll keep the stallions here. And Tom Clifford has offered to collect Dyer and take him off to Hereford Goal before the day is out.' He pushed himself a little wearily to his feet, restless still. 'At present he is locked in one of the storerooms with a guard watching his every move. I shall be relieved to have him away from here in case one of my people is tempted to take a bloody revenge. It was nasty work last night. Lives could have been lost.'

'I hear he already has a black eye and a bloody nose.' Sarah's raised brows begged for enlightenment.

'I know nothing of it.' But Nicholas rubbed the skinned knuckles of his right hand absently.

'No, of course not. I merely wondered if you were as talented with your right arm as your brother.'

'He taught me well.' The soft laugh acknowledged the accuracy of the prompting. 'And Thea. I owe her so much.' Now he looked back from where he stood by the window, face suddenly alight. 'You should have seen her, Sarah. There she stood in a gown as rich as amber, firelight in her hair, her eyes ablaze…' He stopped to savour the memory, his lips drawn back in a snarl as he recalled the pleasure of his personal dealing with Dyer. 'You have a remarkable sister, Sarah.'

Sarah smiled at the dynamic picture. 'Theodora benefited from an adventurous upbringing by Sir Hector and Lady Drusilla. Not by our mother, who could not bring herself to venture into the kitchen if the cook was so much as wringing the neck of a chicken. Lady Drusilla is made of much sterner stuff.'

'I know.' He came to sit again. 'I was so wrong. Last night proved it beyond all argument, beyond all doubts. What it must have cost her to stand within the noise and chaos around her, the men and the horses jostling in fear and panic… She did not flinch. Had no thought for her own safety. She has all my admiration.'

'And you are going to put it right with her, dear Nicholas.' Although she did not understand his reference, Sarah rose to walk round the table and lay a hand on his shoulder.

'Assuredly.'

She watched him with silent sympathy as he came to terms with his own doubts and faults and the enormity of what might have happened, emotions chasing each other across his face before he spoke again.

'I have hated Edward Baxendale with every fibre of my body. I think it is within me to have killed him without compunction for his sins. I would have challenged him to a duel if Hal had not prevented it. He has been the enemy for nearly three years or more, but the passage of time has not lessened that hatred. I despise him today as much as I ever did.'

'I know.'

'And Thea?' Nicholas continued, looking up into Sarah's understanding face. 'Well, she too is a Baxendale. What hope would such a fragile emotion as love seem to have against such destructive power? Against such hatred and bad blood?'

Standing outside the door, Thea listened with mounting horror to the words of condemnation in Nicholas's bleak confession to Sarah. She repeated them in her mind, again, and then again, as if she could not believe that she had heard them. But she had and must accept. Of course nothing had changed. His kiss, his embrace, his heated words of the previous night—she had completely misread them. They had only been in response to the immediacy of fear and shock of fire and violence. And gratitude for her role in the rescue of his precious horses! She was still Edward's sister. That could never be altered. Any warmer feelings, any lessening of the disgust that Nicholas felt towards her, that was simply the result of the desperate circumstances.

It was not love that had coloured his words and actions. Gratitude, perhaps. Obligation. But not love. How could she have allowed herself to so foolishly be mislead? How could *he* have so carelessly, thoughtlessly, allowed her to believe that there was any deeper emotion on his side other than obligation!

Fury surged through Thea, heat replacing the winter cold in her veins. How could he! Before she could change her mind, she pushed open the parlour door, to step over the threshold, to face him.

'Theodora…' Nicholas would have risen to his feet with a smile of welcome and outstretched hand, but was instantly aware that the lady was in no mood for pleasantries or platitudes. Waves of temper shimmered round her. Ice over fire.

'How could you have misled me? How could you have held me in your arms and kissed me? I thought you loved me, Nicholas. And that all could be right between us.' Her voice was low, controlled even, but could barely disguise the flood of anger and despair.

'Thea… No…' Sarah's attempted intervention merely stoked the flames. The flash of Thea's eyes silenced her.

'And now I hear from your own lips that nothing has changed.'

Thea continued to face the man who had captured her heart, toyed with it, and then shattered it. 'Nothing! How could you be so callous—so cruel! You despise me as much as ever—'

'It is not so, Theodora—'

'Do you dare deny it? I heard you tell Sarah… What was it—the fragility of love against—?'

'No… Enough, Thea!' The firm note of authority now crackled in his voice, bringing Thea to a breathless halt. Lord Nicholas compressed his lips, brows drawn into a straight and forbidding line. He stalked to the door and opened it. 'Sarah. I need a conversation with your sister. An urgent, private conversation.' He stifled a sigh at the prospect of explaining to a lady who gave every appearance of being beyond reason. 'If you would be so kind…'

Sarah diplomatically made her exit. This was no place for her. Nicholas closed the door behind her, leaned against it to watch the love of his life clench her hands into admirable fists.

'Say what you have to say, my lord.' She deliberately turned her back against him, to focus on the pink showers of roses that bloomed around the terrace windows. And to hide the tumbling emotions that she feared might slip from her control. She could sense his presence behind her. And she trembled. Why was love so very painful?

Nicholas said nothing, but let his gaze travel over her, her straight shoulders and upright spine. So, she would resist his explanation. He would allow her that self-indulgence for a little time. But not for long, by God! Moving past her to the sideboard, without bothering to ask her preference, he poured two glasses of claret, then walked to her side to hand her one of them. Without a word, she took it with fingers that clenched around the fragile stem. He watched her with, for Nicholas, infinite patience. Her face was stormy. Beautiful. Magnificent in its determination to freeze him to the marrow. Or to fry him in the fires of hell.

Not in a million years!

But he also, to his surprise, saw fear. She was afraid of what he would say, of what she had overheard and what might be settled for ever here in this quiet room. So that made two of them!

His mouth was suddenly dry, as dry as the cinder and ash in the remnants of his stableyard, at the realisation that the outcome here meant as much to her as it did to him.

He glanced at the glass still clasped so forcefully. 'You may throw it at the wall if you wish.'

Thea glared at him before quickly looking away, then putting the glass down out of temptation, because she was sorely tempted. She raised her chin a little. 'I am not so far beyond control and good manners, my lord.' There was no thaw in her expression. Thea was far too busy concentrating on the erratic behaviour of her heart, which thudded hard against her ribs.

Lord Nicholas, with applaudable cunning, tried for a minor distraction. 'I have some property of yours, Thea.'

Theodora raised one brow in polite and glacial enquiry.

Lord Nicholas removed from his coat pocket a small object, which he had carried like a talisman. It lay on the palm of his hand, glittering ice-white and fiery blue in the strong light.

Thea made no move. 'And will you return it?'

Nicholas thought of pinning the little brooch to the bodice of her gown where lace met ivory flesh... No. That was not his plan.

'Not yet.' He placed it on the table amidst the breakfast cups where it continued to sparkle.

Then simply stepped to stand before her. It was time to settle matters between them, with no opportunity for misunderstanding. When she would have automatically taken a pace back, he reached out to frame her face, with his hands so that she could not retreat. Lowered his head and kissed her. Brief and hard, allowing her no escape. Looking down into her face he noted with satisfaction the shocked surprise in the deepening wash of rose, in her widening eyes and parted lips. So he kissed her again, a forceful demand with lips that allowed for no compromise. And again until he felt her mouth quiver, her lips part against his.

Only than did he slide his hands slowly, gently, very much at odds with the masterful demands of his mouth, along the slim column of her throat to rest on her shoulders, thus to hold her still. Only then, when he was certain that he had her attention, did he say what he had to say—needed to say.

'Listen to me, Theodora. You misheard. If you had waited… This is what I need to lay before you—and you need to know. I was wrong—desperately wrong—when I accused you of deliberate deceit. I did not know the true facts—did not even stop to think about the distress that I would cause. And now, because of Sarah, I do know the truth. I should have trusted you, but I let the past with all its bitterness colour my judgement. My treatment of you was beneath contempt, utterly unworthy of a man of honour and integrity. I have no excuses. The blame is all mine. I need to ask your forgiveness. If you cannot give me that, then I must accept that there is nothing between us.'

'Oh.' She blinked. As before with Nicholas, Theodora found herself in unknown territory, lost for words. She had never expected this. That he should take the burden of guilt fully on to his shoulders, when she had accused him of wilful and vindictive hatred without cause, sufficient to destroy their love without evidence of her involvement in any deception. After all, her accusation had been equally as ill-founded as his.

'Consider well, Thea. I don't deserve your forgiveness, but I will get to my knees if it will help.' His fingers tightened against the fragile bones of her shoulders as he waited to hear her verdict. A decision that could shatter his future. Without this lady, this glorious woman, he had discovered his life to be an empty existence, bringing nothing but loneliness and dissatisfaction. His hands clenched further, only loosening when he felt Thea wince under his fingers.

Thea watched him, searching the now familiar lines of his features, saw the lingering pain and uncertainty there. He had hurt her. But so too had she hurt him.

'I could forgive you,' she announced carefully, keeping her voice light.

Nicholas took a breath. And another against the hope that slammed into his belly.

'Then there is more. You are wrong, Thea. I know what you overheard between myself and Sarah, but you are wrong.' He still held her, but more gently, despite the frustrations burning in every tense line of corded flesh and muscle. 'If you had waited longer, you would have heard me tell Sarah what I truly feel. That love is not a fragile emotion. It is stronger than forged metal, certainly stronger than past hatreds and enmities. I love you. I care not whether your name is Wooton-Devereux or Baxendale. I love you. I find that I cannot live without you. I do not *want* to live without you. I can never envisage living without you.'

'Oh.' *Could she find nothing other to say?*

'I once asked you to marry me and you accepted. Later you rescinded your agreement. I will not allow that. I intend to keep you to that promise. You will marry me—I shall speak to Sir Hector as soon as I can. Do you understand me?'

'Yes.' *Of course she did.*

'Since you have already lain in my arms, shared my bed, you are in no position to be maidenly.'

'No.' She blushed a little, for it was the truth.

'You belong to me, Theodora. You are mine. Do you hear me?'

'Yes.' *Was he always so masterful?*

'You will not marry the Earl of Moreton.'

'No.' *So uncompromising?*

A little shake punctuated every point.

'There—I have said it all. Now, what do you have to say?'

What could she say? He had offered her the sun and moon and all the planets to hold in her hands, as rare and costly as a jewelled necklace.

'Do I have any choice in the matter?'

He laughed softly at the unexpected reply. 'No. None at all.'

Suddenly Theodora's face was bright and shining, her eyes aglow as if from an inner flame. She could not hide it. Her lips curved in a smile of utter delight. Nicholas saw it and knew that the battle was won. The relief of it swept through him as a wind through summer trees. So knowing finally that she was his, he retreated a little, allowing her at least a little space.

'You only have a choice, my dearest love, if you do not love me and cannot bear the thought of living at Aymestry as my wife.'

Again she studied him, head tilted, savouring the warmth that touched her skin and tinted her face with delicate colour. She supposed that she would have to put him out of his misery—although the smoothing of the lines of strain around his mouth suggested that he knew the victory was his. But it was *their* victory, as she well knew. Stepping forward, standing on her toes, she pressed her lips to his in the most tender of kisses.

'Very well. I will marry you.'

'Is that all?' One brow rose a fraction of an inch in astonishment.

'Is that not enough, dear Nicholas?'

'It is.' A soft sigh. 'So much more than enough. You can never know.'

He touched her cheek, a light brush of his fingers against the satin curve, as if he could not quite believe her reply. Or when she turned her face into his caress.

'I thought that I would have to persuade you, you know.'

'And how would you have done so, my lord?'

He smiled against her palm, where he had pressed his lips, at her deliberately predictable response. 'Like this, of course.'

Releasing her, he slid his hands up, and up, until he could draw her close, imprisoning her against his chest within his embrace. His mouth was warm and most persuasive, brushing softly at first, encouraging her to accept the delicious caress of his tongue as her lips opened willingly in acceptance of so intimate an invasion. Her skin was soft, so very soft and seductive. Whereas he... He held her body firmly against his, so that she might know her power over him, for the desire made him hard as stone. But who seduced whom? With a little cry Thea stretched her arms to slide around his neck and angled her head to allow his mouth to take even further liberties. So much heat, so many impossible sensations that raced through her body, leaving her totally at his mercy. It stunned her that he could take her over, demanding and receiving every shivered response to his touch. It stunned them both, a mutual joy and possession that stole their breath and raced through their limbs, a promise of even deeper passion. Control was destroyed, replaced by a simple desire to love and be loved, to pleasure and be pleasured. When his kiss became hot, now a demand rather than a request, it demolished her defences against him utterly, as his, too, were destroyed.

Nicholas lifted his head, as sense prevailed to restore some element of self-control in the breakfast parlour in the full light of day, but not before kissing her closed eyelids in gracious acknowledgement of her power over him.

'Would I have persuaded you, do you think?'

'I think you might.' Thea turned her face into the curve of his throat, a little shy of the depth of emotion that had wrapped around, enclosed them like a velvet cloak.

'I thought I had lost you,' he murmured. She felt his lips against her hair. 'The flames still haunt my dreams. It brought me to my senses as nothing else could. I need you in my life, Theodora.'

'Nicholas—are you sure?'

'Of what?'

'That you love me. I think…I think I might be difficult to live with. I like my own way.' Now she looked up into his face as she confessed. 'You may have noticed.'

'I would never have guessed it! But I think I am no easier.'

'But when we argue—will you not call me a *scheming Baxendale*?'

'Never!'

'Good. I would not like it.' The sparkle in her eyes was a delight to him.

'As long a you do not insist on referring to me as one of those *damned arrogant Faringdons*.'

Laughter sprang between them at the lessening of tension, to cauterise the wounds of the past, even though both realised and accepted that they would undoubtedly find space for disagreement. Both were too strong willed to make for a placid relationship. Somehow, it no longer mattered as long as they were together.

'Besides,' Nicholas reassured his love, 'you will no longer be a Baxendale. You will be a Faringdon. Will that be acceptable to you, my lady?'

'Most acceptable, my lord. I think that I have loved you for ever—since the day I struck at you with my riding whip.' Confession came easily, she decided, as she touched his hand where the old scar had long since faded into less than a shadow.

'The scar has gone from my hand, but if you had refused me, my heart would have been scarred for ever.' Meshing his fingers with hers, Nicholas brought their joined hands together against his chest.

'I thought I had ruined everything... And Edward told me such lies. So that when we met at Judith's...' Thea shook her head. That image still had the power to wound her. 'Can you truly love me in spite of all the hurt and malice of the past?'

'Let me show you how much I can love you. Come, my affianced wife.' Only then did Nicholas allow distance between them, but he kept her hand firmly in his as he led her to the door. 'Let me show you the depths of my love.'

The splendour of Nicholas's sumptuous room at Burford Hall became witness to this most private of moments. They stood in the centre, making no overt move, a little shy of each other. The tension in the air sparkled as if an entity in itself, much like the brooch, which now lay forgotten in the breakfast parlour. The rift between them had been so wide and vicious, words spoken so accusing and bitter. But now it was in their power to set all aside and become free of the past. Nicholas took his love's hands in his, the first step to renewing his knowledge of her, to renewing his promises and avowals of love, which had been so cruelly broken.

Her eyes were captured and held in his, in the dark fire. She knew him now. She understood him so much better now, what had driven him to judge and condemn. And she had forgiven. She would trust this man with her life. He had saved her from harm, had given her comfort. He had rescued her from possible death. He loved her. She closed her hands tightly around his wrists, bonds of love and trust. Now she must convince him that the past was indeed dead and would cast no long shadows unless they allowed it.

As he must convince her.

Nicholas wanted nothing more then to take her, to love her. The bed was there, beckoning with its cool sheets and soft pillows. Such a little distance. There was nothing now to separate them, nothing to prevent them reaffirming the love that had been strong enough to withstand impossible strains. But Lord Nicholas Faringdon, for once, was uncertain, his confidence undermined. He knew that he must have a care of her after the pain and hurt of the past weeks. Guilt and self-disgust slicked his skin. The beautiful woman who stood before him, encircling his wrists with silken chains, willing to giver her heart into his keeping, had every reason to turn her back and marry her Earl with her parent's blessing. But she would not. She would not leave him and wed another. She had said that she loved him. She would trust him. And Theodora was not a woman to break her word—or give it lightly. It was more than he could have hoped for. Now he acknowledged in his heart and soul a need to heal the hurt he had caused and to rebuild the trust before they could look to a future together.

So he set himself to woo her again, without words, but with every muscle and sinew of his body, as if he had no knowledge of her nor she of him and it was all new discovery. As indeed it was. As if she were an untried virgin again, who needed—and deserved—the most exquisite care and cherishing at his hands. Which was not so. But Thea, aware of her lover's torment, allowed him with joy the luxury of the tender seduction.

Gilded by evening sun, stroked by its warmth, he set his mind to control the urgings of his body. Dedicated every skilful touch of mouth and hands to create a delight and a pleasure for her. Lovingly. Tenderly. Yet claiming her as his own. For she must be left in no doubt of the strength of his need for her. His unshakable faith in her. His love for her.

Thea stretched and arched languorously beneath this relentless assault, absorbing the weight and fluent power of her lover. Admiring the controlled restraint even as she fought against it. Clever hands and skilful mouth, rediscovering the secrets and textures, the satin sweep of breast and waist and thigh. The perfumed invitation of softest skin. All thoughts were obliterated in that delicate, sensual onslaught.

For Nicholas it was in the way of a promise that nothing should stand between them. Never again. He had allowed fear and suspicion, arrogance and hatred to separate and wound. He shuddered at the memory of it as he traced the line of her ribs with heated kisses, smoothed the warm skin with a slow trail of fingers. Lingering as she gasped on an intake of breath. And poured all the love of which he was capable into that magnificent courtship as he covered her body with his own.

Thea had read her lord well. The depth of hurt and regret. The need to make restitution. So she allowed him the dominance and the freedom to make amends in his own way, seeing his need to do so, as she took on her own delicious role to soothe and reassure. Following the paths he took, the slow, thorough awakening of every nerve, of every desire, she responded to every demand. The choices were his. Yet it was no hardship for her to follow. Or to use her own experience with him to tease and arouse with a delicious sense of power. Passion was built on passion, layer on enticing layer, until Thea's heart raced and her breath sobbed, the heat built her body crying out with desire for fulfilment. She placed a palm against Nickolas's chest, fingers spread where his heart was as tumultuous as hers. Tears sparkled on her lashes.

'Don't cry, Thea. It breaks my heart.'

'They are tears of joy. I do not regret them.'

He dried them with gentle lips, cradling her against his heart.

'I will not break, Nicholas.'

'No. You will not.'

Silent, they smiled, lost in each other in that instant of perfect stillness, the air around them heavy with emotion, knowing at last that the future was theirs to make of it what they would. And then, only then did Nicholas allow the pace to explode into brilliant heat. Patience was abandoned. He claimed the authority for himself, giving Theodora no choice but to allow herself to be swept along on the storm waves of impossible longings. His mouth took and took. She gave all.

With her name on his lips, did he allow his mind to be flooded, erasing all thought but of her, to thrust deep, sheathing himself within her and claiming her for ever, taking her with him as he drove them both to shuddering delight and ultimate release.

Epilogue

In the intervening weeks since she had received her mother's letter, Eleanor's boudoir and bedchamber had lost the intense smell of newly sawn wood, the spicy tang of resin, and gained a certain sophistication, particularly in the way of new furnishings. The lengthy discussions between Eleanor and Sarah, the apparently endless choosing and discarding of fabrics and patterns, had resulted in tasteful curtains at the windows with matching hangings for the bed. It was now a haven of tranquillity in shades of blue and cream, always Eleanor's preferred hues. The deeply cushioned chairs and window seats invited and encouraged one to sit at ease.

But now the bedchamber held an even more recent item of furniture.

'D'you like it, Mama?' Tom traced the intricate carving along the foot with a grubby finger.

'Of course I do.' Eleanor, newly returned to her previously slim figure and her easy tolerance of the heat, smiled at her elder son. Perhaps she looked a little tired, her fine skin pale against the lace of her wrapper as she rested back against the banked pillows, but her eyes glowed with amethyst fire, heralding both pride and achievement. And a fierce love. 'It is quite beautiful.

You are such a clever boy, Tom. How could you guess what I would exactly like?' She leaned to smooth the palm of her hand over the rounded edges of the cradle. Its occupant, astonishingly new to the world, slept on, unimpressed with the surroundings, the admiration or the company.

'We guessed.' Tom shrugged his nonchalance, a miniature copy of a gesture that Eleanor had seen so often in Henry and now made her laugh softly. 'Papa said you like plants…and things.' Tom followed the outline of what might have been a daisy. 'Like this.' The cradle was made from cedar and polished to enhance the grain, the decoration at head and foot a riot of deeply incised leaves and flowers, more to do with enthusiasm than elegant taste, but still a work of love and therefore of delight. 'I chose the flowers,' Tom confided, shuffling impatient feet in pleasure at the success of the gift.

'And you made it? All by yourself?'

'Well…' Honesty got the better of him. 'Papa helped. A bit. D'you think the baby likes it?'

'I am certain.' Eleanor kept her solemnity in place as she pushed the black hair from Tom's forehead. The honesty had cost him! 'Look how well he sleeps. It must be so comfortable for him. I think he looks very pleased to be here.'

'I suppose.' Tom peered in with a frown. One baby, after all, looked much like another.

But not to Eleanor. She was aware only of the dark hair, the straight nose. And she knew that this time their child's eyes were blue, dark as the columns of delphinium that graced the flower borders at Burford Hall. Another Faringdon. Another son.

'I have to go.' Tom abandoned his brother without shame. 'I haven't seen my pony today. He'll be missing me.' He came to a sudden halt at the doorway and turned back. 'The baby won't be able to ride yet, will he?' The anxiety of personal ownership was written across his face, a burning concern. He looked to Henry, a silent and amused observer of the previous interchange, who saw and understood.

'No,' he answered his son's unspoken concern plainly enough.

'He is far too small. The pony is yours, Tom. When the little one is older, we shall buy another for him.'

'Yes. That's what I thought.' Life was as simple as that. Tom took himself down the stairs with a rush and slide of feet on the polished treads. Eleanor did not bother to tell him not to run.

'I fear a pony holds more attraction for our son than a baby.' Henry pushed himself upright from where he had been half-sitting against the open window frame, arms folded, to stride across the room with his habitual long-limbed grace. Moved to sit on the edge of the bed, where he took Eleanor's hands in his, raising first one and then the other to his lips. 'He is very fine, Nell. Was Tom like this when he was born?'

'Oh, yes.' Eleanor tightened her clasp in instant sympathy and a sharp twist of grief to put an edge on her happiness, surprised by a sudden desire to weep. Of course. Hal had missed all the early promise and progress of his firstborn son, but could now relive it through the first weeks and months of the life of this new child.

The baby snuffled in his sleep and yawned, but did not wake.

Henry grinned at the innocent gesture as he bent his head and kissed the palm of Eleanor's hand. 'Richard, then. Are we agreed?' And, when she nodded her compliance, 'We are indeed blessed,' on a little sigh now that the pain and his fears for her safety through the dangers of childbirth were past.

'I would wish the same for Nicholas. And perhaps even the unknown Miss Wooton-Devereux—if he truly loves her.' Eleanor fretted a little at their enforced ignorance. 'We know so little of what is between them now. Do you suppose that she was indeed in league with Edward Baxendale? I hope that she hasn't quite broken Nicholas's heart.'

'I don't know.' Henry continued to hold his wife's hands enclosed in his, as if he feared that she might still be snatched away from him. 'But Sarah will write when she can. All you need is patience, my wife. And confidence in Nick's good sense!'

'Where a lovely woman is concerned?' Eleanor's tone spoke her scepticism of all men in such circumstances.

Henry lifted his hand, palm up in the formal gesture of a swordsman, in acknowledgement of the accurate hit.

'*Touché*. I have never had any sense where you are concerned! But Nicholas has a strong will and a liking for going his own way. He always had. Perhaps he was a little overshadowed as a boy because he was the quietest of the three of us, but his calm acceptance of life disguised a determination to achieve his goals in the way that best suited him.' Henry's mouth curved, his eyes softened at the memories of a happy boyhood at Burford. 'Before you knew what he was about, he had done it—whether it was to persuade our far-from-indulgent father that he could not survive without a new horse, or to charm the affections of one of the maids at the inn in Burford. Whatever the future, Nick will work out his own salvation, with or without the débutante.'

'Well, I am sure that you read your brother correctly. I just hope that the lady is innocent of all subterfuge and that Nick loses his heart to her and has to kneel at her feet. I think it will do him good not to get his own way quite so much!' And then, 'I miss Sarah.'

'I know. But she has her own life to live, and that of John to consider, and it was her decision to make. I do not think that she made it lightly.'

'No.' Eleanor remembered the final leave-taking when Sarah had wept. 'But still she believed that to return to England was necessary to meet with her sister.' Whether Sarah would remain in London—or return again to New York—only time would tell. Eleanor set her teeth. Again a matter for patience! Her somewhat melancholy mood was interrupted by a shout of laughter from below the window as Tom indulged in some childhood pastime. Then the sound of running feet, followed by a distant shriek of joy.

Her face lit, the sadness swept away. 'Tom never told me, you know.' Eleanor smiled into Henry's eyes. 'Your *secret*. Sometimes I thought he would burst with the overpowering desire to do so.' As a smug smile was all the answer she received from her lord, her expression became suspicious and not a little stern. 'How did you do it?'

'I think it would not be honourable for me to divulge my methods to my wife,' Henry replied in all seriousness. 'Not in so vital a matter between a man and his son.'

'So it involved money!'

'You have no confidence in my powers of persuasion, Nell!'

'Oh, Hal. Bribery!'

Henry laughed at her affronted, yet still amused expression. 'What else? It was in an excellent cause.'

'And it is a splendid cradle.'

'As is the child. Both of them.' The pride in Hal's face made her catch her breath. 'Thank you, Nell. Dear Nell. I shall be always in your debt.' He slid his arm around her shoulders to pull her close as he leaned to touch the infant's clenched fingers which flexed in response—tiny fists and perfect nails. 'What a clever girl you are, my love.'

'Shall I tell you a secret?' For a moment she turned her face against his shoulder.

'Is it very terrible?'

'No. Just that I wanted a daughter.' She felt him smile against her hair. 'But I have decided that Richard is quite perfect and I find that it no longer matters.' She lifted her face. 'And he is so like you, Hal.'

'Perhaps next time.' Henry folded his arms around her, touched his lips to hers in the tenderest of caresses. 'We will make a good life here, Nell. Whatever the future holds for us.'

'I have no doubt of it.' Eleanor leaned her head against him and smiled her perfect contentment.

Some months later, far from New York in Herefordshire, Nicholas was indeed working out his own salvation in his own way. Now Nicholas took the steps at a run and strode into the entrance hall at Aymestry Manor, a man at ease in his surroundings and with the life that he had chosen for himself. It was clear that his involvement in that life was complete. His hair was ruffled from physical exertion, his shirt sleeves rolled up, cravat loosened, boots and breeches covered with straw.

'Thea?' No reply. No sound. She could be anywhere at this time in the morning. 'Thea!' His voice echoed. He would have shouted again but then heard her feet, in riding boots, hurrying along the oak boards of the corridor to the head of the staircase. He would recognise the sound of her quick, light footsteps anywhere now. He stood hands on hips, head thrown back, until she came to look down over the balustraded landing above him. As full of vibrant life and as beautiful as the first day that she had struck him with her riding whip and in so doing had turned his life upside down.

'What is it?' she asked. 'Are you hurt?—no of course you are not! You look far too healthy.' Smiling down at him, she was aware of the tingle in every nerve ending as his smile banished the austere lines from his face, the warmth in her blood when his eyes swept over her, even after six months of marriage. He still had the power to make her want him, to need him. To feel herself at one with him, body and soul. And, it appeared—she flushed with delight at the realisation of the miracle—he needed and wanted her just as much.

'Come down!'

She did.

'You are very dirty, my lord.'

'And you are very smart, my lady. I like the riding rig.'

'I like the boots and breeches better.' Her smile was openly teasing. 'But this is more appropriate! I am going to see Mrs Calke at Burford and I must not shock the tenants!' The velvet of the long skirt and closely fitted jacket was in her favourite deep blue. Her eyes reflected its depth of colour and her hair, worn a little longer these days, was a rich gold. Nicholas could not resist sliding his arms round her slim waist, pulling her close, regardless of the dusty state of his clothes. And since she did not object over much—indeed, she wound her arms around his neck and tilted up her face in blatant invitation—he kissed her, hard and fierce.

'I will accompany you.' Nicholas still had moments of sheer horror when he recalled in vivid detail the dangers that she had faced, moments when his blood froze at the certain knowledge that she might have met her death here in his own home. He knew that those fears would never leave him, but chose to say nothing, carrying the weight of care close within him. It must not be a burden on her. His lady must be free to fly if that was her wish. Yet he often found excuses to be with his wife, to accompany her when she rode off estate land.

As if she did not know! Thea hid her smile because she understood and valued his care. Knowing his fears, she would never refuse his subtle planning.

'But before we go—I have something to show you, my lady. Close your eyes.' He pulled her arm securely through his to aid her steps. 'No looking, now!'

The stables! She surmised from their direction when they left the house. Newly constructed, Nicholas's prized horseflesh were once more in residence. They had been brought over from Burford only the previous week and appeared to be well settled into their fine accommodation. Her smile bloomed. 'Can I guess?'

'Of course not! No guessing. No peeping.' He tightened his hold on her arms. 'Take care here—the pavings are still somewhat uneven.'

But she knew why he had come to find her. What he had brought her to see. Her feet clattered on the cobbles of the courtyard. Then soft darkness, intermittent rays of sunshine, with the sweet scents of hay and horses closed around her—but she remained obedient with her eyes closed. Nicholas led her forward.

'Now look.'

Of course. The Zephyr stood in the centre of the large stall. At her feet, a foal, newborn, its coat still damp, but determined to manage its long legs and gain its feet. By their side stood Furness with handfuls of straw with which he had been wiping down the little grey's hot sides. He looked up at Thea with pride and the suspicion of a grin on his lined face.

'Oh Nick.' Thea leaned against the half-door to see the new arrival. It was a roan, the dark bay taken from its sire, Nicholas's recently acquired stallion, but with the arched neck and small head of the Arab mare. Liquid eyes with absurdly long lashes blinked at them as sunshine came through the high windows.

'A colt, my lady,' Furness explained. 'Give him two or three years on his back—he'll be an asset to our breeding programme here at Aymestry. What do we call him, my lord?'

'I think Faringdon Pride. He will be the bedrock of our future.' Nicholas looked at Thea. 'Do you agree, Thea? You have part-ownership, after all.'

'Yes. I approve.'

Thea stroked The Zephyr. Admired her baby. Then Lord Nicholas and his wife walked back into the sunlight to sit on the stone balustrade that delineated the formal garden and look out over the home pastures.

'I feel so happy.' Thea laughed aloud, eyes sparkling.

'Even after all of six months?' Nicholas knew what she meant. Their love was still as new and bright for him too. He stripped a late rose bud from the bush beside them, handing it to her with solemn formality. 'Even though I only married you to stop your taking The Zephyr away from me?'

Thea raised the unfurling flower to her lips as she slanted an arch glance at her companion. 'There now! And I thought it was for my own sake.' Then on a thought, 'Will they ever return, Henry and Eleanor?' Thea asked as she leaned back within the shelter of her lord's arm.

'No. This was never the life that Hal wanted. And although the title is rightfully his, he would never claim it. It would ruin Eleanor's reputation, you see. It is better that the world here continue to see Tom as Thomas's child, rather than Hal's, born without the sanction of marriage.'

'The strait-laced Faringdons!' Her smile was a little sad for all the anguish and scandal of the past.

'True. But Tom might return. One day. When he is grown and can decide for himself. Burford is his, after all.' He glanced down at her. 'Are you content, Thea? Managing acres that are not ours? Perhaps it is no more secure for you than residing in a foreign embassy. You once told me that you had no settled home, had never had one—and that is what you wished for above all else.'

How delightful that he should remember. And was concerned that she should not be dissatisfied with any one part of their life here together. Nicholas's sensitivity to her emotions was something which still took her by surprise. Thea shook her head, eyes clear, meeting his without shadow.

'Aymestry is your own. I am here because it is yours, and thus it is mine too. I feel that it has been waiting for me all my life, and I have come home at last. Just as I felt that you and your love had been waiting for me to discover the glory of it. Fate has determined that we be together.'

He could not look away from the love that shone from her face. 'You can still travel, you know, if you become restless. It was never my intention to chain you to life in rural seclusion. We are not buried here.'

'I know.' And was grateful for his promise, although she no longer needed it. 'But we have a beautiful home here. I predict that Faringdon horses will be famous.'

Lord Nicholas would have risen to his feet, pulling her with him. But Thea detained him with a hand on his arm and a thoughtful expression.

'What is it, my heart?'

Her fingers tightened on his, to the detriment of the neglected rose bud. 'It is just that I have been thinking… Perhaps we should consider securing our own inheritance for the future for Aymestry Manor.'

'I think it an excellent idea,' he replied promptly, as solemn as she.

'Ha! Why do I think that you always manage to get your own way?'

'How can you say that? Certainly, in my younger days I usually managed to do so.' His fleeting grin, devastating as ever, melted her bones. 'Until, that is, I met a certain wayward débutante who challenged all my preconceptions.'

'I cannot imagine what you might mean, my lord!' Thea could

not repress an answering smile as she tucked her hand cosily into her husband's arm with satisfaction at her achievement. 'So we have decided that we need an heir for Aymestry.'

'I believe, my dear love, that we have.'

Which was exactly what Lord Nicholas Faringdon wanted after all.

* * * * *

MILLS & BOON®

The Regency
LORDS & LADIES
COLLECTION

Two Glittering Regency Love Affairs

BOOK SEVEN:
Rosalyn & the Scoundrel *by Anne Herries*
&
Lady Knightley's Secret *by Anne Ashley*

Available from 6th January 2006

Available at most branches of WH Smith, Tesco, ASDA,
Borders, Eason, Sainsbury's and most bookshops.

0206/135/MB148

Amateur sleuth Francesca Cahill sets out to solve a new puzzling – and terrifying - case in 1900's Manhattan...

From New York Times bestselling author Brenda Joyce

Irrepressible heiress and intrepid sleuth Francesca Cahill moves easily from her own elegant world of Fifth Avenue to the teeming underbelly of society. And despite the misgivings of her fiancé, Calder Hart, Francesca cannot turn away from the threat that is now terrorising Lower Manhattan. A madman has attacked three women - and only one has survived.

To solve the case, Francesca must work with her former love, police commissioner Rick Bragg – Calder's half brother and greatest rival. But even as Calder's jealous passions leave his relationship with Francesca teetering on the brink, Francesca stays on the killer's trail – certain he will strike again...

On sale 7th January 2006

FREE!
2 Books
and a surprise gift!

We would like to take this opportunity to thank you for reading this Mills & Boon® book by offering you the chance to take TWO more specially selected titles from the Historical Romance™ series absolutely FREE! We're also making this offer to introduce you to the benefits of the Reader Service™—

- ★ **FREE home delivery**
- ★ **FREE gifts and competitions**
- ★ **FREE monthly Newsletter**
- ★ **Exclusive Reader Service offers**
- ★ **Books available before they're in the shops**

Accepting these FREE books and gift places you under no obligation to buy, you may cancel at any time, even after receiving your free shipment. Simply complete your details below and return the entire page to the address below. You don't even need a stamp!

YES! Please send me 2 free Historical Romance books and a surprise gift. I understand that unless you hear from me, I will receive 4 superb new titles every month for just £3.65 each, postage and packing free. I am under no obligation to purchase any books and may cancel my subscription at any time. The free books and gift will be mine to keep in any case.

H5ZEF

Ms/Mrs/Miss/Mr ....Initials ....
                                                                    BLOCK CAPITALS PLEASE
Surname ....
Address ....

....

....Postcode ....

Send this whole page to:
UK: FREEPOST CN81, Croydon, CR9 3WZ